Sherlock Holmes
and
The Vampires of Eternity

Sherlock Holmes
and
The Vampires of Eternity

by
Brian Stableford

A Black Coat Press Book

Table of Contents

Acknowledgements

An abridged version of the chapters making up the Prologue, the Count's Story and the Explorer's Story appeared in *Interzone* in January/February 1995 as "The Hunger and Ecstasy of Vampires." A version of similar length to the one that appears here, but with numerous slight variations, appeared in hardcover from Mark Ziesing Books under the same title. An abridged and slightly variant version of the chapters making up the Writers Story and the Detective's Story appeared in *Interzone* in January/February 1997 as "The Black Blood of the Dead." An abridged and slightly variant version of the chapters making up the Soldier's Story appeared in *Interzone* in January/February 1999 as "The Gateway of Eternity."

The details of William Hope Hodgson's last recorded days on Earth are mostly taken from *Some Facts in the Case of William Hope Hodgson: Master of Phantasy* (1974) by R. Alain Everts, which had earlier been serialised in *Shadow* 19-20 (April & October 1973). The omnibus edition of Hodgson's novels whose duplicate is consulted in the story by Oscar Wilde's simulacrum is that published by Arkham House in 1946. "The Hog" can be found in the Mycroft & Moran edition of *Carnacki the Ghost-Finder* (1947). An unexpurgated version of "The Baumoff Explosive"–which was published posthumously in *Nash's Weekly* for 17 September 1919–can be found in *Out of the Storm: Uncollected Fantasies by William Hope Hodgson* edited by Sam Moskowitz (Donald Grant, 1975) under the title "Eloi, Eloi, Sabachthani."

In concocting my highly speculative account of Oscar Wilde's last days on Earth, I used data from Richard Ellman's *Oscar Wilde* (1987) and Laurence Housman's *Echo de Paris* (1923). Material relating to the Great Detective was mostly taken from *Profile by Gaslight* (1944) edited by Edgar W. Smith, although almost all of it is ultimately derived from what that book insists on calling the Sacred Writings. I made some slight use of a description of Rémy de Gourmont's living quarters contained in an article by Arthur Ransome first published in the *Fortnightly Review* and reprinted as an appendix to his English translation of Gourmont's *A Night in the Luxembourg* (1907). I found the quotation that includes the phrase "the black blood of the dead" in Richard Howard's English translation of *Michelet* by Roland Barthes (1987, from the French original of 1954).

Some elements of the description of the universe featured in the novel are borrowed from Frank Tipler's *The Physics of Immortality* (1994) and such antecedents thereof as the works of Pierre Teilhard de Chardin and Camille Flammarion's *La fin du monde* (1893; tr. as *Omega: The Last Days of Earth*). Some elements of the vocabulary used by the Engine and the Hog in their attempts to explain the nature of the universe are borrowed from "The Self-Reproducing Inflationary Universe" by Andrei Linde, published in the *Scientific American* supplement *Magnificent Cosmos* (Spring 1998).

Brian Stableford

Prologue

Paris, March 1894

The air above the city was uncommonly clear and the stars shone brightly. The Moon was full, and visibility was good even though the nearest gas-light was 100 meters away.

Jean Lorrain disapproved of the Comte's insistence–in frank defiance of convention–that the duel must be fought before dawn, but he grudgingly admitted to himself that there was light enough. In fact, as he and Octave Uzanne walked across the dewy grass to meet Mourier's seconds, he felt alarmingly conspicuous, as if he had unwittingly exposed himself to some attentive eye whose attention he had done better to avoid. There was something about this business that filled him with a dire and horrible unease. It seemed oddly like a premonition of some future disaster. He had never experienced such a sensation before, even when he had been the one appointed to fire the gun.

This was the very spot where Lorrain had faced Guy de Maupassant not so long after first arriving in Paris, and even though he had known his opponent since childhood, he had not been absolutely sure that the elder writer would discharge his pistol harmlessly into the ground, as modern etiquette demanded. He had been anxious then–near sick with anxiety, in fact–but he had not felt the way he did now, weak at the knees with superstitious dread. Perhaps it was merely a delayed effect of the ether, which had filled his house with ghosts as soon as he had started taking it; not all of them had had been laid to rest when he had stopped.

One of Mourier's men opened the box to display the ancient pistols resting within. Lorrain, who was no expert judge of weapons, did not bother to inspect them closely; he was happy to presume that they were identical. Uzanne likewise waved them away with barely a glance.

Mourier's senior second–a white-haired man whose bearing was sternly military–took Lorrain to one side, with an exaggerated pantomime of discretion, to say: "I wonder if all this is really necessary. Monsieur Mourier has authorized me to say that he had no intention of causing mortal offence. He wishes it to be known that he repeated the rumor only to comment on its utter absurdity, not with the intention of spreading it further. If Monsieur le Comte wishes to deal with the author of the rumor he must look elsewhere."

Mourier is frightened, Lorrain thought. *Because Monsieur le Comte is not a Frenchman, let alone a Parisian, Mourier cannot be sure that he will follow the unwritten law.* Aloud, he said: "I fear that Monsieur le Comte has instructed me not to accept an apology."

The old soldier curled his lip in obvious distaste. At first, Lorrain thought that it was he who had prompted the distaste; he was certain that the man had recognized him, although he, for his own part, had not the slightest idea who the ex-soldier was. He realized when the soldier continued, though, that it was Mourier's instructions that were sticking in the old man's throat.

"Monsieur Mourier has asked me to make it perfectly clear that he does not believe there are such things as vampires," the old soldier said, "and that he used the word in connection with Monsieur le Comte simply to make clear the absurdity of any such belief. He has also asked me to say that he had no intention of implying that Monsieur le Comte is using an assumed name."

Mourier is very frightened indeed, Lorrain thought. *Even his seconds feel that he should not go to such lengths of self-abasement. In any case, he is wrong. France is full of vampires; I have seen them myself, and have joined their company, gathering at the abattoir gate in the rue de Flandres before dawn's first light. As long as consumption runs riot through the land, and as long as there are doctors who believe that fresh ox-blood is an effective treatment, there will be no shortage of vampires here. The doctors are quacks, of course–blood has no more virtue than ether, although it does not visit a man with quite so many phantoms–but wherever there is ill-heath there will always be quacks. As for assumed names, that is a trivial matter. I wear one myself, at my father's command–although, in the end, it was he and not I who dragged the name Duval in the dirt.*

"Well, Monsieur?" snapped the military man, impatient for his reply.

Lorrain coughed into his hand, and felt flecks of bloody sputum hit his palm. He felt almost relieved, although he had not coughed blood for some weeks. It reassured him that the terrible dread that had taken possession of him must be physical after all.

"I fear," he murmured, hoarsely, "that Monsieur le Comte will not depart without exchanging shots. It is all most unfortunate, I confess, but Monsieur le Comte has been pursued by evil rumors through half the capitals in Europe, and these whispers have caused him considerable pain. He is perfectly able to ignore jests of an ordinary kind, which link his name with certain young women, but there is one particular name that causes him particular hurt, and that is Laura Vambery's. He had not thought to hear it mentioned here in Paris, given that the incident happened long ago and in another country, and it wounded him deeply. He would surely admit, as a matter of mere probability, that Monsieur Mourier did not intend to charge him with direct responsibility for the girl's death, let alone of drinking her life's blood, but he feels that unless he responds in a firm and definite way to your friend's carelessness others might feel comfortable in making similarly vile insinuations."

Mourier's second sighed, in a very contrived and ostentatious fashion–but there was real anxiety in his eyes. "Monsieur le Comte does understand, I suppose, that this is 1894, not 1794, and that whatever the situation in his homeland might be, the Courts of France have become very serious in their opposition to private settlements?"

This, Lorrain knew, was the true heart of the matter. "Monsieur le Comte may not be a Parisian," he said, with malicious frostiness, "but he is well enough acquainted with the direction in which the march of progress is taking our society. He knows full well that we are here as a matter of honor, not to attempt murder. I can assure you that if his opponent were, let us say, accidentally to discharge his weapon without fully raising it, so that the ball went harmlessly to earth, Monsieur le Comte would not dream of attempting to fire a fatal shot in return."

The old soldier actually laughed, albeit softly. His relief was palpable. He even raised his open-palmed hand in an amicable gesture. "I confess that I am glad to hear it," he said, his voice hardly above a whisper "In the days of my youth, duels were fought authentically, and the Law knew far better than to interfere–but nothing has been the same since that damned humiliating war. Even the Prussians would be ashamed had they known how deeply France would be scarred by it. What kind of a future are we making for ourselves, when men who meet on the field of honor no longer dare to take aim with their guns? Sometimes, I fear that in refusing to dig secret graves for our boldest and best, we may be digging a grave for all mankind." He turned away as soon as he had finished speaking, as if he regretted his own loquacity.

He is rambling! Lorrain thought. *He is as horridly disturbed as I am–as we all are! All, that is, except Monsieur le Comte.*

By now, the pistols had been conveyed to the combatants by Octave Uzanne and Mourier's junior second, and the selection had been made. It was the military man who placed the adversaries carefully back to back, and made certain that they knew exactly when to walk, and exactly at what point to turn. There was nothing for Lorrain to do now but stand back and watch. Again, that feeling of premonition swept over him, and he could not help shuddering. He hoped that the curious and malevolent imp stirring in his belly was a mere ache, but feared that it might be a kind of thirst–whether for ether or for warm blood, he dared not hazard a guess.

Lorrain watched the two gentlemen take their measured paces. The Comte was not the taller of the two, nor the younger, but he seemed nevertheless to be the more commanding figure. The rumors that pursued him alleged that he was an accomplished mesmerist as well as a fiend, and despite the fact that there was nothing in the least intimidating about his ordinary gaze, Lorrain found that easy enough to believe. The man from the East seemed to be in a kind of trance, as if his mind had slipped into some uncommon mode of consciousness, which permitted a concentration as absolute as that associated with obsessive monomania.

The precision with which he turned to face his opponent at the apposite moment was smoothly mechanical.

Mourier began to raise his arm, trying to hold it as straight as a ramrod but failing miserably. His terror was embarrassingly frank. Long before it reached the horizontal, the progress of the trembling arm was interrupted, and Mourier allowed it to fall back. The arm was limp when the pistol in his hand went off, and the ball discharged harmlessly into the turf no more than a meter from his toes.

After that, there was nothing for Mourier to do but wait. He tried to look his opponent in the eye, but he could not do it.

No flicker of a smile passed across the Comte's face on account of the fact that he could not now be hurt. His own pistol was already raised, and it pointed unwaveringly at his opponent's heart—but then, with scrupulous politeness, the Comte let the barrel droop, so that the weapon was angled conspicuously downwards, pointing at the spot from which the two men had stood back-to-back. He fired.

Mourier fell, clutching his throat.

Lorrain could not restrain a cry of astonishment and anguish—a cry echoed by Uzanne and the younger of Mourier's seconds. Even the old soldier started with amazement and exclaimed in horror.

For a moment or two, Lorrain took leave to wonder whether some cruel supernatural agency had redirected the Comte's bullet. Even when he had realized, belatedly, that the bullet must have struck a stone, he could not help but wonder for one insane moment whether the Comte might actually have aimed at the stone, calculating that the ricochet would strike his opponent in a fatal spot. Such a calculation would be quite impossible—and yet, the Comte still seemed quite impassive, despite the miraculousness of what had happened. Neither surprise nor alarm was yet evident in his stony expression; he stood stock still, as if his bewildered consciousness were waiting for the realization of what had occurred to overtake his unbelief.

Mischance, Lorrain realized, had struck a terrible blow. It would be impossible for the Comte to remain in Paris now. The whole point of making such a show of fighting the duel in earnest had been to ensure that he would not be forced to an ignominious retreat, by making certain that no one would ever dare repeat the rumor that the Comte was a vampire, and that his true name was not the one printed on his visiting cards. Now, he would have to flee, urgently as well as ignominiously. A million-to-one freak of chance had killed Mourier, but the Comte would get the blame.

Mourier's seconds were already hard at work when Lorrain and Uzanne reached them. The old soldier was desperately attempting to stem the flow of blood from the wound that had opened Mourier's windpipe, although his lace-edged handkerchief was woefully inadequate to the task. Lorrain had seen many a bloodstained handkerchief in his time, but never one so red and sodden as this one.

The white-haired man looked up. "Go, you fool!" he said, in a tortured voice. "Get your man away from here–out of Paris and out of France. Send him home by the fastest available route. It matters not that at all that the killing was an accident. There will be Hell to pay, and the story will be on everyone's lips. If your friend does not want rumors of vampirism and the name of Laura Vambery bandied about in open court, he had better not set foot in France for a very long time."

Lorrain ran back to the Comte, resentfully aware of the fact that he and Uzanne hardly knew the man, and had only consented to be his seconds because they had been asked so urgently. The Comte still had the weapon in his hand, and did not drop it when Lorrain urged him to flee for his life–but he condescended to return to his *fiacre* and give the necessary instructions to his German coachman.

Lorrain and Uzanne got into the carriage behind him, and took their places to either side of him as the horses took it away, hurrying beneath the whip.

No one spoke, at first. The Comte offered no explanation or apology–he seemed to be lost in a private world of his own, hardly belonging to this one at all. Before the rumors had arrived in his wake, he had seemed the most charming of men–one of those who sparkled beneath the brilliant light of chandeliers, perfectly at home in the *salons* he graced with his presence–but he was very different now.

When he did speak, it was to say: "What have I done that the Fates should take against me so? *What have I done?*"

Lorrain did not know how to answer that. "Will you go home, Monsieur?" he asked.

"I have no home," the Comte replied, bitterly. "To Le Havre first, I suppose, and then to England. I have met some charming Englishmen while I have been in Paris. Perhaps it was always my destiny to go there, although I cannot imagine why."

"No one can imagine what destiny has in store," Uzanne said, as philosophical as ever. "If it really is determined in advance, its shape ought to be easy enough to detect, but such intelligence as we obtain of it is never more than the faintest whisper, and ever in a foreign tongue. How else could we conserve the hope–or the illusion–that our will is free?"

"I seem to be forever saying goodbye," the Comte murmured. "Sometimes, I feel like that Dutch captain who cursed God and was condemned to fight the wind forever, never able to double the Cape of Storms."

"You will find a place yet where tongues do not wag maliciously, *mon ami*," Lorrain assured him, wishing that he were more confident of the fact. "Or, at least, one where their malice is turned in other directions. In London, no one cares what happens beyond *la Manche*."

"I hope you are right," the Comte declared.

The carriage set the two friends down in the rue de Courty while dawn was just beginning to tint the sky. Lorrain had not seen that first light since the days when he had sought a desperate cure for his perennial fever in the rue de Flandres. It reminded him forcibly of the odor and taste of blood, and of the effort that had been required to force the warm liquid down while his throat rose in rebellion against its foulness.

"I should not like to be a vampire," Lorrain said to Uzanne, as the Comte's carriage drove away in the direction of the *barrière*. "To wear the mask of a common man, while nurturing some dark and precious secret identity, would be one thing–but to live on blood alone would be another. I would rather let the fever consume me."

Uzanne looked at him very strangely–as well he might, considering that he had not been party to Lorrain's train of thought. "You had best be careful in using that word," he said. "We have just seen a man die because he repeated it."

"Have I ever been careful?" Lorrain asked him, only realizing when he smiled that the feeling of dread had left him. As a brighter light possessed the sky, the pall that had briefly hung over him was lifting, setting him free.

"No," his friend admitted, "you never have. Perhaps you should–or one day, it might be you that dawn finds lying there, nourishing the soil with your rich Norman blood. What a tragedy that would be, when you have not yet written your masterpiece! If you find room in it for Monsieur le Comte, as you have found room for so many others, you must be certain to disguise him well."

"I doubt if any writer who would met him could resist the temptation to include him in a novel," Lorrain said. "But you are right: he would have to be disguised, if he were not to take offence at his own image, and not by any mere reversal of his name."

They went into the house together, and drank brandy until *maman* awoke and asked her wayward son exactly where he had been all night.

"Helping a friend in need," he said, although he knew that she would not believe him.

14

The Soldier's Story: Part One

Belgium, near Ypres, April 1918

1.

Between midnight and daybreak on April 19, there was a lull in the firing, which lasted nearly six hours. Grateful for the opportunity, and knowing that it was unlikely to last for long, the signaler took advantage of the quiet period to fall into a deep sleep. Unfortunately, the wound that I had sustained on April 10, when the Germans had launched their big attack, still would not grant me any peace. I had not given it time to heal properly, and now it was getting worse, opening wider than before and weeping red and yellow. I could not sleep.

Since my release from the hospital, I had not slept for more than 30 minutes at a time, and then only fitfully. Supplies of morphine were very low, and there were others whose need was evidently greater than mine. I would not have been reluctant to take advantage of that kind of release had it been more easily available, even though a soldier has a duty to remain alert, and to keep about him a keen sense of danger–and even though, in my particular case, morphine had always suffocated pain only at the cost of nourishing nightmares.

It was my inability to rest, as much as any other consideration, that had caused me to volunteer to man the Forward Observation Post on Mont Kemmel. In the absence of efficient anesthesia, the best antidote to pain is need of fierce concentration. Extreme danger cannot overwhelm extreme discomfort, but it can confer a strange propriety upon it.

At first, the Scottish captain who had passed on the order requiring me to hold myself ready for reassignment for special duties had taken a dim view of my acceptance of the Observation Post. He must have feared a repetition of the terrible events of April 9, when the battery's communications had been cut and the Germans had circled around behind us, forcing a disorderly retreat. Had there been a Forward Observation Post that day, its occupants would have been left behind, abandoned to capture or death–death being by far the likelier contingency. A mere matter of hours after chiding me, however, MacLeod had spoken to me on the land-line, telling me that my position might, after all, be perfectly convenient–and to be ready to accept relief at any moment of the day or night.

I had no idea what the "special duties" might entail, and had been sworn to such close secrecy that I had not been able to discuss the matter with my own commanding officer, but at that time, I could not bring myself to care overmuch what I might be asked to do.

I knew that MacLeod was under the orders of General Hartley, who had taken the trouble to visit me in person–and it is not every day that a General deigns to speak to a mere subaltern–but I no longer felt capable of any powerful curiosity, nor even of any desperate anxiety. Although my family had always called me *Hope*, I had none of my own. All I was able to feel was a dull but deep discomfiture overlaid by a shallow but searing pain.

It is difficult for me to imagine, now, exactly what state of mind I must have been in during the final phases of my part in the Great War–which no longer seems to me to be "great" in any sense of that word. In my youth, I am certain, the same intensity of pain had seemed to me to be Hellish torment; the abuses and indignities I suffered after running away from home had been parent to waking terrors as well as horrific nightmares. The pain of my war wounds, added to the routine hardships of life at the Front, must have been worse, in purely objective terms, than anything inflicted upon me by my father or the brutal mates under which I served, but they never seemed so. The war that had been advertised as "the war to end all wars" and "the war to salvage civilization" was in its fifth year then, and pain was so familiar and so universal that it would have seemed churlish to think my own portion of it extreme or intolerable, even though it forbade me rest or peace of mind.

In days long gone by, when I had been an apprentice at sea, disturbed and fitful sleep had invariably delivered me into the grip of fantastic dreams, but the daily reality of April 1918 was so phantasmagorical and dream-like already that no such evil deliverance could have seemed plausible. While I was surrounded by an actual *Night Land* from which there was no conceivable escape, I had no need to journey to any imaginary equivalent; now that every day was a chapter in the extinction of the Earth, I had no need to venture into the far future to experience it.

Paradoxical as it may seem, my time with the 84th seemed then, as each foul day gave way to another, to be a relatively tedious phase of my life. Whether we were straining every muscle to haul the guns through the treacherous mud, or blasting away at the German lines, my days were equally unilluminated by the kinds of visions that welled up spontaneously from within my dark and desperate soul, and the better kinds which flowed in disciplined manner from my scratching pen. No matter how close to me the shells were bursting, nor whatever stink crept into the crevices of my gas mask, existence itself was dour: grey, bleak and empty. Even the pain of my weeping wound, which spread downwards to the hip and groin and sideways to my ribs and gut, was fire without light, provocation without vision.

If there were a Hell, I sometimes thought, that would be the quality of the circle reserved for men like me: eternal desolation, always horrid but never intense.

Dark as the night of April 19 was, I did not surrender myself to a waking dream; still as it was, I made not the slightest attempt to plan a story; ominous as it was, I did not ask myself whether the secret orders that might reach me at any time would be my death or my salvation.

I remembered my dreams of old, of course, but all I could do during that fateful pause was to mull over the records I had made of their awful imagery; such idle pondering left no trace on my enduring memory. I wish I could remember now exactly which memories teased my exhausted mind that night—whether the glow of fires to the north-west put me in mind of the *Red Pit* or whether I fancied that the trenches at my back might be reckoned the *Road Where the Silent Ones Walked*—but I cannot.

I know now that there *were* Watchers abroad, and that the place of the Abhumans was closer than I had ever dared imagine. Above all else, I know *now* that the long-awaited Gateway of Eternity was yawning wide—but I could not have known it then. Any thought of such things that passed through my stubbornly unsleeping brain must have been mere whimsy, intended for consolation rather than inspiration.

Even so, it would be more difficult to imagine that no thought at all of the *Night Land* had risen up in my consciousness—for I was, after all, in a landscape in which everything had died but despair, and I was a part of that landscape: a lonely and shadowy figure in its middle-distance.

There had been a time when I had imagined that writing my nightmares down, and making fiction of them, might somehow exorcise them and put them away forever, but the process of storification had instead preserved them from further decay, like prehistoric monsters trapped in glacial ice.

I must have known, as I could not help but compare the actual night in which I was suspended to the one I had experienced in vision and re-experienced in scribbling, that what I actually remembered were the words that had precipitated the dreams on to the page and not the dreams themselves, but it must also have seemed—must it not?—that I truly remembered the horrid Sunless world whose Last Redoubt my dream-self had visited. I have good reason now to wish that I were better able to separate vision from confabulation, but in April 1918, I probably did not care at all. I could not care.

In the small hours of April 19, I could not even care that the guns were quiet; everyone knew that when the guns were still, it was because shells were being stockpiled for a new assault. Everyone knew that every lull was the prelude to a storm; the only uncertainties were whether the storm would rain down high explosives or gas—and whether, if it were gas, it would be chlorine or phosgene. Everyone knew, too, that there were worse gases in preparation, against which no masks would be proof. Rumor said so, and we had all learned that rumor was far more reliable than the word of our superiors.

Even without the black laughter of the guns, the night that turned April 18 into 19 was not silent. While the trenches were no more than a few 100 yards apart, there was no silence to be found in the heart of no-man's-land. There was always a susurrus of whispers and footfalls, challenges and cries of pain. Even if every man within a mile had paused to hold his breath, putting a simultaneous end to all the sounds of human activity, the rustling movement of the rats would still have been audible.

The rats won all the battles; it was easy to believe that they would be the only winners of the war.

I knew, as I waited, that the morning would bring a renewal of the action. That was when my position would become vital. It would be my primary task to judge the position of the German guns, and the signaler's to communicate those positions to the battery. My secondary duty would be to observe the falling of our own shells, and the signaler's would be to communicate my estimates as to how their range should be amended. Any shell from either side that fell short of the lines might hit the post itself; a German shell would be counted a very clever shot, while a British shell would be counted a very unfortunate error, but the effect would be the same in either case.

When I heard the sound of someone approaching, I drew my pistol, even though the men were coming from the direction of our own trenches. It could have been a German detail returning from a reconnaissance mission, who had no idea that the post was there. For that reason, I issued no challenge, hoping that if they were enemies, they would pass harmlessly by–but the leader of the approaching party must have had better eyesight than I, for he made straight for my position, and sounded no whisper of his own until he was almost by my side.

"Lieutenant Hodgson?" he breathed, so lightly that the whisper was barely capable of carrying a Scottish accent–but I knew who he was.

"Here, MacLeod," I said, returning the pistol to its holster.

He came to stand beside me, while a junior officer and two riflemen crouched down outside. The narrowness of the post would have forced the Captain and myself into uncomfortable proximity in any case, but he seemed to be anxious not to be overheard and he brought his lips very close to my ear in order to say: "We must leave as soon as we have light enough."

"Have you arranged for my relief, sir?" I murmured, anxious that my duty must be done, even if I could not be there to do it. I wondered why he could not have arranged for me to be recalled to the battery and substituted under cover of darkness.

"I have," he said. "Lieutenant Thwaite will take your place"–he waved a finger in the direction of his crouching companion–"but you must leave your cap and belt behind, and your identity-tags."

The signaler stirred in his sleep, but did not wake. He was no more than 20, and must have been at school when the war began, although he had probably begun some kind of officer training before sitting the Oxford entrance. If he survived, he would go to Oxford far richer in experience than he had ever imagined possible.

"Regulations do not permit it," I said–referring, of course, to my identity-tags.

"If you read your orders carefully before following the instruction to destroy them," the Captain replied, "you will know that the regulation does not apply to this particular case."

I knew well enough that, in what John Buchan and William le Queux were wont to call the "secret service," men shed their identities at the drop of a hat, carrying forward all manner of bold masquerades–but I had always been a mere artilleryman. My French was good, but I could not have passed for a Frenchman, and I certainly could not have passed for anything more exotic, as Buchan's heroes seemed able to do.

"How do you expect to get away unseen?" I whispered. "If we are spotted, the Germans will know exactly where the post has been set up."

"That is a risk we shall have to take," he said–although he must have known that my replacement would be taking the greater risk, and my junior with him. "We must move westwards–we shall not be moving back behind the lines until we have come to the far side of Le Touquet Berthe."

We had been at Le Touquet Berthe on April 9, having relieved an Australian battery; so far as I knew, the Germans had occupied our positions after forcing us to withdraw.

"That seems to me, sir, to be dangerous in the extreme," I told him.

"On the contrary," he told me. "The Germans have regrouped; the position is deserted. We have such desperate need of you that we are exceedingly anxious to protect you from risk, and you can trust our judgment in this matter."

I did not trust his judgment, but he was a Captain and I was a Lieutenant–and the written orders I had burned as soon as I had read them had been signed by General Hartley himself. It was not a matter of trust, but a matter of duty. "Yes sir," I said, meekly. I could not have known that I was sealing the poor signaler's death-warrant, and condemning the meager remains of the man who took my place–I have no good reason to doubt that poor Thwaite *was* a man–to lie in a grave marked with my name.

Men had suffered in my stead before, during my days with the Merchant Marine–a debt I had only begun to make good with the 84th–but their suffering had never rebounded on my own loved ones. This time, it did.

My wife and mother were informed of my death during the following week, and the *Times* recorded it. Owing to a mistaken inference in my commanding officer's report, the world was informed that I had been killed by a shellburst–not on April 19, when the position was actually hit, but on April 17, when the post was unoccupied. So far as history is concerned, therefore, I was already dead during those long hours of quietude–and even though I know full well that I was not, I find it absurdly easy to imagine that I was.

It still seems to me now, even though I know the true and much less plausible reason, that my incapacity to feel anxiety or hope at midnight gave birth to

April 19, 1918 and might have been a symptom of the fact that I had already *passed on*, across the borderland of which I had written so frequently, into a region beyond life and beyond dreaming: a region where anything and everything was possible, and from which eternity stretched forth like a great crumbling highway, dark and derelict and saturated with death.

I thought then that it was the secret service that had conscripted me into a vague and uncertain existence, but I know better now.

2.

It is difficult for me to recall what happened after Captain MacLeod led me away from the observation post into the mists of dawn. Even the earliest phase of the march made the pain of my wound flare up again, worse than it had been before. I am sure, however, that the German sentries could not have caught sight of us; it was too dark. The shell that blew the post to smithereens, no more than an hour after I had sent my last message down the land-line, was presumably a freak of chance.

We had gone no more than 150 yards before we were able to drop down into a deserted trench, and we began to make our painstaking way through the maze towards Le Touquet Berthe. We contrived to cover a few 100 yards more without encountering any significant obstacle–although it was painfully slow going–but when the mists began to evaporate in the heat of the Sun, shells began to whistle overhead in some profusion.

It was the Germans who started the barrage, but the 84th had been making ready to match it for two days and our own guns leapt to action as if they were determined to match Ludendorff shot for shot. It must have been our own shells that began bursting over and around our position because the Germans knew full well that their own forces had re-grouped. MacLeod knew it too, but whoever had given him the news had not taken the trouble to make it clear to the gunners of 84th.

"We must keep going," MacLeod said, as we crouched down in a rain of mud, ankle-deep in filthy water. "Stay low, but move as fast as you can."

The eyes of the two riflemen glared within their spattered faces, lit by fear and by that strangely fervent resentment enlisted men sometimes display when their orders merely state the obvious.

We kept going, staying low but moving as fast as we could. The mist gave us some cover, but I knew that it would evaporate as the Sun climbed higher. I was the slowest, and I became slower still when we had to climb out of the trench and run across a patch of bare ground flecked with shell-holes. There was nothing there at which the guns might have been profitably aimed, but that could not have been obvious to the men crouching behind the field-pieces. I know now that if Thwaite had not been blown to smithereens, he might have got a message back to prompt a more apt alignment, but I did not know it at the time.

One blast knocked MacLeod from his feet. While we paused, another sent shrapnel screaming around us. One of the riflemen waved his weapon vaguely in the direction of the German guns, but it was mere tokenistic ritual. Rifles are snipers' weapons, unless they are fixed with bayonets, when they become mere spears.

I took a piece of shrapnel in my thigh, a foot below the re-opened wound that was causing me such trouble. It was a mere sliver, and seemed no worse in context than a bee-sting, but it was a significant inconvenience. I had been moving reasonably freely before, despite the gash in my side, but once that dart was embedded in my muscle, my whole leg threatened to seize up.

MacLeod cursed roundly, and told the riflemen to stand to either side of me and stay close–not just to help me walk but to shield me from any further harm.

"This man is precious," he barked, when one of them hesitated. "If he dies, there'll be Hell to pay!"

The shells continued to fall, although the vast majority of them were traveling over our heads as the British gunners found the range of their opposite numbers. The world to either side of us was filled with the awful sound of their overlapping blasts, and we seemed to be scrambling through a narrow margin, like a bridge of planks suspended over a chasm.

Half-supported by the two riflemen, I must have walked for more than a mile thereafter before we reached the Allies' lines–which turned out, as we crossed them, to be French ones. Rumor had not informed me that the French had moved into position beyond Le Touquet Berthe, but rumor rarely bothered with such trivia as that–except, of course, to report the advent of Americans, which still seemed almost miraculous. British, French, Belgian and Australian troops had all been homogenized by the common experience of disaster, but the Americans were spectacularly fresh, quite different in the way they looked at the blasted landscape and its human flotsam.

Not unnaturally, we found ourselves in mortal danger yet again once we were among our own side's guns, and we were more exposed than we had been in the abandoned trenches. The soft mist that had blanketed the land since daybreak had gone now, but it had been partly replaced by dark clouds of stinking smoke and stinging dust. Fortunately, there was no gas. The Germans seemed to be preparing for a push, and would not want the ground to be littered with canisters discharging mustard gas if they hoped to be sending the infantry forward to occupy this position.

My doubled wound increased its harassment of my spirit, but I refused to recognize or respond to its depredations. I had tried with all my might to cultivate a state of mind which allowed me to do that, having heard that some men were able to subject their bodies to uncanny discipline, but I had never been more than half-successful, and such success as I had now was as much the product of exhaustion as of strength of will. Infirmity ignored is still infirmity, and I grew weaker by the minute, while the shells aimed at the French guns fell behind us. The shellbursts seemed actually to be following us deeper and deeper into our own territory, but if there was any more to the suspicion than mere illusion they must have been probing for some other target.

I was only mildly astonished when the Captain took the place of the younger rifleman, seizing my arm in a powerful grip and hurrying me on. "It's not much further," he growled, stretching the vowel in *further* in his Gaelic fashion. "You must not falter–we'll get a surgeon to that leg as soon as possible. It's only a scratch."

I meant to assure him that I had not the slightest intention of faltering, and I contrived to utter at least half a sentence before my legs and lungs betrayed me, but my flesh gave the lie to my optimism. I collapsed, and would have fallen had the Captain and the rifleman not held me up; they were bearing all my weight now, although I was still upright.

The loss of blood was making me slightly giddy, but when I looked down at my leg the tear in my uniform hardly seemed visible, and the bloody discoloration below it was a mere streak, as if a dirty thumbnail had been carelessly drawn across the cloth. I knew that the Captain must be right about the relative triviality of the wound, but I also knew that a single straw may break a camel's back if the poor beast has been too long overburdened.

I tried hard to remain conscious, but the cost of the effort was that I retreated within myself to an extraordinary extent. I could not pay more than the most fleeting attention to my surroundings, and hardly noticed when we finally moved far enough beyond the scope of the German guns to find a measure of quiet.

The relief I felt when I was bundled into the seat of a car was profound; robbed of the need to keep account of my awkward progress, my mind felt free to let my senses reel. I slumped in the corner, my eyes looking outwards from the side-window of the car.

The road in front of the vehicle seemed to twist like a coiling snake and occasionally to rear up like a frightened horse, although its curves must in reality have been gentle and its potholes none-too-deep. I heard voices speaking, although I could not have responded to what they said even if they had been speaking to me. Much of the conversation made no impression, but I was afterwards able–when I had motive enough and opportunity–to reproduce a few exchanges.

"You left it too late," the Scotsman said, at one point, adding an indecent accusation that would have been most improper had he been speaking to an officer with sufficient seniority to bring a staff car that close to the front.

"Not my decision," replied a voice whose accent was contrasting, and yet not entirely dissimilar.

"We should have taken him while he was still in England. We could have done it easily, if only the idiots across the water had not dithered."

"Who could have known that he would pass the medical board? Who could have anticipated that they would reassign him when they did–and to Ypres of all places?" I finally placed the second man's accent; he was an Ulsterman.

"Now he has two new wounds to add to the injuries he suffered when that damned horse threw him," the Scotsman said. "What chance does he have, in this state, of making good our losses? If we had only seen the way the wind was blowing before hostilities broke out! Two years we had, to judge the quality of his mind and find him–six if we had only seen the clue in the earlier book. We are a company of fools!"

"He's strong–stronger, I dare say, than you or I, and certainly stronger than Copplestone was when he opened the way. It's not his wounds that require us to be anxious but the long journey that still lies ahead of us. We have to cross the water twice, one way or another–and all England too. When we reach the hospital, he'll be well patched-up, but he'll be dead weight for a while thereafter, and the Boche is not our only enemy."

Something must have happened in my head thereafter to derange my senses. I have never succeeded in remembering anymore, although I know that I continued to keep a sideways watch over the serpentine road as best I could, and that the man who was with me in the back of the car continued to exchange remarks with the Scotsman who sat beside the driver. I know that I ate at midday, and again in the evening, and was given brandy to drink as often as I was given water, but I have not the slightest idea what hospital it was at which we finally arrived. I remember the stained bonnet of a weary nurse, but if I ever saw the surgeon who removed the sliver of metal from my thigh, I could not keep the memory of his face.

I do not remember being injected with morphine, but I must have been injected with something, else my memories could not have blurred so badly. I suppose that I must have slept at last, and therefore might have dreamed, but I do not know when the remains of my uniform were cut away and bandages applied to my side and thigh. Indeed, I lost all track of time and the sequence of events. Such memories as I eventually contrived to recover–even with the unusual assistance that was eventually made available to me–are momentary and indistinct.

I do remember red roses, and freshly-laundered nurses' aprons–but I do not believe that I was ever put to bed. I cannot remember being dressed again after my wounds had been bandaged, in khaki or in civilian clothes. I was certainly put into the back of an ambulance, and I know that I felt very grateful and relieved when I was allowed to lie down there, although it was a mixed blessing. The ruts and potholes in the road had felt bad enough before, but now that I had no forewarning at all of impending jolts they seemed increasingly malevolent. My mind became fixated upon such jarring disturbances: waiting for them, counting them, pulling myself together after each and every one.

I was not alone in the back of that first ambulance; there were at least two men in uniform as well as a grey-eyed nurse. I do not even know if MacLeod was one of them, let alone the Ulsterman whose name I had not been told. What they said, if they said anything at all, made no impression. I cannot estimate how long it was before I finally contrived to sleep, nor how long I slept before waking. It must have been soon afterwards that I developed a fever, which began to burn very hotly in my brain.

I seem to recall that my delirium was stubbornly earthbound, its imagery besotted with rich Belgian soil, furious shellfire and thick red blood–but there was something of the sea in it as well, and doubtless more than I would have liked. I had grown to love the actual ocean, after a fashion–or at least to conquer my fear of its many natural hazards–but the seas of my nightmares were always worse, in their implacable malignity, than the most furious seas stirred up by honest storms. I had taken my camera into the eyes of a dozen hurricanes, but had only ever had a pen to wield against the malign eyes of the swinish things that dwelt beyond the Borderland, in the worlds beyond the world.

By the time we were actually at sea, I was so uncertain of myself that I did not know whether the waves were real or not. Although that first crossing must have been from Calais to Dover, it was long enough and rough enough to raise sinister echoes in my soul.

Of our transit of England, I remember next to nothing, but I must have been on the road to recovery by the time we took to the water again–crossing, I must suppose, from Holyhead to Dublin. By that time, I had grown accustomed to the presence of the grey-eyed nurse, who was distant but efficient. The uniformed man who was with me during that second crossing was an orderly, who hardly ever met my eye.

Having been on the continent for so long, I knew little or nothing of the state of affairs in Ireland. The censors took care to limit intelligence of such events as Sinn Fein riots, although rumor usually had little difficulty filling in the blacked-out lines of our correspondence. I remember asking the grey-eyed nurse, in a faint voice, whether there was more danger or less in Dublin than in Belgium, but I cannot remember what she said in reply, if she deigned to answer at all.

It was not until we had been on the road for some time, in yet another ambulance, that I was able to engage in a real conversation. By then, MacLeod had taken up a position by my side, and he seemed far more kindly–perhaps because he was more obviously solicitous–than the nurse or the orderly.

"I fear that I have been very ill," I said to him.

"Your wounds became infected," he told me, "but the doctor used maggots to clean them. The height of your fever caused some anxiety, but the crisis soon passed. You'll make a full recovery."

I knew of maggot-cleaned men whose bodies had made full recoveries but whose minds had not–but I was perfectly certain that I was made of sterner stuff.

"Has the secret mission for which you recruited me been cancelled?" I asked.

"It certainly has not," he assured me. "It is as vital as it ever was, and you are still the man best fitted for the job. General Hartley is determined to press ahead without delay. We cannot tell when–or even if–another man with your qualifications might appear."

"I can no more pass for Irish than I could pass for French," I told him. "I'm no Richard Hannay."

"You will not be required to pass for anything you are not," he told me, with a slight curl of the lip and a very slight stress on the word *you*. "This is not *Greenmantle*, but something far more profound. Please don't ask me any more, for I have reached the limit of my authority. You will be fully briefed in due time." His accent was beginning to grate on me–but no one could have taken him at his word, however free of irritation his voice was.

"Where are we going?" I asked, disobediently.

"I cannot say," he replied, as he was doubtless bound to do.

By way of practicing my recovered faculties, and in the cause of dispelling the grogginess that still set siege to my intelligence, I tried to make what estimate I could of where we were and where we were headed, but the only windows at the rear of ambulance were set high in the doors, and I was not yet ready to rise from my bed. All I could guess from the altitude and subsequent movement of the Sun, whose rays were angled through those windows, was that we were traveling a few degrees south of westwards. Hours passed while I deduced no more, and the only news which my Scottish companion would condescend to pass on was that Milner had been made Secretary for War. It was not until we had stopped to fill the vehicle's tank, and attend to our own accumulated needs, that I was able to strike up a conversation with the nurse while the Captain was otherwise occupied.

"Milner will make no difference," I opined. "The war has a life of its own, now. Nothing but the mutual exhaustion of both sides will bring it to a close."

She looked at me with a tolerant expression; I saw that her eyes seemed faded, as if the color had been drained out of them, perhaps by too much weeping or too frequent an exposure to sights not meant for mortals. "The Americans have tipped the balance," she replied, hopefully. Her accent was Irish, softer by far than the Ulsterman's. "The Germans are desperate, and their next wave of attacks will break them. It will be 20 years and more before they try to take their revenge, and even that conflict will be a distant prelude to the *real* world war– the war of all against all."

It seemed at the time to be empty speculation, unusual only in the extent of its cynicism.

When the Captain returned, the nurse put her finger to her lips, to signal that she would say no more and would rather I held my own tongue. "What shall I call you?" I asked her, having never heard her addressed by name.

"Helen," she said. "Call me Helen."

MacLeod took note of the fact that I was asking for names and beckoned to the orderly who was driving the ambulance. "This is Corporal Heath," he said. "You know us all now, except for Colonel Wrightman. He was with us in Belgium and England, but he's gone ahead with the General to make ready for your arrival."

Before he closed the door behind him I looked past him for any sign that might have told me where I was heading, but there was none that I could see.

The Soldier's Story: Part Two

The west of Ireland, April 1918

3.

We arrived at our destination that evening. At the time, I did not know what day it was, although I later deduced that it was probably April 25. I did not ask because I was still preoccupied with the question of what the General and his staff could possibly intend to demand of me, given that they had gone to such extraordinary trouble to bring me here even in my enfeebled state.

When I got out of the ambulance–coming to my feet for the first time in several days–that mystery became confused with another.

I have no idea where in the west of Ireland we were. I had certainly never been there before, but I was nevertheless struck by a strange sense of familiarity. It might have been the sound of water splashing as it fell, or it might have been something about the grey stone wall of the house which confronted me, or the wall that surrounded its unkempt garden–or it might simply have been the in-evitable re-emergence of the barely-submerged awareness that the west of Ireland had been the site selected by my imagination-driven pen for the location of one of my nightmare-based romances.

For whatever reason, I became acutely conscious, not merely of the fact that I now stood *on the borderland*, but that the borderland in question was one that I had faced, and traversed, before. There was no tremendous waterfall, no abyssal pit and no ruin on its brink, but I could not shake off the feeling that I was returning to a familiar place, and that I had always been fated to return. The house set beside the road seemed perfectly ordinary, and the flat landscape stret-ching to the western horizon where the Sun hovered, invisibly, behind a cluster of pink clouds seemed positively bland, but I could scarcely suppress a shudder as I looked at them. The sound of falling water was only a sudden shower–there was no stream nearby–but it seemed ominous nevertheless.

"Hurry," said the Captain, ducking beneath the assault of the heavy rain-drops. "We must get inside."

The door was already open. Had I been fit, I could have run to it, covering the intervening distance in a dozen strides or less, but as things were I had to be supported by the Captain and the orderly; it was to the Corporal, not to me, that the Scotsman had addressed his remark.

While they hurried me inside, I had only time to note that the house was a sprawling affair, hardly a mansion, but bigger than an inn or farmhouse. Its roof was slate and its walls showed signs of recent repair; the mortar between its stone blocks had been repointed and the lights in its heavily-leaded windows patched, so that segments of modern sheet glass were mingled with more ancient slabs of cheap pooled glass, transparent but swirlingly unclear.

I was taken along a corridor to a room on the ground floor, where a bed had been made ready for me. It was not a pleasant room–the ceiling was low and inadequately plastered, while the walls had been ineptly painted with a sickly cream gloss–but it was carpeted and seemed a little more like a home than a prison cell.

I was immediately put to bed. I was still wearing my pajamas, although a greatcoat had been put about my shoulders while we crossed from the ambulance to the house. It was Helen who brought me my meal, after an hour's impatient rest, but when she was gone, there was very little delay before I was visited by individuals of far greater importance.

I had been expecting General Hartley and Colonel Wrightman, but I had not been expecting to see another Major-General and a Brigadier. I was tempted to inquire as to whether Milner had left anyone to mind the shop in Ypres, but I did not dare. All four brought chairs from the far side of the room, lining them up beside the bed before taking their seats, with Hartley closest to my pillow.

I suppose, in retrospect, that we lower-ranking officers had nothing for which to thank or glorify the Generals who planned the campaigns of that dismal war, but we could not and did not think like that at the time. I had no reason to doubt that Hartley and his colleague were anything but what they pretended to be, and no reason to doubt that the men they were pretending to be were entitled to my fullest respect and loyalty.

"I am sorry, sir," I told Hartley, "to come to you in such a miserable condition."

"It's not the fitness of your body that will determine the success of your mission, Lieutenant Hodgson," he assured me. "It's the quality of your mind. We have every reason to believe it, at any rate–and every reason, despite all that you have suffered, to hope that your mind is as powerful now as it ever was."

"I wish I could reassure you on that point, sir," I said, "but I am only now recovering proper consciousness–and for a moment, while I stood outside, I felt that I had stepped into the edge of a nightmare."

"The edge of a story based in a nightmare, I think," he said. "It was your waking mind that described *The House of the Borderland*, was it not? The substance of your nightmares merely supplied certain raw materials."

I should have been surprised by his perspicacity, but I was not. My silent response was to think that *raw* was more apposite a description than he probably imagined.

"Are you ready to hear what will be required of you, Lieutenant Hodgson?" the General asked. "You will think it strange, but you may be assured that this is no dream."

"I am," I said, as loyalty compelled.

"Very well," he said. "You understand, I assume, that everything you hear within these walls–including the names of the people gathered here–is a secret, which you must not divulge under any circumstances. This is Major-General Sir Philip Horniman, and this is Brigadier Severn, both seconded from Military Intelligence. We are jointly responsible for certain categories of special operations, involving esoteric scientific researches."

I said nothing, but when he paused, as if for some acknowledgement, I nodded my head.

"We have some reason to believe," said Hartley, "that the war that has sapped Britain's strength these last five years will soon end. We shall reckon ourselves the victors, and punish our enemies harshly for all that they have done to us–but the spoils will be meager. In 1914, Europe was the economic heart of the world, and might have remained so had the continent not been so deeply divided against itself; from now on, the economic heart of the world will beat in New York."

I could not decide how old Hartley was. The lines on his face suggested that he must be well over 50, but there was not a trace of grey in his hair. Horniman seemed much younger, although his features were even more severe. Both were clean-shaven, as was the thin-faced Brigadier, whose hook-like nose reminded me of an eagle's beak. The four pairs of eyes varied in shade, but not in the intensity of their gazes; they looked at me in an expectant manner, which did not quite match the melancholy tone of Hartley's voice.

"Britain went into this war convinced that it might provide the means to secure Anglo-Saxon hegemony over the entire world," the speaker went on. "The intention was to consolidate the Empire and make it safe from the envy of less happier nations. We have not achieved that, nor have we retained such precarious security as we had before. Even though victory is to be ours within the year, Britain and the Empire will be so severely weakened that their future is in terrible jeopardy. Ludendorff is our immediate enemy, but he is by no means the final one. The war has been more terrible than we have been given leave to confess, but we have reason to believe that there is a greater holocaust still to come. We need to know everything that can be known about that threat, if we are to have the slightest chance of averting or ameliorating it.

"There is a great deal that I am forbidden to tell you, not merely by reason of the nation's security but by reason of the nature of the task that lies before you. It is, however, permitted to me to say that experiments have been going on since the turn of the century with a number of drugs whose effect seems to be to allow their users access to visions of the future. The greater number of the reports which have been carried back to us have been direly confused, and where they have tallied at all, they have done so in respect of events so remote that there has been no possible opportunity to test their accuracy. The events of the war have, however, provided a number of checks to be set against data recovered long before its beginning, and we now have enough evidence in hand to be sure that the drugs do have considerable efficacy.

"I do not wish to deceive you as to the risk you are taking, so I will admit from the outset that more than 12 of the volunteers who have taken part in our experiments have died, and more than 100 have suffered some ill-effects. The compounds involved are toxic; I make no bones about that. Three in four of those who have been very ill obtained no advantage whatsoever from their experiences; the visions they experienced were so disordered as to offer no clear information at all. For some years, we selected subjects who were physically robust, on the grounds that they would be best fitted to resist the toxicity of the drugs, but we have had proof enough that this policy was misconceived. We have now concluded–and we are perfectly certain of our conclusion–that those individuals best-fitted to receive the most powerful drugs are those who have already demonstrated an innate visionary power of their own."

I had not been expecting anything like this. Nothing I had learned about the British and German secret services from such ardent propagandists as le Queux had suggested that they had taken to dabbling in the sibylline arts. Nevertheless, here were three men who gave every indication of being wise as well as stern, assembled in committee to lend weight to their spokesman's declarations. Their eyes forbade me even to wonder whether they might be less than wholly serious.

"All men dream," Hartley went on, sonorously "but we do not all dream alike. Three in four of us, at least, find nothing but trouble-less confusion in our dreams. Many of the remainder, if Dr. Sigmund Freud of Vienna can be believed, experience dreams shaped by our inner conflicts and repressed desires. Some men, however, have always believed that their dreams contain awkward intelligence of things to come, which might be infinitely valuable were it not so difficult to decipher. Anthropologists assure us that there are countless primitive tribes whose holy men routinely employ drugs in attempts to obtain forewarning of things to come, and are utterly convinced of the occasional success of their methods.

"Civilized travelers have, of course, taken leave to doubt such assertions, considering themselves intellectually superior to such tribesmen by virtue of their own societies' mastery of mechanical technology. In the absence of written records, the representatives of conventional wisdom have observed, the record of prophesies fulfilled is mere hearsay–and where written records did once exist, as in the case of certain oracular prophesies of ancient Rome, they seem to have been irredeemably vague and probably corrupt. Few have troubled to do as we have done, and subject the claims made on behalf of these compounds to the test. The greatest proof of our success is that the information which has allowed us to refine and perfect these potions, so as to maximize their visionary potential and minimize their undesirable side-effects, has itself been transmitted back to us from the distant future."

Amazing! I thought. I could not help but wonder, having already heard the General refer approvingly to *The House on the Borderland*, whether one of these men might have visited the Night Land, or caught some fugitive glimpse of the death of the Earth. The expression in their eyes seemed less peculiar once I had considered that hypothesis–although I guessed even then that their experimental subjects were probably conscripts, with hardly an officer among them. No doubt the men in question would have been desperately eager for an alternative to service on the Somme, or in the West African Rifles: quite happy to drink poison instead of hanging on the wire, riddled with machine-gun bullets.

"I think you will understand, by now, why we selected you for recruitment to our peculiar cause, Lieutenant Hodgson. We have scoured the Western world for men who have demonstrated visionary power and acumen in their writings. We have approached dozens–including, I dare say, many whose names you would immediately recognize–and have won the limited co-operation of most. Some have consented to become members of our organization–which was not originally founded by military men, although political necessity has determined that military men had to take charge of it during these last four years. It has been suggested that we should have identified and approached you several years ago, as soon as you published *The House on the Borderland*, but we were not in a position then to identify the aspects of that fascinating document that showed clear evidence of prophetic ability. *The Night Land* provided further clues, but even in 1912, its correspondences with other items in our records seemed vague, and their relevance dubious. We can only apologize for our tardiness–and assure you that we now have data that have convinced us absolutely that you are the man for the mission we have in mind. In fact, there is no other in the entire world more suited to its requirements."

"I fear, sir, that I have been very ill," I told him, frankly. "My wounds are healing, but I am not half the man I was when I kept a School of Physical Culture in Blackburn. I was well enough when I first moved to Sanary, intending to make a home in France, but ever since that day, I have suffered as badly as France herself. I was already weakened when I was thrown from my horse, and I have been stricken with infection more than once while my flesh has been scored and scored again by the rigors of battle. I have had to be pumped full of morphine, or some such opiate, to bring me through the last few days–and to be perfectly honest, I dread the prospect of withdrawing from its tender clutch. I do not say this because I am afraid, sir, but only because I fear to fail in my duty. I have already accepted this commission, and have given my tacit consent to anything you may care to do with me, but I cannot in all conscience say that I am fit enough, as yet, to be given a dangerous drug."

I believe that what I said was the simple truth, although I have to admit that the one duty I might have been reluctant to perform on my country's behalf was to dream as I had once been accustomed to dreaming. I had not yet absorbed the full import of the General's assertion that I had been selected for this mission precisely because I had already given unmistakable evidence of a sibylline gift, but I had taken the most oppressive inference. My visions had been fearful enough when I had been able to tell myself that they were utterly false–flying in the face of the gale of conviction that had always urged me to believe otherwise–and to have it confirmed that I had been right to reach for grains of truth therein was not welcome news.

"I know all that," was General Hartley's response to my speech. "Nor can I expect you to take comfort from the fact–although it is a fact–that the clearest visions ever received by our subjects have been recovered by men who were almost at the point of death. What I do insist upon, however, is that it is not in our interests to subject you to any ordeal that might prove fatal. If you are to serve us, then you must return from this mission alive and articulate; if you are to serve us well, you must come through it with sufficient strength of body and mind to attempt further visionary odysseys. If we believed for one moment that the risk to your life was too great, or that it could be lessened by delay, we would take no action."

I was not particularly relieved to hear it, although I followed the logic of his argument readily enough.

"Is there anyone here who has used this drug?" I asked, surveying the General's silent companions.

"Apart from Sir Philip and myself," the General said, "there is no one in this house who has not. Brigadier Severn, Colonel Wrightman and Captain MacLeod are all in a position to reassure you that the experience can be borne, and that it can sometimes add to a man's strength rather than depleting it."

I looked at Severn, and he looked back at me. "It's true," he said. "I only wish I had been better able to serve. Alas, I am not. There is only one person here at present who brought back anything of real value, and that is Miss Flynn. I fear that we have had to ask her not to reveal any of its substance."

It took me a moment or two to realize that Miss Flynn must be grey-eyed Helen.

"We would not countenance this if we did not think that there were rewards to be won," Horniman put in. "We have, however, forbidden everyone here to say anything about the shape of the future as they or others have tentatively sketched it out. Because the expectations and inclinations of the visionary mind might have the capacity to pollute and confuse the content of prophetic dreams, there is no folly greater than to fill a would-be explorer with expectations. If you set forth in ignorance and bring back information that others have already brought, that is proof–were you to set forth already in possession of such information, its supplementation would prove nothing."

"If you have found information in my literary visions which matches news of the future brought back by these and other men," I said, "then I already have grounds enough for thinking that the experience will be profoundly disturbing."

"And we," General Hartley countered, "have grounds enough for thinking that the threats that will face us in the future are too dark and awesome to be let alone."

"But if a vision of the future can be true," I said, having gone over the logical ground several times before in discussion with admirers of H. G. Wells– once with Wells himself–and with Frenchmen I had met in Paris and Marseilles, "that implies that it cannot be altered, even with the aid of foreknowledge. That is a frightening thought, is it not? It ought to make us wish with all our might that we cannot obtain true knowledge of the future–except, perhaps, insofar as we may concern ourselves with the acceptably inevitable." I was thinking of the vision of the Earth's demise that I had recorded in *The House on the Border-land*, which was ultimately unavoidable, but far too distant in time to cause any human being an atom of concern.

"Alas," said Hartley, "our wishing will make no difference. If the future can be known, then we must make it known–and we must hope that having become known, it may also become avoidable. It is, I confess, an odd sort of truth which, in becoming known, may falsify itself–but we must take the universe as we find it, even if we find it strangely mercurial. There is not a man in our organization, I think, who does not hope with all his might that if we can only act wisely on the basis of the dreams we induce, then future users of the drugs might discover far happier news of a much brighter future."

"Do you think that is possible, sir?" I asked him.

"How shall we know," he answered, "until we have tried, with all our might, to make it possible?"

4.

There is no point in my setting down here a further record of my experiences in that stupidly mundane parallel of the House on the Borderland. Perhaps, if I had devoted myself to intensive investigations, I could have discovered a great deal more about its inhabitants and the organization to which they belonged–even the cook and the handyman, it seemed. Perhaps that is what I should have done.

I could have sneaked out of my room at night on exploratory expeditions. I could have bombarded my various attendants with all manner of cunning questions, calculated to obtain information despite their orders. Had I been as great a detective as Conan Doyle's titan of *The Strand*, or even my own dear Carnacki, that is probably what I would have done. I would have smelled a rat even if there had been no rat to smell–but as things were, my nose remained stubbornly clear and I kept it scrupulously clean, except for asking a few very gentle questions of my nurse.

"They say you have taken this drug?" I said, tentatively, when she brought me a glass of laudanum to help me sleep.

"Yes, sir," she said. "But I must not tell you what I saw."

"I do not ask you to tell me anything that you are sworn to keep secret," I assured her, "but General Hartley suggested that you might help to set my mind at rest regarding it effects on my person. Did it make you very sick?"

"No, sir–but I believe that I received a very slight dose, not nearly as great as was given to Captain MacLeod or the Colonel."

"All for nothing, in their cases–so I'm told," I said. "But they look fit enough now. Have you ever seen them give the drug to a man as sick as me?"

"Yes, sir," she said, hesitantly. "And I never saw one die–though they say..." She broke off.

"I know that men have died," I told her, gently. "That, at least, is no secret." I was tempted to add "and you need not call me *sir*," but I did not; if she did not call me "sir", what would she call me? "William" would have sounded odd, "Hope" entirely inappropriate.

I let the matter rest, for fear of causing her to let something slip that would get her into trouble. Perhaps it was foolish to collaborate thus in my own deception–but I had not the slightest reason then to suspect that I was prey to a deceptive conspiracy, and I had other things on my mind.

When Helen came in again to take account of my steadily-improving condition, I thanked her kindly, but did not try to detain her. When the orderly came in to clear dishes or sweep the floor, I was equally polite. When any of my superior officers came to ask me how I was, I took care to assure them that I was as well as could be expected. I sometimes asked for news of the war, and was told of the British victory at Villiers Bretonneux and the apparent end of the German offensive, but I made no attempt to touch on matters of which I and they had been forbidden to speak.

I did once inquire of Brigadier Severn about any lingering after-effects of his own experience with the visionary drugs, and was told that he had none–but he also volunteered the information, frankly enough, that although such effects were normally slight, he had seen more than one man who had been noticeably disfigured, the flesh shrunk back upon the bones of the face so that it resembled a death's-head with staring eyes.

"It is not certainly impossible," he told me, "that you will wake to find the flesh clinging tight to your bones, as thin as a rake–but I have seen a man in that situation recover the greater part of his lost weight within a month. He was not regretful about the remainder, although he had never been unduly corpulent."

I was not unduly corpulent myself, and I felt that my muscles would not benefit at all from any further wastage, but the tone of the man's assurances was nevertheless welcome. He told me, with all apparent sincerity, that he felt sure that the company of experimenters had learned enough from their previous experiments to make the possibility of fatality or serious injury exceedingly remote.

It was not until I had agreed with the two Generals that I was ready to make the attempt–indeed, not until the drug was actually brought into my room–that I raised an issue that I probably ought to have raised earlier.

"You said that you had obtained the services of other men who had shown evidence of visionary power," I remarked to Hartley, "including several whose names I would know. Will you tell me who they were?"

"That might not be wise," the General replied. "If you have read their published works, revealing their names might provide exactly the kind of cue that we are anxious to avoid. I wish that you would try not to think about such matters. It would be ideal, from our point of view, if you were to empty your mind, so far as is possible, of all expectations, however tentative or speculative."

"I can hardly be expected to do that," I told him. "It is like being commanded not to think of a piebald horse. How can I refuse to entertain the thought of such visionaries as Edgar Allan Poe, Camille Flammarion and Svante Arrhenius, when my work has so often been compared to theirs? How can I forget that I have read *The Time Machine*, *The Purple Cloud*, *La Mort de la Terre* and *The Hampdenshire Wonder*? The intervention of the war has inhibited the production of such works, but I have talked about them while on leave in Paris and in London, all the more eagerly because opportunities to do so with men like H. G. Wells or Alfred Vallette came about so rarely. How can I put existing visions of the future out of my mind, when I know nothing of my own future, save for the fact that you wish to send me forth as a visionary explorer? Even if I could put such images aside by some effort of conscious will, they would surely return as soon as my thoughts were free to wander."

"You did not copy them when you wrote *The Night Land*," Hartley pointed out. "We have confidence in your independence of spirit, provided that it remains unprejudiced. I shall not tell you which of the men whose works you have cited have worked with us, although I will admit that there is only one among those who are still living who has *not* been given our most careful consideration–that, of course, is Vallette. We have little interest in mere editors, however hospitable they have been to visionary work."

I let the matter rest. How could I have done otherwise? I even did my level best to let it rest internally, in the interest of cultivating the independence of spirit that was required of me.

I was docile because I was innocent; I suspected nothing, because I had no grounds for suspicion.

When the time came for me to lie down upon my overly familiar bed and accept an injection in my arm, administered by the ever-dutiful Miss Flynn, that is what I did.

"One more thing," said General Hartley, leaning over me as if to speak in confidence, although his words were audible to the other five people who were present. "We have reason to think that some of the individuals you might encounter within your dream might be hostile to us. You must be on your guard–not so much against violence, although it is not impossible that you might be in physical danger, as against deception. It might be in the interests of certain inhabitants of the future to lie to you. Take nothing on trust."

It was a warning I would rather have received before, while I was in a position to seek further clarification, although the mere possibility that I might be told lies could hardly have made any difference to my resolve. As my eyes closed, I did my best to signal with my gaze that I would do my duty as well as I possibly could, and as warily too–exactly as my commander, my country and my King were entitled to expect of me.

At first, the effect of the drug was not unlike morphine. I felt as though I were falling gratefully asleep, released from the burdens of worry and pain. I drifted into a dream in a far lighter manner than had been my habit in recent days, and the images which pressed in upon my quiet consciousness did not seem at all threatening.

Despite my best intentions, I knew that the images I was producing were emerging from the legacy of my reading and my writing, but even notions which had formerly seemed horrific now seemed very ordinary and not at all frightening. The cosmic vision experienced by the protagonist of *The House on the Borderland* had terrified me when I actually experienced it, and the terror had come back to me–albeit faintly–as I first set it down in writing, but the experience of copying it several times and proof-reading it several times more had defused it of all effect save tender familiarity. It seemed to me, as I tumbled into the unknown, that the unknown in question was more welcoming than it had ever been before, and that all its inhabitants were mere whimsies devoid of malignity or ugliness.

For a while, as I fell into eternity, I felt more relaxed than I had in years, and safer than I had ever felt before.

I fell through a colorless spectrum of light and dark which flickered unsteadily, but there seemed to be nothing eerie or disturbing in the oscillatory effect. There were longer periods of darkness too, but the darkness never seemed pregnant with evil.

It was difficult to think clearly, but one idea that did seem to float to the surface of my mind was the possibility that the General had dangled before me: that while the power to remake the future had been increased by warning visions, so the future itself must have been improved and made increasingly hospitable for future visitors.

When the world stabilized around me, that possibility was trembling on the brink of full and active consciousness, ready for application to what I saw–and what I saw, at first, did not in any way defy the optimistic expectation.

The Soldier's Story: Part Three

*The island formerly known as Ireland
and the orbit of the Moon
circa 12,000,000 A.D.*

5.

I found myself lying on ground as level as the bleak plain that had surrounded the house in Ireland, but much more lushly furnished. I was cushioned
by thick green grass, and the profuse boughs of trees extended over me like a
great reckless arch, some dressed in pink blossom and others crowded with mis-
tletoe-like growths. The crowns of the trees were dense but not so opaque that I
could not see the cloudless sky beyond, bluer and brighter than any sky I had
ever seen over war-torn Flanders. Birds were singing, as they never sang in the
scarred landscapes of Belgium, and their tunes seemed perfectly familiar–almost
as if the hidden singers were not merely members of species I knew, but actual
individuals whose songs I had heard before.

My own body, by contrast, seemed distinctly less familiar. I felt very
strange–heavy and awkward–but when I looked at my right hand it seemed far
less substantial than I remembered it, almost translucent. Even more puzzling
was the fact that I seemed to be attired in a dress uniform, which had all the appropriate badges of rank and yet was curiously light, quite *unreal*. As I climbed,
very unsteadily, to my feet, knee deep in the tangled grass, I could hardly believe that I was the same man who had lain in bed in the house in Ireland–nor,
for that matter, the same man who had suffered such terrible nightmares in my
youth.

Perhaps the war has scoured me clean of all my direr fears, I thought, as I
ducked beneath a trailing branch. *Perhaps the horrors of reality have impressed
themselves so powerfully upon me that there is nothing left within me but a delicate fever for beauty and quiet, and a sense of my own insubstantiality in the
face of eternity.*

I tried to draw a deep breath, convinced that the forest must be full of
sweet scents, but that proved oddly difficult. I certainly felt as if I had lungs, but
it no longer seemed to be the case that I could inflate them with an easy gesture
of the diaphragm. I could not smell anything, even when I opened my mouth as
if to taste the air with a moist tongue.

I turned slowly through 360 degrees, searching with my eyes for a path or any other evidence of human habitation. There was nothing, but I could not believe that the woodland was entirely wild. It was too comfortable for that, too mild in its appearance. It was certainly no jungle, and I could easily have believed it to be some covert of a garden: a garden modeled, as so many English gardens have been, on a piece of continental art-work. The greenery that surrounded and overhung me seemed too calm even to be an image of Arcadia, although it seemed too conspicuously European to be made in the image of an artist's Eden. Had the surrounds of Mont Kemmel been like this, I wondered, before the guns had been set for the very first barrage?

I looked around a second time, this time appraising my environment as I might have judged a painting in the National Gallery, hunting for evidence of style in what I had now decided to consider its artifice.

And then, to prove me wrong, the world exploded.

The trees rattled as if their crowns had been strafed by machine-gun fire. The grassy ground beneath my feet, which had seemed so richly clad, peeled back its turf abruptly, and opened lips of loam. Those lips drew back as if in a snarl, to reveal teeth of granite.

It seemed that the whole glade had become an avid and furious mouth, with no intent but to suck me in and chew me into pulp.

When the trap opened beneath me, threatening instant destruction, I felt a stab of alarm–but nothing like the rush of panic I might have expected. As I looked down into the gaping hole the thought that surged into my mind was that I was in a dream, and that as soon as I began to fall, I would awake, safe in my bed.

I did not awake–but neither did I begin to fall. Given that I was in a dream, that did not seem unduly astonishing.

In my less nightmarish dreams I had often floated, in calm and lordly defiance of the dictates of gravity, and I floated now. My body still felt unduly heavy and cumbersome, but I found no cause for wonder that it could also be reckoned light as thistledown.

It was not until I actually began to rise into the woodland canopy that I realized that I was in the grip of some exotic force–that I had been snatched from the brink of disaster by an invisible but powerful hand. When I was taken up, however, I felt the pressure about my torso and abdomen. I looked down, half-expecting to see visible strands coiling about me, but there was only a curious uncertainty in the air, like the heat haze rising from a hot gun-carriage.

The living ground was not prepared to accept defeat so easily, however; it reared up after me.

It was as if some giant sleeping beneath the tangled sward had been awakened by my arrival, and had awakened hungry for the flesh and blood of an Englishman. There was only the least trace of human form in the mass of soil and rock that climbed like a steeple beneath my booted feet, but I could not help thinking of it as a huge hand reaching out for me at the extremity of a Gargantuan arm.

It might almost have been a comfort to look down and see baleful eyes staring up at me, enviously measuring my ascent, because that would have placed me unambiguously in a fairy tale–but whatever sense inspired the growing tower, it was not the kind of sight that required human eyes, and whatever the hunger was that guided it, it was no mere animal impulse. It seemed, as I stared down at the burgeoning tree-studded mass, in which the green was rapidly being devoured by the brown, that the impulse forming and guiding it must be akin to the kind of blind tropism that guides flowers to bathe in sunlight. The avid mass remained quite undifferentiated: an inchoate structure of fluid soil.

For a few seconds, I thought it might actually catch me and snatch me back–but as it extended like a snaking tentacle it was grabbed as I had been grabbed, and forced into conflict with some invisible adversary carved from the very air.

By the time my upward progress was arrested, I was at least 200 feet above the crowns of the tallest trees in the wood–which now revealed itself to be a considerable forest, extending its canopy in every direction to the visible horizon. Now that I was suspended, with no visible means of support, I had the opportunity to become giddy, but I was not nearly as distressed as I might have been. I still had it firmly in mind that this was a dream. I was a dreamer who had dwelt in the Night Land, and on terrible derelicts lost in the Sargasso Sea; I had seen the death of the Earth and the advent of the Dark Sun; the Ab-humans and the Silent Ones were no strangers to me. Why should I be frightened by the thought of being caught in an invisible bubble of force a mere 200 feet above an angry forest?

I watched the flexible tower of Earth do battle with what now appeared to be a veritable host of invisible spirits of the air, writhing madly as if to swat them away. I watched it lose the battle, and the war, and I watched it collapse ignominiously back into the body of the forest, dissolving into the spaces between the trees. It left no scar behind when the canopy closed above the place where it had fallen back.

I tried to shout *Hurrah!*, but when I opened my mouth to let the syllables go, I found that my vocal apparatus was as strangely leaden as my frail flesh, and it took more effort to contrive the least audible sound than I had ever been forced to make before in so trivial a cause. I was not unduly disappointed when I found it convenient to strangle the silly cry.

Then the birds began to rise from the boughs of the trees in awful profusion, the sunlight glinting on polished feathers of every possible hue.

With such brightness about them, I thought at first that they must be parrots and birds of paradise, but they were more like thrushes and finches in form. The great majority of them were very small, and I could not see any that was as large as a crow, but there were so many that it was difficult to pick out individuals within the colored chaos. Their song had struck me while I was on the forest floor as something not merely familiar but intimately significant, but their gaudy appearance seemed far more alien and their intent obviously hostile. They flew at me in a great cloud, fighting for space as if each and every one were desperate to pluck the eyes out of my head.

I lashed out reflexively with arms and feet, although the birds were so many that I could not possibly have shooed them way with such limited instruments. Whatever it was that held me had greater resources, but its ingenuity seemed greatly tested by the storm of wings. The air surrounding me writhed and seethed, contorting some elastic envelope in a manner that was amazingly rapid and topologically incalculable.

The birds were ripped apart in mid-air by the hundred, their feathers exploding in all directions, but hundreds more contrived to collide with my body, pecking madly at my flesh. I had no alternative but to snatch up my hands, using them to cover and protect my eyes.

I felt the pricking of their multitudinous beaks and claws upon my legs and torso, and could not help but think of men I had seen badly tangled in barbed wire, whose struggles had only increased their bloody distress. The stings rained most intensely upon my forearms and the backs of my hands, and I felt sure that my uniform must be in shreds and my skin running with blood.

I felt that I was rising up yet again, more rapidly this time, but I had to trust to subtler senses to tell me how far I had come from the forest canopy; while the vicious birds still flocked around me, I dared not look. For as long as the fluttering shapes battered themselves against my protective arms, I dared not unshield my face.

I tried to breathe deeply, but could not do it. It was that, rather than any of the improbable assaults I had suffered, that gave me my first real thrill of panic. For a moment, I was convinced that, from the very first instant I had arrived in this deceptively pretty place, I must have been laboring to draw breath, and now must be on the very brink of asphyxiation–but then I realized that I was not choking, and that I was quite capable of drawing air into my paradoxical body.

I redoubled my efforts. The act of breathing seemed to take all the strength I had, but I did breathe. As soon as I felt certain that I would not faint the impacts ceased, and the flutter of wings died away. I felt safe again.

When I lowered my arms tentatively, and lifted my eyelids, I saw that there was no blood at all on the backs of my hands, and that my uniform was not in the least distressed, let alone ripped to shreds. I also saw that the air around me was coalescing, becoming tangible–and visible too, despite its transparency. I was captive within a clearly-discernible bubble, or perhaps some softly-faceted gem. The spirits of the air, if spirits they were, had condescended to show themselves.

Within the gem-like chamber in which I was now enclosed, I continued to rise into the sky. When I looked down, I could see a coastline separating the forest from a broad blue sea, but I could not recognize the familiar contours of Ireland; the distinctive shapes of Erris Head and Blacksod Bay were nowhere to be seen. Nor was there the least sign of any human habitation: no towns, no harbors, no ships afloat on the oceanic expanse. The Sun was high, and I assumed that it must be near its zenith; that told me which direction was south. The coastline was to the west, but I could not see the summit of Nephin Beg below, nor the silhouettes of the Ox and Curlew mountains in the east.

The near-noon Sun was exceedingly large and bright, and the refraction of its light through the facets of the cell that confined me sent dazzling rays in every direction, bringing tears to my eyes and forcing me to squint so narrowly that I almost lost sight of the world below–but not before seeing the horizon relax from a near-straight line into a very evident curve. That change of shape informed me that I must be very high indeed. I guessed that I would not be able to breathe at all were it not for the cradle that the spirits of the air had built around me.

The blue of Heaven grew deeper as I climbed, although the brightness of the Sun did not in the least diminish. Indeed, the Sun's light seemed to become whiter, less like liquid yellow fire and more like the pure radiance of distant stars–until it was eclipsed, by a black shadow whose incisive rim was a casual arc like the edge of a parabola.

That plunge into shadow made me shudder as if I had been chilled, although there was no perceptible alteration of temperature. I opened my eyes wider, but my pupils could not adapt to the abrupt transition, and the shape that folded itself around me seemed utterly black. I could not imagine that it would have been much different to have fallen into that awful and awkward grave, which had been so enthusiastic to gather me into the bosom of the Earth.

6.

My eyes had no sooner begun to be reconciled to the darkness, dimly perceiving shapes within the gloom, than they had to fight all over again for accommodation to a flood of bright light–yellow light, this time, no paler than the warm glow of a hooded oil-lamp.

I found, somewhat to my relief, that I was standing on a solid floor, which gleamed like polished silver. I felt very light on my feet, as if I were possessed of a tiny fraction of my normal mass, but after feeling so lumpenly heavy before that seemed an intoxicating release. There was a chair before me, which grew out of the floor upon a squat stalk, broadening out capaciously into cushioned comfort, with broad arms. The upholstery was black and slick, like no fabric I had ever seen before.

Seated in the chair, in a relaxed position with legs lazily crossed, was an approximate image of a man. I say "approximate" because it was like some impressionistic statue cast in pliable metal–metal so elastic that it could move as easily as any creature of flesh and blood. It changed its position, gesturing with its right arm, as if to demonstrate that it was no mere automaton jointed with bolts and axles.

I thought of the Talos of Greek legend, forged by Hephaestus from brass and given to Minos of Crete to serve as a patrolling sentry. This creature's color was closer to bronze than brass; its eyes were like almonds of jet and its ruddy lips seemed soft and moist. The face, in isolation, might have seemed feminine by virtue of its hairlessness and the gentleness of its lazy contours, but its torso was innocent of any breast-like curvature and its naked groin was quite feature-less.

The Talos of legend, I remembered, had made himself red hot in order that he might welcome strangers with a lethal embrace–but this creature did not even stand to greet me politely.

"Can you understand this language?" it said. Its accent might have been trained at either of England's great universities, but its manner of speech was a little hesitant. I could not see how the syllables were produced; its lips hardly moved.

I knew that the Comte de Villiers de l'Isle-Adam, who was still remembered in anecdote and rumor in the salons of Paris, had written a story in which Thomas Alva Edison had made a perfect woman of electrified metal–an *androïde*–to satisfy a nobleman who was tired of the fickleness of actual women. Perhaps, I thought, that *androïde* had been a more voluptuous version of the creature which faced me now. At any rate, the imagination of my immediate forebears had countenanced such individuals as this, and there was no reason to be unduly surprised to find one in my dream of futurity.

"Yes," I said, forcing the word out with some difficulty. Once I had broken my silence, however, I seemed to recover the knack of speech. "I am an Englishman," I was quick to add. "What are you?"

The homunculus gestured again with its arms, and I realized that it was pointing to a chair positioned behind me, identical to the one in which it was sitting. Before lowering myself into it, I looked briefly around the room in which we sat, but there was little enough to see. It was a very narrow room, no wider than was necessary to contain the two chairs. The walls seemed to be metallic, of a brazen hue not much different from the android; they were dressed with an intricate tracery of black and blue lines, which might conceivably have been mere decoration, except that there was no other evidence of a door. The room was illuminated by a diffuse radiance emitted from the whole surface of the ceiling.

"I am a scion of the Engine," the homunculus replied, as I lowered my lightened body into the chair "May we know your name?"

I knew that I would have to make a special effort to formulate my words clearly, and I took care to do so. "William Hope Hodgson," I replied, only a little awkwardly. "Second Lieutenant, Royal Field Artillery, most recently attached to the 84th Battery of the 11th Brigade."

At first, I took the other's response to be a blank stare of incomprehension, but it was not that. The pause was so brief that it might have been mistaken for mere hesitation, but it was not that either. "Second Lieutenant William Hope Hodgson, RFA," the android quoted, in a flat tone, "killed in action on April 17, 1918. Second son of the Reverend Samuel Hodgson. Author of *The Boats of the Glen Carrig, The Night Land, Men of the Deep Waters*, and other books. His early days were spent in the merchant service..."

The impassive tone of the narration was too eerie, and I felt that I had to interrupt. "I am certain that I was still alive and well on April 28, 1918" I said.

The creature fell silent, as if pondering.

"Do you have a name?" I asked. "What year is this?"

"I have no name," the metal man informed me. "There is some dispute about the number which ought to be attributed to the year, had your method of calculation continued, but you have come approximately 12 million years into what you reckon as the future. Was it on April 28, 1918, that you took the drug that projected your timeshadow into this era?"

I could not reply immediately. *Twelve million years*! It seemed utterly incredible, not because I had had any other figure in mind, but because it seemed inconceivable that my name and rank might be recognized after such an interval. Even though some of the information recited by the android had been erroneous, it was information nevertheless and it had been available almost upon the instant! How could that be possible, given that this age was as remote from my own as those epochs of prehistory in which the apeish ancestors of man had not yet mastered fire and flint? But the android waited patiently for my reply.

"I think it was the 28," I said, realizing that I was not absolutely sure. "I had been told of the victory at Villiers Bretonneux three days before, and Alfred Milner's appointment as secretary of war three days before that." I found myself searching its polished features for some sign that it recognized Milner's name, although the attempt was absurd. "Did you say 12 *million* years?"

"Approximately," the other repeated, with absurd modesty. "Who administered the drug to you?"

The General's warning was suddenly recalled to mind; I was supposed to be on my guard against deception as well as open hostility. But why would the creature lie about the extent of my displacement in time?

"Why do you want to know that?" I parried.

"The Archive is incomplete," the machine informed me, calmly. "We would be grateful for any data you can add."

"When will the war end?" I asked, abruptly–only realizing afterwards that I should have used the word *did*.

"World War One," recited the machine. "1914 to 1918. The armistice was signed at the 11th hour of the 11th day of the 11th month."

November! Less than six months! Five seconds passed before it occurred tom me that I had missed the most important item of information.

"World War *One*," I repeated. "How many World Wars will there be... I mean, *were* there?"

"World War Two, 1939 to 1945," said the machine, impassively. "World War Three, also called the First Plague War, 2025 to 2027. The Second Plague War, also called World War Four, 2032 to 2038. You may consult the Archive, provided that we can sustain and protect you. Will you tell us now who administered the drug? We did not expect to receive any further time-travelers, and certainly not in the location at which you appeared–but someone evidently knew better. If you will tell us who it was who sent you..."

"Military Intelligence," I said, seeing no good reason not to give way. "General Hartley."

The machine was silent for a moment; its face remained expressionless. Then it said: "General Anthony Somerton Hartley, Grenadier Guards. 1869-1937?"

I had never heard Hartley's Christian name, but the initial on the written orders I had received had been A. It was plausible that his original regimental attachment had remained on the record when he was seconded to Military Intelligence. I nodded my head to signify agreement with the tentative identification. "I had not expected to travel 12 million years," I said, before the android could ask another question, "but I suppose that I have come as far before, and even further. I have seen the final act of the story of mankind played out against the backcloth of the Night Land, and the death of the Earth itself as it spiraled into the dying Sun."

"Yes," said the metal man, after another brief hesitation. "We know something of your previous visions."

I was surprised by that admission, because my own remarks had been no more than half-serious. It occurred to me that the General might have made a mistake in selecting a dreamer with ambitions like mine, if what he required was intelligence of the 20th century. On the other hand, it was not inconceivable that he knew of the Archive to which the android had referred.

"Why did the Earth attempt to swallow me?" I asked.

"It was a trap," the other replied, serenely. "We do not know who set it, or how they knew where it should be set. If it was an attempt to destroy you, it must have been set by Consolidators. If the intention was to capture you, it may have been Transformers of a more ambitious kind."

The labels were not helpful. "What are Consolidators?" I asked.

"Individuals which seek a decrease in the play of uncertainty, with the eventual aim of negating its effect within this inflationary domain, thus establishing a closed realm of absolute control."

It was an exceedingly unhelpful answer, but I could see that any demand for further elucidation might lose me in a maze of unfamiliar concepts. I decided to try again, regardless. "And what are Transformers?"

"Individuals which believe that the present may be profitably changed by interference with the past. Most Transformers work in the cause of Consolidation, but a fugitive few actively seek to increase the play of uncertainty, for reasons that are unclear to us. We are sorry that we cannot make these matters clearer to you. Many of the words necessary to explain were not part of your language in 1918. The Archive is incomplete; we do not know how best to frame our explanations–but we will take you to a place where there is an individual who may know better."

I was struggling to find a more appropriate phrasing for my questions. "You must be accustomed to visitations like mine," I said, "even though you were not expecting me to appear where I did." It seemed a safe enough inference, if there were names for whole classes of individuals who found such visitations offensive.

"There has been none for half a million years," the android informed me, in the same level tone, "and none by a timeshadow that had the capacity to return for more than two million."

"Am I a timeshadow, then?" I asked.

"Is that the wrong term? Do I mean *ghost*?"

"I was not aware that I was either of those things," I replied. "But then, I was not aware that I was supposed to have died on April 17."

"It was the date recorded as that of your death," the metal men said, "if our source can be trusted. It is not unusual to discover errors and discrepancies, even between the few sources remaining to us. Much was lost, alas, and 12 million years is a considerable interval, even for my kind."

I had never thought to hear a machine say *alas*, but I guessed that a great deal of patient research must have gone into the formulation of its speech. On the other hand, the homunculus did not seem utterly unused to the English language, despite the fact that all the languages of the 20th century must be long dead–and it had mentioned "an individual" who might know better how to frame explanations I could understand.

"What are you?" I asked again–adding, in order to avoid useless repetition: "What is this Engine and what are its scions?"

"The Engine is a company of sentient machines working in collaboration towards a common end," the android replied. "Scions are individualized units with independent powers of discernment and decision."

"Machines made in the image of men," I said.

"This scion was shaped in this manner for the specific purpose of receiving you," it told me. "The remotest ancestors of the Engine were made by man's successors, but not in their image. It would be more accurate to say that the Overmen remade themselves in the image of their best machines."

45

I knew that I would have to ask for more information about the "Overmen" who were "man's successors," but it was becoming difficult to identify the most urgent among the host of questions crowding upon my mind.

"Why did you save me from the trap set for me by the Consolidators, or the Transformers?" I asked. "What do you want from me?"

"We are interested in the past," the android said, very calmly. "We do not seek to reshape it in any way, nor to seek any increase or decrease in the play of uncertainty. We maintain the Archive, and desire to improve it. We have maintained and protected other timeshadows, because we are interested in the phenomenon. We are equally opposed to the Consolidators and the more radical Transformers, and we always react to their more extravagant adventures."

It was strangely comforting to hear that the creature's account of its motivation was so confused. It was the first time it had manifested what seemed to me to be a hint of authentic humanity.

"I apologize for my ignorance," I said, with mixed motives of my own. "I fear that the determination of those who gave me the time-displacing drug not to prejudice my expectations prevented my being told anything they might already know about the possible shape of the future. I must seem to you to be very ill-equipped for the mission on which I was sent."

"I apologize also," the other replied, courteously, "but there is a matter which must be settled now, lest the opportunity be lost. If we take no action, you will be returned to your own time in a matter of hours–but if you will give us leave, we can take steps to extend your stay here. I must warn you that whoever tried to destroy or capture you before will certainly try again, and that any extension of your stay will inevitably increase the risk that the adversary in question might succeed–but if you desire to make any considerable study of the world as it now is, you ought to allow us to strengthen your timeshadow. May we do that?"

I had no way of calculating the risk to which my enigmatic host referred, but it seemed quite obvious which was the brave decision and which the cowardly one.

"What is a *timeshadow*?" I asked by way of procrastination.

"What may seem to you, at present, to be your body is actually a kind of projection, as much image as substance. It is material, and may even feel unwieldy in Earthlike gravity, but it is actually rather attenuated, which is why I offered the alternative name of *ghost*. If you will permit our nanozoons to work upon it, however, we can increase its substance considerably, and its resilience too. That way, you will be able to remain here for several days, and learn a great deal more than you could in a matter of hours–always provided that we can protect you from those who seem to be anxious to destroy you."

I was half-inclined to hesitate for a moment more, knowing that it might prove a Devil's bargain–but I knew my duty.

"Do it," I said.

7.

There are no words in English to describe the sensations that I felt as the android's "nanozoons" set to work upon me. Nor has the language any words adequately to describe the object upon which those infinitesimal machines set to work. It would be wrong to think of a timeshadow as a portion of the host flesh dispatched across the centuries like a parcel, although the inert body left behind by the time-traveling dreamer does lose considerable weight. The loss of weight is more sensibly reckoned a compensation than a mere subtraction: a balancing factor within what the android called "the play of uncertainty."

I deeply regret the fact that I never had an opportunity to learn the meanings of many of the words that I encountered in the future world. The entities I met there had no alternative but to speak to me vaguely and in metaphors; now I find myself in the same predicament. I believe that the atoms composing my "future self" were borrowed by some means from the local environment, shaped according to some self-image held in my mind's eye–which is why the body appeared fully clothed. Some such forcible recruitment of local atoms must also have been involved in the making of the invisible hand that snatched me from the jaws of the trap set to catch me–and, for that matter, in the formulation of the trap itself.

Although the loss of weight suffered by the host body must compensate to some degree for the energy employed in the creation of a timeshadow, there remains a supplementary tax to be paid. The net result of any adventure in time is a loosening of the bonds of causality that bind past and future together. Time travel is a phenomenon that puts a strain on the fabric of the universe itself, and that is why those who will call themselves Consolidators 12 million years in our future–who will think of themselves as heroic protectors of the integrity of the universe–will oppose its every manifestation....but I must not get too far ahead of the story I am setting down.

Suffice it to say that my ethereal envelope was invaded by tiny instruments, half-alive and half-mechanical, and was knitted by them into a sturdier weave. The process took several minutes, during which I was unable to speak, to see or to hear. When my sight eventually returned, the wall of the narrow room behind the android's chair had apparently become a window. The android's chair was gone and the creature was standing to one side so as not to obscure my view of the world beyond the vessel in which we were traveling.

I had assumed, without really thinking about it, that the flying machine that had collected me from the bubble must be making its way to England, or perhaps to continental Europe. Now I realized that our intended destination must be much further away.

Within a field that was filled more abundantly with stars than any sky I had ever seen through the atmosphere of Earth, I discerned a half-lit sphere. It was bright, and vividly colored; having no way of knowing how the scale of its appearance related to its actual dimensions I could not tell whether it was the size of a football or a planet. It was like a multifaceted assembly of precious stones compounded out of emeralds and opals, turquoises and sapphires, flecked with millions of diamonds.

"What is that object?" I asked, when I had my voice again. Now that I had been transformed, it no longer required a special effort to formulate the words distinctly. I stood up as I spoke and moved forward to stand beside the scion of the Engine; I felt a little heavier than before, but was still far more buoyant than I was accustomed to feel.

"It is the Earth's Moon," answered the android. "You seemed to doubt me when I told you that 12 million years had passed; this is not proof, but you can certainly judge that no such transformation could have been wrought in a matter of centuries, or even millennia. It is an image only, but it is an image of what this vessel's exterior eyes can see at this very moment."

"That is not actually a window, then?"

"This vessel has no portholes; it needs none, when it has eyes of its own. But this is what you would see, were you able to look out from its bow with your own eyes."

"And the Moon is where we are headed?"

"No. If you look closely at the field of stars, you might be able to discern other bodies, tiny at this distance but larger than stars. You will be able to see far more in a little while, but you will need to become accustomed to your new powers of sight and it is best not to demand too much of them so soon. *There*! Can you make it out? There are 100 such objects sharing the Moon's orbit round the Earth, and 1000 more sharing the Earth's orbit around the Sun. Not all belong to the Engine, but most do. It is on one of them that the Archive of the Human Species is kept."

As I tried to follow the direction of the android's pointed finger, the multitudinous stars seemed to blaze far more brightly, and their fire fused into a strange whole, as if they were mere elements of a vast and monstrous creature made of light. My head swam, and I had to lower my eyelids. If the metamorphosis of my phantom form had given me new powers of sight, their utility was not yet obvious.

"Why are the records of human history not kept on Earth?" I asked, to cover my confusion.

"Earth has a different part to play in our schemes–and in the schemes of others, for it is disputed territory still."

"Are there any human beings on Earth?" I asked, remembering what the creature had said about humankind's successors. "Or anywhere else, for that matter?"

"The species *Homo sapiens* is extinct," was the laconic but chilling answer, "and has been for a very long time. The original Overmen are gone too, although there are some among the Transformers who still reckon themselves Overmen of a sort, and are anxious to preserve the legacy of their ancestors. There are no sentient individuals in the Solar System who retain more than the faintest echo of flesh and blood, and the only one who identifies himself as an echo of a human being lives within the worldlet where the Archive is maintained; we shall leave it to you to decide whether that individual ought to be reckoned the curator of the museum, or merely an exhibit therein. You shall meet him soon enough."

"So my kind has been relegated to mere relics in a museum," I said, in a tone as level as I could contrive. "We existed for a few 100,000 years, and then were gone, like the ammonites and giant sloths. So much for human vanity." I was slightly surprised by the fact that the news distressed me less than I might have expected–but I had never found cause for despair in the knowledge that man was a product of evolution like any other, whose time would pass as surely as the Earth's and the Sun's, while aeons passed and the universe of stars endured.

"But your heritage endures," the android observed. "Everything your species learned was communicated to your successors, who continued to build upon it. Had you been less inclined to violence, you might have been the parents of the Engine, instead of its remoter ancestors–but your achievements were not lost; our own empire is built upon their foundation."

This time, when the android spoke the word *successors*, I thought of the giant creatures that had clustered about the Last Redoubt in the darkest of all my dreams, and of the Shining Ones, which followed their own mysterious path. I thought, too, of my fleeting vision of the Sea of Sleep, and of the great Green Sun that was the grave of lesser stars, and the dark partner with which it comprised the Central Binary of all Creation. I remembered the celestial globes, and the messenger rays that I had imagined as the source and comfort of all life, which would continue to serve that purpose as kalpas waxed and waned: a greater covenant than any contained in a mere rainbow.

While I remembered, I lowered my eyelids again, but the brightness in my mind's eye only increased. I saw the Green Sun again, as I had seen it in a dream long ago, but the image was sharper by far than any I had formerly retained in my memory–sharper too, I dare say, than the vision I had actually entertained in the ameliorated nightmare that had given birth to the record I had made.

Is this a product of my new power of sight? I wondered.

As I wondered, I had no alternative but to imagine the darker side of such a gift, and I shut my eyes convulsively against the Thing from the Pit and all its swinish kin, lest I be transfixed by the stare of their inhumanly human eyes. *If there has always been truth in my dreams,* I thought, *then there must be monsters here: monsters uglier by far than that Earthborn giant that tried to swallow me.*

I opened my own eyes as quickly as I could, to look upon the android, which now seemed very benign.

"If that is a screen and not a window," I said, hoarsely, "can you show me other images? Can you show me the Sun?"

"The Sun is too bright to behold directly," said the metal man. "In any case, it looks exactly as it did in your own day. You saw it clearly enough, did you not, before the vessel reached you?"

I had–but I had not been told, then, that 12 million years had elapsed since I saw it last.

"When I experienced the first of the nightmare visions that I struggled to preserve in my writings," I told the android, while I fought to recover my composition, "I believed that the Sun was hot by virtue of the gravitational energy of its collapse, and I accepted Lord Kelvin's estimate of the time at which it would fade into a mere ember. Wells did likewise–but I have since been told that we were probably wrong, for the true age of the Earth cannot be accommodated within Kelvin's scheme. If our visions had truth in them, why did they not show us the folly of that belief–and why did they not alert us to the better theory that the science of 1918 was struggling to produce?"

"Perhaps you did not understand what you saw," the android said.

"And perhaps I do not understand what I see now," I answered, wondering how much of this conversation I would remember when I awoke in 1918–if, indeed, I did awake in 1918. "Can you show me the Central Sun of Creation?"

"I think you know that I cannot," the metal man replied. "The universe is far greater than anyone in your time had any cause to think, and far stranger too. We will explain this as best we can."

"What of the Sea of Sleep, where souls go when death snatches them into the abysm of time?" I asked, but not very hopefully.

"There is no such artifact–yet. In time, we hope that the Archive will be perfected, but that of which you speak is at present a fiction: a glimmer in the collective imagination of all the Engines that will some day combine into the Universal Engine. That may come about, even if the Consolidators have their way; they seek comfort in closure, but not in loss."

"And where," I enquired, "do creatures like you seek comfort?"

"We would not like to see an end to discomfort," the scion said. "Our hope is eternal progress; ours is the neverending quest."

"Bravo," I said, softly.

I knew, though, that I had no right to agree with him. Whatever they had held back from me, those who had sent me here were undoubtedly Transformers of a sort, eager to take what grip on future history they could. My duty was to them, to England and humankind–and certainly not to the mysterious Engine that was, it seemed, simultaneously at war with the party that would render history unchangeable and the ones that sought to change it to their own advantage. I already had reason to assume that if I were to find out what my commanding officers needed to know, I must seek enlightenment in the Archive which these impersonal creatures kept on some tiny orbital island to the east or west of the moon. That, I now assumed, was why I had been sent so far–to a time when no one ought to care what I might find out, or what might be done with the information.

Unfortunately, it seemed that there were individuals hereabouts who did care: Transformers of a distinctly different stripe. I wondered if I had seen their like before, in the Beast-gods and other Horrors that beset the House of the Borderland, in the monsters that overran the beleaguered *Mortzestus*, in the Hog that had visited Carnacki, and in the unspeakable creature that had possessed poor Baumoff as he attempted to recapitulate the crucifixion and found himself forsaken.

"You mentioned humankind's successors," I said. "Can you show me one of *them*?"

"I can," said the android. It did not reach out a hand to touch the side wall, but the view from the false window changed. I found myself looking at a creature very like myself, lit by the frail light of a very different moon and stars far fewer in number.

"No huge-brained Hampdenshire Wonder, then," I murmured, although my silent thoughts were preoccupied with the faint relief of finding that the creature was no replica of Set, Destroyer of Souls. "I am delighted to see that *Homo superior* had the good grace to retain our form, and our idea of handsomeness."

"His kind lived among you from the very beginning," the android said, "often seen but never properly observed. This was not their only form, and only common usage established it as their most familiar one. Your legends knew them, but did not fully understand them, calling them vampires, werewolves or elves, deeming them mere demonic spirits rather than patient neighbors. They inherited the Earth when your own species destroyed itself, by means of wars fought with the most terrible of weapons: plagues to which your cousins had better immunity than your own masters attempted to reserve for themselves."

Do Generals Hartley and Horniman know this already? I wondered. *Is this the context of the secret that I am supposed to winkle out? Am I supposed to find a means of averting this future war-to-end-war–or am I supposed to find a means of winning it for humankind?* I remembered, yet again, Hartley's final warning; there might be those here, even at such a vast interval of time, whose first priority would be to destroy or deceive me, presumably lest I should somehow abort the history that gave them birth.

"And these demonic Overmen have been superseded in their turn?" I said. "They have no descendants, save for intelligent machines?"

"That is true," said the android. "I am one of them–but I count you among my ancestors too, for I am the product of skill and art, not the rituals of germ plasm. We take care to preserve the history of the Overmen too, insofar as it survives. Their own archives were devastated by a terrible disaster, which they called the Hail of Hell. Earth was hit by a storm of comets–but that was a long time ago. The Solar System is more tranquil now, and no such accident could ever happen again. The cometary halo is part of the Engine's domain, the raw material of our industry."

The image of the not-quite-human being was replaced by the star-field, as before–save that the half-circle of the Moon was noticeably larger in apparent size, and displaced to one side. It was obvious now that our trajectory would take us to some other destination. Reflexively, my eyes sought out the object that the android had tried to point out before. This time my powers of sight were ready to respond. It was as if I were looking through a powerful telescope. No sooner had my mind focused on our destination than my eye focused too, and it was magnified greatly.

It was shaped like a thick-tired wheel with a dozen spokes and a long spindle-like shaft piercing its hub. The spokes, the hub and the shaft were opaque and metallic, but the bulbous rim was only opaque on its outward-facing surface; the inner was crystalline. It sparkled like a well-polished decanter by virtue of light reflected from a complex array of mirrors mounted on the shaft about which the wheel was spinning. Within the crystal, there were hints of green and blue, even the occasional flash of red.

"Has it a name?" I asked, trusting that my mechanical companion would know what I meant.

"The one who considers himself the keeper of the Archive calls it the Attic of Olympus," the android said. "We named it Utopia, but he did not like the name. He arrived here as you did, as a timeshadow, but he is a true scion of the Engine now."

"Why did he not return to his own time?" I asked.

"He fled from the moment of death," was the answer. "There was nothing left behind that could receive his returning intelligence. He gambled everything on the chance of finding entities willing and able to transform and sustain him."

"And what would have happened to his timeshadow had you not caught it?" I asked.

"Even drug-assisted timeshadows are fleeting by nature," the scion assured me, carelessly dashing the fondest hopes of religious men. "If they are let alone they dissolve within hours into the play of uncertainty, becoming part and parcel of the chaotic play that underlies the precarious order of matter and nourishes the phenomenon of life."

8.

The android seemed to be gaining in confidence and in eloquence. I realized that the scion must have been learning while it had been talking to me, taking cues from my own speeches as to the kinds of words that I would be able to understand, the rhythms and the rhetoric to which I might respond. I thought that the time might have come to demand a fuller account of the "play of uncertainty." Before I could ask, however, the floor on which I stood lurched disconcertingly, and I found myself abruptly dispossessed of the weight that had kept me delicately anchored. I floated free, reflexively flailing my arms–and the flailing made my situation even worse, setting me spinning madly.

From the corner of my eye, I saw that the field of stars had blazed more brightly, and I thought that I must have lost control of my enhanced sense of sight for a second time–but as the android reached out and took hold of me, bidding me to be still, I realized that something had indeed blazed into brilliance in the void: something that was now evaporating into a mist of angry light.

"What was that?" I demanded, as the android held me tight, anchoring me. The scion had not floated away from the floor, although I assumed that it too had lost what weight it had; I guessed that its feet must be held by magnetism.

"An attack," it replied, its perennial calmness now seeming awkwardly inappropriate. "A missile with an explosive warhead. It came too close for comfort, but the vessel is well-defended and it forced the missile to discharge its energy at a safe distance. We had not thought that our rivals had any weapon close enough to fire at us, but it seems that we were wrong again. Earth is disputed territory, and there is much going on there that is beyond our control. We shall not underestimate our enemies again."

I slumped in the creature's arms as my weight was abruptly restored, and I was lowered back into the chair in which I had been sitting before.

"I apologize," the android said, with all apparent sincerity. "No matter how clever machinery becomes, it remains subject to the principles of motion and inertia; no action is without reaction."

I did not want to embark upon a philosophical discussion of Newton's laws. "Why should anyone try so very hard to kill me?" I demanded, roughly. "What harm can I do?"

"I do not yet know how to explain it in terms you can comprehend," the android said, carefully, "but the orderliness of the visible world is built on less orderly foundations. The forces that bind atoms together are oddly mercurial, and there is an irreducible uncertainty about the behavior of the fundamental particles. At that level of perception, causality may run backwards in time as well as forwards. On a grosser level, the counterflow is negligible by comparison with the great tide that determines the directionality of time, and it is not easy for beings of our kind to exert any influence upon it–but it is not entirely beyond the reach of such influences, as the possibility of your return to a earlier era implies.

"The integrity of the universe can tolerate all manner of eddies and undertows within the counterflow of causality, provided they remain exceedingly tiny–but if they were to intensify, precarious order might turn to utter chaos. It is our belief that no such dissolution could be permanent, or even universal, but there are those who do not agree with that judgment–and there are, in any case, some who value their own individual endurance so highly that they are ruthless in opposing any decrease in the stability of local space-time.

"Your arrival here, seen as an event in its own right, is quite trivial, but if you can carry information back to your own time that alters the patterns of causality connecting past and future–even more so if that information assists others to follow your example and further recomplicate the patterns of connection–the tiny ripple might spread and grow. It is possible in principle, therefore, that an adventure like yours might be the seed of far greater disruptions.

"The Consolidators have killed others of your kind in the remote past, and must have hoped for the last three million years and more that they had put an end to the whole business of two-way traffic in time, at least so far as this tiny corner of the inflationary domain is concerned....but there are no ultimate ends in a domain like ours, any more than there are ultimate beginnings. We scions of the Engine understand that; the Consolidators and other Transformers seemingly do not.

"All the Consolidators, and the greater number of the Transformers, believe that disruptions of time can and ought to be knotted into closed circles of causality, rendered harmless if not individually advantageous. They know that at the ultimate level of causality–the domain of the forces that hold atoms together and organize their transactions–there is an inherent and perhaps irreducible uncertainty, but they find the thought intolerable.

"The Consolidators are prideful enough to think that the universe might ultimately capitulate with the demands of their intolerance, so that the whole of existence becomes perfectly determined. They believe that the counterflow of causality will carry that absolute determinism back in time as well as forwards, obliterating the seeds of uncertainty within the ultimate singularity. We believe that would be tantamount to the destruction of life and intelligence–a triumph of mere mechanism–and we fight against it, knowing that the fight must be eternal, because it can never be conclusively won."

"Are you stalwart champions of chaos, then," I asked, "and diehard enemies of order?"

"The Consolidators would classify us as allies of chaos, although they would probably reserve the appellation *champions* for reckless Transformers," the android admitted, equably. "We see things differently. We are interested in everything that happens, everything that *is*, and everything that might be. We desire to live in a world in which the new and the unexpected are possible, and welcome. We desire to be intelligences which can anticipate surprise with pleasure, and do not live in mortal dread of spontaneity. Surely that does not seem paradoxical to a creature of your kind?"

"It does seem strange in a machine," I observed.

"To us," said the android, "it seems strange that any intelligent machine could take another view."

I had lived a substantial part of my adult life in mortal dread. I could easily have wished to be the kind of intelligence which could anticipate surprise with the pleasure of a connoisseur–but, for the moment, I was saturated with astonishment, and my senses seemed to have been dulled by its excess. Had any other man, I wondered, ever found such cause for astonishment as this, or reacted so sluggishly to it? The Engine's nanozoons might have given me strength and new powers of endurance, but they had not sharpened by blunted sensations. I could only wonder what I ought to be feeling, had I sensation enough to react like a human instead of a mere specter.

One thing, however, was obvious: despite avid giants and exploding missiles, this was a future less desolate and doom-laden than those of which I had once been wont to dream.

It was understandable that the dreamer driven by lost love, who had been appointed to serve as my surrogate visionary in the first-written and last-published of my long confessional fictions, had found a future full of darkness and despair. It was understandable, too, that the nightmares I had suffered during my days in the merchant marine had made the sea pregnant with horrors. What, then should I have expected of a nightmare born of Ypres and the double wound in my side and thigh? What should I have expected of a future born of what would apparently come to be recorded as *World War One*? Whatever hostility this future might hold, it certainly did not seem to be a world of ultimate desolation on the brink of oblivion. As yet, I had seen no real monsters, as yet, save for the invisible force that had turned the soil of ancient Ireland into a violent clutching hand.

I was, however, well aware of the gulf of uncertainty that could be contained in such playful, phrases as "as yet."

The view from the false window informed me–accurately, I had to presume–that were falling towards the crystalline inner surface of the floating wheel, which now loomed large even without the aid of my enhanced powers of sight. This, at least, seemed to be a world from which desolation of every kind had been entirely banished–and its builders had called it Utopia!

As we came closer to our destination, I watched the play of light within the crystal canopy, striving to make sense of the blues and greens that danced within. I wondered what else would be here, alongside the Archive of the Human Species and its mysterious attendant. Earth had been "disputed territory" but this, apparently, was not. This was a haven of peace maintained by the protective Engine.

Then my attention was caught by a number of tiny points of light moving against the stellar background. They had to be close by; otherwise, even superhuman vision could not have apprehended them.

"Are there other vessels coming to meet us?" I asked.

"They are coming to defend us," the android said. "We do not know what our adversaries might do next, or to what extreme they might be prepared to go.

We must assume that they knew your identity almost as soon as you gave the information to us; it is possible that they have put their own interpretation on the limited information about you that we have in store. It is conceivable that the other name you mentioned means more to them than it does to us, for we have no record of General Hartley's involvement in experiments in time-travel. They did have some forewarning of the place where you appeared–or so it seems."

"Your Archive has no record of Hartley's secondment to Military Intelligence?" I queried.

"The reference-sources we have are limited, and we cannot be sure that there are no better ones in other hands. If the Consolidators did have information about experiments in time travel conducted in remote antiquity, they would not be inclined to share it with the Engine. We might be better able to judge the seriousness of the situation if you could tell us more."

I hesitated, but I could not see the point of keeping trivial secrets 12 million years after the event. "There was another General," I confessed. "Sir Philip Horniman. There was also a Brigadier Severn, and a Colonel Wrightson. There was a Captain Macleod... and a nurse named Helen Flynn." I knew that I had left out the orderly Corporal, but it seemed far more likely that the Archive would have records of the careers and achievements senior officers."

"Thank you," said the android. Then it, too, hesitated before continuing. "We do not know why the Consolidators are so anxious to destroy you–if, indeed, it *was* Consolidators who set the trap and launched the missile–but it may be significant that official records claim that you died on April 17, 1918. According to your own testimony, you were alive for at least ten days after that, before taking the drug that facilitated the formation of your timeshadow–although that need not be inconsistent with the fact of the report being made. If, however, you were to return safely to your own time, there ought to be some further record of your life and endeavors. It may well be that the Consolidators have decided that in order to protect the integrity of our history, you must not be allowed to return to 1918."

For a moment or two, I could not quite grasp the import of what the android was saying, but then I saw the implication. "If you have no record of my subsequent life," I said, slowly, "and the erroneous account of my death was allowed to stand in the official record, then is it not an established fact that I did *not* return to my own time? Is it not already established that I *cannot* return, no matter how you might strive to defend me from my mysterious attackers?"

"It is not certain," said the man of metal, carefully. "Our records are far from complete, being mere fragments dredged from the ruins of a dead civilization. The absence of any information as to your career after April 1918 may be a mere accident of happenstance. On the other hand, if you do go back armed with valuable information about the shape of your future, your employers might well have felt it politic, after your return, to give you a new identity, leaving the record of your death unamended in order to protect you."

"But I have a wife!" I protested. "I could not let her think that I were dead, if I still lived!"

"We are merely listing possibilities," the android reminded me, "and trying to form a hypothesis as to why certain individuals might be so enthusiastic to see you dead. All possibilities are open; nothing is certain, as yet."

As yet. The words echoed in my mind again, mocking me. I grappled with the tangled web of possibilities for a few moments more. "But what if I were to go back and correct the record?" I said. "What if I were to set out deliberately to alter the history recorded in your Archive? Could I possibly succeed? What would the consequences be?"

"Opinions differ," the metal man admitted. "We believe that we know the answer, but the Consolidators and the minority of the Transformers both take different views. The Consolidators fear annihilation by virtue of the erasure of the chains of cause and effect that produced them. The most extreme among them fear that the entire universe–or this inflationary domain, at least–might be annihilated along with them."

"But surely," I said, having glimpsed some further consequences of the argument, "if traveling in time is possible–as it clearly is–then the method of displacement is bound to be discovered over and over again. What good can it do, in the long term, to destroy one time traveler, or even 1000?"

"There are some who believe the extirpation of all timeshadow-casting species to be a sacred mission of true intelligence," the android said, patiently. "That is the essence of the philosophy of Consolidation: the notion that the ultimate survivor in the universal struggle for existence will be the collective that takes control of uncertainty, eliminating it from consideration by creating a universe in which–unlike this one, in its present state–causality can only flow in one direction. Their aim is to rid the tide of time of all its subsidiary disturbances–and if that involves their taking control of the transactions of the subatomic particles and rewriting the laws of nature, that is what they intend to do."

"I think I am beginning to understand that," I said, hopefully. "But what of the Transformers who are not Consolidators?"

"Many Transformers accept that the universe–or this inflationary domain– is in a constant state of flux, due to the continual extirpation of histories by irruptions of reversed causality, most of which are not the work of mischievous time travelers. They believe that a final state of order *might* be achieved, if and when the primal singularity–what you would probably call the moment of Creation–were to be reshaped in such a way that it gives rise to a universe consolidated from its very inception, but those who are not Consolidators have a different goal. The most radical among them desire to maximize the creativity of the domain, and its fecundity in spawning daughter domains. The most extreme are ambitious to become mass-producers of new inflationary domains, active practitioners of mutation in the physical laws developed by those domains, thus becoming–in the fullness of local time–masters of multiversal proliferation and evolution."

This seemed far harder to grasp than the idea of extirpating uncertainty "Is there no one in this hectic world who has ambitions less than godlike?" I asked.

"Few hereabouts," the creature said. "When your successors put away their flesh, they also put away the limitations of the flesh. When death is no longer a necessity, the scope of realizable ambition inevitably increases by an order of magnitude that is bound to seem godlike to a creature of your kind. On the other hand, the universe is home to many worlds like Earth, and many of them are evolving their own ecospheres. Although humankind is long gone, there are other creatures approaching the same transient stage of their development–some of them, no doubt, possessed of the same perverse gifts of nature. Their ambitions, I dare say, would fit the narrow margin that you consider *less than godlike*."

"What do you mean by *perverse gifts of nature*?" I wanted to know, although I had an inkling already.

"The ability to cast timeshadows," the other replied, equably. "And, in consequence, the ability to spark conflicts beyond your comprehension."

The scion looked around as it spoke, as if searching the star-field with miraculous eyes for evidence of spacecraft at war–but we were descending now into the span of the great wheel. The space beyond the false window was filled by a great curving plain of crystal, like a vast trough roofed over in the manner of a greenhouse: a trough filled with forests and lakes, very reminiscent of the Earth as I had looked down upon it while I was in the grip of the invisible hand.

"Why is this the Attic of Olympus?" I said, remembering the name it had quoted. "The name suggests an abode of the darker gods who were unwelcome at the dining-table of Zeus and his cultured kin–the prison of Prometheus, perhaps, or the refuge of Pan. Not Utopia, at any rate."

"We had better hope that it will serve well enough as a fortress," my friendly captor replied. "Given recent developments, even the Engine might be hard-pressed to keep the barbarians from its walls."

9.

The truth of the machine's words became evident as soon as it spoke, for the image on the wall immediately became blurred, and then disintegrated altogether. The wall itself seemed to be cracking and blistering, and its delicate traceries of blue and black, which had dressed the remaining walls of the narrow room throughout our conversation, were now losing their own distinctiveness.

"What is happening?" I asked my companion–but it seemed that the mysterious infection had spread into its body, for the smooth metallic surface was becoming pitted, as if with rust, and the semblance of human form was beginning to melt into shapelessness.

"Don't be afraid," it said, by way of answer–but how could I be expected to remain calm and confident when everything around me seemed to be on the brink of disintegration and there was nothing without but the void?

Even so, I did feel unreasonably calm. My fear, such as it was, seemed purely intellectual; my strangely-augmented phantom body resisted all the commonplace symptoms of dread. If I had a stomach at all, it was not nauseated; if my false skin had sweat-glands, they remained inactive.

I tried to rise from the chair, but found that I could not. My arms were stuck to the rests, while the seat and back were flowing around my shoulders and thighs.

"You will be....pro-tec-ted," the android promised, as black corrosion swallowed up its surface and its shape alike, almost obliterating the impressionistic mouth before whatever mechanism was within its head could complete the sentence. Ordinarily, my reflex would have been to fight against enclosure, but the situation was so utterly incomprehensible that I made an effort to relax. The material that comprised the chair was now fluid, like molten candle-wax, and it flowed around me in a matter of seconds, closing off my hands and face before becoming more viscous again.

I lost the sensation of my own weight for a second time, but this time I did not float free; I was held securely by a rapidly-setting cocoon.

I felt my supple shell draw me into an erect position, with my arms flat to my sides, almost as if I were reflexively answering a call to attention. The fact that I could not feel my own mass reminded me that I was in a dream, and that my "actual" body was lying on a bed in a remote house in the west of Ireland, but I no longer felt confident that I could regain possession of that body.

I had sometimes had the impression, in my visionary dreams, that I was flying through time and space into distant epochs and remote regions of the cosmos–but I had never felt as thoroughly disconnected from my own time and space as I did at that moment, locked into my plastic prison.

For a few moments after I had lowered my eyelids, in reflexive response to the seeming threat to my eyes, I could see nothing at all. Then I heard a whisper, which must have been released directly into the recesses of my ear, saying: "Open your eyes and you will see."

I opened my eyes, and found that I could, indeed, see perfectly well, although there was something very strange about the world upon which I gazed. Its colors seemed too vivid, its shapes too well-defined. I stood–or seemed to stand–on the floor of the narrow room I had been in before, but its walls had vanished, leaving me in a brightly-lit cavernous space cluttered with bizarre machinery.

The roofless expanse was infinitely greater and more complex than any factory-floor I had ever been on, but what struck me most of all was its astonishing cleanliness. Although the machines were intricate in the extreme, and were certainly not dead although they had few moving parts by comparison with a textile-mill or a munitions plant, there was not a hint of dirt or spillage.

I would have liked to have studied the machines for longer, but even as I looked curiously around, the floor beneath my feet began to devour my encased form. I say "devour" because I had no sense of *falling*–I was still devoid of weight–and was convinced that I was indeed being drawn down into the seemingly-solid mass.

Even before my head was swallowed up, the image before my eyes was abruptly altered. I took the inference that it was a product of some hyper-kinematographic artifice, like the image in the false window.

Now I was looking out over an arching landscape, which I took to be the interior of the floating wheel: a landscape that remained perfectly steady, even though I am sure that my body was turning head over heels, and moving laterally.

The landscape was lush with vegetation, but not as disorderly as the plain into which I had first been delivered by my leap through time. It was more obviously under control, more *decorous*. Its trees were spaced like those in an orchard rather than clustering like wild woodland, and the flowering bushes whose hedges wound around the stands of trees looked as if they had been neatly pruned.

The treeless hills in the middle-distance were gently rounded, with no crag or scree to be seen. The colors were still too bright–the greens and blues too resolutely primary, the violets and pinks too pure–and I could not begin to believe in the very ordinary sky at all. I had seen the wheel from without and knew that I really ought to be looking up at the panes of a vast greenhouse with naught but stars behind. The shapes were too distinct–especially those of distant objects which ought to have been blurred.

"It is a picture," said the whisper in my ear, as if it had somehow divined my skepticism. "You will see the reality soon enough. Be patient, please; the vessel transporting the scion of the Engine has been infiltrated, but the infection will soon be cleansed. You are safe, for the moment, and we shall do everything in our power to keep you safe."

I was not reassured by this; if the last four years had made one lesson abundantly clear, it was the lesson that destruction is a far easier business than creation. I knew only too well that the eternal battle between the forces of annihilation and salvation is far from evenly matched, and that far inferior forces can wreak terrible havoc, if destruction is their only aim and they are careless of their own survival.

I still could not quite credit that my humble presence could urge such forces to action in a world 12 million years after my own time. It was, however, easy to believe–once the first premise had been granted–that a committee of Generals, Colonels and Captains would not hesitate to keep hurling men of lower rank into a breach from which few, if any, could return.

I tried to be glad that the mysterious assembly of machines which called it-self "the Engine" seemed prepared to go to any lengths to make me safe, but I could not help wondering what motive it had, and whether I could lend the slightest credence to any account of its motives that it might condescend to offer me.

Like the image in the false window, the pictorial landscape blurred, and then began to disintegrate into darkness. I was certain that the cocoon enclosing me was still in motion, although I had no way to judge the direction or velocity of its movement. I had no idea whether the vessel carrying me had been able to reach its destination; for all I knew, I might be tumbling towards the sun in a fall that might last for days or months before I were finally consumed by solar fire.

I would have spoken to the whispering voice if I could, but my closed lips were tightly-sealed. Again, it seemed to guess my predicament.

"We have merged with the hub of the wheel," it said. "You will be delivered to the habitable surface as soon as it is safe. The centrifugal force of its spin simulates gravity there, and you will be able to walk and breathe freely. Do not be afraid."

Again, the last injunction was unnecessary. I was not afraid, save in some abstract intellectual sense; it seemed to me that my curiosity was far more piquant than my fear. I wondered whether my years in Belgium and northern France had finally brought me to a psychological redoubt, from whose patiently-hollowed trenches fear had been conclusively banished.

If the intelligence lurking within my flesh could not read my thoughts, it was remarkably clever in anticipating my desires.

"We shall do what we can to help you to understand," said the whisper. "We had hoped to explain in a more convenient way, but time presses more urgently than we had anticipated and our resources are strained. Forgive us this makeshift."

Within the darkness, I saw a globe of light, which was gradually magnified as if I were approaching it from some infinite regress of empty space. At first, I took it for a planet, but then I saw that it was transparent and many-layered. I realized that it was a model of the Aristotelian universe, constructed as series of concentric spheres with the Earth at its centre and the "fixed stars" suspended in its outermost shell. I could see the spheres turning, one within another, although I could not see the gears that moved them.

"This was once the compass of the human imagination," said the whisper. "A droplet universe contained within a tiny space–but when the Sun was shifted to the centre of the model, and the diameter of the Earth's orbit was calculated, the true distance of the stars became calculable."

The sphere dissolved and the stars retreated. I knew well enough how the distances of the nearer ones had been calculated by virtue of the tiny displacement they showed against the stellar background when viewed from opposite extremes of the Earth's orbit.

"At first," the voice said, "the stars were assumed to belong to a single sidereal system."

My viewpoint withdrew again, until the Earth became invisibly tiny, leaving the stars as a host of tiny pinpricks of light, aggregated into an approximate sphere. The sphere was rotating on its axis, as if about a central sun–but I already knew that the vision I had reproduced in my dreams and in my book was outdated, and I had admitted as much to the android.

"In fact," said the whisper. "Stars are aggregated into galaxies, which are at least as numerous as the stars in any one of them." I saw the sphere of stars shrinking and flattening, so that it became a lenticular whirlpool–and the space left vacant by its shrinkage was filled with similar whirlpools.

"It was discovered in your own time that the galaxies were becoming more and more distant from one another," the voice informed me. "The universe is expanding, as if it were the remnant of some primal explosion. The astronomers of your day were uncertain as to whether it would continue to expand indefinitely, becoming emptier and darker as the stars leached away their energy, or whether it would eventually reach a limit, at which time it would begin to collapse again under the influence of gravity."

I saw the cosmic explosion; then I saw it fade into darkness; then I saw the universe collapse. It was all just a play of tiny lights; the true scale of the events I was being asked to imagine was too vast for ready apprehension or comprehension.

"We do not know whether human astronomers ever resolved this question to their satisfaction, although we do know that some had begun to speculate before the 20th century ended that there might be an even greater scale of magnitude, in which the visible universe was merely one aspect of something much vaster."

The perspective shifted again, so that the re-exploded universe became merely a bubble in a foaming mass.

"The model is inadequate," the whisper said, apologetically, "and there are many complications that you might not understand. Be assured that much will become known to your contemporaries, and to their children, that we have not time even to attempt to teach you. The greater part of that knowledge will pass to your successors, and eventually to theirs–who will take their place among the builders of the Engine.

"The architects of the Engine imagined that they might be setting in train the ultimate project of intelligence: the aggregation of all the matter in the observable universe into a single machine, which could orchestrate and supervise its eventual collapse. The ultimate aim of that endeavor, as they imagined it, would be to contrive a new expansive phase that could be *planned*. In the meantime, they presumed, the Engine would become a kind of god, busy with the works which they imagined to be the prerogatives and purposes of gods. They accepted that this universe might be part of something greater, something evolving in its own way and constantly giving birth to new universes one within another, but the architects of the Engine were content to work within their own infinite-but-bounded space."

I knew, as I watched the foaming mass spawning bubbles, that the voice was about to tell me that the so-called architects of the Engine had assumed too much.

"When the intelligences descended from the organic produce of the Earth discovered that there were many other Engines already under construction, they knew that there would be an era of competition," the whisper went on, "but they hoped that the competitive phase would be transient, and that all the entities involved would ultimately consent to be bound into a single project with a common purpose. In fact, the competition had the opposite effect: the existing endeavors were fractured and splintered by the re-emergence of very different ambitions and strategies.

"Perhaps, by now, we ought to have learned sufficient humility to accept that our history, extending as it does over a mere few million years, has not equipped us to plan the future of our own galaxy, let alone our entire inflationary domain. Perhaps, on the other hand, we need great crusades of some kind–and the conflicts they engender–to maintain the dynamic of our own existence. At any rate, as you have now had opportunity to observe, the Engine is locked in a conflict that seems never-ending, whose bone of contention is the ambition according to which our ever-expanding material empire ought to be disposed. Some, at least, of its analogues based in other solar systems are similarly troubled.

"You already know that the conflict is complicated, involving numerous factions–but the most fundamental divide of all is between those who assert that the ultimate aim of intelligence should be to stabilize its own sphere of influence on every imaginable scale, from a single solar system to the entire inflationary domain, and those who assert that the true purpose of intelligence is to innovate, to make change eternal. We are of the latter party, although our ambitions are more modest than those whose ultimate purpose is to work on the largest scale imaginable, to create new inflationary domains in abundance. Our aim is to preserve spontaneity and innovation without facilitating alterations to our own space-time continuum so sweeping that its fabric might be rent apart. Everything we know of human beings suggests that they–or, at any rate, the majority thereof–would immediately take our side in this conflict, and we regard you as a natural ally."

Even if I had not already heard the android speaking dismissively of the endeavors of the Consolidators, I would have known from the very beginning of its discourse which side of the great dispute the whispering voice favored. It was obvious even in the illustrative play of lights that continued to seethe before my eyes. The entity that called itself the Engine–although it had now admitted that it was merely one hopeful seed among many–was trying hard to present itself as the party of sensible compromise. It did not want the Consolidators to consolidate the pattern of past and future, but it did not want the more radical Transformers to employ their transformations of the past in such a way as to produce a dangerous instability; it favored a moderate middle way, and it presumed that I ought to fall into agreement with its sense of balance.

Perhaps it presumed too much.

I had no doubt that the Engine had a reason for wanting to make all this clear to me. It intended to send me back to my own time, if it could, and it had some notion of what effect it wanted my return to have. If its statements could be trusted, it wanted me to help maintain the flow of wayward ripples of cause and effect that disturbed the connection of past and future but did not want me to precipitate excessive changes that might lead to utter chaos.

Ideally, I felt sure, the Engine would want to protect its own existence while weakening the tenure of its rivals, especially the unexpectedly-resourceful Consolidators. But how, I wondered, did the Engine propose to achieve this? Had it grounds to believe that furtherance of the causes to which my own duty would inevitably incline me when I returned–the salvation of humankind from the destructive effects of more "world wars" and our eventual supersession by a cousin species–would inevitably work to its own advantage? Did the seeming fact that the Consolidators were so anxious to exterminate me lend further credence to that supposition?

I knew that I had to keep in mind the fact that, whatever the Engine's ultimate aim might be, I was a mere pawn within its scheme. I dared not believe the account it had given me of its motives for protecting me; I had to assume that it thought me useful, and would not hesitate to lie to me or injure me in pursuit of its own cause, whatever that cause might actually be.

Somehow, I found it more difficult to believe in anarchist machines than it had ever been to accept the existence of human anarchists–and yet, as I pondered the matter, I began to wonder whether vulnerable creatures compounded of flesh and blood had not infinitely more reason to count control and safety as cardinal virtues than any mere "scion" of some vast, protean and impersonal machine. Were not most human beings natural Consolidators, albeit very inefficient ones? Was not the average man possessed by a desperate desire to carve whatever safety and prosperity he could from the constant barrage mounted by the slings and arrows of outrageous fortune?

I could not help but wonder whether I might have fallen into the hands of the wrong party in this conflict. I only had the Engine's word for the fact that it was probably the Consolidators who wanted to destroy me. Perhaps it was not the Consolidators at all. Perhaps the Consolidators, had I fallen into their hands, would also have wanted to lecture me and to use their powers of persuasion to convert me to their cause, so that when I went back in time I would act in *their* interests as well as the interests of humankind. How would I ever know, if I only heard the Engine's side of the story?

I began to wonder whether I might have been foolish to give the Engine permission to remake my timeshadow–although I could hardly have prevented it from acting against my wishes if it had been so inclined–given that I had not the least idea whether any of the changes its nanozoons had wrought might be capable of affecting the behavior of my real body once I had returned to it.

To make matters worse, I still did not know whether or not the Engine might be capable of reading these skeptical thoughts as they crowded the forefront of my consciousness. If so, and if it had presumed too much, it would know it by now, and would presumably be remaking its plans to take aboard the effects of my skepticism.

10.

The motes of light still dancing before my eyes–which had begun as stars, and had then become galaxies, and finally whole "inflationary domains"–faded away into darkness. The cocoon encasing my body flowed away from my face to release my eyes and mouth–but it did not flow away entirely. It became, as it had been before, a chair, and as it left me it folded me neatly into a sitting posture upon its well-upholstered cushions.

I felt solid again, and possessed of a sensible measure of weight. I knew up from down as well as light from dark.

The room in which I found myself was very different from the one in which I had previously been confined, although I was hesitant, at first, to trust the evidence of my eyes. The ceiling was high–12 feet, at least–and the windows were very tall, filling the space with abundant light although my own position was shadowed.

There were many such shadowed coverts, because huge bookshelves jutted out at regular intervals from walls that were themselves covered from top to bottom with row upon row of neatly-bound volumes. I counted sixteen vertical rows, but I could not spare the time to count the sets of projecting shelves or make any estimate of the total number of the volumes housed therein. I was content to feel sure that there were far more books here than I had ever seen in one place before, including the great libraries that I had been privileged to visit.

Standing a few feet away, not shadowed at all, was a tall man in a neatly-tailored coat and well-pressed trousers. He was wearing a cravat and his long hair had been carefully styled; he was carrying a book in his right hand. I was not immediately ready to think him fully human on the basis of such affectations, however, because I had already been told that I would meet an individual who had entered his world as a timeshadow but was now a "true scion of the Engine." I recognized his face from portraits I had seen–and knew that the man who owned them had been dead for many years in 1918.

"Lieutenant Hodgson," he said, airily. "I cannot tell you how delighted I am to make your acquaintance. Words cannot express the relief I feel, to have human company at last after having waited so long. Do you, by any chance, know who I am?"

I only hesitated for a moment before saying: "No, I do not." When I had watched faint expressions of vexation and sadness flit across his soft features, though, I added: "But I know who you resemble."

That made him smile. His teeth were very white and neatly-aligned; the image contained in his timeshadow, which the Engine's nanozoons had presumably labored very carefully to reproduce in every detail, was not entirely honest.

"Yes," he said. "You are absolutely right. They told you, I dare say, that I often refer to this celestial hidey-hole as the Attic of Olympus–but it is very clever of you to have guessed the reason."

I had not quite guessed the reason until then, but I guessed it now that I was able to put two and two together.

I stood up, partly because I wanted to appraise him on equal terms, and partly because I wanted to be free of my over-solicitous chair. I extended my hand to be shaken, and he transferred his book from one hand to the other in order that he might take mine. No sooner had he released my hand than he gave me the book to hold instead.

"I have been attending to my homework," he said.

The book was bound in black, with gold leaf on its spine. My surname was at the top, and beneath it the title: *The House on the Borderland and Other Novels*. The publisher's imprint at the base was not one I recognized.

I felt a curious thrill at the realization that my work had somehow survived 12 million years, outlasting the human race itself. Given the total number of volumes in the room, I had no right to feel uniquely privileged, but it was a precious intimation of immortality to one who had struggled all his life to find publishers for his more ambitious work, and had lived the past four years in the toils of a particularly horrible war. I wondered if I dared ask my companion's opinion of the work contained within the book's pages, but thought better of it.

"How many posthumous volumes have you added to the shelves yourself, Mr. Wilde?" I asked, instead–fully cognizant of the fact that it was a wretchedly inept conversational gambit.

"Too many," he said, "but only one that you will have time to read, alas. And you must call me Oscar, even though–as you have very scrupulously observed–I am not even the ghost of my former self. I am merely his incorruptible image, secured in my attic by the cunning artifice of gods who love beauty, while my decayed body rots in the soil of old Earth. I hardly think that corruption and corrosion can have left so much as a chip of bone by now, do you? I would not like to think that I had become a fossil, when my atoms might have been returned to the stream of life: to the feathers of birds, the petals of flowers and the sweet air, which pink lungs and green leaves breathe and renew, each according to its fashion."

I remembered the greenery that had greeted my arrival in the new world, and the birds which had pursued me into the air. Was it possible, I wondered, that Oscar Wilde's simulacrum had something to do with their presence–or at least their prominence–in the wilderness that now covered the Earth?

"I was told that men of vivid imagination made the best time-travelers," I said, "but they would not tell me who had set forth before me. Indeed, they told me virtually nothing, lest it prejudice my expectations."

"It was a needless precaution," said the image of Oscar Wilde. "I shall be happy to reveal something of the history of your illustrious predecessors, in the hope that you might be able satisfy my own curiosity regarding an intriguing puzzle." He half-turned and pointed a well-manicured finger at a desk, upon whose cluttered leather top a sheaf of manuscript pages had been set. "Don't worry," he added, although I am sure that I cannot have exhibited any sign of dismay. "I am certain that you will find it interesting–and very intriguing, if the puzzle that has confounded me is as obvious and as startling to you as it now seems to me. But first, may I ask you how you feel?"

"Quite well," I told him, "considering that I appear to have been the focus of a considerable battle. I have been shut up in some kind of cocoon for what seemed to be at least an hour, while a machine attempted to acquaint me with ideas I am only beginning to comprehend."

"I wish that you would tell me exactly how you feel, if you can," he said. "There is more than mere politeness in the enquiry."

I was startled by the repeated question, and puzzled, but I thought that I had better do as I was asked.

"I really do feel quite well," I told him. "Much better than I had felt for some considerable time in 1918, when the pain of various wounds–some new, some old–would not give me a minute's true rest. I presume that my freedom from pain is so comforting that it blots out all other possible sensation. I am not afraid, although I suppose I have every right to be, nor am I unduly overawed, although I certainly ought to be. I think, perhaps, that I am reveling in my own lack of sensation, luxuriating in my unexpected freedom."

"Thank you," he said. "I will explain later why I wanted to know–and why the question seems important to me. You are not tired, of course, nor are you hungry–and the absence of such sensations seemed to you to be so unremarkable that you left them out of account. I, on the other hand, have taken great care to preserve the possibilities of hunger and fatigue. I don't suppose that I can tempt you to join me, but would you mind if I took a little wine?"

He was right; I had not the slightest desire to join him–and I saw, as he had presumably intended me to see when he probed into the matter of my lack of feeling, how puzzling that was. After all, I had a body of sorts, which presumably maintained some semblance of respiration and needed some kind of sustenance.

The machine that looked like Oscar Wilde–as I disposed myself carefully to think of the remarkable apparition–went to the desk. Among the clutter that had been pushed back in order to make space for the prominently-displayed manuscript was a decanter of red wine, whose cap only had to be inverted to convert it into a goblet. The simulacrum poured himself a modest measure, and took a sip.

"The wine is rarely less than excellent," he told me, "but one requires the occasional failure in order that one may still treasure the commonplace success."

"Just so," I said, trying to speak lightly and ironically, as seemed to befit such a remarkable meeting of minds. "I had gathered that your mechanical allies are no friends of permanent perfection. It does not prevent their vessels from being exceedingly tidy and their manufactured images a little too sharp and colorful." As I spoke, I took note of the fact that I had never seen another library as free from dust as the one in which I was now standing. The carpet was a discreet shade of dark blue, which was by no means garishly primary, but it was not in the least faded or dirtied.

Instead of joining my host at the desk, I went to the nearest window and looked out. I had expected, without having any particular reason to suppose so, that we would be on the ground floor of a tolerably large but not excessive house. In fact, I found myself looking down from an improbably great height at a wide-flung array of roofs, balconies, skylights and parapets, which even such a builder of stately pleasure domes as Coleridge's Kubla Khan would surely have thought excessive. Nor did we appear to be at the very top of the edifice, which must have been at least 1000 feet tall, surrounded by gardens as grandiose as those at Hampton Court and ten or 20 times as extensive.

Hampton Court sprang to mind as a standard for comparison because the hedges separating the myriad flower-gardens seemed to be arranged in a vast maze, which stretched–remarkably, given my astonishing elevation–almost to the limit of vision. There was no horizon; the landscape curved up instead of down, its appearance decaying into a misty blur within which I could just make out a few mountainous ridges.

A single continuous watercourse wound its way through the gardens, with a path to either side, although there were a number of isolated rectangular pools. The sky was remarkably bright, its light unevenly distributed into a cloud-shrouded trellis of radiance, which obscured every trace of the metal framework holding its gargantuan panes together.

"I had been told that you lived alone," I murmured, to cover up the fact that I had been so easily taken aback.

"I do," said Wilde, a little mournfully. "Had I company, I would not need a palace. Had I *good* company, I might even be content with a mere cottage. Ostentation is not the best counterweight to tedium, by any means, but it has its uses and its charms. When time and energy are no obstacles, the imagination naturally runs to excess."

"But the Engine has its mock-human scions, has it not?" I said, stepping back from the window, "and the entire Solar System is at war, it seems. Can life here be so very tedious?"

"The war extends far beyond the limits of the Solar System," said Wilde, after taking another sip from his glass, "and the Engine would provide guests for every room in the house, if I were disposed to hold a party or a costumed ball. Interesting people all–individuality and idiosyncrasy are easy to manufacture, when one has the resources of the Engine–but not quite the perfect audience, to one of my stubbornly old-fashioned sensibilities. Having had a very long time to ponder the matter, I have become a hardened Darwinist, aesthetically speaking. People deliberately shaped by gods in one's own image seem somehow less worthy than people shaped by natural selection; a contrived imitation of randomness, no matter how assiduous the imitation is, remains a matter of contrivance. Perhaps I should not care, but I do, and am perversely glad of it. I find the scions a little tedious, and the war even more so. I could never have been a soldier."

I came to stand beside him at the desk, thinking that he was lucky to have lived in an era when one had a choice in such matters. I picked up the first page of the manuscript. Its headsheet was inscribed with a title, *The Black Blood of the Dead*, and the signature *Sebastian Melmoth*. I knew that Sebastian Melmoth was the pseudonym Wilde had adopted while living in France after his release from prison.

"Should you not have reverted to your own signature, Mr. Wilde?" I asked him. "Surely you no longer have any reason to employ a pseudonym?"

"If I were certain of who and what I am," said the individual who had asked me to call him Oscar, "I would have more confidence in signing my work. Tell me, Lieutenant Hodgson–did you and the man I resemble ever meet?"

"No," I answered. "I was only 23, having spent much of the previous seven years at sea, when Oscar Wilde died. I visited France more than once in the last years of the century, but our paths never crossed. I have heard far more about you during the last three years than I ever heard before, both in England and in France–I have spoken to people who did know you, and you certainly have not been forgotten in 1918."

"That I know," he said. "Take time to read, now, if you will. You will find that your enhanced powers of perception will make it easy to do. I shall return in a little while."

So saying, he strode towards one of the shadowed coverts, where I saw a door that I had not noticed before. He nodded to me before passing through it and closing it behind him, but I was too slow to answer the gesture.

It did not occur to me until he was gone that there were 1000 questions I ought to have asked, whose answers I ought to have been burning to know–but I felt, as I had confessed to him, a little *too* well to be anxious. Now that I had entered into surroundings that had been shaped to give the impression of safety, comfort and near-familiarity, I had allowed myself to become lost in the luxury of a better numbness than morphine had ever given me. I seemed incapable, for the moment, of feeling any real urgency. "Well," I murmured, "I came here to be educated, and time is pressing."

I carried the manuscript back to the no-longer-ominous chair, and did not hesitate to set myself down thereupon.

I began to read.

The Writer's Story: Part One

Paris, September 1900

1.

There is something magical about artificial light, especially when its effects are combined with those of absinthe; it brings out the true colors which properly define the nature of things. Sometimes the result is unendurable, sometimes redeeming.

The yellow lamplight in my room at the Hôtel d'Alsace had the strangest effect on the wallpaper. Lit by the Sun, its sprays of foliage and liliaceous blooms were dingy and apologetic–but contrived radiance made their verdance subtly malevolent and caused the flowers to open, shedding intangible but disturbing pollen into the air.

Never in the course of my hectic career had I encountered nefandous wallpaper–the walls of the cells of Reading Gaol are, of course, sullenly and insultingly naked–and I felt that there was a certain monstrous unfairness in the probability that my final days in earth were to be spent in such company.

As the summer died and autumn damp descended on Paris like a catarrhal contagion the walls of my bedroom became the walls of the world, surfaced with symbols of everything inimical. I felt, more than once, that I had already passed from the final year of the nineteenth century into a nightmarish eternity.

I know now, of course, that such feelings were premonitions; perhaps I had reason to trust them even then, but my reserves of trust had run dry. I am not sorry on that account; it is one thing to know that one must die beyond one's means, quite another to know what means one will have beyond one's dying.

I was not really well enough to go out on the night when I first caught sight of the Grim Reaper, but while I still had strength enough to walk I felt that I simply had to go in search of a kindlier light whenever darkness fell. On other occasions I had had friends to help me, but even Robbie and Reggie had lives of their own to lead, and when they were about their own business I had perforce to go alone.

There is nothing like isolation to bring a sick man into brutal confrontation with his own mortality. I was always careful to carry a book with me when I fled the horrid walls of my room, but books are imperfect defenses, even when their pages are lit by a redeeming light. I was not at all surprised, that night, to see

Death; nor could I doubt for a moment, when I saw him, that he had come to find me.

My pilgrimage had brought me, slowly and painfully, to the *Vieille Rose*, a small café on a side-street of the Place de l'Opéra. By day, its furnishings were unrepentantly magenta, but when the gas was lit, it justified its name. Roses are not always to be preferred to lilies, and there is something essentially effete about pink roses, but there were no actual roses to be found in the *Vieille Rose*; there was instead a general and piquantly elusive atmosphere of rosiness which, in falling upon a whitely powdered cheek or a hollow eye, could produce a naïve impression of health. I had come to that interval between life and death where such illusions are cherished.

In the interval before the Reaper appeared, I happened to catch an accidental glimpse of my reflection in a glass. Usually I was quick to look away when that happened; by day, I reacted to the sight of my features exactly as the greater number of my former acquaintances did–except that I had to content myself with looking away, while they had the oft-exercised option of turning on their heels and vanishing. In this instance, however, the generous gaslight lent my leaden jowls a welcome semblance of healthy flesh. For the briefest instant, I could almost have believed that I was my old self again–but even absinthe has its limitations. Although the illusion bravely refused to collapse, I remained acutely aware of the mottled skin beneath the pale facade, and even more acutely aware of the fact that the superficial rash was itself a mask for the hidden corruption that was killing me.

The invaluable Monsieur Dupoirier was still injecting me every day with what he claimed to be morphine, but the itching would not let me go and the deeper pain was positively scornful. I could have forgiven the bad mussels that had afflicted my entire skin with crawling spite, if only that effect had succeeded in distracting my attention from the patient wrath devouring my heart and soul.

I had just taken a sip of wormwood–a libation to the alien power that possessed me–when I saw Death.

Less than half a second passed before he saw me, but the interval was enough to give me the advantage of measuring his response. I was interested to observe that he seemed reluctant to expose himself to the magical light of the *Vieille Rose*. When he did catch sight of me, his instinct was indistinguishable from that of my Earthly acquaintances: he recoiled. As soon as his shadowed gaze lighted on my face, and was immediately arrested, he stepped back, removing his cowled head from view.

"How magnificently discreet!" I thought. "Even Death does not care to be seen with me in public. He has decided to wait for me in the darkened street, to save himself embarrassment."

I did not hasten to meet my destiny. While I finished my glass, I studied the other patrons of the strange establishment in which Death was reluctant to set foot. The opera had not yet disgorged its crowds upon the street and the whores were bored with waiting. Like me, they had powdered faces; far too many of their masks were hopelessly intent on hiding the same sad corruptions that worked within my own body and soul.

I tried to count my blessings, but in the circumstances I could think only of wreaths. That I had survived Queensberry might be reckoned a blessing, but I had survived Constance too, and Aubrey Beardsley, and Ernest Dowson, not to mention Lewis Carroll. Who could have imagined that I would outlive Beardsley, Dowson and the creator of *Alice in Wonderland*? What a wayward course Death used to follow as he navigated his sharkish way through the human shoal!

Although I had lately become expert in the art of procrastination, I had never grown fond of its exercise. I was sick enough, and drunk enough, to be confident that I could not long remain awake. The threat of the ominous wallpaper weakened in the face of irresistible slumber, and I would have been ashamed to fall asleep in a café like any common-or-garden derelict.

In any case, I thought, *if Death is waiting for me at the threshold of the* Vieille Rose, *that is where my particular appointment in Samarra must be. How can I possibly avoid it?*

Little did I know what possibilities the world still held.

I picked up my book, surrendered my last few *sous* as a *pourboire*, and walked unsteadily to the waiting door. The patient darkness awaited me, and the hooded figure of the Reaper. The book I carried was *La mer* by Jules Michelet, and I could not help but remember, as it nestled warmly in my hand, the epitaph that Michelet had wisely laid in store for his own demise: "*I have drunk too deep of the black blood of the dead.*"

What a bold admission! What a beautiful boast!

I, alas, had drunk too much *eau de vie*. Unlike Michelet, who used work as a weapon against his migraines and penned every sentence as if it might be his last, I had disarmed myself in brilliant conversation and had written every line of my verse as if I had eternity at my beck and call.

Now, it seemed, I was about to add my own stagnant blood to the waters of the Styx–or, at least, to a damp Paris side-street.

Many men would have opined that the Reaper had already waited too long, and ought to have cut me down *en passant* the day he called on London to collect poor Lugard, while my fame was at its height.

When I first stepped out on to the rainswept street, it seemed that Death had gone, but I was not deceived. As soon as I began to walk in the direction of the rue des Beaux-Arts, I heard his footsteps echoing my own. At the corner, I hazarded a surreptitious backward glance and saw him scuttling along from shadow to shadow like some predatory spider. His skull-like head was invisible within its hood, but there was no mistaking his improbable thinness. He was not carrying a scythe, but he had something clutched in his arms, which looked suspiciously like a briefcase.

I was relieved to know that even Death had a sense of place and occasion. In the great gaslit cities of the *fin de siècle*, Death had no need for a scythe; he was far more aptly equipped with a diary of appointments and a wad of warrants of arrest–and where should he keep such instruments, if not in a lawyer's brief-case?

Death did not seem to be in a hurry. He followed me, but he kept his distance. Had it been a year earlier, I might have led him a merry dance from café to café–from the *Vieille Rose* to the *Calisaya* and from there to the *Chat Gris*– but I had lost my ability to climb hills and Montmartre was beyond my powers of attainment.

I could not help but remember an occasion when I had paused on the Pont des Arts and noticed a poorly-dressed individual lost in contemplation of the murky water. "*Alors, mon pauvre Monsieur,*" I had called to him, as one lost soul to another, "*êtes-vous désespéré?*" He had looked at me with such perfect melancholy while he replied, without the least hint of surprise or irony: "*Non, Monsieur. Je suis coiffeur.*"

Would that I had been a hairdresser myself, eternally spared the toils of desperation.

Death's footsteps came closer as I tired. I looked back for a second time, and caught a glimpse of my pursuer's face as he passed the brashly-lit display-window of a modish boutique. I do not know why I should have been startled, but I was. I had already glimpsed the face, which was so nearly fleshless as to suggest a naked skull, but I could not have guessed that his accusing eyes would shine so diamond bright as they caught the gleam of stray limelight.

Perhaps it is not Death, after all, I thought, becoming desperate at last. *Perhaps it is a guest late for a private masque, or perhaps it is that phantom who is rumored to haunt the Opera, driven from his favored box by the incompetence of the performers. Is* Faust *playing tonight or* Don Giovanni?

I remembered, then, that the playbills in the *Vieille Rose* had been advertising *Orpheus in the Underworld*. I became afraid to look back again; I had already lost too much that I had loved too well.

I cannot say why I hastened my steps. It is natural to flee from Death, and only to be expected, but I had always done my best to shun the natural and the expectable. What had I to fear, after all? What had I to lose but my pain, my ignominy, my incapacity? I wish I could say that I turned to greet him gladly as a friend–or even as a fiend–but I did not.

I should like to believe that I hurried for the same reason that I continued while it was within my power to traipse from café to café every night, courting the accidental encounters that were far more likely to shame me than bring me relief from loneliness. I should like to think that I had no motive in mind but to continue to be *noticed*, to continue my irritation of the shameful eyes and guilty hearts of those who wanted to forget me. Alas, I fear that there was no such stubborn reason in my flight.

The humble truth is that I fled because I was in the grip of panic.

All I could achieve, within that grip, was a feeble impulse to represent my cowardice as virtue. *If he wants a race, should I not oblige him?* I said to myself, a dissimulator to the last. *If he wants to match strides with a sick man, a man already defeated, a man with nothing to gain by winning, why should I not give him that meager satisfaction? If he wishes to pretend that this is sport and not mere savagery, should I not support his illusion?*

With this excuse in mind, I made what haste I could. It was all in vain, of course.

He caught up with me just as I reached the threshold of my lodgings. I cast one hopeful glance at the door of the hotel, hoping to see the loyal Dupoirier hurrying down the steps to greet me, but there was no help at hand at all. Panic or no, I had to turn to face the creature in the monkish habit, to meet those terrible eyes.

"Damn you, Wilde," said Death, with a petulance that seemed wonderfully pathetic. "Why didn't you wait for me?"

2.

Because I was lost in astonishment at the ridiculous manner of the Grim Reaper's complaint, I had no reply ready. Devoid of dignity and breath, I could only whisper: "Here, Monsieur, I am known as Sebastian Melmoth!"

He must have been less astonished than I, but he blinked in surprise nevertheless. "Indeed?" he said, in a voice so hoarse that he seemed to be on the brink of extinction himself. "Well, for that matter I am registered at my own hotel under a false name."

I wondered what *nom de guerre* Death would choose in order to preserve his *incognito*. I had named myself for Maturin's tragic hero, Melmoth the Wanderer, but it was difficult to identify a soubriquet that would suit the Grim Reaper as well. Chartley, after the Fatalist in James Dawson's novel, was too recondite and Varney, after the Vampyre in Reynolds' penny dreadful, would have been rather tasteless.

In his place, I decided, I would have shunned the frankly melodramatic and opted for Marius, after Pater's epitome of Epicureanism, or perhaps even Jude, after Hardy's paragon of Obscurity–but I could not say so, because I was still trying to recover my breath. I felt utterly dreadful; I expected him to reach out a skeletal hand at any moment to clutch my heart and claim my soul.

"You don't recognize me," he muttered. "Well, I can hardly blame you for that. I have changed a great deal–more than you, I think. We did meet, briefly, in January 1895."

He paused then, to give me space to consider.

I realized, belatedly, that the apparition was not the Grim Reaper at all. The hope that I had dared not entertain was, after all, justified–but I knew that he was no mere masquerader. His imitation of death was far too convincing for that. He was not Death, nor even dead, but there was something unearthly about him, which whispered insistently of destiny and mysterious worlds beyond the world.

He waited, wanting me to put a name to him without too much prompting. I supposed that he was in search of reassurance that he was not *entirely* a monster: that the human being was still recognizable within the ravaged mask. I tried, in spite of my dying panic and enduring debility, to rise to the occasion.

In January 1895, I had had one play in production and another in rehearsal; I had been near the height of my success. I had met 1000 men that month. Alas, the flesh of this creature's face was so shriveled that he might have been the relic of any man in the world, or no man at all. I wanted to see the human in him, but I could not. All I could see, despite what I now knew, was the face of Death.

"It was at Edward Copplestone's house the night before and the night after his death," he said, eking out his clues and pleading for my inspiration.

There had been eight of us at Copplestone's house on those two fateful evenings. Lugard, whose name had crossed my mind only a few minutes before, for the first time in a year, had died a few days later–allegedly a suicide, although the exact circumstances had been, as the saying goes, "hushed up." Bertie Wells was famous now and I had recently heard complimentary rumors of Matt Shiel's latest literary endeavors. Nothing like this could have happened to Sir William Crookes or Nick Tesla without it being reported as a scandal–which only left the dutiful doctor and his grey-eyed friend, the model for the Great Detective of *The Strand*. Unless he had grown endways, while shrinking sideways, this could not possibly be the doctor. Having eliminated the impossible, there was only one name left in the hat.

"I had always assumed that your reputation as a master of disguise was overstated, my dear sir," I said, weakly. "I must apologize. Your present performance is truly remarkable." I had never felt less capable of cleverness, but I felt obliged to muster what wit I could.

Always the perfect Victorian, he was not amused. "I wish this *were* a disguise," he said. "As things are, I must wear theatrical make-up to go abroad in daylight."

That was a tactless thing to say, as it must have been obvious to him that the same was true of me. He might have lost a substantial fraction of his flesh but he presumably still had his talent for observation. A brief flux of resentful bile put new impetus into my power of speech.

"You need not have been afraid to come into the café and sit down with me," I told him. "Even the whores would have been resolute in refusing to see us. I knew, of course, that your friend the doctor had brought your *alter ego* back from the dead, but I had not appreciated the price that you had paid for the privilege. I never realized that a sojourn in Tibet could take so much out of a man. No wonder the French prefer Algeria."

It finally came home to me then that I was not about to die. Not only would I live to fight another day, but I was still capable of striking out with my most lethal weapon. I knew that I would not long survive the 19th century, but I felt a burst of sudden confidence that I might yet find and appropriate valediction with which to usher the *siècle* to its appointed *fin*.

"I come as a friend, Mr. Wilde," he said, in a wounded tone. "I have a tale to tell and a letter to deliver–but first..."

He unbuckled the straps of his briefcase and threw back the flap. It was full of papers collected into several distinct bundles, each one tied with green ribbon. He took out the thickest and held it towards me. As he did so, the loose sleeve of his black robe slid back a little way, exposing the skeletal wrist and forearm. There was so little flesh on them that every bone and sinew was clearly outlined, but his muscles were not without strength and resolution. His hand was steadier than mine as I took the package from him, moving *La mer* from my right hand to my left in order to do so.

"I don't need your testimony," he said, gruffly, implying by his reluctance that he probably did need it, or would at least be glad to have it, "but I do need your understanding. Read it, I beg of you. There is much more to be added. I suppose there is no chance that you could pack your bags and meet me at the Gare du Nord tomorrow?"

If he imagines that I could return to England, I thought, *he must really have been in Tibet, or somewhere equally remote*. "Quite impossible," I croaked. "I am bound to Paris by fate and mortality alike."

Now that he had had time to study me he must have been able to appreciate my meaning.

"I see," he said. "It might be wisest, in any case, to improvise an audience here, as soon as is humanly possible. The doctor's literary agent has given me a letter of introduction to a man reputed to be one of the cleverest in France, and he has a colleague here who numbers another among his patients. I'll make what arrangements I can, with all possible haste, and I'll send a messenger. I'm truly sorry, Wilde, to find you in this condition..."

He broke off when the door behind me opened. It was only my guardian angel, Monsieur Dupoirier, anxious for my safety–but Death's double did not know him, and his instinct was to retreat from curious and censorious eyes. He stepped back immediately, shrugging his shoulders so that the cowl of his habit slid forwards, hiding his awful face.

As Dupoirier came closer, Death's simulacrum moved away, anxious to fade away into the darkest shadow he could find and to make good his retreat. He scuttled away–no predatory spider now, but something far more circumspect and far less menacing. Even so, I wondered what kind of subtle web I might be holding in my hands.

"Who was that?" Dupoirier demanded. Like Moréas and Tailhède, he always spoke to me in English, not because he intended any insult to my French, but because he thought the English language an instrument that none could play more delicately than I, and felt a duty to encourage my use of it.

"It was a living legend," I told him, my voice diminishing again to a mere whisper. "Do not be deceived by his resemblance to the infamous Erik. He has the reputation in England of being the greatest detective in the world, although some of the published accounts of his adventures are greatly exaggerated. He has asked for my help in solving a particularly difficult case–but I must ask you to be discreet."

Dupoirier took my intended inference, although he could not help curling his lip in slight contempt. Where great detectives were concerned, the French remained fiercely loyal to their very own Monsieur Lecoq and the Chevalier Auguste Dupin; they were unimpressed by English Johnny-come-latelies.

"No one will hear of his visit from me, Monsieur Melmoth," Dupoirier assured me, with a solemnity which could only signify that he thought I needed to be humored. Perhaps, after all, there *was* morphine in the daily syringe he presented to my mottled and near-veinless arm.

"This is not a dream," I murmured. "Nor did the magic of artificial light produce it out of nothing."

I would have said more, but I could not. The exertion of my flight through the rainswept streets had reduced me to an unsteady wreck, hardly able to stand without assistance. Dupoirier had to take me by the arm and lead me into his precious haven; I felt nothing in his supportive grip but honest generosity.

He helped me up the stairs and along the corridor. He used his pass key to open my room, in order to save me the ignominy of groping in my pockets. In any case, both my hands were full, one with *La mer* and the other with the mysterious manuscript that Death's reluctant deputy had commanded me to read.

I think Dupoirier was a better man than any I had known. If only he had not chosen to decorate his hotel with such appalling wallpaper!

I thanked him very kindly when he had completed his work by helping me into bed and pouring a little laudanum into a glass. "Leave the lamp, if you will," I said, as he reached out to stifle it. "I should like to read for a while."

Dupoirier glanced at the copy of *La mer* I had laid down on top of the manuscript on the bedside table. He nodded his head sagely, as if to judge that I could be safely entrusted to the company of an earnest Frenchman who had drunk too deep of the black blood of the dead. Then he withdrew.

I pushed *La mer* aside and took up the manuscript, riffling through its pages. The first page was blank, serving as a protector for the rest. When I had untied the ribbon and set the blank page aside, I found that there was a title and a signature on the second leaf. The text began on the third leaf; it was written in a strangely punctilious hand, which did not seem to me to have been learned from any tutor in England or France.

The title was *The Hunger and Ecstasy of Vampires*; the signature was *Lucian, Count Lugard*.

I had thought of Lugard and the curious persecution to which he had been subject when I had read Bram Stoker's *Dracula*, some little time after the commencement of my exile, but I had not thought of him again until tonight. Even then, my consideration had been cursory; I knew that he was safe from any further slurs upon his name. I wondered how, and when, the Great Detective could possibly have come into possession of such a document as this.

I began to read, and immediately found myself present on the page. Curiosity mingled with, and was then briefly displaced by, nostalgia.

I had been at the height of my powers in those days. How beautiful the world had been! How could so much have changed, to such a terrible extent, in the space of five years?

When I read further, however, curiosity returned in fuller force–and by the time the lamplight began to flicker and fade I was well and truly spellbound.

The Count's Story: Part One

London, January 1891

1.

"Do you know Professor Edward Copplestone?" Oscar Wilde asked me, as he sipped appreciatively from his glass. It contained absinthe, which I had smuggled in from Paris for his delectation. We were dining at Roche's in Soho, but our host made no objection to the absinthe. *An Ideal Husband* had just started its run, to universal acclaim, and Wilde could do no wrong within those or any other walls.

I had been less than a month in London, and knew hardly anyone, so I denied it almost without thinking.

"He dines here sometimes," said Wilde, "but he cannot really be considered a member of our set. He is a great traveler, and tells extravagant tales of his adventures in parts of the world of which most of us have never heard. Some of his stories may even be true, although that hardly matters. He is the only man I know who can speak with casual familiarity about the hinterlands of Siberia and the Mongol lands."

That struck a chord. There was another man I knew who was widely travelled in the Far East, and liked to tell dubious traveler's tales. "Perhaps I *have* heard the name," I conceded, controlling the impulse to scowl that always assailed me when anything recalled the name of Arminius Vambery to my mind.

"You will find it extensively acknowledged in the notes and bibliographies of Tylor's *Primitive Culture* and Frazer's *Golden Bough*," said Wilde, airily–although I suspected that he had read neither book. "He is a self-supposed expert on primitive religion and magic, with particular reference to shamanistic cults, but he's by no means an academic Dryasdust. Quite a dreamer, in his way. No stranger to the opium dens of Limehouse, it's said–and rumor can usually be trusted...except, of course, when it turns its attention to me."

This news was mildly reassuring. It was entirely probable that such a man might know Arminius Vambery by repute, but Vambery was unlikely to have gone out of his way to pour out his troubled heart to a man reputed to be a dope-fiend. Like most sober madmen of impeccable reputation, Vambery had little tolerance of delusions born of conscious artifice, or of those accused of courting them. Vambery was the kind of man who trusted rumors–especially those he had invented himself.

"Why do you ask whether I know this Copplestone?" I asked.

"Because he has written me a curious letter saying that he has a very strange report to make and would be grateful for my presence. He goes on to say that he considers me one of the three most intelligent and open-minded men in London–I cannot imagine who else he has in mind–and that he would prize my opinion of what he has to say most highly. He requests me to bring an acquaintance as wise and as wide-eyed as myself. It is a description that could hardly apply to Bosie, or even to Robbie, so I naturally thought of you. Will you come with me, if you are not busy? The invitation is for tomorrow evening."

"You hardly know me," I murmured. "How do you know that I fit the requirements?" I was fully in agreement with the estimate of my intellectual acumen, but I suspected that Wilde had only *naturally thought of* me because I happened to be dining with him that evening.

"I was impressed the first time we met, in Paris," he said. "You seemed to have a view of the world of men so clear and so cynical that I could hardly believe you were part of that world. It is true that we have never talked at great length about deep matters, but I am always impulsive in my judgments and I am very rarely wrong. Will you come?"

I agreed to go with him. How could I possibly have refused? In any case, I was becoming hungry for new amusement. London seemed unbelievably dull after Paris, which I had left with such a sudden wrench. It is never a good idea for an individual of my kind to stay in one place for long, but I never regretted leaving a city more than I regretted leaving Paris. On the other hand, London was not entirely devoid of advantages. One could buy a slumgirl for a shilling, and a passably pretty one at that; we who are obliged by restless nature and the harassment of vile slanders to be forever on the move must be grateful for every opportunity which a city has to offer.

"Who else will be there?" I asked.

"I really have no idea. The only other name Copplestone mentions in his letter to me is Bram Stoker's–and that is only to say that Stoker is in Ireland just now, and cannot possibly come. Copplestone does not explain why he thinks Stoker might have been a suitable candidate for inclusion; personally, I have always considered his mind to be conspicuously second-rate."

I had laid down my fork rather abruptly at the first mention of Stoker's name. I had, in any case, only been toying with my food. I sipped a little water from my glass, but the attempt to cover up my reaction failed. Wilde must have seen my reaction immediately, and was wise enough to be surprised. He did not know me well, but he had observed that I rarely react intemperately to anything.

"Do you know Stoker at all?" he asked, curiously. "He's Henry Irving's factotum–his strong right arm, I suppose he would say."

"I have never met him," I said, in a neutral tone.

"I've seen little of him lately myself," said Wilde, "although I was a regular visitor to his home when he first moved to London. He was at Trinity before me, you know, and he was still working in Dublin when I went up. My father befriended him, and even my mother condescended to like him a little. He married a girl of whom I was exceedingly fond, and I was never able to forgive his temerity. The fact that we are now in rival camps, theatrically speaking, only serves to add new insult to the old injury."

I was not in the least interested in the petty politics of the English theater. I had heard far too much gossip about theatrical matters while staying with Jean Lorrain, and I had had my fill of paeans of praise offered up to the divinity of Sarah Bernhardt. I knew, though, that Stoker was one of the people Arminius Vambery had talked to when he was in London; Stoker had invited him to address a meeting of the Beefsteak Club, where he had waxed lyrical on the subject of vampirism. If Stoker and Copplestone were acquainted, it was possible that Copplestone might have been present. After what had happened in Paris, I wanted to steer well clear of anyone who might conceivably have occasion–with whatever motive–to mention the name of Laura Vambery. On the other hand, I had already accepted Wilde's invitation, and it seemed that Stoker would not actually be present. I thought it best to change the subject.

"Shall we share a carriage?" I asked. "I shall be happy to collect you, if you wish. Where does Copplestone live?"

"On the south side of the park–Regent's Park, that is, not Hyde Park. Yes, I'd be grateful if you could collect me from the Haymarket; it will be easier to tear myself away from my friends, my duties and my admirers if I know that I am impatiently awaited by a stern aristocrat. We are expected at eight. I do hope that it will be amusing. Travelers' tales have become far less interesting since Mungo Park and the indefatigable Stanley let so much dismal light into the delicately dark heart of Africa, and the steady march of geographical science is slowly strangling the spirit of wild romance–but if there is any forgotten corner of the globe still rich with gorgeous mystery, Ned Copplestone is more than likely to have found it. If he intends to test our credulity, we may be reasonably sure that it will be well and truly tested, perhaps to delicious destruction."

Even though I knew full well that there were more things in Heaven and Earth than were dreamt of in Oscar Wilde's philosophy, I did not think of myself as a gullible individual, and I was inclined to think that listening to a story that tested my credulity to destruction would be a waste of time–but I put my reservations firmly aside, and resolved to do my very best to play the part allocated to me: that of a man of the world, clear-sighted and open-minded.

I little suspected what unprecedented demands that role would make of me in the nights that followed.

2.

I called for Wilde at the appropriate hour but he was–as always–late. I had to sit in my carriage for a quarter of an hour, watching the crowds go by.

The famous London fog had condescended to leave the city unblanketed for once, and the frost had not yet begun to glitter upon the pavements. The chestnut-roasting season was well past by now and most of the brazier-men were hawking baked potatoes, whose odor was not quite so astringent. The crowd was as good a quality as one could expect to find in London out of season, but they seemed a tawdry gaggle by comparison with the excited throngs of Paris's Latin Quarter. My mood was such that they seemed more than usually like cattle trooping to the barn, or laying-hens milling about their carelessly-scattered corn. I was glad when Wilde finally consented to appear.

As we bowled along Regent Street, Wilde lost himself in some interminable anecdote, and for once his brilliance seemed slightly off-key, but he was in such good heart that he slowly roused me from my torpor of indolence. By the time we reached the fringes of the park I felt quite ready to face the challenge of the long winter night.

Inevitably, we were the last to arrive, although my coachman had contrived to make up some of the time we had lost by showing his usual scant regard for the convenience of other road-users.

Wilde's enthusiasm seemed to falter slightly when he saw the remainder of the company gathered in Copplestone's waiting-room. He doubtless wondered what judgments had been made of their intelligence by way of polite enticement. He introduced me to Copplestone, who–mercifully–showed no flicker of recognition at the mention of my name.

Copplestone was a tall, gaunt man who had doubtless been more solidly-built in his younger days, but who seemed to find the advancing years uncommonly burdensome. He was not unduly wrinkled, but his complexion seemed curiously jaundiced and his handshake was far from firm. Politeness forbade me from saying so but he really did not look well, and I wondered whether he ought to have postponed his story-telling until he had recovered more of his color and strength.

I had to concur with Wilde's unvoiced judgment that our fellow-guests did not appear at first glance to be a coterie of the most intelligent and open-minded men in England. They seemed, in fact, to comprise an assembly of eccentrics. I dare say, however, that there was more than one among them who felt that Wilde and I increased the bizarrerie of the gathering rather than adding a necessary counterweight of wise sobriety.

Wilde proved, once he had removed his coat, to be dressed as flamboyantly as usual, although the green carnation in his lapel was made of silk and crêpe paper. I, of course, was a foreigner–and a Count to boot–and needed no artificial aids to appear exotic in English eyes.

While Copplestone introduced me to the others I searched anxiously for any sign or symptom which might testify to the arrival in London of scurrilous gossip, but there was nothing. If any of them had heard of the Mourier affair they were models of discretion.

The first man to whom I was presented was a stout and stolid doctor who had served in India. He seemed a man of common sense rather than exceptional cleverness, but he was the only man present who seemed to have been long acquainted with Copplestone. Copplestone referred to him as an "invaluable supporter" but also as an "unwilling collaborator," and I gathered that the doctor had his own reservations about our host's physical condition.

Like Wilde, the doctor had been invited to bring a companion, and the man who accompanied him was tall and distinguished, though not particularly well-dressed. He seemed grave almost to the point of melancholy, and I was struck by the strange acuity of his grey eyes. Nothing was said concerning his station in life, but he greeted me politely.

I was then introduced to two young men, perhaps not yet out of their 20s. The first of them was a study in contradictions. He was not thin, but the peculiar softness of his flesh gave the impression that he had recently been very lean indeed, and was filling out for the first time. His complexion was naturally pale, but he pinked very easily, and a hectic flush seemed to be continually ebbing and flowing from his cheeks. There was a slight feverish glint in his eye, which suggested that he was not entirely well, although he was by no means as debilitated as our host. It was evident that Copplestone had never clapped eyes on him before, and that it was his companion to whom the professor had actually written.

The second young man could hardly have looked more different. He was dark and curly-haired, with perhaps a touch of Creole about him. Copplestone explained that he had but recently returned to London after spending some time as a schoolmaster in Derbyshire, but that Wilde knew him slightly and would doubtless be glad to see him again. Wilde obediently pantomimed the pleasure of an old acquaintance joyously renewed, but it did not seem to me that their friendship could have been very intimate. Wilde knew so many young men that he must have found it hard to remember their names.

I judged from snippets of conversation I barely had time to overhear that the two young men were not very well acquainted with one anther, but that they had many interests in common. Both seemed to have studied medicine, or at least biological science, and both had apparently served as teachers before finally choosing to devote themselves to the precarious life of the pen.

There was only one man in the room who presented incontrovertible evidence to the naked eye that he was older than Copplestone; he seemed to be in his mid-60s, and his flowing beard was white, but he was still healthy. He was clearly a man of means, and also a man of science. I would presumably have recognized his name immediately had I been well versed in science, but science has always seemed to me to be very much a day-time product, and those who invariably keep late hours–as I do–tend to be thrust more often into the company of men of Wilde's or Jean Lorrain's stripe. This was the only man in the room with a title of any sort, but Copplestone did not say whether it was a baronetcy or a knighthood earned by public service; he did, however, mention that the old gentleman was as well-known for his exploits in association with the Society for Psychical Research as for more material work. This did not make me any more enthusiastic to cultivate his acquaintance.

The final member of the party, who had been brought as a companion by the white-haired man of science, was a dark-haired man of science. Copplestone seemed to think that we might get along famously together, presumably because we both had European accents, but it was obvious to the two of us, if to no one else, that we came from nations that had so little in common as never to have gone to war against one another. In any case, this mustachioed worthy candidly explained that he was an American by adoption, and had renounced his European identity in order to give his allegiance entirely to the American spirit of free enterprise. I was not sure exactly what this implied, but I gathered that it had something to do with the profits one could make out of the sale of patents.

I concluded, on due consideration, that although we comprised an exceedingly peculiar crew, we nevertheless constituted a team as well-qualified as any to pass judgment on an exotic and challenging report.

When I had the opportunity to stand aside for a few moments with Wilde he was quick to give me the benefit of his own judgment. "We can expect little in the way of ready wit from the men of science," he told me. "They will play their part very earnestly–but some such counterweight of sanity may be necessary, given that our remaining companions have no shortage of romance in heir souls."

"Have you read the work of either of the young men?" I asked.

"Not a word. I have heard rumor of them both, and the more personable of the two has urged me more than once to look at some of his tales, but I never quite found the time. The one who blushes so hectically is said to have produced some very pretty fancies about the future evolution of the race and the probability of its extinction. He has studied Darwinism under Thomas Huxley, I believe, but he has absorbed the ideas without the rugged optimism of a Winwood Reade. The third literary man is far more famous than either. *Everyone* has read his work."

It was news to me that there was a third literary man present. "Are you talking about the grey-eyed man?" I asked.

"No–that is, not directly. I meant the doctor, who has published several novels and a long series of short stories in a periodical called *The Strand*. The stories chronicle the adventures of a consulting detective: a master of ratiocination, who solves puzzles by observing clues that less sensitive men invariably miss. The appearance, quirks and mannerisms of the detective in question are said to be very closely based on those of his grey-eyed companion. Like your friend Lorrain, who annoyed Guy de Maupassant by putting him into one of his novels, the doctor prefers to paint his pen-portraits from life."

"Unfortunately, the doctor's friend is said to have become so entranced with the doctor's literary confections as to have convinced himself that he really *is* a great detective. He is only recently returned from a rest-cure in Switzerland. Rumor has it that the cure was forced upon him by a breakdown which he suffered when the doctor–perhaps hoping to dispel his delusion–killed off the character a little over a year ago by sending him tumbling to his death over the Reichenbach Falls. Perhaps he is cured, but it is conceivable that he has convinced himself that the Great Detective is not dead after all and is merely in hiding, awaiting his chance to emerge from obscurity by solving a mystery deeper and more deadly than any he has ever faced before. Did you remark the strange glint in his eye?"

"I did. He certainly has a disconcerting stare–if he has the intelligence to go with it he must be a man to be reckoned with."

"It is more likely to be the effect of a new drug–not a derivative of opium, but something equally powerful. He is supposed too have broken the habit while he was away, but...some habits are hard to break. Has poor Lorrain given up drinking ether, by the way?"

"I believe he has," I reported. "I think he has had enough of physicians, for now, and is more disposed to place himself in the hands of a good surgeon. As you say, though, some habits are hard to break."

"I am interested to see that Copplestone has invited no clergyman, nor anyone of the legalistic turn of mind," Wilde said. "To my mind, that is evidence that he has an altogether sensible notion of trust and trustworthiness."

That was a judgment with which I concurred, but I did not have a chance to say so; we were already being ushered into the dining-room.

Copplestone had the grace to feed his guests well, and to lay out a burgundy of very tolerable vintage before setting forth to tax their credulity. I, as was my habit, ate very little and drank even less, but I made a polite show of participation in the pleasures of the meal. I had been seated between Wilde and the younger man of science, directly opposite the grey-eyed man, so I was not ideally placed for conversation. Fortunately, Wilde soon took charge of the occasion and held the entire company in thrall with anecdotes regarding the production of *An Ideal Husband*, the writing of *The Importance of Being Earnest* and the appalling behavior of the Marquess of Queensberry.

It was not until the port was being passed that the professor introduced the serious business of the evening–by which time he seemed a little stronger than he had before the meal. I settled back in my oaken chair, ready and eager to be entertained–although I suspected that Wilde's might be a difficult act for him to follow.

I need not have worried. Despite the enormous difference in their styles, Edward Copplestone proved easily capable of putting on a fascinating show.

3.

"Some of you," Copplestone said, "will already know something about the studies that have been my life's work. Some of you may even have read one or other of my monographs on the religious rites and magical practices of various exotic tribes. We are inclined to call such tribes primitive, partly on account of the fact that they indulge in un-Christian rites and un-scientific practices, but it has long been my opinion that our condescension is not entirely justified. In my admittedly-blasphemous view, Christianity has no more claim to truthfulness than any pagan faith, while modern science, in so savagely condemning the occult studies which not so long ago gave birth to it, has thrown out more than one baby with the bathwater.

"My published writings on tribal magic and divination have always been scrupulously skeptical–my reputation as a natural philosopher would have been reduced to tatters had they shown the least trace of credulity–but my private thoughts have ever been prepared to entertain hypotheses as to the shy truths which might lie hidden in the undergrowth of superstition. I have been particularly interested in the various means used by tribal magicians to obtain knowledge of the future.

"The history of prophecy is littered with ignominious failures–and the prophecies in which, as Christian men, we are supposed to invest our faith are as ignominious as any–but I have seen enough in my travels to convince me that there are indeed some men who have the innate gift of foresight, and that there are chemical methods by which such natural gifts may be enhanced. I have long thought it probable that the application of proper scientific method to the study of such men and such chemical compounds would rapidly produce a way of inducing more accurate and more far-reaching visions of futurity."

"A bold ambition," Wilde put in–but Copplestone only frowned, resentful of the interruption.

"A hopeless ambition," the American murmured, for my ears alone, "given the rapidity with which new technology is changing the spectrum of possibility."

"In saying this," Copplestone went on, insistently, "I remain well aware of certain philosophical problems that arise in connection with the notion of precognition, and of certain psychological problems that inevitably confuse the visionary process. I have no wish to insult the intelligence of men like yourselves by lecturing you, but I would like to comment very briefly on both these kinds of problems in order to prepare the ground for the story which I have to tell.

"Throughout my adult life, I have held firm to the belief that if the principles of causality that we have recognized since Newton's time are true, then the future must–at least in principle–be foreseeable and predictable. I have always taken it for granted that, if the future flows from the present by virtue of inviolable physical laws, it must do so according to a destiny that has been *mapped out*, as it were, since time immemorial. I take it for granted, too, that if the future really is mappable, then there must be a sense in which it already exists; if its shape is already fixed, then that shape must in some sense be *perceptible*, not in the uncertain fog of the speculative imagination, but in actuality. In the book of destiny, the moments making up the history of the universe must lie next to one another like slender leaves, each one ready for inspection, if only a man–or any other sentient creature–were somehow able to step outside the ordinary course of his own temporal procession."

The white-bearded man leaned forward at this point and opened his mouth to interrupt–to protest, I suppose, that there was a contradiction here, in that one could not simultaneously hold a belief in destiny and yet speak of creatures stepping outside it–but Copplestone held up a hand to forestall him.

"I am aware of the paradoxes implicit in the idea," said the professor, "and of the vicious circularity inherent in the supposition that a man may step outside the course of his destiny if, and only if, he is destined to do it. I was never satisfied with that, and have ever been impatient with the twists and turns of the labyrinth of pure conjecture. I always desired to make an experiment that might guide me to the heart of the philosophical maze. Rather than be content with demonstrating the impossibility of looking into the future *a priori*, I wanted to make the best effort I could actually to do it, so that I might have the leisure afterwards to examine the implications of what I had been able to do.

"It seemed to me, on the basis of my studies of drug-enhanced precognition in tribal societies, that these magicians sometimes did obtain true knowledge of the future, but were almost never able to profit from it. One reason for this, I perceived, was that any true knowledge they obtained was invariably alloyed with extraneous material, which frequently led to its misinterpretation. After long study, I concluded that the organ of foresight–the sixth sense, if you will admit the term–is that which engages in the ordinary business of dreaming, and that its sensory function is confused by other expressive functions linked to the passions. In brief, our usually-meager powers of precognition are so polluted, perverted and confused by our hopes, fears and fancies that it is normally impossible to separate truth from fantasy until the event that was dimly foreseen actually comes to pass, thus revealing the previously-hidden meaning of the precognitive vision."

I have heard all this before, I reflected. *It has been the substance of countless intoxicated debates in inns and coffee-houses. Can there really be anything new to add to it?* I glanced at the paler of the young men, and saw that he too had the look of one who had heard it all before. He seemed to find its repetition here and now a little annoying. I permitted myself a little smile; he had not yet learned the virtues of patience and relaxation. Were he lucky enough to live as long as I had, he would doubtless become less hectic of temperament.

Copplestone had not paused; he was fully in the grip of what seemed to me suspiciously like alcoholic eloquence. "It was evident to me from my extensive studies of shamanistic and related practices," he went on, "that the enhancement of visionary precognition by appropriate drugs could not entirely filter out this psychological pollution, no matter how powerfully the compounds increased the power of the sensory function–but I hoped that it might at least be minimized, if the optimum combination of drugs could be found.

"Each of the tribes that I studied had to rely on the bounty of nature to supply enhancing drugs. The Siberians use agaric mushrooms, the Mexicans use *peyotl*, the Mongolians use opium derivatives. I, by contrast, had the double advantage of being able to collect and combine all these different kinds of compounds, and of being able to refine and modify them using the recently-evolved techniques of organic chemistry.

"This was what I set out to do: to discover the mechanics of a modern Delphic oracle, more powerful than any known to history. I set out to find the most reliable possible means of dividing the curtain that normally confines me within the sequence of my living moments, so that I might peer through the breach into the world which is to come. By this means, I hoped to discover, among other things, whether what I had long taken for granted was actually true: whether the future glimpsed by authentic seers is, in fact, an immutable future of destiny, which they are quite unable to affect in any way despite their foresight of it, or whether it is merely a future of contingency, which might yet be altered or averted if they were able to act upon their precognition."

This time he did pause, and he rang a bell to summon the manservant who had single-handedly carried the food we had consumed from the kitchens, and had cleared the dishes after each course. Copplestone apparently had no other servants, except for an aged cook.

The servant must have been warned that the summons was imminent, for he immediately came in, carrying a large tray. On the tray was a wooden rack which held a series of test-tubes and glass-stoppered vials, and a large manila envelope. These items the servant carefully placed in front of the professor–who was, of course, seated at the head of the table.

"These," said Copplestone, indicating the test-tubes, "are the various vision-enhancing drugs which were my raw materials." He touched one of the sealed vials, which was marked out by a ring of red paint. "Here is the last and best of the many mixtures which I made from them. Needless to say, it is not a simple mixture, and the complex series of treatments to which I submitted the various compounds is carefully set out in a formula, which I have placed in this envelope.

"As you have doubtless observed, my experiments have taken their toll of my health, and I fear that I may have done myself irreparable damage in the course of the expeditions I intend to describe to you tonight. In order that my discoveries may be made available to other interested parties, I will give the formula to my good friend the doctor–and I will gladly give the remainder of the compound to any one of you who might care to volunteer to follow where I have led, in order to prove that what I have to tell you has at least some truth in it. There is enough for a single moderate dose, similar to the one I employed in the second of the three dream-journeys I shall describe to you."

Copplestone gave the envelope to the doctor, in an appropriately ceremonious fashion. The doctor placed it dutifully in the inner pocket of his jacket.

"Perhaps, Doctor," the professor said, "You would be kind enough to tell the others what you observed while you have attended me these last few days.

Our attention shifted to the doctor, who coughed rather gruffly. "I can only tell them what I saw, Copplestone," he said. "Nothing else."

"Nothing else is required, I assure you," said Copplestone.

The doctor seemed uncomfortable, but he nodded his head. "I observed Professor Copplestone on three separate occasions," he said, awkwardly. "On each occasion, I watched him inject the drug whose remnant you see in that vial into his arm, and I did not leave him until its effects had worn off.

"After taking the drug, Copplestone fell into a deep sleep, which quickly gave way to an unusual form of coma. His heartbeat slowed down to some 28beats per minute and his body temperature fell by some 12 or 14 degrees Fahrenheit. His body suffered a considerable but not-quite-consistent loss of weight, amounting to slightly less or slightly more than three stones, although its dimensions were not altered commensurately."

"What a pity," Wilde murmured. "Copplestone might otherwise have hawked his discovery as a convenient cure for obesity."

The doctor spared him a brief frown, but continued doggedly: "This condition persisted for the same length of time–approximately three hours and ten minutes on each occasion–even though the professor increased the dosage at each stage of the experiment. As the end of each period approached, the professor's body was subject to tremors, which increased considerably in violence over the course of the three experiments. On the third occasion, I was fearfully anxious lest the convulsions should cause his heart to stop. When the professor regained consciousness he was noticeably weak. His body did not recover all the weight which it had lost; the first coma resulted in a net loss of seven pounds, the second 10 and the third 16. It would be unwise in the extreme, in my opinion, for the professor to attempt any further experiments along these lines–and I must say that anyone who is prepared to give serious consideration to Copplestone's invitation to continue this work must bear in mind that he might do himself considerable harm."

The professor seemed quite unperturbed by this dark warning.

"Thank you, Doctor," he said. Then, addressing the whole company again, he continued: "I will not bore you with a lengthy account of my preliminary experiments, nor with any elaborate presentation of my discoveries in organic chemistry, fascinating though they are. As to the nature of the mechanism involved in the process of precognition, even I can only speculate. However, it may be worth bearing in mind that, although the locus of the individual mind is normally limited to the body at a particular moment in time, this does not mean that the mind has a particular location within the body. Sir William will, I think, bear me out when I say that there is now an abundance of evidence that the mind is capable of extending its function beyond the body, producing in the process what we normally call *apparitions*?"

The white-bearded man of science nodded his head. "The evidence for the survival of the mind after death, and its ability to formulate a fragile envelope for the purpose of earthly manifestation is now overwhelming," he agreed.

"Not all apparitions are vestiges of that post-mortem kind," said Copplestone, "as my story will demonstrate. The naturally-occurring compounds traditionally employed to induce visions are limited in scope, and the perceptions they permit are invariably distorted. However, such compounds do indeed allow the human mind to extend its perceptive range in both space and time. Space and time are, of course, merely two different aspects of the unitary fabric of the cosmos. Perception of any kind would be impossible without some kind of physical presence, so projections of this kind require the synthesis of a body of sorts, sometimes misleadingly called an *astral body*.

"The compound which I eventually refined and perfected increased the powers of the natural compounds very considerably. The range of achievable projection was increased, and–perhaps more importantly–the degree of conscious control which I was able to exercise over my remote manifestation was very greatly enhanced. After a few preliminary experiments, I was very eager to employ what I had begun to call my *time machine* in the exploration of the future of mankind."

"You don't care to tell us, I suppose," said the pale young man, rather rudely, "what will win the Derby this year?" He seemed curiously hostile, almost as if he had been insulted in some obscure fashion.

"Alas," said Copplestone, "my machine is so very powerful that it would require an impractical precision of dosage to travel 60 years, let alone six months, and I have reason to think that it would be impossible to remain in such a near future for more than a split second. In order to achieve a vision of reasonable coherency, and to take advantage of the conscious control which this compound allows, one must work in terms of thousands or tens of thousands of years."

"Not *hundreds* of thousands?" asked the young man, intemperately. Now that he was no longer schooling his speech so carefully his lower-class accent was discernible even to my untutored ears.

"The dosage required to journey as far as that might easily prove fatal," said Copplestone, whose equanimity was unconquerable by irony. "I did not dare to venture as far as that."

The young man scowled, and muttered something barely audible, which seemed to include the word *plagiarism*. His companion placed a soothing hand on his wrist, bidding him be patient and listen.

"My sketchy explanations have clearly strained your credulity too far, although my story has not yet even begun," said Copplestone, looking around at the uneasy faces which confronted him, "but I will press on regardless. Perhaps, though, some of you would also like to make preliminary statements about your opinions as to what I have said regarding the possible perceptibility of the future?"

I certainly did not, and felt uncomfortable to be asked, but some of my companions were not so shy.

"I don't believe in your damned native seers," said the American, brusquely, "and I don't believe in Sir William' apparitions either, although he's promised to show me a few while I'm here. I believe in causality, so I accept that certain aspects of the future might be foreseen, but we live in an era when new discoveries are changing the world with unparalleled rapidity, and we can't know today what we might discover tomorrow. Drug-induced dreams can't show us the shape of things to come."

"That's true," said the pale young man. "The future is subject to the determination of causality, and is hence potentially discoverable, at least to the extent that we can gather the relevant data, but it will need a better instrument than mere hallucination to calculate our future."

"I'm not so sure that there's anything *mere* about authentic visions," his curly-haired companion objected. "The origin of motion, which was the primal Act of Creation, must already have contained the plan of universal evolution–and the plan must still exist, in some form, within our bodies and our minds. It might well be accessible to the imagination, if only we could master the trick of it."

"But what of free will?" the British scientist put in, impatiently. "Men have the power to choose what they will do, and their choices determine the shape of their own futures. The future of mankind will be the sum of those choices, not the product of any merely mechanical laws. Consciousness is immune to the laws of causality that apply to inert objects. There are such things as premonitory dreams, I know–but we must consider them as warnings of what *might* happen, not as glimpses of something immutable that *already exists*."

"I agree with Sir William, at least about the freedom of the will," said the doctor, gruffly. "Even if human beings are part of some unfolding plan, they have the power to alter it. The future of mankind depends entirely on the force and competence of the human will. We were not impelled here tonight by some irresistible force of necessity, and not one of us really doubts that he might be somewhere else entirely if it had pleased him to go."

"Neither Milton nor Mill could find a contradiction there," said Wilde, mildly. "Both would argue that our choices are real, and yet their outcomes would be known with perfect certainty to an omniscient mind. Yes, they would admit, we *do* have the power of choice–but the choices we make are determined by our powers of reason, our characters and our interests, and are therefore predictable. When our friends act unexpectedly, Mill says, we do not shrug our shoulders and attribute our surprise to the inevitable consequences of the freedom of the will–we simply conclude that we did not know them as well as we thought, and did not fully comprehend the causes of their actions."

I noticed that Wilde did not offer an opinion of his own, but was content with introducing the relevant ideas of others. I also noticed that the doctor's grey-eyed companion made no effort to intervene in the discussion, even when a momentary silence fell.

Copplestone turned to me, and said: "Do you have an opinion, Count?"

"I have an opinion of sorts," I said, a little reluctantly. "I hold that there *is* an inescapable destiny that faces us all, and the universe itself: it is death. Perhaps we have the power to delay our course, or attain to the end by different routes, but in the final analysis, there is no other fact, no other absolute."

I had always been a fatalist, and could not conceive that anything Copplestone might say would change my mind. How arrogant, how unimaginative and how wrong I was!

"Death is not the end," said the pillar of the Society for Psychical Research. "That is proven; we need not doubt it."

I saw the excitable young man shake his head vigorously, but for once he had discretion enough not raise his reedy voice in protest. Copplestone lifted a placatory hand.

"Enough, gentlemen," he said. "Let us not fall to squabbling. When I have said what I have to say, you might be better informed to carry this argument forward–if you can believe my story."

"Is there any reason why we should not?" asked the American, ironically. He, at least, seemed fully prepared to disbelieve it.

"Only that it is incredible," said Copplestone, soberly. His tired eyes shone with reflected firelight, and he suddenly seemed to me to be extremely sad as well as debilitated–as if the world that had once been a comfortable home to him had turned traitor, and cast him into some private hell of unbelonging. I felt an altogether unaccustomed pang of sympathy, and looked down at the wine in my glass, which had not the power to intoxicate me.

"If it were not incredible," said Wilde, pleasantly, "it would not be worth the ceremony. I am hoping for something very extraordinary indeed, Ned, and I trust that you will not disappoint us. As for myself, I am sufficiently realistic to be eager to believe anything, provided only that it is an obvious and grandiose lie."

Copplestone had the grace to smile at this, although it could not have been the kind of support he wanted. "In that case," he said, "I will proceed to describe the three expeditions I undertook while the faithful doctor patiently stood guard over my *residuum*."

The Explorer's Story: Part One

The island formerly known as Great Britain,
circa 5,000 A.D.

1.

The first subjective sensation induced by the compound whose external effects the doctor has described is one of dizziness and disorientation. As the drug spreads through the bloodstream, the mind is invaded by images of a bizarre and rather incoherent fashion. I am certain that, if I could only train myself to concentrate upon a few elements of the torrent–thus making them selectively captive in the net of memory–useful information might be derived therefrom, but I have not so far managed to master the trick.

After a time, however, the flood of inchoate images eases, and there is a process of settlement attended by a sensation of *coming together*, which corresponds with the formation of what I shall call, for want of a better word, a *timeshadow*. This is an actual, corporeal entity, visible to the inhabitants of the space and time in which it appears, but it is considerably less substantial than an ordinary body.

My timeshadow was not sufficiently attenuated to pass through walls, although the much fainter shadow-selves projected by means of naturally-occurring drugs might be....but I ought perhaps to leave further discussion of that topic until I have described the manner in which I learned about the odd properties of my projected self.

I should explain in advance that the time that elapsed while the good doctor was standing watch over my unconscious body and the time experienced by my timeshadow did not run in parallel. A timeshadow's attenuation has a temporal as well as a physical aspect, which has the effect of stretching its subjective experience. An hour of real-body time corresponds to a longer period of timeshadow time, but the actual proportion varies somewhat according to dosage–and hence, I think, in proportion to the time-difference involved. I was therefore present in the world where my timeshadow coalesced for considerably longer than three hours.

When the world about me first came into clear focus I found myself on a lightly-wooded hillside. The Sun, which stood high in the sky, seemed identical to the one with which we are all familiar, but the trees were not the familiar trees of the English countryside. The green of their leaves was more vivid, and their smooth bark was lustrous, as though varnished. Their trunks were stout and very little gnarled. I could hear birdsong, but I caught only the most fleeting glimpses of the birds themselves as they fluttered from crown to crown, and could not easily compare them to the species I knew.

I was surprised to find no trace whatsoever of the city of London, for I had assumed that I would remain in the same place while moving in time; apparently, I was so far displaced in time that all vestiges of the world's greatest city had been quite obliterated. I knew immediately that thousands of years must have passed, if not tens of thousands.

Not without difficulty, I raised my hand to place it before my face. I half-expected that I might find it transparent, or at least translucent, but it was opaque, and lined in a familiar fashion. I looked down, and–somewhat to my surprise, but greatly to my relief–found that I was not naked.

I was not clad in the kind of suit in which I had left my true body, but I was wearing a thin white tunic and trousers. These were designed according to no model I had ever actually seen, and I could only assume that they were a minimal concession to my sense of modesty. This seemed to confirm what I believed about the ability of my own mind–without, apparently, any actual exertion of my conscious will–to interfere creatively with the sensory aspect of the drug's operation. This was not altogether good news. If a sense of propriety could alter the content of my prophetic vision, I thought, what might more powerful agents like fear and hope make manifest?

The grass that grew to between ankle- and knee-height in the open between the trees was as vividly green as the foliage of the trees. I could not help but reflect, ironically, that if this futuristic grass really were greener than the grass of the 19th century, it must be a good omen–but I could not, of course, be certain that the difference was in the grass rather than in the sensory apparatus of my unusual corpus.

There were a few colored flower-heads raised above the grass, mostly blue or purple, and there were insects paying court to them: bee-like humming creatures and patterned butterflies. I did not pause to study the insect-life of the period into which I had come; I wanted to seek out more interesting sights.

From my vantage-point half way up the hill, I could see a road, and in the distance a village, or perhaps the outskirts of a town. The road was very smooth and regular, as though it had been hewn from a single strip of soft stone, and the distant buildings seemed very clean in the bright sunlight, with roofs neatly tiled in brown and green, and walls mostly pale grey or pastel blue. There were no vehicles on the road, but there were people–human beings, I assumed–walking in either direction, in pairs or small groups.

When I tried to move down the hill, I realized why it had required such an effort to raise my hand. A timeshadow may walk, run or jump like any other body, but the habits ingrained by ordinary experience must be modified. Although one might expect the opposite, a timeshadow seems to its tenant to be unusually heavy and rather sluggish. I found that what seemed to me, on the basis of ordinary experience, to be an effort adequate to take a step forward had to be considerably increased if I were to make headway, and that the headway I made was moderate–although, perhaps by way of compensation, once my time-shadow was in motion it had unusual momentum. My stride was slow, and required more than the usual thrust, but it was also long. My gait must have seemed very peculiar at first to the inhabitants of that future land, although I gradually learned to modify my actions to produce a less awkward result.

I made my uncomfortable way down the hill. The people on the road must have caught sight of me, but no one stopped or turned to stare. It was not until I too was on the road that I was able to meet anyone's gaze or command attention.

They were dressed even more simply than myself, each in a single garment not unlike a short nightshirt. I could hardly tell whether any one of them was male or female, although they differed in individual appearance as much as we do–given, at any rate, that not one showed the least sign of a beard. Most of them were conspicuously plump, and even the thinnest was certainly not slender by our standards. There were children among them, though none very young, but there was none who showed any marked sign of old age.

While I stood for a few moments upon the road, recovering my breath, 12 or 14 people must have passed me by in one direction and nearly as many in the other. All of them glanced at me, but only a few looked me up and down or reacted to my presence. The children seemed most curious, and one or two of them pointed, and spoke to the adults with them. I could not understand the language they spoke, but its sounds seemed to me to be softly Oriental. Their hue was oriental too–not exactly that pale shade of brown which we misrepresent as "yellow," for it was far too ruddy, but by no means white. The cast of their eyes was Caucasian, though. Their complexions seemed very ruddy, and I noticed that the blue tracery of veins on their bare forearms was very thick and outstanding.

Why are they so incurious? I wondered. *They see me, but despite the fact that I am not at all like them, they find nothing remarkable about me. Why are they not as excited by my appearance as men of my world would be if a ghost were to walk down Oxford Street in broad daylight? Can it be possible that timeshadows are so familiar in this world as to constitute a trivial nuisance, best ignored?*

I tried to raise my hand to bid a group of them to pause, but I was not yet master of my muscles and the gesture went wrong. Any thought of correcting it, however, was driven out of my mind when I tried to speak. My voice was very low indeed, and the words I was trying to form seemed exceedingly hoarse and hollow. At first, the syllables which I was attempting to string together ran into one another in a hopelessly inarticulate jumble.

The passers-by seemed more startled by my voice than by my appearance, but the effect on those I had been trying to interrupt was the opposite of what I had hoped. They speeded up, hurrying on their way, and others began to alter their courses so as to steer clear of me. When I stepped towards them, they moved–much more gracefully–to increase the distance. I tried to protest, but it was futile. I could not blame them; had I heard another man speaking as I was, no matter that I could understand the language in which the words were, I would have taken him for a madman or a freak. It seemed sensible to hold my renegade tongue, at least for the time being.

I began to walk along the road, heading–as the greater number of the natives were–towards the nearby village. My gait gradually became smoother as I went, and even at its worst did not alarm the indigenes as much as my distorted voice. Even so, they kept their distance, and were careful not to approach too close. They were by no means mortally afraid, but they were wary of me.

I was soon among the buildings of the town–which did indeed seem to be a town, for once I was there I could see no further limit to it. It was laid out in a remarkably orderly fashion, its streets curving to follow the contours of the gentle slopes but otherwise very regular in their spacing. The houses differed slightly from one another in size and style, but the overall impression I got was one of astonishing uniformity. So far as architectural design was concerned the limits of variation were narrow, and there seemed to be an absolute uniformity of building technique.

At a closer range I could see that the walls were made out of pale bricks supported and separated by thin layers of mortar, laid with awesomely mechanical regularity. The houses had glazed windows set in frames of some substance I had never encountered; these were all exactly the same size, as were the doors, which were constructed of the same substance as the window-frames.

There seemed to be only one other kind of edifice apart from the houses, at least in this part of the town: every now and again I would pass a much larger construction, like a huge low barn, with numerous doors but no windows at all. I often saw people going into the houses or coming out of them, but in the course of that first stroll through the streets of the town I never saw anyone go into or come out of the windowless buildings.

I suppose that I had always tacitly expected that the world of the future would be cleaner and more orderly than our own, and that life would have become less chaotic, if not entirely free of strife. I had expected, too, to find life more leisurely–but the image with which I was confronted now seemed to take all these things to a discomfiting extreme!

As I looked about me at the people in the streets, I could see hardly any real evidence of purpose in their movements. No one was in a hurry, and no one was carrying anything. None of the children had toys, and none seemed to be involved in the playing of any kind of game. Although they moved in groups, never as individuals, their conversations were dilatory. Members of one group never paused to exchange greetings or information with members of another.

There were no vehicles to be seen, nor any domestic animals. The houses had no gardens.

This does not make sense, I thought. *But if it is a fantasy conjured up by my mind and superimposed on a much richer reality, what on Earth can my mind be about? Why should it deprive the society of the future of all its verve and intelligence?*

I paused as I passed some of the windows and peered into the houses. I saw laden tables, and chairs drawn up around them, sometimes occupied and sometimes not, but I never saw anyone engaged in any activity except serving or eating food. I saw unfamiliar fruits being eaten with the fingers, and I saw people using spoons to draw various different liquids or solids from bowls, but I never saw a knife or a fork, or a plate. Everything was simple; life here seemed as carefully minimal as my clothing.

The inner walls of the houses were as plain as the outer ones. I saw no pictures or hangings, nor any other kind of ornamentation. I saw no books or shelves. I saw cribs containing babies, and sometimes heard the babies wailing, but I could detect no signs of distress among the children who were old enough to walk.

If the people inside a house became aware that I was looking in they would look back, evincing the same signs of mild alarm that the people on the road had showed when I tried to make contact with them, but they never tried to shoo me away, and did not seem overly offended by my invasion of their privacy. No one came to investigate my presence, even though it must have been obvious to everyone who saw me that I was not merely a stranger but an alien.

At first I had thought the town rather pleasant because it was so neat and clean, but it quickly came to seem direly uncanny. The impression which grew upon me was of one of those miniature towns which are sometimes constructed as toys for the children of the very rich, where everything is present, but dramatically simplified.

This is not human life. I thought. *It is a mere simulation of it. These are not people at all, but mere imitations of people: automata of some kind, which can maintain some pretence of walking and talking, of eating, and perhaps excreting, but cannot do these things in any authentic sense.*

I gave serious consideration to the hypothesis that everything I saw might be nothing but an illusion, conjured up by a sadly jejune imagination, but when I looked at the slowly-setting sun, and the display of color it created by its effects upon the slightly-humid atmosphere, I could not believe that this was other than an actual world. The breeze, hardly perceptible in any case, felt odd upon my attenuated flesh. I could not tell whether the dearth of scents was likewise an illusion of dull sensation, but when I recalled the hillside where so many natural things had deployed themselves in such a natural fashion, I could not help but starkly contrast the lifelessness of this crude forgery of human existence.

Eventually, I became bolder, and I went into one of the houses, having first peered in through the windows. The people who lived there were seated at the table, enjoying a meal–and I do mean *enjoying*, for they seemed to relish what they were eating until I arrived. When I came into the room, they stopped immediately, and got up. They were so obviously disconcerted by my invasion that I almost expected them to fall upon me and throw me out, but they did not. Instead, they twittered at one another in their strange language, and backed up against the wall. The adults extended their arms protectively to the children.

When I had come far enough away from the door, the people of the house moved towards it–sidling rather than dashing–and went out, leaving me alone with their half-finished repast. In my attenuated form, I was not sure that I could taste food properly, and I had not the slightest hunger or thirst, so I contented myself with inspecting the contents of the bowls by eye. Considering that everything else was so simple, the diet these people enjoyed seemed unusually rich and varied. But where, I wondered, were the fields and orchards that generated this produce? Where were the markets in which it was traded? How was it brought into the houses?

The inhabitants of the house had gone out into the street, and I watched them through the window to see if they would call for help. They did not. They waited, and they watched. They talked to one another, but not to other passers-by.

I went to investigate the other rooms in the house. There were several rooms upstairs, each containing a low bed and a closet in which half a dozen tunics hung. There was a bathroom downstairs, and a separate water-closet with a flushing toilet. The pipes that carried the water were not metallic and I could see no joints of the kind which might have required a plumber's attention. The taps in the bathroom were mere levers, and I could not open the cistern of the flushing toilet to see what kind of ballcock it contained.

The kitchen had a sink too, but it had no range, no fireplace, no kettle, and no boiler. Hot water ran from one of the taps but I could see no apparatus for heating it. There were cupboards for bowls, spoons and some foodstuffs, but no utensils which might have been used in its preparation. There were, however, no less than three dumb-waiters, whose shafts disappeared downwards into impenetrable depths–a fact that seemed all the more remarkable when I concluded, after assiduous searching, that the house had no basement or cellar that could be reached from the ground floor.

It is all mere surface, I thought. *This whole town is but a toy, whose appearances are controlled from below by hidden mechanisms. But if it is all artifice, who or what can the artificers possibly be?*

That was the question which preoccupied my mind as I went out into the gathering dusk, to see the last few fugitive rays of the setting Sun as it sank beneath the colored horizon, leaving the world to blue-grey twilight.

2.

I had half-expected that nightfall would put an end to activity within the town. Just as our children must put away their dolls' houses when the day is done, so it seemed appropriate that the mysterious owners of this sham of life might put their charges to bed, and leave their habitat to silence and inaction. I was quite wrong. The family whose home I had invaded made no attempt to reclaim their territory as the twilight faded, and I observed that many more people were emerging on to the streets. Soon, a far greater throng had assembled out of doors than I had seen in mid-afternoon.

Darkness did not fall. As the sky became black and the stars began to shine through, the streets lit up. I do not mean that lamps were lit; it was the actual fabric of the roadway that began to glow, with a white, cold luminosity. I could see a similar light within some of the windows of the houses, but the lighted windows faded away as their inhabitants came out to join the gathering crowds in the street.

I guessed that some surface within each room–a wall or the ceiling–must be made of some material similar to that of the roadway, and that there was some kind of control mechanism which ensured that light was released only when someone was actually in the room. I inferred that the light was a kind of artificial phosphorescence, or possibly a domestic bioluminescence akin to that which one sometimes sees faintly glimmering upon the surface of the sea.

A half-Moon had recently risen above the eastern horizon, and was slowly climbing higher. I studied its face closely, and was oddly relieved to find it quite unchanged. However many thousands of years had passed since the era of my birth, some things had evidently remained constant and inviolable.

As the people in my immediate vicinity began to move past me, it seemed that they were moving with genuine purpose for the first time. All those nearby were moving in the same direction, as if they had a common destination. Lit from below as they were, their marching figures seemed rather eerie, but curiosity impelled me to fall into step without delay, following those who moved ahead of me.

I did not have far to go. I soon perceived that the crowd was heading for the nearest of those larger buildings with which the houses were interspersed. As I approached, I saw that all of its many doors now stood open, and that an orderly queue of people was forming at each one. I suppose that I could have barged ahead, but it seemed impolite to do so–and in any case, the queues were moving with reasonably rapidity. I simply took a place in one of them and waited for those in front to enter.

In the meantime, I studied the people. As on the road, I could see no very young children, and no old people. The babies I had glimpsed in one or two of the houses had not been brought out. There was no talking in the lines, although people who arrived in groups always joined the same queue. My presence caused not the slightest disturbance even to the man who was directly in front of me or the woman who was directly behind. There was no hurry; patience ruled supreme.

The light inside the barn-like building was as wan and white as that which illuminated the roadway, but it shone down from the ceiling and cast its shadows in what seemed to me to be a more ordinary way. There were plenty of shadows to be cast, for the building was crowded with machinery of some kind, much of which loomed up to a height considerably above that of a man.

The vast room reverberated with a low humming sound, but there was no whining as of turning wheels, no clattering as of pistons and no hissing as of steam engines. It was, I guessed, an electrical hum, and I concluded that the whole town must run on electrical power generated in some subterranean region. I resolved to look closely at the machinery so that I would be able to describe it minutely to someone like Sir William or Mr. Tesla, but I fear that I was unable at the time to make the most of that resolution, for reasons which will shortly become apparent.

The queues, which remained as orderly within the building as without, extended into narrow corridors between the hulking masses, there vanishing from my sight. I stayed in my place, more fascinated for the moment by the machinery than the people. I could see that there were glass-faced dials set in the sides of the machines at eye-level, and levers and switches positioned as though for the human arm, but no one made any attempt to read the indicators or activate the levers.

There was a slight pulse in the floor beneath my feet, which implied that there was indeed more machinery at a lower level, and I could see steps leading down at various positions along the inner wall of the building. There were also upward flights of steps, made out of what looked like wrought iron, which led to catwalks that ran all around the inner walls. These were connected by a sparse webwork of railed walkways, which bridged the gap between the longer sides of the rectangular space.

Distributed about these catwalks, leaning casually on the guard-rails, were a dozen human figures, distributed in groups of two or three. As soon as I caught sight of them they commanded my attention. For the first time I thought: *Here are real people, at last. Here are the masters of this vast charade.*

From where I stood, the men on the walkways were mere silhouettes, limned against the evenly-lit ceiling, and I could not hear a word of their conversation. Nevertheless, I had not the slightest doubt that they were not of the same kind as the docile cattle which swarmed around me. Their postures were lazy, their attitudes too obviously negligent for them to be anything other than people engaged in a desultory fight against boredom. They were evidently in charge of whatever was happening here, and yet their presence was hardly necessary; the whole process was working automatically, at least for the time being.

I was tempted to step out of line and go to one of the flights of steps, in order that I might ascend and try to make contact with the real inhabitants of this strange future world, but I hesitated. The line in which I had taken my place had now progressed so far that I was on the point of entering the narrow corridor between the ranks of machines. I knew that, in a minute or two, I would be able to see where the queue was heading, and what the people in it had come to do. I decided that there would be time enough to go upstairs when I had satisfied my curiosity on that point.

The narrow corridor extended for about forty yards between two rows of compartments or stalls. Every few seconds someone would emerge from one or other of these stalls and the person at the head of the queue would go forward to take their place. Each stall was occupied for several minutes at a time, but there were so many of them that the queue was kept moving and a moderate pace. When the man ahead of me moved–as chance would have it, into the first space on the left–I did not stand patiently by waiting for my own turn. I went with him, to watch what he did.

Within the dimly-lit compartment there was an outward-facing chair, on which the man sat down. He could see that I was standing before him, watching him, and he hesitated momentarily, but the inhibiting effect of my presence was insufficient to deflect him from his purpose. He reached behind him to pull something from the wall.

As he pulled, a long tube of what looked like transparent rubber was drawn through an aperture; on the end of it, which he had gripped, was a metal device which was headed by a slender needle and from which dangled a number of threads. Hitching up the skirt of his brief tunic, the man casually thrust the point of the needle into the flesh inside his thigh, and with practiced ease, he distributed the threads so that they adhered to his skin and held the needle in place. He then pressed a small switch set in the wall behind him, and sat back listlessly. He did not bother to watch the blood that rapidly filled the transparent tube and disappeared into the wall behind him.

I can hardly convey the horror which began to grow in me as I watched all this happening. The bovine nonchalance of it all was quite chilling.

Another stall became vacant further down the line, and I squeezed myself further into the compartment in order to let the woman who had been standing behind me in the queue move past. She showed no disinclination to do so, nor any resentment of my failure to take my turn. The man–to whom I was now standing very close indeed–looked up at me with an expression I could not evaluate. It did not seem like anxiety or loathing, but I had lost confidence in my ability to make such ready judgments of people who were clearly far more alien than I had assumed.

As my horror increased, I began to see new significance in the fact that all the townspeople seemed so plump and so full-complexioned, and so curiously docile. It burst upon me with all the force of a revelation that this barn-like edifice was indeed a barn, and that these humans I had likened in my mind to cattle were exactly that: domesticated creatures of little intelligence and less independence, who came to be "milked" at dusk instead of dawn, giving a copious yield of the good red blood that they had been selectively bred to produce superabundantly.

I understood, belatedly, that the "houses" in which these "people" lived were not really houses at all, but merely animal-shelters, whose plumbing and heating had perforce to be controlled from elsewhere, by the herdsmen who kept such livestock.

They are vampires! I thought, with an awful thrill of superstitious dread. *The masters of this world are vampires, which feed on human blood. Nor are they predators haunting the night, but careful farmers. They have enslaved mankind and reduced the human species to a status hardly above that of the goats and sheep the earliest human nomads kept.*

3.

As I realized what was happening, I shrank back against the partition separating the cubicle from the next in line. My sudden timorousness was not the result of anything the creature with which I shared it had done, but rather because it had occurred to me to wonder what might happen if the watchers on the catwalk overcame their burden of tedium sufficiently to notice that I was there.

I looked up hastily to see how many of the silhouetted figures were visible from where I stood, and realized that I was shielded by the surrounding walls from all but two of them, who were positioned on a bridge some 60 feet away, at an angle of 30 degrees or so. They were facing the other direction, and I realized as I became calmer again that it would not have been so very easy for them to catch sight of me had they been looking my way, unless they had unusually sharp eyes. Save for my head and shoulders I was completely hidden from their view, and because the diffuse light was above them the entire floor area must have been rather gloomy. Even so, I began making plans as to how best I might make my exit from the building unseen.

My earlier enthusiasm to make contact with these masters had evaporated now that I knew that they kept other human beings as livestock. Perhaps this was cowardly of me, but the sudden rush of terrible enlightenment I had experienced had come as quite a shock. I did not know what to do.

The man in the chair began again to address his attentions to the device attached to his leg. He detached the adhesive strips, withdrew the needle, and held it carefully while it was drawn back into the wall. He took a piece of lint from a dispenser and used it to mop up the bead of blood which formed upon his thigh, discarding it into a repository set low down in the wall. He seemed to be glad that the time had come for him to be gone, but that might have been a result of my presence rather than the kind of relief which might follow the conclusion of a painful ordeal.

As another came to take his place, I was pleased to slide myself out of the way so as to offer no obstruction. This one was a girl, seemingly no more than 10 years old–one of the youngest I had seen in the queues. I had no wish to distress her with my presence, nor to watch her making her donation of blood. I began to walk down the corridor in the direction that all those went who had performed their function.

I felt sure that all I had to do was to follow the others, and behave exactly as they did, so that anyone who caught sight of me from above would not see that I was not one of them. It seemed easy enough. At the far end of the corridor, there was an open space much like the one from which I had come, but somewhat narrower and far less crowded–for there were, of course, no queues here. The nearest door was only 15 paces away, but so was the nearest ascending staircase. Standing on the seventh step of that stairway, looking down at the people who had done their duty and were going home, was a lone man clad in black.

Immediately after catching sight of him, I attempted to step back into the corridor, to hide myself behind the angle of the wall, but it was too late; as soon as I had seen him, he had seen me–and at this range, he could be in no doubt that I was different from the rest. The absurd clothing I was wearing, which my scrupulous psyche had seen fit to invent for the sake of my modesty, was enough to mark me out instantly. My height, thinness and coloring would surely have been enough, even if I had contrived to conjure up a tunic of exactly the kind the human cattle wore.

The man in black was not brightly-lit, and I could not make out his features very well, but the way his body shifted made it apparent that he was by no means as incurious as the people I had tried to speak to on the road. This was a thinking being, but I had every reason to believe that he was no more like me than those who had come here to be milked of their blood.

However human his form might be, I thought, *he is a monster*.

I know well enough now that it was entirely the wrong thing to do, but panic took over. I could not escape by turning around and running back along the corridor, because there was too far to go and little hope of unimpeded progress, and I certainly did not want to emerge at the other end with more of the black-clad watchers waiting patiently to catch me. I ran forwards, taking a course diagonally away from the stairway where the watcher stood, towards one of the open doors that allowed the human cattle egress from the building.

I had not practiced running, and the moment I began to move in a new way all my former awkwardness returned in full measure. My body felt heavy, more lumpen and leaden than before, and it seemed to me that the strides I was taking were very slow and very painful. The confusion of these alien sensations served only to amplify my panic, but the more effort I exerted to hurl myself forward the more ungainly I seemed to become.

I felt myself begin to fall, and experienced a sharp thrill of terror as I realized that my reflexes were incapable of compensating. I could not regain my balance.

The impact I suffered as I met the floor jarred me, but did not knock me out, and I scrambled to regain my feet. By the time I had done so, however, the individual I was fleeing had come down from the stair and was moving swiftly towards me.

I could see his face more clearly now. It was even paler than my own, save only for the lips, which seemed red and full. His eyes were peculiar, with a hint of luminous green about them; they, at least, seemed manifestly inhuman.

I lurched unsteadily towards the door, but I could not have reached it had not my pursuer been impeded. As it happened, his path crossed that of a woman who had emerged from the corridor to his left. She walked dazedly in front of him and they collided. She let out a wail of anguish as she realized, too late, what had happened. He tripped, and fell as heavily as I had, howling as he hit the floor.

Desperation lent me the skill I needed, and I managed to accelerate my progress towards the doorway. I hurled myself through it just ahead of another of the cattle-men.

It was not until the cooler air struck my face that it occurred to me to wonder what to do next. Where could I run to? Where could I hide? The urgency of these questions over-rode any sober consideration of the degree of danger I was in. I firmly believed, on the basis of a very plausible intuition, that if anything happened fatally to wound the attenuated body which currently housed my consciousness, then I would really die, and would lose my chance of slipping back through time into my own body.

I stumbled away from the doorway, determined to reach the shadows beyond the illuminated strip of roadway, which seemed to offer shelter of a kind–but even as I did so I realized that the dull humming sound which had filled the huge shed had not given way to the gentle silence which had reigned out here before I entered the building. Far from it; the night was now filled with sound, which came from above rather than below.

Having taken no more than three or four steps into the darkness beside the roadway I looked up into the starry sky, and saw to my astonishment that it was full of shadows, as if a great flock of huge and monstrous bats were wheeling above the town.

For a moment, I thought the flying things really were predatory haunters of the night, but they were not alive. They carried lights to signal their position to one another, and their wings were rigid. It was impossible to make out their exact shapes, although they were no more than a few 100 feet above the ground, but the thrumming noise of their engines was unmistakably similar to the sound which had filled the huge barn. They were machines.

The sky was so full of stars that their temporary occlusion was both obvious and disconcerting, but I perceived that the machines were not as numerous as I had first thought. There were dozens rather than hundreds, but even dozens seemed astonishing and alarming.

In God's name, I thought, *what mad kind of world is it into which I have been delivered?*

Sheer confusion must have brought me to a standstill, for I was no longer running. I was impotently staring upwards into the sky when rough hands grabbed me from behind.

I heard voices exclaiming. Although I could not understand a word of their language, I was sure that I could read frank amazement in their tone. I found time to wonder what these solid mortals felt–if these were, indeed, solid mortals–when they took hold of my attenuated form. Now that my flight had ended, panic had lost its tyranny over my processes of thought; as I was dragged back towards the doorway through which I had come I felt perversely free to delight in contemplation of the puzzle I might pose to my captors.

4.

I was carried by my captors into a curious Underworld. It was illuminated, apparently by the same method that the houses were illuminated, but not so brightly. The light had an odd hue, somewhere between blue and violet. I suppose that there was as much light as there is on a clear English night when the Moon is full, but its peculiar color made it seem altogether alien. My own eyes adapted well enough, when a few minutes had passed, to allow me to see what was around me, but I understood that eyes for which that level of light was optimal must be quite different from mine.

It was futile to struggle against the strong arms that held me. It was obvious that, no matter how heavy my limbs felt to me, I was not much of a burden to my captors. They held me very gingerly, as though my insubstantial body felt strange and unpleasant, but there was no prospect of my breaking away, and now that I knew that they were not bent on my immediate destruction I began to think more clearly again.

I realized that, if I were to come to a fuller understanding of this world, I would have to descend further into the Underworld, in order to see what manner of troglodytes dwelt there and what kind of existence they maintained.

While I was taken down the stairs, I tried to inspect my captors more close-ly. As my sight became clearer, I confirmed my earlier impression that they were very pale of face, and that their eyes glowed faintly green. I saw now, though, that these eyes were very much like cat's eyes, with lenticular pupils. They had full lips, which now seemed more nearly black than red. They were all male, but all beardless, and their faces were curiously unblemished; it was im-possible to guess how old they might be. Their dark clothing was more elaborate than that worn by the people of the town, but simpler than the conventional suits of our own era.

They took me down two more flights of stairs, with a winding corridor in between, and then through a further maze. I knew that I would not be able to find my way back again, but I had recovered control of my emotions by now and I was far less afraid than I had been. I reminded myself that my time in this world was strictly limited, and that I was certain to return to my body in due course. From the viewpoint of my captors, I would simply vanish into thin air. In the meantime, the task before me was to find out as much as I possibly could about the vampires and their empire of the night.

On the other hand, I remained sharply aware of the probability that I could be permanently injured by any violence they might inflict upon my attenuated body. I decided that I must oblige my captors as far as I was able, so as to en-courage them to handle me kindly. Fortunately, they seemed to have no inten-tion of causing me pain, at least for the time being. When I ceased to struggle, they ceased to treat me so rigorously, and by the time we arrived at our destina-tion, I was virtually walking alongside them, with their hands guiding me.

They brought me into an extraordinary room, whose walls were mounted with numerous rectangular screens. Most of these screens were inert, but four of them were active, displaying moving pictures of various kinds. I could make no sense of two of the images, which were diagrammatic, with associated printed text of a kind I could not decipher, but the other two were pictorial. One showed several persons in conversation–not people like those I had seen in the town, but beings like those who had seized me–while the other showed machines in flight: not huge airships like those that are so often described in popular fiction, but contraptions like those I had briefly seen outside, far more akin to rigid-winged birds or bats.

Beneath the screens there were complicated panels decked with countless buttons and switches. I would dearly have loved to make sense of all this appa-ratus, but there was simply too much. It bore some faint resemblance to the cab of a railway locomotive or the bridge of a steamship, but I could not imagine how any human being could cope with the sheer profusion of it all.

There were three persons already in the room, and when I was brought in, they became very excited; the two who had been seated instantly stood up. They fired questions at my captors while they moved around me, inspecting me very curiously. They also attempted to fire questions at me, but I could not understand their language and my attempts to reply sounded grotesque even to me because of the hollow laboriousness of my pronunciation.

I realized, numbly, that they had difficulty believing in me. They prodded and poked me in a manner which suggested that they doubted their own senses. They seemed astonished by my speech, perhaps as much by the curious distortion that afflicted my voice as by the unfamiliarity of my language, although they were probably not aware that I would have sounded quite different had it not been for the distorting effects of my attenuation.

After several minutes of animated discussion, their attitude changed. Solicitously, and with much ceremony, they ushered me to a chair situated before one of the screens, and invited me with a mime of exaggerated politeness to sit down. When I had done so, clumsily, one of them began moving his fingers over the control-panel before me, with incredible speed and dexterity.

The image of yet another cat-eyed person appeared on the screen, and it was clear from his attitude that my image must have been simultaneously relayed to him. A voice that I assumed to be his emerged from a disc beneath the screen. There was a long and rather confused exchange of staccato conversation between the person on the screen and the persons clustering about me.

Eventually, one of my captors began signaling to me furiously, gesturing with his hand in front of his mouth. I inferred that he wanted me to speak, and I did so, haltingly at first but more fluently as he encouraged me to continue. In the meantime, two others left the room.

I am not sure exactly what I said. I told them that my name was Copplestone, and repeated the syllables for emphasis, pointing at my chest in order to make their meaning clear. I then tried to give some account of the experiment which had brought me here–although I knew well enough that I might just as well have been reciting nursery rhymes. If I hesitated, my interrogator-in-chief resumed his urgent signing, so I knew that they wanted me to keep talking whether they understood me or not.

Just as I had earlier mastered the art of walking by dint of practicing, so my speech improved by degrees. Within a few minutes, I was enunciating clearly enough, although my voice still sounded unreasonably deep and slow. By that time, I had little more to say about myself, but every time I faltered, I was urged to continue.

I could not quite bear to revert to nursery rhymes, so I began quoting verse–snippets of Shakespeare, Shelley and Tennyson. That seemed to suffice for their purpose, and after some 12 or 15 minutes, the one who had taken charge held up his hand to give me permission to stop. He then began playing with the control-board again, displaying his incredible dexterity once more.

After a few moments, I heard the sound of my own voice emerging from the speaker from which the voice of the man on the screen had earlier emerged. I recognized words that I had earlier spoken, and winced at their uncouth tones. Embarrassment left me little space to wonder at the fact that my words had been so accurately recorded–and any wonderment I might have felt would have been banished entirely when the recording was interrupted by another voice, which said, as nearly as I can reproduce the words: "Anglish. Is Anglish."

I looked up at the image of the man on the screen, but he was not speaking. Like me, he was listening–but he was looking at me eagerly, avid for some response. The voice that had spoken was as hollow and hoarse and distorted as mine, but that was presumably mere imitation.

The one who had appointed himself my principal interlocutor gestured once again, demanding that I speak, and I presumed that he wanted some confirmation of the identification. "English," I said, trying to correct the pronunciation. "The language is English."

The words were immediately repeated back to me, adjusted so that they reflected exactly the syllables I had spoken. The voice, I now realized, was a calculated echo of my own, presumably produced by a machine which, with the resources I had provided, had contrived to identify the language which I spoke. That was the moment when it finally came home to me what resources these people had–and gave me to wonder whether they were, indeed, people at all, or whether they were creatures from some other world, which had conquered, subdued and made prey of mankind.

"Can you understand me?" I said, hesitantly. "Do you know what I am saying?"

There was no immediate reply. Instead, the speaker let loose a rapid burst of the alien tongue that my captors spoke, and I judged from their reaction–part astonishment, part delight–that it was a translation of what I had said. Then the man on the screen spoke, and there was a brief pause before what I assumed to be a translation of his words emerged in English from the speaker: "We understand. Your language is preserved in the memory banks. How did you come here? What manner of being are you?"

I gathered from this that the information I had given earlier had simply been used for the purpose of identifying the language that I was speaking. Presumably, they could and would recover the recording at a later time–but in the meantime, it would be simpler to respond to their questions. The ensuing conversation was unusually cumbersome because of the delays involved in the mechanical translation, and there were several hitches caused by mistranslation, but I will try to reproduce the bare essentials of it.

"My name is Copplestone," I said. "I am a timeshadow. My own body lies unconscious..." I intended to say *in the city of London, in the year 1894*, but I was not allowed to finish my sentence. This may have been a stroke of good luck, although I did not realize it at the time.

"What is a *timeshadow*?" demanded the machine, sharply. "Explain!"

"I am a man of the past," I said. "Your world is my future; this timeshadow–the strangely attenuated body which I present to your senses– is the means by which I can look into it."

This was translated, but the person on the screen seemed deeply confused. His frown seemed entirely human, and I was comforted by the readability of his expression. There was a sharp exchange between the person on the screen and one of those who had seized me outside the barn, which was not translated for my benefit. In the end, the man on the screen uttered a single brief syllable, which the machine rendered into English as: "Impossible."

"As you can see perfectly well," I retorted, stiffly "it is not impossible. I am real; I am a timeshadow; I am here. Will you tell me what kind of man you are?"

"I am no *man*," replied the other, with apparent contempt, as soon as the machine had translated my words. "Men make blood, but have no minds. You are no man. You have a mind, but make no blood. We are Overmen."

It was my turn to say: "What are *Overmen*? Explain, please!"

It was, I think, the translation machine itself that responded, not the man on the screen. "Members of the dominant species," it said. "End-products of Earthly evolution."

"What year is this?" I asked. "How long has it been since *my* kind were emperors of the Earth? How many thousands of years?"

The man on the screen–or, rather, the *Overman* on the screen–shook his head slightly in bewilderment. I took what further comfort I could from the fact that whatever technical miracles were his to command, the science of casting a timeshadow did not seem to be among them. He did not answer my question, but the mechanical voice of the machine did: "Approximately 3000 years have passed since *Homo sapiens* became extinct."

The man on the screen reached out then, presumably to flick an invisible switch. "You are a strangely solid illusion," he said, "if you are indeed an illusion."

My first impulse was to take offense, and deny that I was an illusion, but I realized that he was not trying to insult me. He was talking more to himself than to me, giving voice to his incomprehension.

"I came to this world," I said, "to see what time would make of *Homo sapiens*, man the wise. I came to see what triumphs and glories lay in store for our descendants. It seems to me that if the Earth has passed into the care of *Overmen* who use their own kind–their fellow humans–as mere cattle, and milk them of their life-blood, then the news that I must carry back with me is dire and terrible." I added, as my resolution faltered and I remembered that I had at least as much cause for doubt as he did: "I must hope, I suppose, that you are the strangely solid illusion, and that this is nothing but an opium-dream."

While he waited for this speech to be translated, the person on the screen grew much more thoughtful–and so did the others who clustered around me. When he replied, he spoke in a level tone which the translation-machine reproduced.

"You do not understand," he said, speaking for the first time as though he were attempting to explain. "The lovers of daylight are not our own kind. The descendants of humankind are not our fellows. In the long-gone days before they became our docile herds, humans were our deadliest enemies. Is that truly what you are: a wild and savage human, miraculously preserved since the dawn of history?" It seemed that the translation machine was having some slight trouble with the concept of a human being, and I judged that the implications of the situation were only now becoming evident to the person on the screen.

"Some of the humans of my own time are wild and savage," I told him. "Some, it is said, still have the cannibal habit, and will slay their fellow men for food. But I am a civilized man–a man of intelligence and culture."

While the translation of my words was being relayed, the door opened again, and the two who had left returned, the first of them carrying an empty syringe mounted with a long, glittering needle. I knew at once that he intended to use it to extract blood from my body–or whatever fluid was circulating in my shadowy *corpus*.

I opened my mouth to protest vigorously, and leapt to my feet in alarm, but the syllables I had tried to pronounce never sounded, and when I lashed out with my arms, they failed to connect with anything solid. The world had turned to mist, and was already dissolving into darkness.

I felt that I was falling into an infinite abyss. I lost consciousness....and when I awoke again, I was all a-tremble in my true body, and my good friend the doctor was busy reassuring himself that I was fit and well, or at least alive and sensible.

The Count's Story: Part Two

London, January 1895

4.

When he reached this point in his story, Copplestone paused. It seemed that the memory of what he had experienced–or, rather, dreamt–had made him shudder convulsively. I could see sweat standing on his brow, and his color had grown worse. I wondered whether he had enough strength to reach the end of his account–and I wondered, too, whether I had the stomach to hear him out.

I had not expected to hear anything like this. Wilde's passing mention of the name of one of Vambery's English acquaintances as a potential member of the audience had awakened my concern, but had not informed me that there might be some danger of embarrassment were I to come in his stead. I dare say that my own color was almost as unprepossessing, in its own way, as Copplestone's. I must have been as white as a sheet, and it was all I could do to keep myself from trembling with wrath. Had all this, I could not help but wonder, been set up expressly for my discomfort? Was it all a drama planned to taunt and threaten me?

A few moments of careful reflection assured me, however, that I was being oversensitive. There was no connection whatever between the kind of fantasy that Copplestone was spinning out and the rumors that Vambery had spread, save for the use of the word *vampire*. I reminded myself that the notion was common enough, nowadays, because it was so frequently employed in literature and shallow conversation. Science had not killed off the old folktales popularized by Dom Augustine Calmet and his inquisitive kin; it had merely served to make them seem quaint, and therefore interesting. In he meantime, literature had taken them up and made free with them, turning vampires into symbols of forbidden but fervent erotic desire.

I looked around at my companions when Copplestone paused, to satisfy myself that there was no one seated at the table who could possibly believe in vampires. The only pang of doubt I experienced occurred when I met the eyes of the man sitting opposite my station: the doctor's eccentric friend. He was looking at me with a most peculiar expression.

He has been ill, I reminded myself. *He is an addict of sorts, and prey to delusions. It would not matter what he thought, if he thought anything untoward at all.*

I was able to meet the grey-eyed man's stare quite frankly, although it did not seem that my openness set his troubled mind at rest. As Copplestone's pause extended, however, he returned his attention to the speaker, just in time to see him dissolve into a fit of coughing.

The doctor got up from his seat then, and rushed to Copplestone's side. The professor's tremors now grew worse, and it seemed that he was on the brink of some kind of fit, but he grew calmer again as the coughing faded. After a brief lapse of time, the doctor suggested that the rest of us should move from the dining-room into the smoking-room, while he saw to the needs of his patient. He promised that the story would continue as soon as Copplestone was fit enough to tell it.

As we rose from the table, moving to do as we were bid, Wilde was engaged in conversation by the American, and I found myself moving to the door alongside one of the two young men. It was the one who had seemed–and still seemed–to be rather agitated.

"You do not seem to be enjoying yourself, Mr. Wells," I remarked, as I stood aside to let him precede me. He looked at me with perverse annoyance, as if my politeness might somehow constitute a veiled insult, but he obviously thought better of his suspicion.

"I beg your pardon," he said, in his awkwardly-distinctive voice. "I am confused. I must confess that this whole evening has the appearance of being a joke at my expense."

I was slightly startled. I was still wondering whether Copplestone's story might be an elaborate joke at my expense, and it had not occurred to me that anyone else might have grounds for a similar suspicion.

"How so?" I asked, curiously.

"Do you read the *National Observer*?" he asked.

"I fear not," I replied, making no real effort to sound apologetic.

"I suspect that Copplestone does. I suspect that he has been an avid reader of a series of articles I contributed to the journal, couched in the form of a story told by a time-traveler to a group of his acquaintances, concerning his exploration of future time. And yet, he showed no sign that he recognized my name when Shiel introduced me, and Shiel has assured me that Copplestone could not possibly have guessed that he would invite me to be his guest. The professor certainly cannot know–unless, perchance, he is intimate with Henley–that I have already rewritten the articles into a form more akin to a novel, for serialization in *The New Review*. But what is the purpose of this apparent plagiarism? I cannot fathom it."

Nor could I. "Perhaps you are a trifle over-sensitive," I suggested. "Are the resemblances between your story and his really so close that there is no possibility of coincidence?"

"They are," he said, positively. "It is true that my time-traveler uses an actual machine to transport him into the future rather than a drug, but that makes it all the more significant that Copplestone uses the term 'time machine,' which I have adopted into the title of the newest version of my story. What my protagonist discovers in the first future era he visits is so similar to what Copplestone has described, save for certain cosmetic alterations, as to be an evident copy."

I found this news strangely disturbing. To discover one story-teller dabbling in nightmares of this particular kind was puzzling; to find two was verging on the uncanny. "You have also foreseen a future in which the human race serves as the cattle of a race of vampires?" I said.

He blinked in perplexity. "Oh no," he said. "Not *vampires*, as such. But the difference is inconsiderable. In my vision of the year 802,701, the human race has divided into two separate species. One of them–the Eloi–lives meekly upon the surface, enjoying a life of ease, while the other–the Morlocks–lives underground, tending the machinery which sustains the apparent Golden Age. They are, you see, the ultimate descendants of the two great classes of our society: the leisured and the laborers. But in my story, the wretched and ugly Morlocks have their revenge upon the lovely Eloi, for they emerge from their caverns by night to prey upon their one-time masters, feeding upon their flesh. You see, sir, that Copplestone's story is merely a simple transfiguration of mine–although there is one detail that does seem uncanny, for he cannot have obtained it from the *National Observer*.

"What detail is that?" I asked.

"The frame-story of my latest version of the story describes a situation very much like this one, in which the time-traveler invites a group of friends to listen to his tale. I feel as if have been trapped in my own story, as if I were no more than a character."

I could not help thinking of the people who had been distressed to find themselves adopted as characters by Jean Lorrain, and the manner in which Oscar Wilde had inserted obvious versions of himself into *The Picture of Dorian Gray* and *An Ideal Husband*. I glanced sideways at the grey-eyed man, wondering how *he* had felt when he first discovered himself as a character in the doctor's detective stories. According to Wilde, it had unhinged him slightly–just as Dorian Gray had been unhinged by the sight of his own portrait.

"That is hardly case for great regret or resentment," I told young Wells, in a quasi-paternal manner. "All the world's stage, as Shakespeare tells us, and we are all mere players, often forced to play parts scripted for us by others in spite of our free will."

"That's not what I resent," Wells insisted. "What I resent is the theft of my ideas. There's no copyright in ideas, I know, but Copplestone's story is plagiarism pure and simple. There's no other possible explanation."

"Pardon me," interposed another voice, "but I believe there is."

"We both turned, neither of us having realized until that moment that anyone else was listening to our conversation. It was the older of the two men of science: the white-bearded Briton, Sir William Crookes.

"I should be interested to hear it, Sir William," I murmured, while the young man merely gaped.

"Even skeptics like my friend Tesla must admit," said the old man, equably, "that it is possible that all men are capable of a degree of precognition. Many men of science accept that there is good evidence that our dreams routinely bring us news of the future–which is admittedly confused by our own minds with other materials. Must we not admit the possibility that you, Mr. Wells, have something of the innate ability possessed by the best of Copplestone's native shamans, and that your mind is capable of reaching into the future even without the kind of chemical assistance that Copplestone requires. You, not unnaturally, construe your vision as a pure product of your own imagination–a story that you have invented, shaped and polished–but perhaps it is a true, if somewhat blurred, vision of the actual shape of things to come. Perhaps, sir, you are a modern Sibyl, and the story you have written is the produce of the contemporary Delphic Oracle: an authentic prophecy, differing only in the idiosyncratic literary details which you have used for its embellishment, from Copplestone's equally authentic vision."

It was difficult to judge from the man's tone how serious he was. He spoke lightly, as though he were elaborating a hypothesis rather than stating a belief, and there was a hint of gentle flattery about the way he offered the young man the opportunity to pass himself off as a seer more gifted than others of his kind. The young man seemed to me exactly the type to nurse such delusions of grandeur, but his response to the argument was conscientiously skeptical.

"That is every bit as fantastic as Professor Copplestone's story, Sir William!" he exclaimed.

"Which is," the old man pointed out, "every bit as fantastic as your own."

"But mine is pure invention!"

"If what you said earlier about the future being determined and discoverable is true," I murmured, playing Devil's Advocate, "there may be no such thing as *pure invention*. If everything has a cause, then who is to say whether the similarity between Copplestone's story and yours arises because yours is the cause of his, or because both have a cause in common? I think Sir William is joking, though–it was he, after all, who suggested that the future is implicitly unpredictable, because its form will depend on the exercises of free choices yet to be made."

"That is true," Crookes agreed. "But I also argued that premonitory visions are real. My case is that they need to be construed as warnings of what *might* happen, rather than inevitabilities that we cannot prevent."

"I can agree with that, to some extent," the young man said, cautiously, "but it creates a difficulty, does it not? In the philosophy of determinism, causes must be prior to their consequences. If visions of the future can influence the present, allowing us to act in such a way as to prevent their fulfillment, the argument is trapped by a vicious circularity."

At that moment, Professor Copplestone came into the smoking-room, seemingly revived and revitalized by whatever treatment the doctor had administered. He suggested to us that we take the seats that had been set out for us around the fireplace. The doctor protested, but to no avail. Young Mr. Wells, Sir William Crookes and I had no option but to postpone our argument and take our seats, as the dutiful guests we were. Copplestone sat down too, in an armchair that offered him better support than the dining-chair he had occupied before.

5.

"I know that some of you will already have formed opinions as to the significance of my strange experience," Copplestone said, looking around at all his listeners doubtfully and rather apologetically. "I suppose most of you will be inclined, at least for the moment, to the hypothesis I suggested to the Overmen in the course of my first encounter with them—that my experience was but a delusion. There is much in it, I know, that is reminiscent of perfectly ordinary dreams. You may well think that vampires are imaginary beings, whose mythical origins must be sought in equally ordinary nightmares, and which have no place in rational visions of the future—but I have much more to relate, and I beg you to reserve your final judgment until you have heard accounts of my second and third adventures in time."

He still seemed reasonably strong, and his voice was steady, but his body was slumped in his armchair in a fashion that betrayed considerable fatigue. As I looked around, I could see that I was not the only one anxious on his behalf. I saw, too, that the young man who had spoken to me about the resemblances between Copplestone's tale and his own was very eager to make his complaint generally known. His curly-haired companion—who had taken a seat beside him—took the trouble to restrain him, whispering something I took to be an entreaty to be allowed to speak in the other's stead. The excitable young man reluctantly gave way to his friend.

"I think, Professor Copplestone," said the dark-complexioned young man, "that it might be as well to clear up one puzzling point before we hear the continuation of your story. My friend and I have been struck very forcibly by the manner in which your account of the far future duplicates certain features of a series of speculative articles that has been published recently in the *National Observer*. We cannot help but wonder whether your visionary experience might be reproducing—unwittingly, no doubt—a distorted version of these articles, which you might have read or heard discussed."

I watched Copplestone's face very closely. If this were true, I thought, then the distortions of his tale might also have a commonplace source. The parts of the story which most interested me might also have been borrowed—wittingly or not—from Arminius Vambery, presumably *via* Bram Stoker.

The professor, however, seemed genuinely surprised by Shiel's suggestion. "I fear that I have read no such articles," he said. "There are so many periodicals in circulation these days that I can hardly keep track of their titles, let alone their contents. My experiments have taken up almost all of my time these last few months, and I have had little contact with anyone save for my servants and my physician. I certainly do not recall discussing anything of this kind, or hearing it discussed–and I am certain that I would have paid very careful attention to any such discussion. There were, I recall, some articles issued a little over a year ago–in the *Pall Mall Budget*, I believe–which the good doctor did bring to my attention. One was entitled 'The Man of the Year Million,' another 'The Extinction of Man.' I thought them fascinating, but..."

"They too were mine!" the pale young man interposed, unable to keep silent any longer. "All of this is mine!"

"Yours?" Copplestone's amazement seemed sincere enough to me, but I could not trust my judgment well enough to be absolutely sure. "I am sorry, Mr. Wells, that I did not immediately recognize your name when you were introduced to me. Your presence here is a happy coincidence."

"It is not entirely coincidental, Professor Copplestone," confessed the pale young man's friend. "I suppose that you contacted me because you remembered my interest in certain matters on which your story has touched, expressed en passant in the conversations we had before I went to Derbyshire. Having so recently returned, I had no intimate acquaintance I might bring with me, so I, in my turn, wrote to Mr. Wells–whom I hardly know, save by repute–because I knew of his very similar interests. I dare say that there are others here who came with some kind of predisposition to be intrigued. Sir William and Mr. Tesla presumably came to hear your accounts of the electrical machinery of the future. Mr. Wilde and his friend might well be interested in your visionary method–although I have had some experience of opium myself, and I must say that your experience does not seem to me to have the least resemblance to an opium-dream."

"I think he has confused you with Stenbock," Wilde whispered to me. "A man born and nursed in the colonies can hardly be expected to be able to tell one Count from another."

I had avoided meeting Stenbock, although I knew that he had asked after me when I first arrived in London. I wanted to avoid encouraging any association between our names that might be ready to take root in the minds of the unwary. No such automatic association could have arisen had the English aristocracy boasted Counts of its own, but the English mind does have a tendency to think of men who bear foreign titles as a kind of tribe, and I was most certainly not the same kind of madman as Count Stenbock.

"I agree," Copplestone said, in reply to the young man's remark about opium. "Perhaps it was foolish of me to introduce the simile. My time machine is a compound of a very different chemical class, which sharpens very different sensibilities. I wonder if it is possible that Mr. Wells has the kind of natural gift which can perceive the future–albeit dimly–even without such assistance. Except that..."

I saw the white-bearded man of science nod with satisfaction at hearing his own hypothesis repeated, but his companion scowled. Mr. Tesla's opinion seemed to be that improbability was being heaped atop improbability. Given that there was a perfectly ordinary way in which Mr. Wells' ideas could have influenced Professor Copplestone, I was half-inclined to agree with him–and yet, Copplestone's story did seem sincere.

"May I ask you, Mr. Wells," Copplestone said to the excitable young man, "whether your story continues beyond a point parallel to that which my own has reached?"

"Yes, it does," Wells replied. "I have now completed a revised version, which is somewhat longer than the *National Observer* text, but the extension is merely a matter of fleshing out the detail. My time-traveler explains to his own patient audience that he continued into a future far more remote than the one you have described, eventually witnessing the extinction of life on Earth as the Sun cools–but there are other intermediate stages along the way."

"My story does not progress nearly as far as the end of the world," Copplestone said. "It will be interesting to discover, though, whether its continuation has anything in common with the intermediate stages of your own."

Wells seemed to be repenting his impetuosity. "The timescales of our accounts do seem very different," he admitted. "Mine extends for hundreds of thousands of years rather than tens of thousands, and if the schemes were similar, your Overmen would be very distant ancestors of my Morlocks. Is it the case that in your subsequent visions they suffered a gradual degeneration towards bestiality?"

"Quite the opposite," Copplestone said. "They continue their ascent towards powers of which our kind can only dream."

"In that case," the young man conceded, "I may have been mistaken about the extent of the resemblance between our stories." He paused, but added: "In the long run, of course, the extinction of all life on Earth is inevitable, as the Sun gradually dies. Our ultimate descendants might find habitats elsewhere, but an ultimate degeneration of life on Earth is unavoidable."

"I dare say that you are right," Copplestone said, judiciously. "The span of time involved in my adventures does not, I fear, extend to millions of years. The Earth does not become uninhabitable within the scope of my vision, and man's successors–who are not quite what I deduced as a result of my first expedition into the future–continue to thrive both here and elsewhere. If you will agree to be patient for a while, you might well find that all the resemblances between your story and mine will disappear entirely."

The young man was gracious enough to accept the request to be patient, and I could see that several other members of the company were glad of it.

"If premonitory visions are warnings of dire possibility," Crookes observed, "they might well warn of different possibilities, while still retaining certain elements in common. Mr. Wells and Professor Copplestone might both have seen truths of a sort, whether they are the same truths or not."

"In that case," said Tesla, seemingly keen to distance himself from Sir William's suggestion. "Anything we dream might be true, after a fashion. No vision of the future would actually need to come to pass to prove its worth; those that fail need only claim to have been more powerful as warnings than those that succeed. In such a scheme, the notion of *truth* loses all semblance of meaning–in which case, it will not matter what anyone else who takes your drug might experience, Professor Copplestone. They will be unable either to confirm or deny the accuracy of what you have seen."

"Gentlemen!" Wilde protested. "We are wasting time. If we do not hear the resumption of Professor Copplestone's story soon, we shall be here till dawn."

"I hope we shall not be delayed so long as that," I murmured, supportively. "It would be most inconvenient."

"You are right," said Copplestone, hastily. "I am glad that Mr. Wells has brought the matter of the similarity between my story and his to our attention, and I readily admit the relevance of what Sir William and Mr. Tesla have said, but I do think that we should press on. There will be time enough to discuss the import of my story when it is fully told. If there is no objection, I shall continue my account of the further exploits of my timeshadow."

There was no objection. I was evidently not the only one who did not relish the thought that the business might take all night.

The Explorer's Story: Part Two

The island formerly known as Great Britain,
circa *15,000 A.D.*

5.

For the purposes of my second excursion in far futurity, I increased the dosage of the drug by a third. The good and dutiful doctor expressed strong reservations about the wisdom of this course, but the after-effects of my first expedition seemed to have been relatively mild, and in my enthusiasm for discovery I thought the risk justified.

I had no way of knowing exactly how far into the future my first expedition had taken me, and I had no way of knowing how much further the increased dose would impel me, but I believed that I would be able to span several times as many years. Although no firm evidence had been presented to me in the course of my first expedition, I judged that it must have taken me at least several thousand years into the future. I now hoped to see what might have become of the Earth after several tens of thousands.

The sensation of displacement followed the familiar pattern, and I found myself once again standing on a hillside, lit by a warm summer Sun that had passed its zenith. I was reassured by the fact that it was daylight, but I knew that I would have to face nightfall eventually, and that, if the world were still ruled by the vampire race I had encountered in my first expedition, then I was almost certain to encounter them again.

I was dressed exactly as I had been before. My timeshadow seemed even heavier, and when I touched my breast it seemed perfectly solid. The slope on which I found myself was densely wooded, and there was no way to tell whether or not it was the same spot on the Earth's surface to which I had come previously.

I was surrounded by the sound of birdsong and the faint hum of insect wings, and I must admit that I experienced a sharp pang of disappointment because I could see nothing in my immediate vicinity to assure me that this was not my own time. Although I could not name the various species to which the surrounding trees belonged my knowledge of botany was inadequate to make me certain that they were alien to my experience, and in their general features they were very similar to those one might find in any of the woodlands of the shires.

I began to walk in the direction which I had taken previously, heading for the place where I had joined the roadway which had taken me into the town where the human cattle lived. Although my timeshadow was more cumbersome, I now had some ready-made understanding of how to adapt myself, and it was not long began to feel reasonably competent and fairly comfortable. While I cultivated a normal gait, I practiced pronouncing familiar syllables, schooling my deep and awkward voice until I could produce what sounded to my own ears like an acceptable version of the English language. I did not suppose for an instant that anyone I met might be able to understand any words I spoke, but I wanted to avoid the embarrassment of seeming stupidly inarticulate to anyone I did happen to meet.

After 10 or 12 minutes of walking, I became aware of the fact that a particular insect, about the size of a house-fly or honey-bee, was always close to my head. I tried to shoo it away, but it easily evaded my flapping hand, and circled around just beyond my reach, stubbornly refusing to depart. When I walked faster, the insect accelerated; although it made no attempt to settle upon my person, it insisted on keeping close attendance with me. I could not see it with perfect clarity because it was perpetually on the move, but its species was unknown to me; it certainly was not a house-fly or a bee, although it had a dark, rounded body and a small head bearing what seemed to be two complex antennae. In the end, I decided to ignore the creature.

When I reached the floor of the valley, where the road might or might not have been in much earlier times, I found a sluggish and murky stream. It was not very deep, but it was wide enough not to be jumped with perfect safety, and in any case there seemed to be no particular reason why I should want to get to the other side. I turned to my left, following the direction of the stream's flow.

I followed the course of the meandering stream for several 100 yards. I had fallen silent by now, and I was moving fluently enough to make very little noise. Eventually, I came to the rim of a little waterfall, where the stream tumbled down into a pool some five or six feet below. The rim of the little cliff was bordered by bushes, but I was tall enough to see over them—and in the hollow below, I saw a strange figure kneeling to drink from the stream. I stopped instantly, frozen by shock. I had been fully prepared to find the world utterly changed, and had thought that there was nothing I might find in such a far future which could astonish me, but I had not expected what I actually saw.

It was a satyr: a creature with the torso and belly of a man, and hindquarters that would have been more fitting on a goat.

The creature's head was very hairy, and two small horns projected from his forehead. The only thing that did not quite match the classical image of a satyr was his feet, which were far more massive than a goat's, although they seemed as horny as hooves and certainly bore no toes. He was slight of stature and slender in the body, no more massive than a healthy 13-year-old boy, but his face, strangely compounded out of human and animal features, somehow gave the impression of extreme age.

How can this possibly be the future? I asked myself. It could not even be the past, into which I might have slipped had my timeshadow been displaced in the wrong direction, for satyrs never really existed. They are figments of the human imagination: creatures born of superstitious fantasy. One species of fabulous creature might be explicable, but to encounter fauns as well a vampires is surely proof positive that all this is a mere dream, that there is nothing in it but the produce of mere fancy.

My disappointment was, however, alleviated by curiosity. *Well then*, I thought, *if I am removed to Hesiod's Age of Gold or Silver, I must make the most of it. If satyrs have replaced vampires as the dominant species of my delusion, then I must be careful to study satyrs more closely and more competently than I was able to study vampires.*

I must have been staring at the creature for about ten seconds before he suddenly became aware of my presence–I cannot say how–and turned to look up at me. I could not easily read his expression, so I could not tell how astonished he might be by the sight of me, but at least he did not start with alarm and flee in panic.

He stood up slowly, and turned slightly so as to face me squarely. Then he proceeded to stare at me as steadily as I was staring at him. After 10 or 12 seconds, he threw back his head and uttered a loud sound, which seemed far less human than his head or legs. It was a sound that human vocal chords could not have made, more closely resembling the note of some huge musical instrument like a church organ. Like a phrase from some atonal composition it rose and fell, echoing eerily from the bank on which I stood.

Afterwards, there was silence. For a few moments, I did not know whether he had sounded a warning or an expression of feeling–but I quickly realized that it must have been a summons, or at least an invitation. From the trees around the clearing other figures appeared.

In Greek myth, if I remember rightly, fauns and satyrs were exclusively male, and their chief delight was the pursuit of delicately human-seeming nymphs. Here, by contrast, there were females of the species too, and children. The females were less shaggy in the shanks, and the hair on their heads was less coarse, but no one seeing them in daylight could possibly have mistaken them for humans, Their features were a similar compound of human and animal, and their feet were every bit as strange.

Within the space of a few minutes, a company of 13 had gathered, five of which were little ones–one of them a babe in arms. They did not menace me in any way. Like the one who had summoned them, they simply stared, with what I took to be frank curiosity. They did not beckon to me, but I received the impression that they were waiting for me to join them.

I found a place where I could scramble down the bank, and did so, though very awkwardly. At the bottom, which I reached rather too hurriedly, I sprawled in a most ungainly fashion. I was not winded, but I could not immediately rise, and one of the fauns approached me tentatively, his hand outstretched. I took it, and he helped me up. I was more than a foot taller than he, but he seemed very strong.

"Thank you," I said, letting go of his slender, warm fingers. The sound of my voice, so different from his own, did not alarm him. He continued to stare up into my eyes, so intently that I wished I could read his unhuman expression.

"Are you mere animals in human form?" I said, speaking in what I hoped was a reassuring tone. "Or are you intelligent beings whose mode of thought is too alien to permit sensible communication?"

The bushes parted again, and another creature came out. This one was of another kind, and for one brief moment I though he might be a man. He was very much taller than the dwarfish fauns, and far more manlike in the face. As his hindquarters emerged from the undergrowth, which at first concealed them, I saw that he too was only half-human.

He was a centaur of sorts, although his lower body did not much resemble that of a horse; it was more like that of a sleek brown bear. Like all the rest, he stood still and stared at me from a distance, reaching up with an oddly delicate hand to stroke his lank brown beard. Then he spoke, or seemed to speak, to the satyr who had sounded the summons. His voice was not in the least manlike, nor did it resemble the whinnying of a horse; again, it was like a series of profound notes sounded by a musical instrument.

The faun replied. I could not tell for sure whether their speech was meaningful; it might or might not have been language.

Again the thought occurred to me that perhaps I had made a mistake and cast my timeshadow into the distant past, before the race of men came into being, and that my mind had seen fit to populate its emptiness according to the imagination of the first story-tellers. It took only a moment or two, however, for me to understand that I might have it all the wrong way around. I realized that the images of the past which ancient societies possessed might well have been based on misinterpretations of the glimpses of the distant future which their seers had caught.

I already knew, of course, that the priest-magicians of ancient societies had used much the same drugs which gave their modern equivalents access to premonitory visions. The most gifted among them, I knew, must always have had the power to journey into the farther reaches of time, but they had never been able to stabilize their timeshadows as I had contrived to do. Even I was unable, as yet, properly to calibrate the impulse of my time machine, and did not know exactly when in time I might be; it was, therefore, entirely understandable that those ancient visionaries had located the Golden Age in the past rather than the future, and made it part of their fantasies of Creation and Descent.

This conclusion raised my spirits considerably. I became convinced that I was in the future, and that it was an actual future–at the very least a future of contingency, and perhaps the one and only future of destiny. But were there more inhabitants of this future, I wondered, than gentle and uncommunicative chimeras? Had I any chance of finding out what had happened during the vast gulf of time which separated this seemingly-happy era from the age in which vampires had ruled the world?

Impulsively, I stepped towards the centaur, and reached out my hand as though to clasp his. He did not shy away, but nor did he reach out in friendship. His face showed no detectable expression.

He is an animal, I thought, *despite his human features–but he does not fear me! Either he is perfectly tame or he thinks me one of his own kind, a freakish cousin.*

I stepped back so that I could look at all the assembled crowd. I raised my arms, palms open, in a gesture intended to signal farewell and reassurance.

"I must go on," I said to them, apologetically. "I have not much time, and I must see as much of your world as I can, even if I cannot reach the edge of the forest before the elastic thread that attaches me to my own time snatches me back again."

I felt a slight thrill of triumph as they copied me, one and all. With the sole exception of the tiny child, they raised their arms, exactly as I had done–and their imitation suggested to me a kind of kinship which ran far deeper than any partial similarity of form.

At that moment, however, I was reminded once again of the insect which had kept close company with me since the moments immediately following my arrival. It descended to fly around my head, buzzing more loudly than before– and it was no longer alone.

Within a few seconds there were a dozen of the tiny flying things, and within a few seconds more, there were hundreds. I flapped my arms at them reflexively, as fearful as I would have been had I been attacked by a whole swarm of stinging bees. Although I half-closed my eyes against the imagined assault, I saw that the satyrs and the centaur had similarly begun to swat the air. This time, their gestures were not mere imitation; the hollow seemed to be filling up with a coalescing cloud, and the air itself seemed to be abuzz with a vast, all-pervading sound.

The centaur and his companions turned to run away, possessed now by the panic which the sight of me had failed to induce. They ran away from the stream, into the depths of the wood, but I ran a different way, continuing along the course I had set, parallel to the slow watercourse.

I, and I alone, was pursued by the swarm. It was as difficult to run in this world as it had been in the earlier one, and I was once again painfully aware of the difficulty. I must have known almost immediately that I could not possibly outrun the tiny things which buzzed around my head if they were disposed to follow me, but my fear was unreasoning. I have always been afraid of bees and wasps, and the behavior of the insects now seemed to me to be exactly that of a swarm of angry bees, so I ran in terror.

I must have blundered on, ineffectually, for several 100 yards. My frightened mind could not quite grasp the fact that I had not been stung, and that not one of the insects had actually settled upon me. But I could not run for long; I was too clumsy. I caught my foot upon a trailing root and stumbled. I managed to stop myself sprawling full length, but I fell to my knees, flailing my arms. It seemed that my flailing was not without effect, for there were not so many of the insects about my head now. They were moving ahead of me, as though to anticipate the resumption of my headlong flight, and I cursed their apparent determination to block my way.

While I remained where I was, trying hard to catch my breath, I saw that the whole vast swarm was now coming together. The vague cloud, assembling itself some 10 or 12 feet away from me, began to take on a definite shape, which became ever more distinct.

As I lowered my arms, because there seemed no further need to defend myself, I saw that the shape which the cloud of insects was assuming was approximately human. While I watched, far more astonished now than I had been before, it seemed that they ceased to be insects at all, and became the cells of an upright body: a human figure, which looked like an animate bronze statue, with a surface as smooth as silk.

The terror I felt did not in the least abate as I watched his miracle. I could not conceive that any being supernaturally distilled from a horde of noxious insects could be anything but loathsome and malevolent. Whereas the fauns and the centaur had never seemed anything but harmless in their docile innocence, this monstrous homunculus struck me as a veritable demon.

In the course of my unusually eventful life, I have been in many hazardous situations, and have often survived by virtue of keeping my head when others might have lost theirs–but on this occasion, I confess, I lost my head completely. When I managed to get to my feet, convinced that the monster intended to impede my further progress, I hurled myself at it, striking out violently with my fists, as though to batter it to the ground. I was a fool, of course. My timeshadow-arms were woefully weak and the object of my attack was less than solid. My blows passed clean through it, not because it was as insubstantial as a ghost, but because its myriad components simply gave way and flew momentarily apart as I stuck at it, presenting no resistance.

I fell again, more heavily this time. I felt bruised and sore, and wondered once more how direly the damage I suffered as a timeshadow might be communicated back to my body when–or if–I became whole again.

The swarm coalesced once again into that hideous golem, which now seemed to be a mocking reflection of my own form. It had my height and my girth, and it did not seem to me that this was mere coincidence.

Then, in a seeming travesty of the gesture the faun had made when I slipped down the bank into the hollow, it stretched out a "hand," offering to help me up. I could not bring myself to take it; I simply stared at the horrible thing, paralyzed by fear. It seemed as solid as a statue now; there was no indication of the fact that it was compounded out of thousands of ubiquitous units.

It slowly lowered the proffered arm. Then it opened its brazen mouth and spoke.

The syllables were as deep and as hoarse and as hollow as the words that had spilled from my own mouth while I practiced the art of pronunciation, but they were quite distinct and there was no mistaking the word they pronounced– the name they pronounced.

"Cop-ple-stone!" said the monster, laboriously. "Cop-ple-stone!"

6.

Had my anxiety been capable of increase, the fact that the monster could pronounce my name might have sent yet another thrill of terror coursing through my attenuated form, but I felt that nothing further could be added to my distress. I seized upon the golem's use of my name as a puzzle to be solved.

While I asked myself, feverishly, how such a miracle could be, the creature compounded out of the swarm of false insects stood stock still, waiting for me to rise. As time passed, moment by moment, without my being rent or crushed by those metallic hands, the puzzle was able to take command of my thoughts and drive the panic out.

My sense of physical danger was still acute. I knew, however, that there was little to be gained by trying to run away from the golem, and that it would be a better use of my time and effort to discover its purpose.

"How do you know my name?" I demanded, breathlessly, amazed by my own temerity. "Can you read my thoughts?"

The mechanical golem waved its arm in what seemed to be a negative gesture.

"Copplestone," it said, speaking with a little more assurance now that it had heard my reply. "Are you Copplestone?"

"That is my name," I admitted. "I ask again–how do you know it?" The golem took a step towards me, but I did not flinch. It was not so much the words it had spoken that had calmed me, but that I had spoken to it, tacitly accepting it as a thinking being. It reached out its hand again, and this time I took it.

It felt as hard as polished metal, but it was not cold. It did no more than support me while I pulled myself up, but I had the impression that it was very strong. The tiny things that had combined to make it had knitted together perfectly to make a single seamless body.

"Thank you," I said. "What are you?"

It did not reply to my question. I stood face to face with it now, and I looked into its eyes. It did have eyes of a sort–black orbs, of a subtly different texture from the surrounding bronze–but they were infinitely more alien than the eyes of the faun or the eyes of the centaur. Its face now seemed less hideous to me than it had been; indeed, its features seemed very ordinary, though not particularly handsome. Its cheeks were contoured like a man's, although I could not believe that there were similar muscles beneath the outer tegument, and it had a nose of sorts, but devoid of nostrils. Its mouth was a black slit, whose border was shaped to give a sketchy impression of lips. Its metallic complexion was nearer to the color of mahogany than to bronze.

When we had stared at one another for a few seconds, it hesitantly extended its hand again, plainly unsure as to whether I would condescend to take it or not. I remembered that the centaur had not been able to respond to my similar gesture. I took it, exactly as though I were shaking hands with a new acquaintance. Its grasp was gentle enough, not at all like a grip of steel.

"Copplestone," it said, yet again. Its powers of communication were evidently rather limited. "You are Copplestone."

The fact that it could pronounce those syllables was a miracle beyond compare–provided, of course, that I really was in a future thousands of years further from my own time than the one I had visited before. Yet again, I began to doubt that. A man may always be recognized in his dreams; whatever phantoms are conjured up in his imagination may have access to his most intimate secrets.

"How do you know me?" I asked, again. My fear had by now transmuted itself into a keen sense of absurdity–and this too seemed reminiscent of the emotional confusion that often afflicts a dreaming man. Could something as strange and bizarre as this automaton compounded out of insects be a product of my own fevered imagination? Could it possibly be anything else? And what of the fauns and the centaur? How could such as they possibly belong to a true future?

The golem opened its arms wide, as if to embrace me. "Come," it said. "Do not be afraid!"

I stood where I was.

"Do not be afraid!" it repeated. There was little or no inflection in its mechanical voice. It could not contrive to sound reassuring, nor could it plead.

"Come where?" I asked. It was the wrong question. The golem did not want me to go with it; it merely wanted me to step into its embrace. When I would not do so, it stepped forward to take me. As it did so, its countless units came apart again, but it did not break up into a flying swarm; instead, it flowed around and over me, enclosing me.

It formed a new body, around my own, fitting itself about me like a suit of living armor.

I understood then why it had instructed me not to be afraid, but the instruction was impossible to obey. I was all too well aware of the fact that it could crush the life out of me by a slight adjustment of its shape.

I tried to protest, but no words came forth–but it had the courtesy, or the common sense, to leave my face uncovered. I could breathe and I could see.

If this is a dream, I told myself, sternly, *you will surely wake up before anything too terrible can happen. If it is not, and this really is the future, you will come to no harm. Your name is known, and your coming must have been awaited for thousands of years. You are precious here, infinitely precious...*

I began to move. I was not, of course, moving by virtue of my own volition, but according to the will of the entity that enclosed me. It began to run, swiftly accelerating its pace to a sprint. Had I tried to achieve such a velocity using the ghostly muscles of my timeshadow it would have required enormous effort, but because the motive force was provided by my captor I felt for the first time that I really was a kind of phantom, lighter than the air.

I could have spoken aloud. I could have asked "Where are we going?"–but how would the golem have responded, now that it no longer had a mouth?

Thus cocooned, I was taken through the forest for many a mile–or so at least it seemed. But we came before very long to a clearing where stood a huge iron mast, more than 100 feet high, and a number of low huts, and several strange machines with rounded bodies and long tails, each with four long horizontal vanes on top and four much smaller ones arranged vertically at the extremity of the tail.

I expected to be taken to one of the huts, but I was taken instead to one of these machines. My suit of armor opened a hatch in the belly of one of them, and climbed in. It was very dark inside–there were no windows, and little light crept in from below–so I could only judge what happened next by means of touch. This was very difficult at first, for I remained enclosed inside my mechanical shell, insulated from direct contact, but after some wriggling I ended up in a sitting position, and I felt my armor flow away again, to leave me largely uncovered, but not free. I was still secured by bands about my arms, legs and waist, so that my movements were severely restricted.

My ears were filled with a sound like the droning of a million insects, and I wondered if the swarm of golem-parts was breaking up again, but it came from all around and it did not abate. A sinking sensation in my stomach told me that the machine in whose belly I was now enclosed was lifting from the ground, and I knew that I had simply been transferred from one prison to another: from a running-machine to a flying-machine. My journey was not ended; it had hardly begun.

The hatchway through which I had entered into the machine was closed now, and I was in pitch darkness for two or three minutes, but then light returned. It was not diffuse light, like the artificial phosphorescence which had lit the town and the Underworld of my previous vision; it was highly localized within a space in front of my head. It was almost as though I were looking into an illuminated aquarium, for the illuminated space had a curious liquid quality about it–but there were no fish swimming there.

Instead, there was a disembodied head.

Although disembodied, the head was far from dead, and seemed quite undiscomfited by its detachment. Its features were animated and not unhandsome, but I knew immediately that it was not a man. I recognized the pallid complexion, the blackish lips and the cat-like eyes. It was an Overman–or, at least, the image of an Overman. I knew that there was nothing really there, and that even the impression of three-dimensionality must be an illusion. Either this was someone speaking to me from afar, his image relayed by some mechanical process of reproduction which ignored his body, or it was a synthesized image, a mere simulacrum of life.

"Are you truly Copplestone?" the face asked. At any rate, those were the words that came from a speaker somewhere above the image; the dark lips moved to pronounce quite different syllables, and I inferred that some kind of translation machine was again being used.

"I am," I replied, hoarsely.

"From what time do you come, Copplestone?" he asked.

"From the 19th century Anno Domini," I told him.

The expression on his face shifted, and he seemed perplexed. There followed a long hesitation. I leapt to the conclusion that he had no idea what Anno Domini meant, but did not know how to ask for clarification. I realized that if he somehow had access to the substance of the conversation which I had had with his remote ancestor, so many thousands of years before, he might know a little about me, but not very much.

"I am Edward Copplestone," I told him, proudly. "I am the pioneer of the exploration of the future. Others will doubtless follow where I have led, but none can come from any earlier time for more than the fleetest moment, nor bring more than a faint echo of substance with them. Is that why you set your insectile machines to keep watch for my timeshadow? Is that why I am a miracle in your eyes?"

The face reacted to my words, but the essence of the reaction still seemed to be perplexity and puzzlement. I realized that, although I could hardly claim to have the upper hand in the exchange, my interlocutor was struggling under a burden of ignorance and incomprehension as great as my own.

He does not understand, I repeated to myself, trying to reason through the difficulty. *Although he knows my name, he does not know who or what I am. For whatever reason, my example has not been followed by countless others. Visitation by timeshadow is not a commonplace of this future. It must be the case that these so-called Overmen, unlike the mere men they have displaced, have no innate capacity for precognition?*

"Tell me the exact day and hour from which you came," said the disembodied head, in a fashion which might not have been intended to sound peremptory, but did.

I was suddenly struck by a fit of suspicion, and hesitated before replying. "Why should you want to know that?" I asked. "You can only have the vaguest notion of what the phrase Anno Domini means, so what use would exactitude be?"

He frowned–and no matter how vast the expanse of time was that separated us, or what differences there might be between his species and mine, it was an unmistakable gesture of annoyance. "Answer," he said.

I resented the implication of command.

Perhaps my secret was lost, I thought. *But if so, how? What prevented me from making it known, from giving all mankind the power of clear foresight. Is it possible–is it even imaginable–that this bodiless thing desires to know my point of origin in order to take action against me, to prevent my revealing what I know about the fate which awaits mankind? Can these Overmen be so worldly wise that they can now reach backwards through time to annul events which threaten their reality?*

These thoughts were, of course, very confused. There was far too much to think about, and the head still wanted its answer. I decided that I must be cautious, at least until I knew more.

"I have many questions of my own," I retorted, "and I have not much time to ask them. You must know a great deal already about my world, while I know nothing at all about yours, save that your kind once reduced mine to the level of mere cattle, which you milked for blood. Why are you so curious about me, when all the curiosity should be on my side?"

He looked at me very carefully, as though he could not make up his mind what to say. He seemed remarkably unintelligent, considering all the marvelous machines which he had at his disposal. Was he, I wondered, no more than a machine himself–another golem, able to reproduce the semblance of a person, but only capable of limited intellectual performance?

"Do not be afraid," he said. "I desire to learn."

"I repeat that there is much more for me to learn about you than you could possibly learn from me," I said. "I do not even know what manner of man–or overman–you are. If appearances can be trusted, your forefathers bred mine for their blood, and hence were vampires of a kind. Given that, how should I begin to trust you, and why should I tell you anything at all?"

He frowned again, but I could not read any wrath in his frown.

"Answer," he said, impotently. "Do not be afraid."

I knew him then for some kind of parrot, trained to talk but not to make proper sense. "I am not afraid," I lied, "but I am not a fool. I refuse to talk to golems and disembodied heads, if they cannot tell me what I ardently desire to know. I am your prisoner, forced to go wherever you care to take me, but I have

nothing to say to you unless you will condescend to contribute to my enlightenment. You must answer me!"

The image flickered, as though the "fluid" in the "aquarium" had been rip-
pled by the current of my displeasure. The features of the face shifted eerily, but
then were reconstituted.

"Ask," said the head, emotionlessly. "Ask, and I will answer."

I felt a surge of triumph, but restrained my exultation.

"Is yours truly a race of vampires?" I asked. "Did your kind enslave mine,
at some point in our mutual history, and reduce the descendants of man to mere
animality? Is mankind now extinct?"

"In a time of trial, 12,000 years ago," the head reported, "your descendants
fought with my ancestors, and were subdued. Once subdued, they were bred for
blood and not for brains, and in the space of a few 100 generations, became as
docile and as unintelligent as cattle or swine. Overmen no longer need the blood
of such beings, but there was no way to return to the descendants of humankind
what they had lost: sentience, intelligence, free will. My more recent forefathers
chose a different way: they remade the descendants of human beings in the myriad images of ancient human dreams, and gave them a garden in which to live
contentedly. One day, that garden will span a continent–perhaps, in the very
distant future, it might cover all the Earth–but the descendants of the human race
can never recover intelligence unless that garden becomes a wilderness of a very
much harsher kind. The descendants of humankind will only make progress if
they first rediscover the constant threat of pain and death."

This recitation was delivered as though it were a dull lecture of no particular substance. There was no trace of emotion in it, nor of apology.

I am, of course, thoroughly familiar with Charles Darwin's theory of evolution by natural selection, and I had no difficulty in following the argument that
had been so starkly laid out for me. For the same reason, though, I was sorely
puzzled as to the origins of the race whose members now called themselves
Overmen.

"If your forefathers were not mine," I said to him, "where did they come
from? Were they invaders from the planet Mars?"

"Your kind and mine had common ancestors," he said. He did not elaborate, and I felt slightly frustrated, wondering whether the inadequacy of the answer was deliberate dissimulation.

"Are you, then, the children of the vampires of legend?" I said, wondering
if his translation-machinery was capable of detecting sarcasm. "Were your distant ancestors the reanimated corpses of wicked men, returned from the grave to
feed upon their brethren?"

"No," he said, flatly. "Not that. When do you come from, Copplestone?
What moment? What place? Your language is English–did you come from England?"

I knew that I ought to honor my bargain, but still I could not help but wonder why he wanted the information, and whether I might endanger myself by giving it. "English was the language of the greater part of the globe," I told him, feeling free to exaggerate the truth. "It was spoken throughout an empire on which the Sun never set. It was the language of Australasia and North America as well as the British Isles."

"But it was England from which you came?" he persisted.

"Where are we going?" I countered. The question was prompted because the flying machine had begun to descend again, and I was aware of a progressive deceleration. "Where have you brought me?"

"You are here," he answered, sourly. I wondered how much comfort he took in the triviality of the answer.

I felt the bonds which had restrained me flowing away. By the time that the belly of the machine began to open beneath my feet, I was free, and a ramp extended itself so that I might let myself down to the ground. The disembodied head disappeared, and when I reached out my hand I found that there was nothing there but a blank wall.

Illusion, I said to myself. *Thus far, all has been illusion. Thus far!*

Then I stepped down from the flying-machine, ready to meet the true masters of this alien future in the flesh."

7.

The Sun had set, and twilight had all but faded from the sky. Even so, the vista that lay before my eyes was visible, and utterly breathtaking. The perch to which the bird-machine had brought me was high on the side of a mountain, and I only had to move three paces away to look out over a huge plain, which was covered from horizon to horizon by a vast city. All of its streets and most of its buildings were richly illuminated, and the tallest buildings loomed up above the streets with an awesome grandeur.

In the largest buildings light shone within hundreds, if not thousands, of windows. This was brighter light by far than the diffuse illumination that had leavened the gloom of the barn where the overmen of old bled their human cattle, but it had the same curious blue-violet tint, which my eyes still found uncomfortable.

I could see tiny flying-machines moving between the buildings, some lit from within by the same eerie light. Many were like the one which had delivered me here but others were differently-designed. I moved closer to the edge of the cliff in order to study the city more closely. There was a guard-rail there, and I rested my hands gingerly upon it. From this coign of vantage, it was easy to see that the streets were laid out with remarkable precision, in a vast rectangular grid. Traffic flowed along each and every street in an endless stream, but it was difficult to see any details of the vehicles even though each one lit its own way with twin violet beams. At each intersection, the passage of the vehicles was restricted by changing lights that shifted from turquoise to vivid blue to pale violet and back again, in endless succession.

"Copplestone?" said a voice behind me, and I turned.

There were two of them; one male and one female. Their faces resembled the disembodied head that had questioned me during the flight, but these were real individuals of flesh and blood. They had no lantern with them, but the light shining from the windows of the solitary house from which they had come allowed me to see them reasonably clearly. They were dressed entirely in black, the male in a suit which displayed his contours as closely as my white "clothing" displayed mine, the female in a narrow ankle-length skirt. That touch of quasi-human femininity struck me as a remarkable oddity, and I had to wonder yet again whether it was not the sort of detail which betrayed the influence of my own imagination–evidence that this was, at least in part, a dream rather than a true vision of the future.

The male spoke again, in a voice redolent with wonderment: "Are you truly Copplestone?" He was speaking English, and the words came from his own lips without the aid of any translation-machine, but he pronounced the words as if he were uncertain whether they could possibly mean anything. To him, I inferred, I was as much a creature of myth as the satyrs and the centaur had been to me. In a world that was to him a long-lost antiquity I had appeared, and disappeared, and there had been no way of knowing whether I would ever return–and yet, there had been hope enough that I might to warrant keeping some kind of watch, even for millennia. And there were Overmen with leisure enough–and interest enough–to have learned to speak a long-dead language, in order to immerse themselves more fully in the study of a long-dead culture. The machines–the golem and the flying-machine–must have brought me to the one place on earth where there were overmen who could speak to me, who could answer the questions which I so desperately wanted to ask.

The female came closer, and reached out a delicate hand to touch my forehead. I permitted it. Her fingertips felt slightly damp as she rested them on my brow for half a minute. She said nothing, as if she simply wanted to make sure that I was real, with substance enough to be touched.

I felt quite calm, now. All my fear had ebbed away, and I was perfectly composed. Later, I wondered whether I might perhaps have been mesmerized, but at the time, I simply accepted my condition as natural, and I cannot say that I saw anything at all in her catlike eyes to make me suspect that her gaze might be making a captive of my soul.

It was the man who led me inside the house, when his consort stepped back again. I did not study the house very closely, but I know that its walls were all curved, without a single corner to be seen, and that its tiled roofs were like conical turrets.

They took me into a room lit by violet light, but caused the light to be muted so that it would not hurt my eyes. There were no screens on the walls here, and no control-panels–only furniture of a fairly commonplace kind, and a strange device like a fountain enclosed in a globe of glass, where some dark fluid circulated in an agitated manner. Because of the peculiar lighting, I could not judge its true color, but they did not intend to mislead me. They took me to stand before it, and told me frankly what it was.

"We no longer need living beings to manufacture our sustenance," said the male. "We are masters of all flesh now, and could alter ourselves if we wished it, so that we might eat any and every food–but we are what we are, and this is the nourishment for which nature and history shaped us."

He let some out into a goblet, and drank it, so that I should be certain what he meant, and what he was–but he did not offer the cup to me. There was no renewal of my former horror. I knew now what kind of a world I was in, and I understood. My hosts indicated that I should seat myself on a low sofa, and I complied. They apologized for the awkwardness of the conversation which I had had with the disembodied head, explaining that–as I had already deduced–it was a mere simulacrum of a living being, a machine whose capacity for action was limited. They went on to explain a great deal more.

I learned that the spies set to watch for me were tiny machines of a very cheap and endlessly patient kind, which represented no considerable investment of effort. Even so, it was an effort that only a handful of persons out of the billions who dwelt on the Earth thought worthwhile, and the machines had been designed in such a way that I might be brought to people who might be able to speak with me, rather than taking me to some public place where I might be paraded before crowds and exhibited as the marvel I undoubtedly was.

They explained to me very earnestly that my species had long ago given way to a higher and better one, according to the dictates of the laws of evolution, and was now known only by fragmentary relics. They assured me, however, that there had been no war of conquest, in which their kind had risen up against and defeated mine. According to their account, the human race had destroyed its own civilization, and all-but-obliterated its own heritage in a long series of increasingly-destructive wars, which had blasted apart the legacy of the Industrial Revolution even before that revolution had attained its climax. Everything mankind had built was destroyed, in the space of little more than a century.

Their grasp of our chronology was a little vague, but they believed that the chain of disasters began in the 20th century and was complete by the end of the 21st. After that, they said, there were no calendars left to chronicle the disastrous decline of once-civilized men into utter barbarity. According to their judgment, the intellectual flowering of our race had been hardly less brief than the life of a mayfly; their civilization, by contrast, had lasted for more than 10,000 years.

I accepted this news with perfect equanimity, and did not doubt then that I was being told the truth. What they were saying–that humanity had destroyed itself, reduced itself to a savage existence before the Overmen had restored the march of progress–did not seem in the least incredible while I bathed in that purple light, listening to the susurrus of the blood which swirled in the ornamental fountain. I understood that the civilization which provided men of my kind with all the rewards of comfort had been a very fragile thing, because the division of manual and intellectual labor that made factory production and scientific progress possible had robbed individual men of the elementary knowledge which would be essential to survival were the support of the complex productive system of modern society ever to fail.

So muted had my own incredulity become that I was not surprised when my hosts told me that they would have the utmost difficulty persuading their contemporaries that I really had visited their world.

"You cannot begin to understand," the male told me, "how incredible it is that we are sitting in our own home, conversing with a ghost from the remotest antiquity. No one now believes in the reality of ghosts; we have long since cast such superstitions aside. It will be very difficult indeed to persuade our contemporaries that your appearance here is not some kind of cunning deception on our part. The machines we use nowadays are so very clever in manufacturing appearances that there is no conceivable proof we could offer that you really are what you seem to be. Indeed, we are acutely aware of the possibility that you are a hoax perpetrated upon us by malicious acquaintances."

"I am real," I said, oddly helpless in the face of his apparent need for reassurance. "I wish I could prove it to you." But he looked at me so strangely that I knew I could not–that so far as he knew, this really might be a practical joke.

"Can you possibly imagine," he said, very softly, "how little has survived into our world from yours? It is not merely the passage of time that has erased the record of your civilization–for I assure you that our archaeologists have been very assiduous in preserving every shard and fragment they could find–but the extremes of destruction achieved by your own wars. We know only a little more about your 19th century than we do about periods 2000 or 3000 years earlier. We have less than 1000 texts written in the language we are now speaking, and almost all of them are incomplete."

I could not help but think of Shelley's poem about the ancient Pharaoh whose shattered statue rested half-buried in a sea of sand, vainly bidding its discoverers to look upon his works and despair.

"What are you, really?" I whispered. "How did it come about that your kind became lords of the Earth, feeding on the blood of men like me?"

He was enthusiastic to persuade me that I ought not to think of his ancestors as evil creatures. He was anxious to emphasize that it was to his ancestors that the descendants of mankind owed their survival. Had the descendants of humankind not been domesticated, he said, the line would have become extinct– and when I protested that all the things which made us human had indeed been extinguished, he reminded me that there still remained a possibility that our ultimate descendants might once again become sentient, in a future as remote from his present as his era was from mine. If that came to pass, he said, those new men would reckon his kind the saviors of mankind instead of its destroyers.

"It is the law of life," said the female. "New species emerge, achieve dominance, and are superseded in their turn."

"As you, too, will no doubt be superseded," I said, with neither irony nor bitterness.

She shook her head. "Not so," she said. "There is an end to the sequence, when a species becomes master of its own evolution, by obtaining direct technical control over the hereditary material. Your species came close to attaining such control, but your descendants destroyed the civilization they had built before they were able to make use of what they had learned."

"And you can be perfectly certain that yours will not do likewise, I suppose," I said.

"I do not mean to insult you," she assured me, "but my kind is better than yours. We are considerably more rational, and much less violent. We are not warlike by nature, and we have far less capacity for hatred than your kind had. What we have built we will certainly keep, and our mastery of the Earth's biosphere is so complete that we can never be replaced. As you have seen, we have long since ceased to be dependent on the foodstuffs supplied to us by men, and we have adapted ourselves so that we are able to walk abroad in daylight quite comfortably–although we naturally still prefer the night-time."

They went on to tell me about the origins of their own kind. They admitted that their remote ancestors were predators who fed on the blood of mammals, including humans, but denied that they were vampires of the kind which featured so luridly in human folklore. They dismissed as mere superstitious nonsense the idea that their ancestors had been evil spirits which took possession of human corpses. Theirs, they said, was a natural species which lived invisibly on the margins of human society by virtue of its powers of mimicry. When I objected that their eyes would make it impossible for them to pass for men, even in the darkness which they favored over daylight, they assured me that they could alter far more than the shape and color of their pupils–and they proved their point.

I have not taken the trouble to describe either of these individuals in any great detail, because their most distinctive features had made other differences seem trivial. The female had not appeared to me to be unusually pretty or unusually ugly by human standards, simply because there was little in her face which could command my attention save for her peculiar complexion and her disconcerting eyes. When she began to change, however, she first exerted herself to become more attractive–at least by human standards.

The green light in her eyes faded, and the pupils became rounded, set in dark brown irises. The luster of her flesh faded, and the paleness of her skin suddenly seemed much more ordinary. A few faint blemishes appeared, seemingly at random–but at the same time, she became startlingly beautiful. Her cheekbones shifted, and the lines of her face became more distinct; her eyebrows grew darker and her eyelashes longer. The changes were subtle, and yet quite devastating.

She laughed delightedly when she saw my reaction. "So I can do it," she said, as if she had not dared to believe it. "What an atavism I am! Is this truly the lure that my foremothers used for the seduction of human brutes?"

They went on to explain that mimicry of this sort was a talent they had almost lost in the period of their first ascendancy, and that none among them really knew how adeptly their forebears used it–but that since they had learned the mechanisms which controlled all their bodily faculties, they had recovered the art and carried it to new extremes.

"Our minds have much greater authority over our bodies than yours," the male said, "for which reason we have no disease, and easily repair injuries which would be sufficient to kill one of you. Watch!"

The woman began to change again, and this time far more ambitiously. I watched emotionlessly as her skin coarsened and became hairy, as her nose was elongated into a snout, as her hands changed into paws and her legs shriveled. She completed the transformation into the appearance of a huge wolf, but began to change back almost immediately. As soon as her face was once again capable of bearing a smile, she grinned very broadly. She clearly felt very pleased with herself.

I took the appropriate inference readily enough; I understood what various means her remote ancestors had used to capture their prey, and why the only record of their existence which existed in the 19th century was a mere whisper of legend, heavily polluted by nightmarish fantasy. I understood the awful truth–and the hidden danger which lurked unseen in my own world.

"So your ancestors were not merely vampires but also werewolves," I said to my hosts. "It is a wonder that you did not rule the world long before my own day. Or were the rumors of your invulnerability greatly exaggerated?"

"Not so very greatly," said the male. "The crude shapeshifting abilities our ancestors had were associated with considerable powers of self-repair as well as virtually immunity to all disease, but....how well do you understand the mechanisms of evolution?"

"I understand the theory of natural selection very well," I told him, perhaps more haughtily than I was entitled to do. "I met Charles Darwin 14 years ago, a year before he died, and I discussed the implications of his theory with him." After I had said that, of course, I realized that I might easily have given away the information I had determined to keep secret when the face on the flying machine's screen had tried to discover my point of origin, but it no longer seemed important–and in any case, the vampire did not react to Darwin's name.

"In that case," he said, "you will understand that in the economics of evolution there is a correlation between lifespan and reproductive fecundity. Most natural species invest almost all of their energy in profligate reproduction, because it is easier for an organism to give birth to 1000 egg-cells, some few of which will survive to become new self-reproducing individuals, than it is to preserve the existing individuals against all the destructive pressures of the environment. At the same time, however, evolution has gradually produced organisms that are far more long-lived because of the reproductive advantages of parental care. Humans invest a far greater proportion of their energy in self-repair and self-preservation than most lower organisms, but they are only able to do so because of the protective care which they devote to the very few offspring they produce. I dare say that you can easily see the benign circularity of the argument, and can therefore appreciate that the species destined to replace mankind would be even longer-lived but would produce even fewer offspring.

"For several hundred thousand years, while humans lived as hunter-gatherers, their total numbers were stable, and the number of my ancestors steadily increased. But when humans underwent the spectacular population explosion which followed the discovery of agriculture, and which continued exponentially–despite the limitations of disease–until the beginning of what you call the 21st century, my ancestors were ill-equipped by nature to keep up. Although their absolute numbers continued to increase, they did so very slowly, and it was not until the catastrophic fall of the fragile human empire that my own ancestors were enabled to emerge from hiding and claim their birthright."

I regretted my boastfulness regarding my understanding of the logic of evolution, because there were certain features of this argument I had the utmost difficulty grasping, but its general outline seemed clear enough. I understood that, in my own time, the species known to us only through fancy-polluted tales of vampires and werewolves had been rare, because they multiplied so slowly by comparison with human beings–and although they were much less vulnerable to disease and injury than humans, they were by no means immortal.

On repeating this to myself, I realized that I had acquired information which might be of incalculable value, provided only that the future which I had contrived to see was a future of contingency rather than a future of destiny. If I could warn my fellow men of the fate which awaited them, I thought, and prompt them to take action against the race that was waiting to enslave them, their reduction to the hideously ignominious status which I had glimpsed during my first expedition might yet be avoided.

"I believe I know what you are thinking," said the female, then. "But I urge you to remember that, were it not for my kind, yours would have become extinct. If you really are what you claim to be, you must abandon all thought of alerting your fellows to the presence in their midst of my kind. At best, they would think you mad; at worst, you might make certain the extinction of all intelligent life on Earth."

"But our kind will triumph," added the male, "for are we not here?" He, evidently, believed in the future of destiny–but how, I wondered, could he believe otherwise, even if his world were no more than a phantom of contingency? He could hardly be expected to accept the unflattering possibility that he, the history that had made him, and the entire cosmos which contained him, were mere figments of my imagination–although it was a possibility that seemed perfectly plausible to me.

"That is not important," said the female, who seemed to favor a different strategy of persuasion. "You must understand, Copplestone, that the only hope for the future of your species rests with ours. We are masters of nature now, and it is in our power to make of mankind what we will. What you saw today in the forest is but one more chapter in a continuing story, and there may yet be a new ascent of man to sentience and civilization."

Why, I wondered, was she so anxious to make me concede this point? It was then, for the first time, that I wondered whether I might have been mesmerized, and that my two generous hosts might be exerting themselves to impress some kind of command upon my dulled mind.

"No!" I said. "I will not..."

At that precise moment in time, however, my timeshadow began to fade out, and I felt myself slipping away from that peculiar discussion into darkness.

"No!" cried the male. "You must not go! Please stay! There is so much more we have to say, so much more we need to learn....Stay, I beg of you!" He did not seem to realize that I had not the least control over the duration of my stay. He must have thought that my departure was a voluntary retreat and a calculated betrayal–but there was nothing I or anyone could do.

I awoke, and found the doctor beside me, anxiously assisting me to wakefulness. I was, I fear, in a parlous state...

The Count's Story: Part Three

London, January 1891

6.

Copplestone had paused twice during the second part of his narration. Whatever medicine had been used to revive him, its effect had worn off long before he had finished. He was more haggard and drawn than before, and all the excitement that had possessed him had drained out of him.

The first pause had passed readily enough, but the doctor had risen during the second and had gone to the professor's side before being waved away. My companions had moved uncomfortably in their chairs, and I knew that some of them must have been convinced by that time that Copplestone was deranged–but no one other than the doctor had shown any sign of wanting to cut the narration short. We had all waited for Copplestone to resume, I more eagerly than any. My anxiety had vanished, and keen curiosity had taken its place.

What if it is true? I thought. *What if he is right, and there is truth in this– truth, perhaps, polluted by fear and fancy, but truth nevertheless?*

I, at least, did not want the professor to stop. I wanted to hear more, if he were able to offer us more. I wanted to hear the story's conclusion, whether it required all night to reach it or not–but this new pause had come at the end of the second of the three parts into which his story was divided, and the doctor rose to his feet with more determination this time.

It seemed that the memory of the parlous state of which Copplestone had spoken was sufficient to recall it; even as he spoke the phrase, he began to perspire very freely, and the tremor in his hands grew into a convulsion which shook his whole body. He picked up a brandy-glass from the table but it slipped from his hand and shattered.

Although he tried with all his might to remain where he was, Copplestone slid from the chair on to the carpet, his body folding up into a quasi-fetal position. The doctor and the curly-haired young man both ran to his aid, but they could not immediately straighten him out, let alone deliver him from the fit which had possessed him.

"Tomorrow is another day, Ned," the doctor said. "You can't continue to-night."

Copplestone recovered himself sufficiently to release a hoarse and bitter laugh, which dissolved into a fit of coughing. "Pour me another brandy, my dear fellow," he murmured.

The doctor was on the brink of refusing the request, but something about Copplestone's eyes would not let him do it. He went to the side-table where the servant had set the decanter and the crystal glasses. He took up the one that I had refused, and poured out a stiff measure. "Anyone else?" he said, as he took it back to Copplestone. Wilde got up to take a glass himself, but no one went with him.

"I must go on," said Copplestone, to all of us. "There is so much to explain. You must forgive me if I sometimes say too much, and sometimes too little, but I must explain."

I could not help but wonder whether he feared that the inhabitants of the far future might be able to reach back through time and snuff out his life like a candle-flame. Why would they want to, even if they could? Did he think that this was the one and only chance he would have to communicate the secrets he had learned? Could he possibly be arrogant enough to suppose that the entire future of the human race might depend on what he said to us tonight–that the march of destiny might be interrupted if he could only empower us to act, and save the human race from the fate which awaited it?

Suppose it were so, I told myself. *Is it not a wonderful conceit? It ought to be true. It ought to be the case that the world itself is hanging in the balance, weighed by this strange company, composed of men of letters and men of science....and me.*

Whatever the reason for his urgency might be, Copplestone was very determined not to bring his discourse to a close while he still had the strength to speak–but he could not do it immediately. The doctor had to hold the glass while he sipped, and the liquor did not seem to be capable of reviving him. His guests waited, with some embarrassment and a good deal of uncertainty.

It was Oscar Wilde who took the trouble to break the silence, making an observation that must have been on the mind of everyone in the room. "If what the professor is telling us is true," he said, laconically, to no one in particular "then, the ancestors of these Overmen must be alive today, hidden in the midst of human society..." When no one answered, he added, mischievously: "There might be one of them within this very company, holding his breath in fear of discovery." He made a show of looking around, to see if anyone were indeed holding his breath.

"They would believe it readily enough in the country of my birth," the naturalized American opined, "and doubtless in yours, Count Lugard. Indeed, I know communists who think that all aristocrats are bloodsucking vampires. We are wiser than that, I hope."

"Was there not a tale put about regarding a soldier who served in Paris during the Second Empire?" asked the doctor's grey-eyed friend, softly. "A Sergeant Bertrand, was it not? Do you recall the case, Count Lugard?"

"Why should I recall it?" I answered, coolly. "It was last year that I was in Paris, not half a lifetime ago. Was this sergeant a shapeshifter, then?"

"The reports were unclear," the grey-eyed man replied, in deadly earnest. "He might have been a werewolf, or a ghoul–but the Protean nature of the accusation would not be inappropriate, if he really were a member of some predatory semi-human species like the one the professor has described."

As he heard this remark, Copplestone smiled, very wanly. He seemed to me to be on the point of collapse, but he was still determined to continue his story if he could–to tell us what he had discovered in the course of his third excursion into the far future.

So completely had the professor's narrative captivated me that I could not help but wonder whether his distress might be the wrath of the unborn inhabitants of an unmade future, recoiling from the uncertain mists of time to strike at the man who threatened the very possibility of their existence. It was absurd, I knew, but what a marvelous absurdity it was!

I understood, then, what Oscar Wilde meant by his ostentatious praise of gaudy lies. How poor a thing it was that common men took for common sense and common knowledge! How narrow a vision it afforded them, how meager and inadequate a meal!

In that instant, I realized that I wanted everything that Copplestone had said to be true. I desired with all my heart to be part of a crucial moment in the history of this world and the million futures that might conceivably proceed from it. I yearned to forget my petty embarrassments and heartaches, and to set aside the awful power that names had to disturb and injure me.

It cannot possibly be a tissue of petty lies, I told myself. *What an adventure the man has had! Even if it has wrecked him, body and soul, has it not been worth it? What traveler has ever had such a fine tale to tell? It should be true. It must be true.*

I arrived then at certain conclusions, and made certain decisions. From that moment on, whatever the destiny of the world might be, mine was set in stone. I knew exactly what I intended to do, and how jealously I must guard the secret of my intention.

"I am very sorry, gentleman" the doctor said, addressing the entire company, although his words must have been intended primarily for Copplestone. "I think you have all realized how desperate Professor Copplestone is to communicate the whole of his story to you in the space of a single night, but I do not believe there is the slightest possibility of his being able to continue at present, and I feel obliged, speaking as his doctor, to forbid him to make the effort. He must be allowed to sleep, and recover himself. Perhaps I might suggest that any of you who have no other engagements–any of you, that is, who are sufficiently interested–might care to return here at 8 p.m. tomorrow, so that the professor can acquaint you with the substance of his third...I dare not say expedition, although that is the word he would probably prefer....shall we say his third vision?"

I could not find it in my heart to admire the man's pedantic caution. He was not a fool, but he was blind to the riches of Copplestone's achievement. They all were–even the most brilliant of them. The men of letters could only see the professor's story as a bold fiction, the men of science as a wild farrago of superstitions. I was the only one who saw hope in it.

Copplestone tried to object, but he no longer had the strength. He was all-but-unconscious.

There was, inevitably, a certain amount of confusion in the company, although everyone present had in the end to agree that what the doctor proposed was the best possible solution.

The manservant was summoned, and he and the doctor removed Copplestone to his bedroom while the rest of us made preparations for our departure.

The pale young man no longer seemed so excitable now, and the hectic flush had long since faded from his features. He seemed a trifle dispirited; I guessed that, however his own oracular vision had proceeded, it had evidently not progressed in any direction similar to what he had just heard. The two men of science had already begun conversing in hurried whispers, while the other young man and the doctor's taciturn companion were staring deep into the glowing embers of Copplestone's fire, lost in problematic contemplation.

"Well," Wilde said to me, not quite sotto voce, "we have had our money's worth, have we not? And a good supper too! What a magnificent fantasist the man is! If only he had not told us of his long experiments with mind-addling drugs I would immediately have proclaimed him a genius, but I fear that he has relied too much on the power of chemical hallucination to be given all the credit for his accomplishments. Even so, it is a fabulous tale–a truly fabulous tale! I wish I had the courage to steal it, but the altercation between our host and young Mr. Wells makes me wary of the consequences of such a theft. Still, it might be worth doing, given that the deftness of my hand could improve it out of all recognition..."

"Be careful, Oscar," I said, making a feeble attempt to mimic his witty manner of speech. "You might start a new fashion, and then where would we be? Every Tom, Dick and Harry would be producing visions of the future. Within a dozen years, we'd have a thousand different fever-dreams to choose from."

"True," he said. "Probably best to leave such things to that sot Griffith-Jones and young Mr. Wells–that way, the fad will surely die stillborn."

As we bustled about, putting on our coats and hats, the conversation continued in a muted but not unfriendly fashion. Apart from myself, only the British scientist had brought his own carriage, and when this became clear he and I swiftly became adamant that we could accommodate all our fellow guests in our spare seats, thus saving them the trouble–which might have been considerable at that hour–of summoning hansoms or risking the terrors of the underground railway.

Upon comparing destinations it became obvious that the most convenient use of resources would be for the two young men of letters to travel with the two men of science, while Wilde and I played host to the doctor and the grey-eyed man. The physician and his dour companion were headed for Baker Street, which was very near, and only a little out of my way, given that I had then to deliver Wilde to his selected home-from-home. For my own part, I resolved to pay a short visit to Piccadilly before going to the house I had rented.

There was some delay while the doctor convinced himself that Copplestone could safely be left to the care of his servants, and in the end, he had to hurry out to the carriage, where his friend had already taken his seat. I tried to dismount, for politeness' sake, but the doctor—who was fumbling at his buttons—cannoned into me and dropped his bag. We both bent to pick it up, and collided yet again.

I took advantage of the confusion to pluck the envelope containing Copplestone's formula out of his jacket, as neatly as the best pickpocket in Paris, and I slipped it unobtrusively into my coat.

7.

As soon as we were under way, I asked the doctor what he thought of Copplestone's remarkable adventures.

"I must reserve my judgment," he said. "I have made the man a promise, and must keep it. But I'll say this much—if he cannot be persuaded to give up this damnable drug, I fear for his very life. He does not know—or will not understand—how ill he is."

"And you, sir?" I asked his friend. "What is your opinion?"

The Detective looked at me very steadily with his solemn grey eyes. "It is the strangest tale I have ever heard," he said, gravely. "If one were to accept its truth, if only as a momentary hypothesis, it would raise many interesting questions and a host of curious possibilities. But I pride myself on my scrupulous use of logic, and I would find it difficult to accept the reality of the art of prophecy without firmer proof. I suppose it would be easier by far to believe that it was the record of a sequence of hallucinations....but I would be interested to hear your opinion of what we have heard."

"I hardly know what to make of it," I said, in a calculatedly off-hand manner. "I fear that I have neither Wilde's love of fabulation nor Mr. Wells' intense interest in the distant future of mankind—and I must admit that I had great difficulty following parts of the narrative. English is not my first language, you know."

"Nor, I think, is French," said the doctor's friend, "although your accent has far more of Paris in it than echoes of your native land, and your clothes were purchased there. Some of your consonants sound Slavic, but whatever its origin might really be, Lugard is certainly not a Slavic name. Your coachman is unmistakably Bavarian, of course. I have known only one other man with a physiognomy similar to yours, and he claimed to be Russian–unfortunately, his name and title proved to be false, and I never did manage to ascertain his true origins. Like yourself, he was an uncommonly fastidious man, who took little or no pleasure in food and wine, and found tobacco smoke distasteful."

I was not amused by this remarkable speech, which seemed more than slightly insulting–and, in any case, implied that I had been closely observed during the course of the evening without my realizing the fact. It was on the tip of my tongue to say that I hoped he did not suspect my name and title of being false, but I knew only too well that one should never tempt fate in such a fashion.

"I say, old friend," said the doctor, uncomfortably, "this isn't one of my infernal stories, you know." He, at least, was fully aware of the fact that acceptance of the hospitality of my carriage carried a certain burden of obligation.

"It is ingrained in the nature of Englishmen to dislike everything foreign," observed Wilde, with mocking disingenuity. "You would not think an Irishman a particularly exotic creature, but everyone in England seems to think me a specimen fit for the Zoological Gardens on the far side of the park. I fear, Count, that you will find many people in London who are morbidly fascinated by the fact that you hail from somewhere east of Calais."

"I meant no offence!" protested the doctor's friend, with all apparent sincerity. "I fear that careful observation of everyone I meet has become a constant preoccupation which I cannot easily abandon for politeness' sake. I am curious, merely curious. I really would like to know what you thought of Professor Copplestone's adventure, Count Lugard."

"After all," Wilde chipped in again, "your opinion as an authentic man of the world is worth a great deal. There is not an Englishman in existence with sufficient romance in his blood to appreciate the story we were told tonight, and I fear that the adoptive American–who is, like all adoptive Americans, trying very hard indeed to be utterly and completely American–is listening with an organic instrument which can only pay attention to matters of electricity and gadgetry. Even the young man from the Caribbean found his attention deflected by his friend's anxiety over the apparent borrowing of his ideas."

"You are, as usual Oscar, quite unjust," I said to him–truthfully enough. "The young man with the high-pitched voice evidently has a soul overfull of romance, and Sir William Crookes is broadminded enough to place equal credence in cathode rays and ghosts. As for Copplestone, who is surely as English as Stonehenge....who could possibly charge him with a lack of romance? The man is an amateur storyteller, to be sure–but what a story he tells!"

"For all its bizarrerie," Wilde said, "the narrative lacks color, wit and action. Were I to tell the tale, how much finer it would be....oh, the temptation!"

"It is a perfectly fascinating tale," I retorted, taking care to sound insincere. "Perhaps I have not your refined aesthetic sensibilities, and perhaps I am the worse for it, but I find Copplestone's vision of the future quite entrancing."

As I spoke these words I glanced at the doctor's friend, challenging him to read the truth of my remarks.

The grey-eyed man said simply: "We will doubtless learn tomorrow whether the human race is to be regenerated thirty thousand years or more from today. I would like to think so–I find Mr. Wells' anticipation of a dark, dead world so very bleak."

"Young men often dally with an extreme bleakness of outlook," said Wilde. "They think it romantically interesting. In fact, it is merely the measure of their own cowardice, in the face of the stings and darts of outrageous fortune. If they are fortunate, they learn to grasp life's nettle. If not, they gradually transform themselves into pusillanimous old men weighed down by acrid regret–and need no shapeshifting gift to accomplish the metamorphosis."

I thought that the doctor shot him a darkly resentful glance, but he said nothing.

"The real point, of course," the grey-eyed man put in, "is not what will happen thousands of years in the future, but what will happen tomorrow and the day after that. Whatever the action of Copplestone's drug is, it is a very remarkable compound, which will certainly repay further study. We may dare to hope that its discovery might be a great boon to mankind, even if it is nothing more than a manufacturer of vivid hallucinations."

"What could mankind possibly need more than a manufacturer of vivid hallucinations?" asked Oscar Wilde–but he was talking about himself, not Copplestone's formula.

"Here is Baker Street," I said to the grey eyed-man, with scrupulous mildness. "Tell me when you want to be set down, and I'll alert the coachman."

"Anywhere above number 200 will do," he replied, as if he were wary of telling me the precise address.

Our au revoirs were polite enough, but a trifle frosty.

"Forgive them, dear boy," said Wilde, once we were under way once again, "for they know not what they are. A consulting detective, indeed! I am by no means devoid of conceit, as you know, but such a frail delusion must be very difficult to entertain! And yet the doctor is as famous a literary man, in his way, as I am. *The Strand* has a huge circulation, the envy of all its competitors and imitators." He sounded more than a little envious himself–he was never a man to conceal his deadly sins.

"As Copplestone rightly says," I observed, sympathetically "there are so many periodicals these days."

"But the only ones really worth reading are in French," he said, mournfully. "Even Lane's *Yellow Book* is conspicuously thin-blooded. I wish it were not so difficult to obtain the *Mercure* in London. There one may find dreams which have delicacy of form as well as bravery of vision. The best French writers always display an appropriate nicety, even when they treat such brutal themes as vampirism. The French vampires of Nodier and Gautier are far more beguiling than their English kin."

"Are there any English vampires?" I asked.

"Not so very many," he replied. "In prose, there has been little more than that ludicrous excrescence of Polidori's, which he tried to pass off as Byron's, and the interminable penny-dreadful adventures of the appalling Varney. Le Fanu's 'Carmilla' is infinitely better than either, but le Fanu is yet another graduate of Trinity, like Stoker–and hence not really English, like myself. Stoker, I believe, is enthusiastically researching the history and folklore of vampirism, so that he might write another 'Carmilla.' If he carries through his intention–and he is nothing if not assiduous–the literary world will doubtless have its due ration of Anglo-Irish vampires. You will not understand this, being a civilized man of the world, but Trinity is a Protestant college in the heart of a Catholic country, built on an ancient cesspit, and it provides uncommonly fertile ground for the growth of feverish tales of exotic outsiders. The Anglo-Irish sometimes think themselves more English than the English, because they have to strive so hard to avoid being Irish, but the English will never support our pretence–they insist that we are outsiders even more firmly than the Irish do."

I could not fully appreciate the bitter undercurrent of feeling which underlay this flippant commentary, but the mention of Stoker recalled to my mind the fact that Copplestone had thought of inviting him to hear the story he had just related. Wilde's revelation that Stoker might be thinking of writing a vampire story might provide the explanation of that fact, but I was by no means happy to learn it. What unfortunate inspiration, I wondered, might Arminius Vambery have communicated to the man?

"Do you know anything about this project of Stoker's?" I asked.

Wilde shrugged. He had turned his face away, as though to look out of the window of the carriage. "Not a great deal," he said. "I told you earlier–we were close once, but we no longer see one another."

"Oh yes," I murmured, without thinking. "You once liked his wife."

"Loved," said Wilde, acidly. "I would have married her myself, but for being haunted by the twin specters of poverty and the pox. And now..." He trailed off.

I was amazed that he said so much. He was tired, and he had had more than a little to drink, but even a man as naturally garrulous as he would surely never have said such a thing in the normal course of conversation with a man he hardly knew. It was not difficult, though, to follow the abandoned line of argument. *An Ideal Husband* had been running for a week and *The Importance of Being Earnest* was in rehearsal. Wilde was set fair for great fame and fortune, and his future was surely brighter by far than Stoker's, whatever their comparative prospects had been 10 or 20 years ago. As for fear of the pox, if he meant by that what I thought he meant, then he must have laid that particular ghost by the time he married Constance Lloyd. Conventional wisdom, I knew, taught that a man diagnosed with syphilis must take the mercury treatment and suffer two years abstinence from sexual intercourse–although I had my doubts, personally, as to whether the mercury treatment had any more effect on that disease than poor Jean Lorrain's blood-supping and ether-swilling had had on his.

"Oscar," I said, on impulse, "I fear that I may not be able to remain in London very long."

"Why is that?" he asked.

"Because certain rumors will doubtless follow me, in time, from Paris. I think your friend Stoker might have heard them already, and he is sure to repeat them if he discovers that I am here–and I fear that the man who just left us is not the only man in London afflicted by infernal curiosity. One such as he would easily root the rumors out, if he had the inclination to try."

"I wish I could say that I never listen to rumors," said Wilde, carelessly, "but you know perfectly well that I always do. I am the subject of so many, and although I pretend to like it....as it happens, I am thinking of going away myself. A clairvoyante I know has foretold that I shall make a pilgrimage to Algeria, and now I have Copplestone's assurance that such prophecies ought to be taken seriously I dare not flout my destiny. Perhaps you ought to come with us."

"Us?" I queried.

"I could not think of going alone to such an uncivilized place," he said, "and poor Bosie is so cut up about Drumlanrig's death. His brother, you know. Even Queensberry liked Drumlanrig, a little."

"I never go so far south," I told him. "I cannot abide the Sun, and its light is so horribly fierce in those latitudes. I like London's grey light much better, and I shall be very sorry to leave."

"You might stand fast against the rumor-mongers," he suggested, mildly. "Let them say what they like, and be damned–or haul them into court for libel. Either would be better than a shooting-match, don't you think?"

I looked at him long and hard, wondering how much he knew–and how much he cared.

"Sometimes," I murmured, "I wish that poor Mourier had fired at my heart, and found his mark."

"But only sometimes," said Wilde, with patient understanding. "We all think ourselves monsters, occasionally–but once we look away from the stubbornly unflattering mirror, there is the world awaiting us, in all its welcoming glory. If nothing else, a tale like Copplestone's puts our petty woes into their proper perspective, does it not? A thousand years hence, you and I and all our world will be mere dust, not even a memory–and no one will know or care what we were, or what we did, or even what we wrote. Let us to our playground, my friend, to amuse ourselves while we may. We'll be long enough dead, when the time comes."

I wished that I could take matters so lightly, and bring such eloquence to the cure of my own heart's sickness, but he and I were not the same kind of man.

"Shall I pick you up tomorrow?" I asked him, as he got down from the carriage.

"I would not miss it for the world," he assured me. "The same time, the same place. I promise that I shall not be late."

Of all his promises, that was worth the least.

8.

It was so late by the time my faithful Bavarian set me down in Piccadilly that the vast majority of the night-birds had returned to their roosts, but I knew by now that the street never quite died, even on the coldest and foggiest of nights. Tonight the fog was very slight indeed; there was nothing but a few stray wisps of mist drifting about the gas-lamps, seemingly gathered there for the sake of the yellow light. The raucous music that spilled from the closed doors of the all-night drinking-dens was muffled only by the doors and curtains set firm to keep the winter cold at bay.

I found the particular night-bird I sought at her station beneath one of the wrought-iron lamp standards. She smiled as she saw me approach.

She was very pale, and her pallor bore the subtly lustrous bloom that is the unmistakable badge of consumption. She made no attempt to cover it with powder; there was no real need, for the smallpox, which had visited her in youth as it visited all the city's poorer children, had left but a single visible scar on her face: an oddly star-like mark on the cheek beneath the left eye.

Her dark eyes were bright, seemingly almost luminous by virtue of the way they caught the lamplight. She had lovely hair, which she kept in very neat trim, and to look at its careful arrangement one might have thought that she had only just descended to the street.

"My Russian Count," she said, as I halted before her. Her voice was low and her pronunciation perfect. I had first been attracted to her as much by her voice as her features; I could not abide dropped aitches and revolting pet-names, and could never understand why so many English whores took such a pride in Cockney vulgarity.

I took her hand in mine, and raised it momentarily towards my lips, although I did not complete the gesture. The hand was very cold.

"You should not stand outside for such long periods," I said, hypocritically. "On a night like this you should retreat indoors, as your sisters do, and place yourself near a blazing fire."

I was at least partly responsible for her chill. She had chosen to remain outdoors because she was waiting for me, although she had no reason to believe that I would come to her tonight–or ever again. She was bound to wait for me, by virtue of the mesmeric spell I had put on her when first we met.

"Will you walk with me, my dear," I said, and she nodded, although not very eagerly.

We strolled off in the direction of Green Park, whose Stygian darkness obligingly provided a curtain to mask the most elementary commerce of the district. Her lack of enthusiasm was easy enough to understand; the ground would be iron-hard and icy, and she had every right to expect greater comfort from a man of my station. She might have objected, but that would have taken a little more courage than she had.

In fact, she had nothing to fear. I had not the slightest intention of taking her into the darkness and laying her down upon the turf. I escorted her along the pavement to a spot equidistant between two of the street-lights. I had no difficulty in making out her features, but she must have been nearly blind to mine. I looked long into her eyes, but it is a cliché of cheap fiction which alleges that a mesmerist must use the authority of his gaze, and it was it more for my sad and somber pleasure than to extend my dominion over her spirit.

I knew that I had only to stroke her cheek a little, and fold my protective arms round her, to make her completely mine.

"Oh my love!" she murmured. It was not a trick of the trade. Perhaps she did speak softly to more casual acquaintances–perhaps she used those very words–but there was no dissimulation in her voice now.

"There is something you must do for me," I whispered, my lips just a breath away from her delicate ear. "I believe that you have the cunning for it. It should not be difficult–the manservant has no company in the house save for his master and the crone who is mistress of the kitchen."

"Anything," she said, almost imperceptibly. She wanted nothing other than to be my slave. How could she?

I pressed a sovereign into her hand, but had to close her nerveless fingers around it to make sure that she held on to it.

"There will be more," I said. "Do this for me, and I will give you everything that is within my power to give." There was hypocrisy in this, too, but there was a kind of honesty too. For once–perhaps for the first time in my life– there was a measure of substance in my seductive promises.

"Tomorrow," I told her, "I will take you home with me. It may be late when I come, but I will come. Trust me, Laura. Trust me."

"My name..." she began–but I put a finger to her lips to silence her.

"Your name," I told her, "is Laura. It has always been, and always will be Laura."

She had tilted her head back, neck bared in that curious instinctive gesture of submission which civilized humans somehow retain: the purely animal gesture of surrender, which offers the throat to a conqueror as a demonstration of faith in the mercy of the strong.

Her name was Laura, and always would be. She accepted that. She was completely in my power.

The situation was familiar, but I was afflicted with an altogether unfamiliar uncertainty as to how it might proceed and develop. I felt that I simply could not go on any longer in the same deep rut—that I had no choice but to step aside from the path which had so far seemed to be my undeniable destiny. After all, had I not told Edward Copplestone that the only destiny was death—and implied without saying it that, outside of death, all things might yet be possible?

I lowered my head slowly, and kissed my darling very gently on the throat, to seal our pact. Then I went home.

Needless to say, Wilde was not ready when I arrived—exactly at the appointed hour—to collect him. By way of apology, he explained that he had been run ragged all day, in a hopeless attempt to catch up with his belated start. I deduced from his sketchy explanations that the rehearsal itself had not gone awry, but that something else was amiss: something he did not care to spell out.

I took the inference that he had seen Lord Alfred Douglas, and that the meeting had come to friction almost immediately. Wilde really did look tired, but it was an exhaustion of the spirit rather than the body—the kind of distress that creeps into the corners of a life that is lived to the full and then beyond.

I was anxious on his behalf; lives lived to the full, let alone beyond, too often fracture under the insidious stress, and fall apart. I wondered whether the day might soon come when he would feel as much need as I for the secret which I had stolen from Copplestone's doctor—but I dismissed the thought. I had suffered the corrosions of Vambery's slanders for many years; wherever I went there was at least one pair of catlike eyes in every crowd which stared at me from beneath lowered lids, and one pair of lips which whispered: "Impostor! Vampire! Monster of depravity!" Oscar Wilde, I thought, was surely insulated from any such fate by his charm and his fame—and, above all else, by his genius. No panther in the world could drag him down and rake him with its claws, even though he was not in the least afraid to feast with their kind. He was tired now, but he would wake more fully than any common man; I was awake, but I had nightmares lying in wait for me every time I closed my eyes.

He saw me studying him, and roused himself; he had a reputation to maintain, even in the security of a carriage with no audience but a foreign friend.

"Irregular hours do not seem to disturb you in the least," he observed, with only the slightest hint of feigned resentment. "You could not have got to your bed before five last night, and yet you seem perfectly refreshed. By way of adding insult to injury you look 10 years younger than I do, although I cannot believe that you are."

"Nonsense," I said, knowing full well that the last thing he wanted was a confirmation of the fact that I was older than he—although of course I was. "You are as handsome as ever, and, now that night has fallen, the gleam is returning to your own eyes. We are two of a kind, you and I; we only come to life after dark, when even the workers of the world must retreat from their toil to the world of thought and imagination: the world where truly human life is lived."

More hypocrisy, I thought, more seduction. But how could one possibly have a conscience about lying to a man who prized great lies far above the humble truth?

"All the workers of the world do not toil by day," he remarked, as my trusty Bavarian took advantage of a rare stretch of clear road to whip his team to a fast trot. "Actors work by limelight, and even playwrights sometimes find inspiration in what common men would call insomnia."

"That is not work," I said, "no matter that it is the means by which some men earn their coin. Work is what happens in the fields and in the factories, producing the bare necessities of life. Wheat and meat, clothing and shelter, are the means of physical survival; their production alone qualifies as authentic toil. The theater belongs to the life of the mind, to the fabulous realm of luxury and whoredom, which is merely the means by which men make life worthwhile."

He looked at me curiously, but did not smile, as I had hoped he might. Perhaps he felt insulted by my implication that what playwrights did was a kind of whoredom rather than a species of true labor. What he actually said, however, was: "Modern factories take no account of day or night. Machines do not care for the sun, or for sleep, but only for power–and because machines are blind and tireless, the men and women who attend them must work shift after shift around the clock. Perhaps it was young Wells, and not Ned Copplestone, who read the meaning of their common dream correctly. Perhaps the tribute of blood was in truth being paid to the machines themselves, not to the overseers whom Copplestone carelessly called vampires."

Wilde's was the fashionable socialism of the upper classes, scrupulously benevolent and safely abstracted from over-extravagant demonstration–but it was by no means insincere. He might have felt a deeper and more painful hatred of social injustice had he been apprenticed to a blacking factory or a draper's shop, but his vision could not be faulted on grounds of clarity.

"I had not thought to find you in such a serious mood," I said, half-apologetically. "I hoped that the anticipation of more gorgeous fabrications would have helped you to be gay."

He made a visible effort, then, to throw off his tiredness and the slight peevishness with which it had infected him.

"You are right, my friend," he said, "as you almost invariably are. We are two of a kind, despite that you are nobly born and I am not. We are true aristocrats of the mind and of the heart. Forgive me for envying your composure. Ever since I wrote the terrible parable of Dorian Gray I have become acutely conscious of the aging process, and there are times when I simply cannot help feeling old. My mind is brilliantly young, but my flesh...."

"I would readily trade my sturdy flesh for an artist's soul like yours," I told him.

He looked at me in the strangest way. "I once wrote a tale of a fisherman's soul," he said, "which was cast out to roam free, rather as Copplestone's soul has roamed, but was so corrupted in he process....oh, enough of this dour allegorization! Let us look forward; let us fix our minds on the remotest future, on the world of the overmen, whose mastery of nature has permitted the transcendence of all frailties. Tell me, Count, do you suppose that the gift of thought will be restored to poor, deprived humanity in Copplestone's third vision? Do you think that they might somehow turn the tables on their vampire conquerors?"

"The good should end happily and the bad unhappily," I quoted, casually. "That is what fiction means. But Copplestone so ardently desires to present us with truth, not fiction, that he will surely disregard such elementary rules. No, I cannot believe that he will end his story as conventionally as that. I trust, however, that he has kept the best of his surprises up his sleeve, and that he will have something to reveal which none of us could possibly anticipate."

I permitted myself a private smile as I said it, thinking that there might be one surprise which I could anticipate–but I spoke more truly than I knew. Because of Wilde's tardiness, we were the last to arrive at Copplestone's house, and because of that we were the last to learn of his death.

9.

We were shown into the dining-room, where the others awaited us. The table was not laid but they were all seated around it, very solemnly. The doctor had taken the place at the head of the table which Copplestone had occupied the night before, and he beckoned us impatiently to be seated. Apparently, they had been waiting for us for some little time.

"This is terrible news, doctor," said Wilde. "How did it happen?"

I, meanwhile, was wondering why we were taking our places, given that the man who was supposed to complete his story was no longer able to discharge that duty. Were we, perhaps, to undertake our planned discussion of the enigmas of destiny after all, as some kind of tribute to the dead man?

"I fear that Professor Copplestone, having fallen asleep last night, simply never woke up," said the doctor. "I had given his manservant an instruction that he was not on any account to be disturbed, and it was not until noon that he finally crept into his master's room and found him dead. He summoned me immediately. The body has been taken away to King's College Hospital, where a *post mortem* examination will be carried out, but I have no doubt of the cause of death. Professor Copplestone poisoned himself with his damnable drugs."

"We cannot be absolutely certain where the responsibility lies," his friend put in. His tone was mild enough, but harbored a fugitive element of threat.

"Why should you doubt it, sir?" said Wilde, less sarcastically than he probably intended. "Surely you can't think that poor Copplestone was murdered?"

"If that were the case," said the Great Detective, soberly, "I doubt that we could ever prove it, given that he was so ready to take poison by his own hand. But he was robbed, and on that account I think we must reserve our judgment as to the precise manner of his death."

"Robbed?" said Wilde. "What was stolen?"

"The vial that he showed to us last night," the grey-eyed man reported. "The vial he intended to offer to us, so that one of us might venture to confirm that his supposed visions of the future were accurate."

"But that surely cannot matter," I put in, smoothly. "Your friend the doctor still has the formula."

"I fear," said the doctor, blushing beneath his whiskers, "that I have not. As soon as I became aware of the theft from Copplestone's laboratory, I checked my pocket, and found that the envelope had disappeared. There is no possibility that I could have dropped it accidentally; it must have been removed from my jacket by a thief, probably while it hung in the closet last night."

"That is not possible, old friend," his companion said. "Had someone entered our rooms, I can assure you that their visit would have left clear evidential traces. I know how reluctant you are to admit that your pocket might have been picked while you were fully awake and alert, but there is no doubt in my mind that that is exactly what happened."

"But who would do such a thing?" asked Wells. "And why? It could not have been one of us, because any one of us could have had the contents of the vial for the asking–there was no need to steal it."

"Perhaps the thief did not care to compete with others for the privilege," said the detective, who clearly felt that he was now getting into his stride. In is own fashion, he was as anxious for an audience as Oscar Wilde.

"I doubt that the competition would have been fierce," said Sir William, drily. "Had the thief known that Copplestone lay dead in his bed, he could have been reasonably certain that there would be a dearth of volunteers."

"Perhaps the professor's worst fears were justified," I suggested, cynically. "Perhaps the vampires who rule the world whose secrets he penetrated did indeed contrive to find a way to reach back into time, so that they might cancel out his discovery, thus promoting their contingent future to the status of destiny. Perhaps we are all in deadly danger now that we have heard the story–or part of it, at any rate; I suppose there is no hope now of our hearing the rest."

"Not so," said Shiel. "It seems that we shall indeed hear the rest, at least in an abridged form. That is one reason why we have not dispersed. We have been waiting for you and Mr. Wilde to join us."

"And what is the other reason?" asked Wilde.

This time, it was the grey-eyed man who answered. "It is not impossible that we might yet be able to shed some light on the mysteries of the stolen vial and the missing formula."

I could see that the detective was doing his best to be diplomatic, but Wilde was not the only person present who bridled at the implication that we were all to be interrogated on suspicion of being thieves.

"Aha!" said Wilde, sourly. "So we are to have the privilege of watching the Great Detective at work! And will you, Mr. Shiel, be pitting your methods against his?"

It seemed that the curly-haired young man did not know whether to smile or frown, but I observed that the great detective was honestly puzzled.

"How did you know that...?" the young man began—but he stopped even before Wilde interrupted him, having divined that the answer was obvious.

"I have my methods too, dear boy," said Wilde, airily. "I have an indefatigable ear for gossip, and nothing that happens at the sign of the Bodley Head escapes my notice. Every aspiring writer in London—with the possible exception of Mr. Wells—has been impressed by the awesome success of the doctor's reportage. I dare say that you are not the only one to have a book of detective stories forthcoming, although I am quite positive that you are the only one to have modeled his detective on dear Count Stenbock."

"Count Stenbock!" exclaimed the doctor, incredulously.

"I merely tried to remain true to the spirit of Edgar Allan Poe," said the young man, disingenuously. "He, after all, is the true father of the detective story. If I have been a little fanciful—well, even the good doctor is fanciful in his own way, and..."

He was interrupted by the grey-eyed man, who called for order by rapping his knuckles sharply, and rather rudely, upon the table. "This is a serious matter," the pretended detective said, sternly. "Copplestone is dead, and the remainder of the drug that induced the remarkable dreams whose contents he confided to us last night has certainly been stolen. I accuse no one, and it is certainly not beyond the bounds of possibility that rumors of his achievements have escaped, despite his determination to quell them, but the fact remains that the only people who knew in any real detail what Copplestone believed he had discovered are here in this room. The doctor and I have questioned the servants, but my friend is quite sure, on the basis of his long acquaintance with Copplestone's household, that neither of them had any real idea of the nature of their master's work, and hence no evident motive for the theft."

"I cannot see that any of us had an evident motive," said the American. "There was nothing in what we heard last night to suggest that Copplestone's visions were anything more than mere delusion, and Mr. Wells gave us some reason to suspect that the delusion may have had a perfectly ordinary seed in something Copplestone had read or heard about."

"Quite so," I agreed, savoring my hypocrisy. "I cannot see that any one of us could have concluded that there might be profits to be made out of this drug, nor that any one of us would have been inspired to take out a patent in order to corner the market."

Tesla's eyes narrowed, but he said nothing. He was not sure whether or not I was insulting him by implication. In fact, of course, I was merely introducing a red herring into the discussion.

"As far as I can see," Wells put in–apparently in much the same spirit, though doubtless without any covert motive to compare with mine–"there are only two people in this room who had ample opportunity to seize both the vial and the formula. Has anyone here been to this house today, except for the doctor and his friend?"

"That," said the Great Detective, seemingly untroubled by the back-handed accusation, "is one thing we ought to ascertain."

Understandably, no one confessed to having visited the house. I assumed that no one had. I had not; there had been no need, when I could so easily send another in my stead.

"Are you quite certain, doctor," said Wilde, "that Copplestone never woke again after falling asleep last night? Is it possible that he got up and went to his laboratory? If it is, then he might have removed the vial himself. Perhaps he discarded the compound, having thought better of his offer to let us poison ourselves with it. Perhaps he quaffed it himself–surely it is possible, if not more than likely, that the contents of the vial provided the dose which killed him?"

The doctor considered the hypothesis. "I cannot prove that he never woke up again," he admitted. "If, perchance, he did drink the contents of the vial...I have to admit that it might have killed him. I begged him not to increase the dose again following the second experiment, but he would not listen. As he came out of his coma for the last time, he suffered a severe physical disturbance. I could not credit his own explanation of this phenomenon, and I think it not unlikely that Copplestone's brain had become permanently vulnerable to fits like the one that apparently caused his death. Any dose, however small, might have finished him off."

"But we could not find the marked vial," the grey-eyed man pointed out. "It certainly was not beside him when he died, as it certainly would have been had he drunk its contents. That implies..."

"Excuse my interrupting," said Shiel, who was perhaps overkeen to find an opportunity to display his own instinct for detective work, "but exactly what was this explanation which you could not credit, doctor?"

The doctor shook his head, but not in denial. "Copplestone imagined that he was somehow being attacked," he said, in a slightly uncomfortable tone. "He could not shake off the suspicion he had formed while he was aboard the flying machine–I mean, while he dreamed that he was aboard the flying machine–that the face on the screen was urgently desirous of finding out where and when he

156

came from in order that the men–I mean Overmen–of the future might attempt to reach back into the past....just as Count Lugard has suggested, albeit in jest."

"Rumor has it that many a true word is spoken in jest," said Wilde, smoothly. "Perhaps the Count is right. Perhaps Copplestone was murdered by the inhabitants of a contingent future in order to prevent his setting in train the chain of causality that might have nipped the victory of the Overmen in the bud and condemned their entire future history to the oblivion of non-existence. Perhaps we are all in danger."

"This is a complete waste of time," said Tesla. "If we are here to listen to the third part of Copplestone's story, then let's hear it. Otherwise, I for one intend to be on my way. I've no intention of sitting here while some amateur sleuth interrogates me as to my movements because he thinks I might be a thief."

"How is it, exactly," I inquired, curiously, "that we may hear the third part of the story, given that poor Copplestone is no longer alive to tell it?"

"I have discovered," said the doctor, "that there is a written version of Copplestone's third dream, which he must have made almost immediately after the experience–as soon as I let him alone, in fact. His suspicions regarding the attempts which might be made by the people of the far future to prevent his publicizing his discoveries, however absurd they may have been, were quite real. The verbal accounts that he gave us of his first two dreams were, of course, much fuller and more considered than this written version of his third dream, and I am certain that had he had the chance to tell the story himself he would have elaborated considerably upon it, but..."

"Oh, get on with it, man!" said Wilde, intemperately.

The doctor looked around for moral support, but there was little to be found, even from his friend. The majority opinion obviously agreed with Wilde. The doctor, somewhat shamefacedly, left the room to fetch the relevant document.

"Let us leave the matter of the theft to one side, for now," said the amateur detective, equably–exactly as if it were his own idea and his own decision to do so. I noticed, however, that his eyes were fixed on me. I could not help wondering what he might possibly have deduced or found out that had inspired him to favor me with such a glance, but I told myself sternly that it was only coincidence, and I was very careful to meet his gaze without giving the least hint of any discomfiture.

10.

"You must remember," said the doctor, "that these documents were not intended for publication. They are, in effect, hurried aides memoires with a few supplementary notes of a very brief nature. There is doubtless much of Copplestone's experience that is omitted altogether, or referred to only obliquely, and what passes for straightforward reportage is continually interrupted by comments, questions and what I can only describe as philosophical rhapsodies. The contents of the conversations I had with Copplestone following his experiments provide a context that sometimes allows me to interpret his meaning a little more easily than an unprepared reader, but there is much herein which remains wholly mysterious to me."

In the privacy of my thoughts, I echoed Wilde's admonition–but the doctor was ready at last, and he began to read:

"What confusion! What astonishment! I must be calm. I must at least try to make a sober and intelligible record. To put pen to paper is to diminish the experience ludicrously, perhaps to distort it utterly, but I must try.

"The beginning. The hill again; the slope was not as steep, perhaps because of the erosions of wind and rain, perhaps due to an altogether arbitrary shift in the pattern of the land. The forest was very different: huge trees, far taller and straighter than anything known on Earth in my own time; the foliage, seen from below, presented mixed colors ranging from turquoise to purple; the light filtering through the canopy was subdued and bluish–presumably comfortable to the eyes of the overmen.

"The purpose of the forest may be–must be–to make the daylit world as comfortable a place for Overmen as the world by night....but there were no Overmen there, only machines. Machines everywhere! Many were tiny metal cells, which were able to associate, as the golem did, in order to transform themselves into complex 'organisms.' What are the limits of their virtuosity? How many different kinds are there? Why did organic life not evolve according to this pattern, so that hordes of protozoans might come together to take whatever form might suit their temporary circumstances?

"Perhaps it did, for a while. Perhaps the shapeshifting Overmen were the product of some such evolutionary sequence.

"The machines immediately responded to my presence. This time, I expected it. It matters not at all that it had been 10,000 years or more since my last manifestation; once a society has true history, nothing can be lost or forgotten, and machines are exceedingly patient. It would not have mattered to those watching for me had I never embarked upon my third expedition–they would have waited forever, without impatience, without disappointment.

"No flying machine this time. No journey. No confrontation. No locking of curious stares by Man and Overman, victim and vampire, primitive and sophisticated. Had I realized what was happening I would have been frightened and appalled, but the process of possession was invisible and painless. The insectile machines came, saw, associated, did their work and dissolved.

"The touch, when it came, was almost imperceptible.

"What the machines did, essentially, was to make more machines, even tinier than they: ephemeral machines whose magnitude was akin to that of those bacterial organisms which are, as Pasteur has recently proved, the agents of disease. Having done this, they infected me with the 'artificial germs' they had made.

"Were the mechanical germs specifically designed to infect a timeshadow rather than a whole body? If so, how? Does the ability of the machines to employ this mode of communication imply that the Overmen have now added this kind of precognition to the repertoire of their mental abilities? How complete is their mastery of time? Have they, at last, become managers of contingency, architects of destiny?

"There are, of course, other questions that have now to be added to those which occurred to me as the knowledge of what had been done to me was slowly made clear. Did the infectious agents bind so intimately to my timeshadow that I brought them back with me? Might they be the seeds of my destruction?

"That is difficult to believe–far more likely, I think, that only the material making up my timeshadow can possibly return–but perhaps this is mere wishful thinking. In 30,000 years, what might men not accomplish?

"I mean, of course, not men but Overmen....if the Overmen are to be believed, mere men are too violent to be capable of much achievement, too ready to destroy one another and hence to destroy themselves...

"What, in the end, did I actually do in the course of my third excursion into the future? Nothing–or nearly nothing. I walked to the top of the hill, where I found a gap in the forest canopy, beneath which green grass grew (left there for my benefit?–surely that is too narcissistic an interpretation?) There, I was able to see the blue sky I had always known, and the white clouds, and the yellow halo of the Sun.

"Later, I was able to see the stars....the same, fixed stars. I was able to see everything that was constant, everything that linked my world to the world in which I had come. I was allowed to see that nothing truly fundamental had changed.

"All I actually did, with my absurdly heavy-seeming half-body, was to walk to the crest of a hill and sit down on the grass, for half a day and half a night, or perhaps a little more. And yet I saw the world of the Overmen, in all its grandeur and glory!

"It was surely not an experience planned and executed solely for my benefit; it was, I must accept, a kind of adventure available to any and every inhabitant of that fabulous era. In that far future, no mind will require the carriage of the body to go wandering, nor will any require the kind of crude separation which my time machine induces. Perhaps the Overmen have finally mastered the art of timeshadow projection (far more cleverly than I, if so), but it is more than likely that they have not bothered, because they have something far better. They have machines that can infect a body like the agents of disease, but are designed for creation rather than malaise. They have machines too tiny to see, which breed in the blood and swarm about the brain–yes, even the anemic fluids that course throughout a timeshadow, even the shadow-brain that preserves a time-shadow's intelligence–and which, in time, induce the brightest and most brilliant of fevers: the fever of synthetic experience; the fever of artificial memory; the fever of knowledge.

"I wish I could say 'wisdom' instead of knowledge....and perhaps that was what the machines were designed to give me, had I only had a complete body. Perhaps what they did give me was incomplete and distorted, by virtue of my attenuation. Perhaps, if I had only been whole, the Overmen could have filled me with all their wealth of understanding....and perhaps they tried to do exactly that.

"Perhaps, on the other hand, they do fear the vicious circle that might result from the communication of too much knowledge from future to present (or present to past). Perhaps they were very careful to give me a vision without coherence....a vivid dream censored of all that might enable me to hasten its actualization.

"There is no way of knowing. What I have is what I have. What I did, within the spaces of my skull, while I sat in the clearing in that alien forest, is what I did...

"I have walked on the surface of the planet Mars: the Mars we see but dimly through our telescopes; the arid, near-airless Mars of pink sands and jagged ridges, awesome clefts and gouged-out craters; the Mars of my today. And I have walked on the surface of their Mars: the Mars of the Overmen; the moist, scented Mars of purple skies and blue-black forests; the Mars of seemingly-eternal half-light; the Mars of gargantuan gliders and gossamer-winged skycraft; the Mars of their today...

"I have walked on the surface of Titan, satellite of Saturn: the Titan that is to us a mere point of light; the Titan entombed by many kinds of ice; bare, brutal, lonely Titan. I have walked, too, on the Titan of the Overmen: the Titan of crystalline cities; the Titan of domed jungles; lush, lovely, hectic Titan. And from both stations, I looked up at Saturn itself; at Saturn's rings; at the gaseous face whose features had, in the second instance, at last begun to change, to harden, to become distinct...

"I have seen the worlds inside the asteroids: the hollow worlds whose inhabitants had remade themselves, four-armed because they had no need of legs. I had no need to walk there either, and so I flew, on wings that were a part of me, and danced their four-handed jigs all around the decorated walls...

"I have seen the Earths which orbit other stars: the myriad Earths, the countless Edens. I have trod the streets and soils of worlds where life has followed other paths than ours. I have seen and known sentient creatures made in every pre-existent image, and in none, some like earthly animals or plants, others seemingly mineral, and some without fixed form at all. I have heard their speech and their music–and I have seen too that these species, like the Overmen, obtain in the end command over their own forms, their own attributes, their own ambitions...

"I have seen the wonderful wilderness of life in the sidereal system: the life of a million worlds; the life of 1000 starfaring cultures; the life that fills the great gaseous clouds between the stars; the life that is irrepressible, uncontainable, ever-changing. I have watched the many meetings of the minds and bodies of different species, have been party to their communions, their mergings and their separations...

"I have not seen humankind. In all of that, I have not seen humankind.

"The satyrs and the centaurs passed into oblivion without eventual issue; the descendants of my own kind never found an upward path of progress to follow for a second time. Homo sapiens will die, and will be gone for ever; ours is a broken strand upon the loom of destiny, but it does not matter. Our kings and queens, our capitalists and merchants, our servants and factory-hands, will give no children to this vast unpatterned confusion, but all that we truly are and represent–our every thought, our every property–is there.

"In this great scheme, the Overmen are our brothers and not our conquerors; they are our other selves, our heirs, our ambassadors to the universe. In this vast overarching scheme, all species are our brothers, our other selves. We are life, and life is everywhere, the image of God in which we are made is neither a face nor a form nor even a soul, but a movement, an impulse, a will to exist, to grow and to change, to be and to become...

"I have seen the worlds which the Overmen have come to know, and I have seen that I belong there no less than they...

"Is it an illusion? Is it simply an effect of my infection by the tiny machines that they left to tutor me?

"Perhaps. How can I know? How can I know whether any of it is more than mere illusion, or some feverish effect of this infection which I have unleashed upon myself with my seer's potion, my subtle poison, my loquacious oracle?

"While I lay down on that hillside, I was dreaming. It was all a dream, and a dream inside a dream at that....but within the dream within the dream there were further dreams, worlds within worlds.

"Like a spark of light, and as fleet, I soared among the stars.

"I saw the sidereal system from without, and from its light-filled heart. I saw stars born from dark dust, and I saw stars die, in vast explosions which left behind mere shrinking embers, which collapsed and collapsed and collapsed until nothing was left of them but the purest form of nothing, the ultimate blackness, the shadow of eternity.

"I saw, outside the sidereal system, other such systems, each one surrounded by a cage of darkness so huge and so dense as to beggar the imagination, and I saw these systems extending into unimaginable distances, millions upon millions of them, all flying apart as if they were the debris of an explosion which was the universe itself...

"It is oddly easy, now, to believe that the universe itself is not something still, something settled, something made and left for dead, but rather something happening, and happening violently, something growing and changing, and that time itself is a headlong rush.....

"We think of ourselves and our world as calm things–nearly tranquil, almost still–but we are not. We are universes ourselves, filled with tiny creatures, sometimes fevered by their intangible attentions. There is so much darkness in the world without, and in our inner being too, that we think of existence as a faint and flickering thing in a great illimitable void, but it is not–for the darkness of the void without and the void within likewise reflect the limitations of our senses, and not the absence of process.

"Within and without, we and the world are far more alive than we know, and it does not matter, in the end, that each and every one of us will die, that the race of men will die, that the race of overmen will die, that the universal explosion itself will leave behind nothing in the end but the purest form of nothing, the ultimate blackness–because everything is a part of everything...

"That is the one and only truth, the one and only destiny.

"Did I truly dream all that, or did I simply come to know it? Is it a conclusion reached by my own effort, or something the machines fed into me, already whole, roiling rhetoric and all? Does it matter, given that it is there inside me, woven into the fabric of my soul, capable of flowing from pen to page?

"How shall I tell others what I have seen?

"Above all, slowly and gently, one step at a time. Were they to read this without adequate preparation, they would simply think me mad. Perhaps I am mad. Perhaps the function of the machines which invaded me was to derange me, to destroy me, to make certain that my glimpses of the future could not change the past. But that would probably be unnecessary. Is there any hope at all of alerting men to the presence in their midst of those whose descendants will be the Overmen? If they could be alerted, could they do anything to alter their fate? Could they become less warlike, less self-destructive, less blind to their particular destiny? Would it make any material difference, in the longer term, if that were so? Should we not simply be glad that our heritage of intellect will not die with our brutish instincts, but will pass into minds at least as wise, and hands at least as clever?

"What should I do with my discovery? Am I already fated to bury it, given that the futures I have visited seem unaware of any timeshadows but my own? Or am I free to give dozens, hundreds or thousands of others the ability to flood the future with timeshadows, emanating from my own era and many later ones, augmenting and overlaying the possibilities that I have glimpsed.

"This is a conundrum that I cannot hope to solve alone; I must have help.

"I saw....how can I possibly record all that I saw? How can I even remember it? It is fading already in my consciousness, dying like a dream which the waking mind tries with all its might to trap and hold, but loses in the end....and after all, what I actually did was to lie upon the grass, staring up into the darkening sky, watching the stars come out. All else was but an illusion, a disease of the brain, a disturbance in my soul....except, of course, that it was true.

"All true, and all real: preserved, synthesized, packaged, projected into the theater of my mind by some infinitesimal phantasmagoria or kinematograph, but quite real.

"I have walked upon the surface of the planet Mars, today and tomorrow. I have seen the planet dead and I have seen it brought to life.

"I have seen tomorrow's creators laboring in their laboratories to make and reshape life. I have seen the hustle and bustle of Creation: not the work of a mock-fatherly God overfond of prohibitions and petty acts of vengeance, but the work of men who are able to manipulate germ-plasm, who have mastery of the mysteries of the flesh. I have not seen the maker of stars crying *fiat lux* into the darkness, but I have seen the makers of Overmen and the remakers of worlds, busy in the crucible from which all the Golden Ages of the future will be born.

"I have come face to face with the black eyes of the infinite, and met their terrifying stare–not bravely enough, I confess, but not so steeped in terror as to be struck blind...or dumb...or dead.

"It was not all seeing and hearing, of course. The things that infected my brain, to bring the news of infinity and eternity directly to my synapses, were masters of all the senses and all the emotions. I felt the texture of the future, the rhythm of the spheres, in the secret chambers of my heart....

"What nonsense! Am I not a man of science, a man of precision? What respect will anyone have for me if I descend to such fatuous nonsense? And yet....the machines which undertook the task of my education did try to make me feel what no human could ever feel for himself; they did try to communicate to me what the existence of an overman is like, from the standpoint of an overman's self-regard.

"What little did I salvage from that, and how can I possibly describe it?

"How indeed?

"Very well...I have looked at the world with an Overman's eyes. I have responded as he would respond. I have stood in the shoes of an Overman of my own day, of my own present, and have looked at my fellow men with his eyes, with his fearful and resentful heart, with his hunger.

"I have felt the hunger of vampires....the hunger and ecstasy of vampires.

"I am the prey, privileged to have felt the anticipatory surge of the predator's blood; I am the unwary, privileged to have felt the uncalm consciousness of the hidden; I am the human, privileged to have felt the triumph of the superhuman.

163

"I have tasted and understood the hunger and ecstasy of vampires. I have seen the altar on which humankind is to be sacrificed–and I have worshipped at that altar.

"I have stood in the shoes of an Overman of the far future, too. I have known what it is to have tamed hunger and ecstasy, to have brought them to heel, to have made them docile.

"They wanted me to stay! Whatever possessed me begged me to stay and not return, begged me to consent....but I could not. I could not do it. I dared not do it. My sense of duty was stronger, in the end, than their temptation.

"Perhaps I am mad.

"I have known the peace of the ultimate Overmen, and would not accept it as a gift. I have been in Heaven, and threw myself out, like a sinful angel, to fall through all eternity into the blackness of the pit.

"Yes, I am mad...but I have known ataraxia, the perfect peace of mind–which comes not from the strangulation of emotion, nor from the transcendence of the passions, nor from mechanization or denial or anesthesia, but from discipline, from control...and I have understood what it was and is in human beings that needed and needs to be been extinguished, lest humankind itself should die....and, of course, did die....to be replaced by something gentler, kinder, wiser, better....something that emerged from the dark edges of nightmares, from the anxious recesses of myth, to be–when seen in its own light–something merely different, and not so very different at that: a blurred mirror-image, but recognizably akin. A brother.

"A blood-brother.

"If only we could recognize what we truly are, we would surely be less afraid of what we are not.

"If only we could see the monster that we are making of ourselves, we might be able to see that the images of fear and hate that our minds conjure up, so vividly and so prolifically, contain something good and wise...

"I might have stayed, but I could not. I might have stayed, but I did not. I chose to return, to my poor poisoned self, my poor dying body, my time of tragedy.

"If only...

"I am ill. There is no doubt about it. Not because I have carried back any vestige of that glorious delirium with which the machines of the far future infected me so carefully....they are gone; I cannot doubt it. I am ill because of what I have done to myself.

"The good doctor was right about the dangers, the convulsions. I am poisoned. In seeking to gain intelligence of the future, I have cut myself adrift from the present. Did the seers of old understand that there was a price to pay for overmuch success? Did the sibyls who served the ancients fully understand their self-sacrifice?

"Why did I not stay? Why did I not accept the gift that was offered?

"God, how my arm aches! What a rack my grip upon the pen has become!

"I ought to write all day and all night. I ought to write and write, until I have wrung from my inarticulate heart every last vestige of the knowledge by which I have been possessed....but I cannot. Forgive me, but I cannot.

"If I am to tell my story at all I must tell it verbally, all of it–tell it in a single night, if I can, to men that I can trust....men who might understand. If only I knew 100 who might begin to understand....

"If only I knew ten.

"If only..."

11.

The doctor looked up from the manuscript. He had been reading like an automaton, but with evident effort.

"I fear," he said, uneasily, "that Copplestone had reached the limit of his endurance by this time, and the limit of his legibility. He did try to continue, but there are only a few more words I can decipher. He tried, at least, to make a list of some kind....perhaps a list of topics accessory to what I have just read, which were to be added to a later draft. I will read those which I can make out. To the best of my estimation, the list includes the following:

"*Hist Reconst. Great War. Wire and Gas. Vampires don't kill. Hide in Comfort. Atom Bomb. Fusion. Birth Pills. Silicon Clips. Vs love flying. Thrive in cities–art light. Land on moor. Great Plague War. Clathrates. Oceans die, then rise. Ozone shield. Shapeshifters immune to rad poison. Proofs. Electricity. Cathode rays.* There are half a dozen other words, of which I can make no sense at all.

"At the foot of the last page, separate from the rest of the text, a list of five surnames has been scribbled. Mine is one–the only one not followed by a question-mark. Sir William Crookes is another; Wilde's and Shiel's are there also. The last is, I think, Stoker."

My overloaded train of thought was jolted very slightly by that name, but there was far too much to wonder at without bothering with such an insignificant reflex.

What a reward I have reaped by following my instinct! I thought. What a wise providence it was which led me to steal the elixir and the secret of its making! How could I ever have doubted my impulse or my destiny, even for a moment? Everything is clear now, everything settled, everything right. All my life– all my wicked, wretched, willful life–has been naught but an enigmatic prologue, a prelude to this moment. How can I doubt it? Even before I heard the summons loud and clear, I did what I had to do. All my life I have been groping towards the kindly light, hardly knowing how blind I was. And now, it is clear. At last, it is clear.

Even Wilde, I knew, could not possibly complain about a lack of imaginative excess in the peculiar diatribe we had just heard...but even a man like Wilde might struggle in vain to penetrate the meaning of the bolder half of it. Infectious machines! A universe of teeming vermin! Existence as explosion! The ultimate nothing! Was even Wilde, I wondered, capable of seeing it as something more than a mere fever-dream, not far removed from gibberish? Was Crookes–or Shiel–or the imaginatively ambitious Wells? I was all agog to find out.

As for myself, I had no doubts at all. If Copplestone had not seen the future, he had certainly seen something immeasurably valuable: something that no man of this or any earlier time had ever seen before. Let it be the future! I said to myself, silently. Great Father of us All, let it be the future of destiny, unalterable by any human deed or freak of chance!

"No doubt Copplestone would have give us a much clearer account of his final adventure had he been able to do so," said the doctor, awkwardly. Clearly he had had only the vaguest notion of what the manuscript contained before he began to read, and now had not the slightest notion of what it all signified. "No doubt he would have prepared us far better to discuss its implications..."

"I am not sure that any elaborate discussion is necessary," his friend put in. "We have all heard the story–or as much of it as Copplestone contrived to reveal–and each one of us will doubtless make of it what he will. There are other matters which require our immediate consideration."

"On the contrary," Wilde said. "We are here at Copplestone's invitation, for a purpose which he defined. He has gone to some trouble to make his story known to us, and our first duty is surely to do what he required of us: to make our reactions known to one another, and exchange views as to the precise implications of what he had seen. We have accepted the man's hospitality, and we owe him that, even though he is not here to listen to us."

The Great Detective threw up his hands. "Oh, very well!" he said. "There is time to waste, I suppose. Justice is rarely swift, but it is inexorable." He looked at me as he pronounced this blatant lie, but I looked calmly back.

"Perhaps," said Wilde, effortlessly usurping the doctor's role as chairman, "Mr. Wells would like to begin, as he has been enthusiastic to point out certain similarities between Copplestone's vision of the future and his own."

The young man was embarrassed, but the proffered opportunity was not unwelcome to him. He took a deep breath. "I freely admit," he said, slowly, "that the similarities between Copplestone's vision and my story are, in the final analysis, less striking than the differences. Nevertheless, the similarities are still a matter of some interest to me. I will accept. for the sake of argument, that no conscious or unconscious imitation was involved–although the possibility remains, I think, that someone who read the first version of my story in the *Science Schools Journal* might in the course of the last few years have communicated its contents to Professor Copplestone in such a manner that he built a fantasy of his own upon their foundation.

"I regret, however, that I cannot seriously entertain Sir William's hypothesis that I am a true seer who has glimpsed–as through a glass, darkly–am alternative variant of the future that Copplestone has seen. I would rather fall back on the less dramatic but more likely hypothesis that Copplestone and I are both products of our milieu and our moment. We shared the same present day for some 30 years, and probably acquired much the same understanding of it. Although he was older than I, and born into a different class, he must have undergone broadly similar educative experiences. He discovered Darwin's theory of evolution, as I did, and realized with a shock as profound as any religious enlightenment what it implies about the precariousness of man's tenure upon the earth. He came to appreciate, as I have, that the rapid advancement of technology will very soon equip our armies with weapons so powerful that we might easily destroy civilization before learning to curb our primitive impulses. If he and I have visited the Delphic Oracle of the modern imagination and come back with similar prophesies, it is because the Age of Reason has now reached the stage at which secure rational foresight is possible–albeit foresight steeped in anxiety and dread."

Wells paused for thought, seeming very young and very frail as he struggled with the burden of his intellect, but he was swift to take up the thread of his argument. "There is bound to be much in any man's vision of this sort that is the product of idiosyncratic interests and anxieties. Copplestone knew it, and freely admitted the probability that his vision would be polluted, in the way that all our dreams are polluted, by random imps of perversity. Within each and every one of us, a constant battle is fought between a higher, rational fraction of our being and a lower, animal part. Copplestone's vision is clearly haunted by a strange darkness of the soul, which persists in populating his imagined future with phantoms–the phantoms he calls vampires. I do not think that we should take Copplestone's vampires any more literally than we take Polidori's Vampyre, or Christina Rossetti's goblins. They are, I think, symbols: symbols of something deep-lying within all of us, but which we feel, in concert with the prudery of our times, that we ought to exorcise or deny.

"I believe that Copplestone protests far too much when he insists that his Overmen are not human beings at all, but some other species that has lived since the dawn of time among us, mimicking humans in order to prey upon us. I think that we should look for the source of Copplestone's imaginary vampires in the blood that is supposedly their nourishment: the blood that carries the chemical substance of our feelings, our desires and our passions. It is clear, I think, from the tenor of the professor's narrative–especially in the final part, which is surely the product of a purely subjective delirium–that he could not quite escape the essential truth. Despite all his attempts to distance himself, he ended up identifying with the vampires, seeing as they saw and feeling as they felt. What he saw in that final vision is far more closely related to his private mental life than to any meaningful picture of what the future could or will be like. The heavy emphasis on the idea of infection proves that, to my mind, beyond the shadow of a doubt.

"In brief, I think that there may be some truth in the earlier phases of Copplestone's story, but I cannot believe that it arrived there by any occult means, and I do not think that the story has any special relevance to the question of whether the future which will come to be is already destined, or merely contingent on decisions and discoveries we might or might not make. Yes, of course we have important choices to make–choices that we must make under circumstances that are not themselves of our own choosing, and are at least partly beyond our control–but we need not and must not search for scapegoats to bear the burden of our own inadequacies. We must look to ourselves, for it is ourselves that we must reform."

It was an impressive speech, in its way, and I was glad to hear it. I suspected that it would set a sober and sententious tone for what would follow, and might well draw the entire discussion into a blind alley. I had not the slightest objection to such a deflection.

"Thank you," said the doctor. "Mr. Shiel, would you like to comment on what your friend has said?"

The curly-haired man hesitated before replying. His experience, I think, had been a little closer to mine than to his friend's. He had felt the same shock, the same thrill....but he was young, and did not yet know how to trust the wisdom of his soul.

"It might easily take half a lifetime," he said, eventually, "fully to digest the implications of what we have heard these last two nights. In broad terms, Wells is probably right. We cannot doubt that Copplestone really experienced these things, and we must be prepared to consider, if only as an hypothesis, that there is some truth in his vision. It does seem probable that the vampires of his dream are not what Copplestone took them to be....but I wonder whether it might not be the case that the final vision was the most rather than the least truthful: the one least confused by the impish froth of pure dream. I wonder whether that incredibly hectic and vivid vision might not have been the grasping of the very essence of evolutionary process and universal destiny...."

The young visionary was warming to his task now. "If there is a lesson to be learned from this dream," he went on, "it is a lesson in the politics of evolution, and the irresistibility of progress. If there is a revelation in it–and I am certainly prepared to entertain the notion that the mind of God is occasionally reflected in the tinier thoughts of man–it is a Nietzschean revelation that speaks to us of the way in which life is forever destined to climb towards dizzy heights of enlightenment.

"The arrogance that once informed men that they were at the centre of creation, that the Earth and the universe entire had been made for them, is something that must now be put away, with other childish things; we must realize and understand that there will indeed be Overmen, whose task it will be to take up the torch of progress when our imperfections lead us to exhaustion. We should not see this supersession as a terrible thing, but as a confirmation of the fact that our sojourn upon this earth has not been in vain, and that the gift of our blood–which is surely symbolic of the heritage we shall pass on to our successors–is well worth the giving. The fact that our species is, indeed, doomed to disappear should delight us rather than disappointing us, once we understand that we are to give way to another that will be better and bolder, which will build so magnificently on foundations that we have laid as to become godlike in ambition and achievement.

"If what we have heard is a dream and only a dream, then I will say this: men who can dream such dreams are already Overmen in embryo. To the extent that the future is not predestined, it must be built out of the dreams of the present; if men were not capable of dreaming such dreams as Copplestone's, they would be unable to produce futures of any kind akin to that previsioned here–and that would be a tragedy. Let us not worry unduly as to the exact extent of the truth or falsehood of this particular vision; let us be profoundly glad that a man has proved himself capable of dreaming thus, and let us hope that we ourselves might not be incapable of similar triumphs."

I saw one or two of the others–including Wilde–smile indulgently at Shiel's wild enthusiasm, but the doctor's friend was the only one whose eyes were raised impatiently to heaven.

It was Crookes who took up the thread.

"I am naturally disappointed," he said, gravely, "that the insights into the nature and possible applications of electricity, which Copplestone hoped to offer us, have not in the end materialized. But I have more than one field of scientific interest, and Copplestone's adventure bears on the other as well. We are on the threshold of a new era of discovery in the science of apparitions and communication with the spirits of the dead, and it seems to me that what Copplestone has achieved is yet another proof of the reality of apparitions.

"If this story is to be taken seriously–and like these young men, I cannot doubt its sincerity, although I certainly doubt that its conclusion was any more than a delirious episode–then the intriguing possibility has been raised that at least some apparitions may be objects temporarily displaced in time rather than the enduring shades of the departed, and it may well be that some of the confusion that presently arises in the course of communication with what are assumed to be spirits is accountable in these terms. I would certainly like to bring Copplestone's story to the attention of my colleagues in the Society for Psychical Research. I think some of them may be better qualified than I to speculate about the possible reality of vampires. Tesla, of course, will not agree with me..."

This was an unwise inclusion in what might have been a much longer discourse. Tesla, as Sir William had anticipated, did not agree, and wanted to make his disagreement clear.

"It'd take more than a few suggestions about the nature of ghosts to recompense me for the loss of Copplestone's supposed discoveries in electrical science," the American said. "When a promise like that is made and not fulfilled, an American begins to smell hokum. I know this guy is a professor, and I know all about your English regard for the word of a gentleman, but can we at least take seriously the possibility that this whole thing is a straightforward hoax, or at best a tissue of fantasies generated by monomania?

"It seems to me that Copplestone exaggerated his understanding of Darwin's theory of evolution, if he couldn't see that any ability to see the future, drug-assisted or not, would be so advantageous to any creature that had it that it would spread through the relevant population like wildfire–and yet we're supposed to accept that men, who do have it, will be replaced by vampires, who don't. I guess he intended to get around that with the help of this shilly-shallying about the future of destiny and the future of contingency, on the grounds that the prophetic gift would only be useful if it actually allowed us to change things, but I don't buy that. I think we've been taken for a ride here. I don't know why, but I think we've been fed a pack of lies, just like Mr. Wilde here has said."

"I fear," said Wilde, "that my earlier comments may have been open to misinterpretation. When I referred to Copplestone's story as a lie, the word was not intended as an insult. Quite the contrary; the modern world's dedication to vulgar truth is something I deeply regret–not because I have anything against the truth, but because the modern notion of what truth is has become so very narrow. The modern obsession with petty facts and meaningless measurements distresses me almost as much as the triviality of modern mendacity–for I would never dignify the banal deceptions of politicians and advertising men by calling them lies.

"Lies, to my mind, are grandiose products of the imagination, which enlarge the truth rather than diminishing it. When I describe Copplestone's experience as a lie, I only mean to imply what he attempted to convey by speaking of it as a vision or a hallucination, admitting its inevitable pollution by the hopes and fears hidden in the recesses of his inmost soul. Even if it had been a lie, in the sense of being a manifest fiction–like the story that Mr. Wells has described to us–I would not say that it could not, in consequence, function as a veritable fount of wisdom. Any man who did say such a thing would be a fool, and I am sure that Mr. Wells will agree with me on that point. Let us not occupy ourselves with the vulgar matter of whether Copplestone's account is false in any trivial sense–rather let us concentrate on what it has to teach us, because and in spite of the fact that it is a lie of unparalleled boldness and magnificence, and therefore potentially truer than any accurate account of mundane experience."

Tesla was clearly unconvinced, and the grey-eyed man's expression was openly contemptuous. Wilde, of course, continued regardless. "What Copplestone tells us, in brief, is that the universe in which we live is a more wonderful place than our half-blind senses and meager minds can easily perceive or imagine. That is surely true–or, at any rate, we ought to hope fervently that it might be. He informs us, too, that we should not be overly vain about the accomplishments of humankind, which might easily evaporate in a reckless moment, or overly regretful of the possibility that we might one day yield our hegemony over the earth to a better species, the fact of whose supersession would naturally embody both our most intimate fears and our most daring ambitions. That too is true–or, again, we should certainly hope so. Perhaps most importantly of all, Copplestone tells us that we are capable, each and every one of us, of adventures of the mind far bolder than any we have so far dared to undertake–and that, however dangerous or confusing such adventures may turn out to be, the brave man will not shirk them. Can anyone, even for a moment, doubt the truth of that–or doubt, at any rate, that they ought to wish with all their hearts that it might be true?"

I looked around. There seemed to be some who did doubt it.

"I could not have put it better, Oscar," I said, drily. I did my best to sound flippant and ironic. "Indeed, no one could have put it better. There is not a word to add."

Even Wilde–whose appetite for flattery was insatiable–frowned a little, as if to say that he had meant what he said more seriously than my casual endorsement implied.

The Great Detective was still impatient to turn the discussion towards matters of his own concern. "I have a keener appetite than Mr. Wilde for the separation of the improbable from the impossible," he said. "For myself, I am less interested in the possibility that Copplestone's story may contain hints about the actual shape of the far future than the probability that it contained clues as to a motive for robbery. We know that Copplestone intended to offer all of us the opportunity of using his drug to put his story to the proof–and we know that someone has taken the trouble to reserve that privilege entirely to himself. I cannot help wondering why–what motive could possibly have impelled someone seated here to do such a thing? If Sir William or Mr. Tesla really believed that the drug might disclose new insights in electrical science, one of them might have thought it worth while monopolizing the advantage–but they have not been given adequate grounds for believing that. If Mr. Wells or Mr. Shiel felt that the drug might be an invaluable aid to the furtherance of their budding literary careers, one of them might have thought it worthwhile to take possession of the formula–but they are young men, and I think they have confidence enough in their own powers of invention. Mr. Wilde is not so young, but he has the confidence of 10 men in his ability to lie effectively."

"Whereas I," I put in, smoothly, "have no conceivable motive at all. It is clear, therefore, where and when the theft took place. It must have you who picked your friend's pocket, after he had taken off his jacket, and you who removed the vial while your friend was busy with Copplestone's corpse. It only remains for you to tell us why on Earth you did it!"

There was a ripple of laughter, not so much because what I had said was hilarious, but because everyone was embarrassed by the man's dogged insistence that a crime had been committed and that someone seated at the table must therefore be a blackguard. The detective's scowl deepened, but he must have known that, had he charged me with the theft, the laughter would have increased. Even so, I was grateful that we were interrupted at that moment, when Copplestone's manservant brought in a message that had been delivered to the door. He gave the message to the doctor.

"It is from the doctors at King's who conducted the post mortem examination," the physician said, when he had scanned it. "They attribute Copplestone's death to the general deterioration of his vital organs caused by his use, over a long period, of certain poisonous compounds. Analysis of the contents of his stomach revealed no evidence of any ingestion of poison within the last 24 hours. There is a separate note to the effect that, in the absence of any evidence of breaking and entering, Scotland Yard will not be mounting an investigation of the missing vial. The matter is officially closed..."

He trailed off, leaving something unsaid.

"It may be officially closed," said his friend, darkly, "but it is not ended."

It was Sir William who took it upon himself to prompt the doctor, although I too had guessed what it was that had perplexed him. "How great was the deficit?" the man of science asked.

The doctor looked up, clearly embarrassed. "What deficit?" he said, although he knew very well.

"Come now," said Crookes. "The doctors at King's may not have considered the matter significant–after all, the weight of a body is a simple datum, if you have nothing with which to compare it–but you have been weighing Copplestone before and after his experiments for some little while. How much weight had Copplestone's corpse lost?"

"About three stones," said the doctor. "It seemed very light when I examined it, of course, but..."

"Death is not the end," Sir William said, triumphantly, as if he were quoting the final line of a mathematical proof. "This we know."

"But he did not take the contents of the vial last night," the doctor said. "The *post mortem* confirms that."

"Perhaps," said Crookes, "he no longer needed the drug. Perhaps the drug merely helped him to teach himself the art of astral projection."

"You aren't saying, I hope, that he might yet come back?" said Tesla.

Crookes shook his grizzled head. "He said once that the body left behind by a timeshadow would probably not survive any mortal damage to the timeshadow–but it is possible, is it not, that a timeshadow might survive the death of the body? It is, I think, very probable that some such phantom always does. Is it possible, do you think, that whatever Copplestone encountered in the farther reaches of his expedition could reach back to his point of origin, not to destroy but to save him? Perhaps, in the end, Copplestone overcame his fear of attack, and found himself able to accept the invitation issued to him in the world into which he went–which may well have been something other than the far future. Perhaps, in the end, he could not resist the temptation of Heaven."

"This is madness," said Tesla. Crookes did not take offence–it was he, after all, who had invited Tesla to accompany him. He simply shrugged his shoulders.

"This exchange of views does not seem to be getting us anywhere," said the grey-eyed man, acidly.

"Perhaps you are right," said Wilde. "Perhaps we expect too much of reasoned discussion–or of our own ability to make use of it. We are only human, after all. Each of us is locked within his own theories, imprisoned by his own prejudices....and there can be no proof of anything that we have heard. Even if we still had the drug, and one of us had the courage to use it, there would be no proof. It is, and must remain, a lie: a rough-hewn, but nevertheless brilliant, lie. Even if we undertook to believe it, it would become a lie again as soon as we tried to persuade anyone else of its truth. Professor Copplestone might have done well to remember the story of Cassandra–the wise parable formulated to remind us that prophets, no matter how accurate they may be, can never command belief."

He looked around to make sure that everyone appreciated the point he was making, and I looked around with him.

They do not care! I thought, as I studied the expressions on their faces. *They are prepared to be serious about it, and to play at philosophy, but they do not really care. It is too remote from their ordinary lives. Wells, Shiel and Wilde are as forward-looking as any men in the world, but even they regard this as an intellectual game. They can see no relevance to themselves–and that is why it has no relevance to them. I alone had the vision to steal the vial. I alone had the intelligence to steal the formula. The future is mine, and mine alone, because I was the only one among them who cared enough to steal it.*

"Very well," Wilde concluded. "We must be content with what we have, and each and every one of us must make of it what he can. Now, sir, do you have some specific charge to bring against one of us, or will you let us go to our homes?"

"I have no charge to bring, at present," said the master of ratiocination, "but you may be sure that the matter of the formula and the vial will not be forgotten."

I offered the Great Detective and the doctor a lift in my carriage, but the detective declined. I was not overly surprised. I suspected that I had not seen the last of him—and that the next time we met, it would not be as friends.

12.

The inevitable came to pass a little more than 72 hours later, when I returned in the early hours to the house I had rented in a quiet cul-de-sac off the Edgware Road. The Great Detective must have been lying in wait, watching the house, for some considerable time. He did not show himself immediately, but waited until the carriage had been driven round into the mews. As I set down my burden in order to bring out my keys he called my name from the bottom of the flight of steps leading up to the front door. I turned to confront him.

"How pleasant to see you again," I murmured.

"The pleasure is mutual," he assured me, with even greater insincerity. "I'm sorry to come calling at such an hour—had I been able to find you earlier in the day I would have done so. May I help you with your case?"

"No thank you," I said. "It is not heavy, and its contents are delicate. I would rather have charge of it myself."

"I presume that it contains the last of the ingredients required to make up Copplestone's formula," he said, carefully maintaining the same conversational tone.

I smiled—a little wanly, no doubt. I pushed the door open before turning to meet his gaze again.

"Would you like to come in?" I asked.

"I would."

"In that case," I said, standing away from the open door, "Please do. Enter freely, of your own will, I beg of you."

When our coats and hats were hung up in the hallway, I conducted him into the sitting-room. The fire had burned very low, there being no servants in the house to maintain it. When I had lit the candles, I added more wood, and stirred it with the poker until the embers flared. I offered my visitor the armchair to the right of the hearth, but before lowering myself into the one to the left I went to the sideboard, where a decanter of whisky had been placed.

"Would you like a drink?" I asked. "I have no liking for alcohol myself, but I keep a little for my guests."

"I think not," he said. There was an edge to his voice now. Apparently he suspected that I might poison him, although my only desire was to help him to relax. Lest that should prove impossible—I did not know how seriously to take his reputation as a man with a preternaturally sharp mind—I opened the right-hand drawer of the sideboard, shielding the action with my body. I took out the gun that rested there—but when I turned round with the weapon in my hand, I saw that the detective had a gun of his own. He was touching his chin lightly with the barrel.

"I fear," I said, with a theatrical sigh, "that we have reached an impasse."

"Hardly," he said. "What you have there is an antique dueling pistol, which can only fire one shot even if it happens to be loaded. What I have here is the doctor's old army revolver, which is a more accurate weapon by far and is fully loaded with six bullets. I think I have the advantage, don't you?"

"Can you be fully confident of the efficacy of any gun?" I asked him, mockingly. "Have you spoken to Arminius Vambery about me?"

"The professor is in Budapest," my adversary replied. "But I spoke to someone who was at the Beefsteak Club five years ago, when Vambery entertained the party with bloodcurdling tales of the vampires of Eastern Europe."

"Then you must know that garlic and a crucifix are supposed to be better tools than a pistol to keep a vampire at bay. Have you doused yourself in holy water? Have you a sharpened wooden stake about you, perchance? We have quite a while to wait until dawn, I fear. I suppose you will be anxious, at least until you see that I will not vanish away, nor shrivel to dust beneath the rays of the Sun."

"You never go out by day," he said, off-handedly. "That much I have ascertained for sure."

I sat down, not more than eight feet away from him. I did not point my gun at him, nor did he point his at me, but neither one of us laid his weapon down. I knew that it would be some time before he relaxed sufficiently to be mesmerized, but the hour was late and his chair was comfortable.

"My skin and eyes are extraordinarily sensitive to sunlight," I told him. "London's grey pall is far less of a menace than the bluer skies of Italy or Greece, but my habits were formed in brighter climes and London's night-life is so much more interesting than its daylit routines."

He looked at the candles on the mantelpiece, and at the unlit gas-light on the wall. "Even indoors," he observed, "you seem to like gentle light. Would you prefer it, perhaps, if the candle-flames burned bluer?"

I laughed. "You seem confused as to which kind of vampire I might be," I observed.

"There is no such thing as a vampire," he informed me. "There are no undead monsters stalking the streets for prey, and there are no patient mimics skulking in the hills waiting for mankind to destroy itself. I am not a superstitious man, Count Lugard. Still, it would be interesting to hear your version of Arminius Vambery's slanderous story–and an explanation of your reasons for stealing Copplestone's formula from the doctor's coat when you collided with him as he was trying to board your carriage."

"Where is the good doctor?" I asked. "According to his accounts of your adventures you rarely go anywhere without him–except, of course, to that sanatorium in Switzerland to which you retired a little while ago for a rest cure. How are your nerves now? Have you managed to overcome your addiction to co-caine?"

"Copplestone's manservant eventually confessed his misdemeanor," the Great Detective said, blithely ignoring the fact that we seemed to be talking at cross-purposes. "I know that the girl was in the house, and I know that she had the opportunity to take the vial. She had no motive, of course–she was naught but a common whore–but she was simply executing a commission. She was seen talking to a person of your description on more than one occasion, but she has not been seen in Piccadilly for three days. The other ladies of the night thought that odd, given that she had stuck so religiously to her pitch for some weeks previously, regardless of the winter cold. On the lookout for someone, they said. Someone special. Not the usual kind of customer."

"What do you suppose I have done with her?" I asked, lightly. "Do you think she scratches even now at the lid of her coffin, desperate to escape, in or-der that she might slake her hunger for human blood?"

"What have you done with her, Monsieur le Comte?" He spoke the phrase as if it were the deadliest of insults, at last abandoning his show of scrupulous politeness.

"Much as I did with Arminius Vambery's daughter," I murmured, tiring of the game. "No more–and certainly no less. I can tell you where to find her, if you really want to, but she will not tell you anything about the vial. She would not even if she could."

"But you do have the vial," he said, "do you not?"

"Arminius Vambery is quite mad," I said, quietly. "You must have realized that, even if your informant did not stress the fact. Not in every respect, of course. On all subjects but one he plays the savant to perfection, and without dissimulation, but on that one subject he is the victim of a terrible delusion. If only he were not so anxious to talk about it to anyone and everyone...but that is the form and fabric of his madness. The preposterousness of the story does not detract from its fascination as a tale, more's the pity. As Oscar Wilde would doubtless observe, a vivid lie is so much more memorable than a dull and naked truth."

"It is the dull and naked truth," he assured me, "that I have come here to-night to ascertain."

I was not overly grateful for that. It might have been easier, in a way, had he come fully prepared to hear wild fantasies.

"Very well," I said. "I will tell you the dull and naked truth. I debauched Vambery's youngest daughter. I did not bother to persuade myself that I had fallen in love with her; I did not propose marriage to her. I used her as I had used others. It was heartless, perhaps cruel. I was a villain. I say nothing in my defense, not even that I was educated in a hard school. I have always been a vil-lain, by instinct and by inclination. None of that matters. The naked truth is that I seduced the girl, in a spirit that had nothing to do with love. I learned, later, to regret it–to regret it very bitterly–but I claim no credit for that; I know that it cannot excuse me.

"Vambery swore revenge, and would have tried to take it in an altogether ordinary way, had he any competence with sword or pistol, but he had not. He had nothing but the mind and sinews of a professor of languages, and the capacity for obsession that academic study requires and rewards. The seduction of his daughter drove him half-mad; her suicide completed the process. He could not fight me, or murder me, so his burgeoning obsession found other ways to strike out at me. I have regretted ever since that he was not a bigger, braver man. I would far rather he had aimed a bullet at my heart than done to me what he has done these last ten years.

"The dull and naked truth is that my name really is Lugard; the notion that I obtained it by reversing the name Dragul is Vambery's fantasy, as is the absurd proposition that I am some kind of reincarnation or resurrection of the voivode Vlad Dragul, called Tepes, or the Impaler, whose name is usually Latinized as Dracul and sometimes rendered Dracula–that is, 'son of Dracul'–in order to distinguish him from his like-named father. It is also Vambery's fantasy that I am one of the undead, who subsists by drinking human blood, and that what I did to his daughter was utterly unnatural and accomplished by magic. The dull and naked truth is that what I did to his daughter was entirely natural, even if a little of the mesmerist's art was employed in its accomplishment. They do say, do they not, that no one can be persuaded by mesmerism to do anything that flatly contradicts their own will? The professor, alas, was quite unable to accept that, and felt compelled to invent an alternative account which absolved his beloved child from all hint of blame.

"As the late Professor Copplestone scrupulously pointed out to us, a man's vision is ever apt to be polluted, perverted and confused by his hopes, fears and fancies. Vambery made himself vulnerable to fears and fancies of the worst kind. He has pursued me throughout Europe with dark rumors and direct slanders. He has done his best to ruin my reputation, and to make a demon of me in the eyes of my fellow men. No one believes him, of course–not literally–but the lie is so very gaudy, so very entertaining that it is repeated anyway. No one really believes that I am Dragul reincarnate, nor that I am an actual vampire who feeds on the blood of my fellow men...but that does not prevent the whispers and the sly glances, and the near-universal acceptance of the notion that, however I accomplished the feat, I did worse than murder Laura Vambery. Vambery has succeeded, after a fashion, in making a vampire of me in the eyes of my fellow men. His caustic lies have stripped me by degrees of every vestige of the respect that is my rightful due by virtue of birth, wealth and station.

"If Wilde's friend Stoker really is writing a book based in the supposed occult wisdom of Arminius Vambery, I shudder to think what a further shadow it might cast upon my life. You ought to sympathize with that, as one who has some experience of the manner in which a real life can be confused by myths. If it is difficult for you to live up to a heroic reputation, think how much more difficult it must be for me to live down a monstrous one!"

He would not respond to that, but he was sitting less rigidly now. As his curiosity was fed, he was possessed by a soothing tranquillity. What a strange being he was!

"In a way," I told him, lowering my voice almost to a whisper, "I wish I were a vampire. It would be better, I think, if everything that Vambery has said about me were true. Then, I could not be hurt by his lies–and Laura Vambery could have risen from her grave to become my kin and my consort. Furthermore, I would far rather be the kind of vampiric overman that Copplestone described than any kind of human being. In my inmost heart, I wish that every word which Copplestone spoke might be true–that all humanity might be doomed and damned, so that vampires might inherit the Earth, and worry no more about the stupid hatreds of blind, mad men. I fear that Copplestone may have been no less a victim of his fears and fancies than Arminius Vambery, and that the dull truth and the dull tragedy is that you are absolutely right...but can you blame me for wanting to believe otherwise? Can you really blame me for wanting to take the risk that I intend to take?"

"I do not judge you," he said, with what was clearly intended as devastating simplicity. "My part is merely to establish the truth–which is that you did steal the professor's formula from the doctor's pocket, and that you did send the girl to steal the remainder of his drug. Justice is for others to administer, should the need arise."

He was being so lumpenly ironic, and seemed so stubbornly blind to the import of what I had been telling him, that I almost called him a fool–but that might have jolted him out of his quiet mood.

"Of course it is," I purred. "Justice is a rare and precious thing, and must be carefully reserved to the province of the law. There is no such thing as poetic justice. I am a mundane law-breaker and nothing more. It was merely my villain's instinct that made me steal the vial and the paper; once I had concluded that I wanted them, it was the most natural thing in the world for me to take them.

"For a little while, you know, I seriously considered the possibility that the impulse was not entirely my own. I wondered whether it might have been planted in my mind by one of Copplestone's Overmen, a rival of his more cautious fellows, reaching back through time to make sure that the secret would not die with him. But that is mere romance, is it not? You and I know better than to traffic in such nonsense, for we are practical men."

I knew that I was on safe ground. Was this not a man whose watchword was: When you have eliminated the impossible, whatever remains, however implausible, must be the truth? In pedantic fact, I suppose, that was the watchword of the doctor's literary invention, but I knew by the haunted expression in his eyes that this man was trying desperately hard to live up to his legend. I, on the other hand, knew perfectly well that, when you have eliminated the apparently impossible, if you are left with something unworthy of consideration, then you must start re-examining your assumptions regarding the limits of possibility.

"You took the vial, although you already had the formula, out of simple dog-in-the-manger selfishness," the Great Detective said, thinking that it was his own idea rather than one I had planted in his mind.

"Of course I did," I said, very gently. The man had little understanding of the true wellsprings of human action; he could not have begun to understand the true complexity of my motives, because they could not have met his crude standards of rationality. He could not have begun to comprehend what I had become, in consequence of the fatal combination of Arminius Vambery's malicious madness and the belated love for Laura Vambery that I had belatedly discovered in my desolate heart. He was certainly not incapable of obsession himself, but he did not have enough imagination to see where obsession might lead a man with a soul as dark as mine.

Oscar Wilde might have understood, but Wilde was about to set sail on the morrow, headed for the desert Sun with his handsome Judas, leaving me alone and friendless.

"I must ask you to return the formula," said my would-be Nemesis, formally. "You may keep the vial, I suppose, but the formula was consigned to the care of Copplestone's personal physician, and certainly is his by right."

"The written formula no longer exists," I said, regretfully. "I have destroyed the paper I took from the doctor's jacket. The formula itself is safe in my memory, but there it will remain."

"I can't believe that," he said–but he said it mechanically, like an automaton. He was mine, now, and I could play him as I wished.

I leaned forward. "You might yet be surprised," I said, "by your own capacity for belief."

"Might I?" he asked, uneasily. For the first time, the barrel of his gun was directed at my heart, but there was not the slightest possibility that he would fire.

"You ought not to despise my weapon," I said, softly. "I have already killed one man with it."

"It was a freakish ricochet that killed Mourier," the detective said, displaying the extent of the inquiries he had made. "You aimed at the ground. You had no real intention of wounding him. It was a matter of bizarre mischance."

"It is a curious circumstance," I said, "that one often achieves one's best ends obliquely. You are right; I had no intention of leaving Paris, but generous Destiny forced my hand, employing the prerogative it has to engineer bizarre freaks of chance. Fate brought me here, and delivered me to Roche's on one auspicious night, so that Oscar Wilde might be taken by a whim and I might be taken to Professor Copplestone's house....and thus brought face to face with my own wonderful future. That is what destiny means, if it means anything at all: the improbable chain of happenstance and coincidence that brings a man to the one and only place in all the world where he might be...shall we say in-spired...with a vision of his true self, and his only conceivable future."

My guest was staring at me now, wide-eyed. I did not have to meet his gaze; no true mesmerist requires an awesome stare or a bright and spinning object to captivate the imagination of his victim. As to whether a mesmerized man can be instructed to do something flatly contradictory to his own will....who can know what a man's will might permit, and what it might forbid? I felt that I could tell the Great Detective any lie I cared to, now, and make him believe it.

I was in a mood to be bold.

"Listen to me, my dutiful friend," I said, in a velvet-smooth tone. "Listen to me, and I will tell you the real truth..."

I told him, very painstakingly, that everything Arminius Vambery had said about me was true: that I was a vampire, and must be destroyed. I told him that his nagging doubts would linger for a while, but that he would be possessed by a perfect conviction, once he had left my house, that the only course of action open to him was to do what needed to be done. I told him that, once the conviction came upon him, he must make his plans accordingly. I instructed him to return, between one and three hours after dawn, armed with a wooden stake, which he must drive through my beating heart.

I told him not to be afraid–that he would find me unconscious and unresist-ing. I assured him that I would not crumble to dust, but that he would find my body lighter by a least three stones than it was at present, and that this would be an unmistakable proof of all that I had said. I told him that he would be doing the world a great service in freeing it from an unholy evil, and that the act of my destruction would make him the hero he had always longed to be, even though no one would ever know what heroism he had shown.

By the time I finished, he was nearly asleep. It was apparent to me that his rest cure had been terminated too early, and that he ought to have remained a little longer in that happy inactivity. I was able to take the revolver from his un-cannily steady hand. I checked the chambers; it was indeed fully loaded. I put it back in his hand, and gently roused him from his trance.

"Go now," I told him, gently. "Come back after dawn. You will know then what you must do."

He looked at me in bewilderment. For a few moments, he did not know quite where he was or why. He put the gun in his pocket, but I had to help him with his coat and hat. When I opened the door for him, he departed meekly–but he recovered himself sufficiently as he descended the steps to turn and face me, and say: "This matter is not yet finished, Count Lugard. Depend on it."

"I do," I assured him, as I raised my hand in a salute of farewell. "I do de-pend on it."

I watched him from the doorway while he disappeared into the shadows of the night. Three hours of darkness still remained before the dawn.

13.

I collected my case, took a candle from the sitting-room, and went down the steps into the cellars of the house. The ones nearest to the foot of the stairway had been wine-cellars once, but I had stripped out the racks when I had installed the false doors, and had thrown them away. What need had one such as I of vulgar intoxicants?

Laura lay in her coffin, perfectly at peace. Her wan face was lustrously clear and her dark eyes seemed almost luminous. The small star-like mark on the cheek beneath her left eye stood out very clearly. Her lovely hair was neatly gathered about her finely-chiseled features.

"Soon," I whispered. "Soon, my love!"

She did not wake while I did my work; she might as well have been truly dead. She did not even wake when I pricked her arm with the needle, and slowly injected the drug into her arm.

"Never fear, my love," I said to her. "There is a better world for such as you and I, and a path that shall lead us there, hand in hand. I have sown the seeds of my last nightmare, played my last cruel trick, and now the time has come for expiation and redemption. I have found my destiny, and I know at last that it is within my grasp."

I found that I was weeping, and wiped the tears from my eyes with my sleeve. How could I, or any other man, ever have thought that I was heartless? How could I, or any other man, ever have condemned me as a monster, forever doomed to remain outside the human community: a thing made shabby by mockery and misfortune?

I filled the syringe again with the remainder of the portion of Edward Copplestone's elixir of life that I had so carefully made up and measured out. No one else would ever be able to use it, I assumed, unless the world produced another man with Copplestone's peculiar fascinations–and even then, the colonial powers would need to have refrained from obliterating the ancient but precarious wisdom of the tribesmen he had visited.

I could not believe that there would be any such man, or any such reprieve for the custodians of wisdom. The future for which I was bound was indeed the future of destiny. Nothing could threaten its masters now, whether or not they had the power and the wit to take protective action on their own behalf.

I had saved them.

I had made the world safe for vampirekind.

I was as certain that no one else could follow us into that glorious world–where violent, vapid mankind was nothing but a myth and a memory–as the Great Detective was that I was a vampire, who could and must be destroyed by a stake through the heart.

Before taking my appointed station and injecting the drug into my own arm I reached out to touch the cold forehead of the lovely victim of my lust. I wanted to feel the faint warmth of her forgiveness before I escorted her into the misty reaches of the worlds beyond the world.

"We leave nothing behind but a sunless world of dismal madmen," I told her, softly, "and we are bound for the vivid and effulgent future, when we shall revel and rejoice in the hunger and ecstasy of vampires!"

The Soldier's Story: Part Four

A Habitat in the Moon's orbit,
circa *12,000,000 A.D.*

11.

Oscar Wilde's graven image had been correct in his estimation of my enhanced powers of concentration, but I was still capable of confusion. I laid the manuscript down, having reached what seemed to be a significant break in the narrative, because I felt in dire need of a pause.

I had no idea how long I had been reading–there was no clock in the library, so I could not keep a proper account of the time. I felt not the slightest hint of any physical cramp or stiffness, but my mind was abuzz. I was curious to know what else this remarkable library held, so I stood up and went to the nearest set of bookshelves.

The fact that they towered over me to such an inordinate extent gave the books a more awesome substance than they might otherwise have possessed, but they would have had authority enough simply by virtue of their number and their astounding endurance. The whole heritage of human understanding was here! This was, apparently, our monument–our particular contribution to the evolution of intellect and to the wisdom of the various species that came after us! How long would it take to read through it all? Had Wilde's immortal simulacrum yet had the time and inclination to do that–or had it rationed itself, preferring to keep a precious residuum of ignorance for future address?

I did not recognize any of the titles or authors' names inscribed on the spines of the shelf at head height, which seemed to consist entirely of books on a subject whose very name was unfamiliar to me: ecology. I took this to be the name of a science unknown, or at least unnamed, in my own day.

I took down a book from the shelf and riffled through it. The pages seemed to be perfectly ordinary paper, and if the binding was not cloth it was a very good imitation. How long, I wondered, could a book like that be expected to last? In 1918, there were numerous books in the British Museum and the Bodleian that had survived from the 16th and 17th centuries, many of them still usable, if only with great care, but every one I had seen had been clearly marked by the forces of decay. I could not believe that those books would have been able to sit on open shelves for another century, or that any of the books mass-produced in my own day would last much longer.

Here, I had to presume, the forces of decay had been rendered impotent; these pages would not be easy prey to the invasions of worms, silverfish and microbes. Even so, it was impossible to imagine that these actual volumes had already endured for tens of thousands of years, let alone more than ten million. The characters printed on their pages must, therefore, be copies of copies of copies–like the manuscripts handed down to the first printers by monks whose forebears had copied them over and over since Classical times. Even in this age of machines, could such copying be accomplished endlessly without loss or error?

I remembered that the Talos-creature had had no book in which to look up my name, and yet it had recovered the information–right or wrong–still associated with that name almost as soon as I had spoken. I looked around again, with a slightly different gaze, realizing that I was wrong to think of this strangely stocked and distorted library as something separate from the figure that had left me alone within it. The room and the android were part and parcel of the same phenomenon: the same calculated echo of a world long gone.

Could all this have been made for my benefit? I wondered. Was it all devised and erected while I was aboard that strange vessel, for the sole purpose of making me comfortable–of providing me with an impression of surroundings that are not merely intelligible but seductive? Might this monumental edifice, and the worldlet that contains it, be nothing but a stage erected to lull me into a false sense of...

The train of thought was derailed by the impossibility of adding the word security–and I could not imagine what other false sense the inhabitants of this astonishing future might be trying to induce in me, or why. They certainly seemed to be doing everything in their power to demonstrate that my arrival here was very relevant to their own affairs–and hence, by implication, that what I might do if and when I was returned to my own time might be of considerable importance not merely to those who had sent me but to all those who came before and after them.....but I could not fathom the mystery of it all.

I replaced the book I had taken down and began to move from shelf to shelf, scanning the titles. I found books on other sciences of which I had never heard–electronics, tribology, genetics, virology, quantum mechanics–and took some down to riffle through their pages, marveling at the intricate diagrams and enigmatic mathematical formulas that some of them contained. I began actively to search for books on history, but had not found that particular section when the library door opened and closed again.

The entity that resembled Oscar Wilde came to meet me, smiling broadly. It was not a simulacrum of Wilde as he must have been when the pox finally killed him, nor even Wilde as he actually was at the height of his powers, but rather the vision that Wilde might have entertained of himself at his bravest and most adventurous. The real Wilde, I had been reliably informed, had very bad teeth, spoiled by the mercury treatment he had been forced to take after contracting syphilis from a college whore at Oxford. This smiling machine was Wilde re-cast as Dorian Gray, magically incorruptible by any conceivable oppression of existence–but even he acknowledged, in referring to his home as the Attic of

Olympus, that he was more like the portrait than the living man, and that he existed now in the time beyond the climax of the story, when the exhausted and desperate Gray had stabbed the corrupted image and reclaimed the burden of his sins into his own frail flesh.

"Are you finding the tale amusing?" he said.

"Somewhat," I replied, ungenerously. "It is confusing, partly because of the excessive number of first-person narrators, and partly because of a certain parsimony in the matter of calling men by their names. When it is difficult to remember who is supposed to be whom, it becomes all the harder to figure out the whats and whys of the plot. On the other hand, tales told according to the Galland method, intricately interwoven one within another, always have a certain dash and flair. The narrative certainly has a good deal of entertainment value, despite its anachronicity, but I cannot imagine why you should offer me a work of fiction to read when I have come so far. There must be a great deal of knowledge on these shelves that I could usefully transport back to 1918."

"Is it so obviously a work of fiction?" he asked. The manner of his asking suggested that he had not expected me to come to any other conclusion–but also that he intended to challenge my incredulity.

"Very obviously," I said. "I suppose you expected it to fit so well with my own experience as a timeshadow that I would readily grant every word, but there are certain aspects of it that forbid me to take it seriously as anything but a gaudy scientific romance closely akin to my own."

"Would you indulge my curiosity by listing the aspects in question?" he inquired.

"One is sufficient," I told him, still convinced that he knew it already. "There was no real person resident in Baker Street on whom Arthur Conan Doyle modeled his most famous literary character."

"The archive patiently assembled by the Engine from the ruins of the civilization of the Overmen is reasonably unambiguous on that surprising point," Wilde's simulacrum admitted. "I hope you will forgive me, however, if I press you on the matter. Is there anything else in the manuscript that you know, beyond the shadow of a doubt, to be untrue?"

I hesitated, wondering what might qualify.

Wilde's simulacrum waited for a moment or two, but his patience soon ran out. "Did you ever hear of Count Lugard?" he asked. "Did you ever hear his name mentioned, in London or Paris?"

"No," I said. "So far as I know, he might be an invention of the writer of the manuscript–but he might equally well be real. Most of the other persons cited were real enough. I know Wells quite well, and have met Shiel. Every educated man has heard of Crookes and Tesla. I never heard of Lugard, but that certainly does not mean that there was no such person in London in 1895."

Wilde nodded, although he did not seem delighted by the news that I had never heard of his erstwhile friend. "Did you ever hear of Professor Copplestone?" he said, a trifle anxiously. "I am sorry to challenge you, but I need to be sure. Did you ever hear his name mentioned, or see it in a book of traveler's tales–or perhaps the footnotes to a book on the primitive tribes of Africa and the Far East?"

"Never, so far as I can recall," I told him, hesitantly–but then something that had temporarily slipped my mind rose again to the surface and I hastened to correct my false denial. "Wait! Yes, I believe I did hear it spoken, once. It was while I was in the ambulance, on my way to the house in Ireland where I was given the drug that sent me here. I was ill, and dosed with morphine, and thought nothing of it at the time, but I am certain that the name I heard was Copplestone."

"What was said?" asked Wilde. "Please try to remember the exact words."

"Wrightson and MacLeod were speaking. One of them was chiding the other for not fetching me sooner; the other was defensive. 'He's strong,' the defensive one said, stronger, 'I dare say, stronger than you or I, and certainly stronger than Copplestone was when he opened the way.' Then they went on to argue over the implications of my wounds. I never heard the name mentioned again, once we had reached the house. Why are you so anxious to know?"

"I will explain that when you have read the rest of the manuscript," he assured me. "Before you do so, however, the Engine wishes me to show you more of my little world. Suffice it to say, for now, that I remember that evening at Copplestone's house very well. I distinctly remember the detective with grey eyes and his fussy friend. I remember Lugard just as distinctly, and the rumors that had been spread about his vampiric inclinations, and I remember Ned Copplestone, and all that had been said of him. I do not think that there was ever a mention of Edward Tylor, or any other student of exotic humanity, in any country house in England, that did not lead to some anecdote about Copplestone's adventures. Lugard was only notorious, but Copplestone was, in his own sphere, quite famous."

I knew that the Wilde-machine was telling me that he believed that his own history had been changed: that the fears expressed by Copplestone in the course of the Count's story had been justified, and that some of the key players in the little drama had been wiped out, leaving no trace behind save for the Detective's supposed avatar, the greatest of the *Strand*'s multitudinous heroes.

In that case, I realized, the graven image that stood before me was claiming that he was not the semblance of a man who had lived and died in my world, but rather of some alternative version of that man, who had lived in a subtly different world, with a slightly different human population. But if his own history had been wiped out, how could this particular Wilde be here, rather than one who remembered the world as I knew it? If testimony to the effect that his remembered world had never existed was unambiguously contained in the books on his own library shelves, how could the paradox of his co-existence with those books possibly be resolved? Should he not have vanished from existence as soon as his own history had been cancelled out?

I looked back at the desk, at the manuscript I had set down half-read. I guessed that the remainder of the story would explain how a further supply of the drug that Copplestone had created had been manufactured or found, and how Wilde had eventually used it himself, in order to venture into a future even more distant than the ones that Copplestone had allegedly visited. Then, presumably, he had found it impossible to return to his own time, either because he had escaped from a body on the point of death–as the android had claimed–or because "his own time" had been shunted into the mists of oblivion, relegated to the standing of a world that never was.

This is a dream, after all, I reminded myself. *In a dream, the pattern of events is perfectly free to make no sense, and to defy any explanation. And yet, I am obliged to try to make sense of it.*

I looked at my tall and handsome companion, speculatively.

"I remember my own fate perfectly well," he remarked, perhaps misreading the puzzlement in my face. "I did not have to read it on a cruel and merciless page. I came here from the final year of the 19th century, not from 1895. I avoided Death's relentless scythe by a matter of minutes–an hour at the most. The details of my own biography have not been altered in the historical record–more's the pity–but men I knew have been erased therefrom, or reduced to the status of mere fictions. You cannot believe that, I know–not yet, at any rate. You cannot believe anything, at present, for you have no reason to think that this is anything more than a hallucination. All I ask of you is that you retain an open mind, so that you will not be unprepared if you are ever disposed to change your mind."

I thought about that for a few moments, but there was too much confusion in my mind for me to respond directly to his plea. I thought it best to approach the issue from a more objective viewpoint.

"What would happen if the Engine's enemies were to win the battle that is supposedly raging in the vacuum of deep space, and sent me back equipped to change history in some wholesale fashion?" I asked him. "Would you and this whole worldlet vanish? Might the Engine itself disappear, because its earliest ancestor was never built?"

"I would dearly like to know the answer to that question," my companion admitted, "and if the Engine were capable of greater feeling, it would probably be prey to a desire far more fervent than even I can entertain."

"The Engine's so-called scion gave me the impression that it had nothing but contempt for the schemes of its adversaries," I told him, "and the precipitation of such vast changes does not seem to sit well with the idea of Consolidators."

"The Engine is no more capable of contempt than of fervor in desire," the simulacrum replied, "but it is capable of desire, and of curiosity too–as you are, despite your condition. As to the likelihood of Consolidators making vast changes–that surely depends on exactly what they are trying to consolidate"

I could not see the full import of his statement comparing the Engine's capacity to feel desire with mine, although I took note of the fact that the subject seemed to be something of an obsession with him.

"When shall I be able to continue reading your own story rather than the ones it encloses?" I asked.

"Soon," he promised. "The more you know of all these stories of human time travel, the better equipped you will be to assess your own situation, as well as mine–but I ought to follow the instructions that the Engine has issued. I resent its insistence on treating me as if I were merely one of its scions, but I do not like to hurt its feelings, strange and shallow though they are. I hope you will forgive me for declining the Engine's offer to supply us with a flying machine, but I prefer to travel in a more leisurely fashion–and I am, after all, your host."

He extended his arm to indicate that I should precede him to the door, and I moved obediently towards it. I had no idea what to expect when I stepped through it, although I knew that we were a long way above the ground and suspected that it might take us some time to descend.

"The Engine seems very enthusiastic to show me what it has done for you," I remarked, as I opened the door and stepped through.

"On the contrary," said Wilde. "Whether it knows it or not, what it is very anxious to show you is what I have done for the Engine. It is desirable that you judge it in the right frame of mind, or you might be seriously misled about the nature of the lure that is being dangled before you."

"Lure?" I echoed. I realized, even as I pronounced the syllable, that, in my attempts to reason out the Engine's motives, I had only been thinking one move ahead, when I ought perhaps to have been trying to anticipate two. If the Engine succeeded in sending me back to 1918, I had to suppose that the possibility would then be opened up for me to come forward in time again, perhaps to an even more distant future than this, and to become the kind of creature that Wilde already was. What the Engine intended to offer me in return for my co-operation with its schemes, it seemed, was a kind of immortality–and my own Utopia in which to spend a million years of life, and more.

It was not merely the opportunity to return home that I stood to lose if the wrong side won the struggle that was raging around me, or if I failed to make the most of whatever opportunity I might be given. Disembodied souls, I had been assured, were more ephemeral than living men; the only humanly accessible Heaven was here, in the future empire of clever machinery–or so the Engine and its scions wanted me to believe.

12.

I thought at first, as we stepped out on to the landing of Oscar Wilde's palace, that I might be expected to walk down the staircase that proceeded in a square-sided spiral into the depths of a staggeringly precipitous well. After allowing me to look over the banister-rail, however, to measure the abyss with my eyes, Wilde led me across the carpeted floor to a pair of sliding doors. These allowed us access to a grey-walled elevator, which proved far less noisy in its operation than the ones in the hotels in which I had had occasion to stay.

The descent seemed to be reasonably swift but it was not soon over. As we stood side by side, facing the doors, Wilde said: "Your father was a clergyman, I believe?"

"He was," I confirmed. I said no more; it was not a subject I liked to pursue.

"I had time to notice that many of the most imaginative men of our era were the freethinking sons of clergymen," he said. "Shiel was another, of course, and Grant Allen. Griffith too–do you remember Griffith? He was journalist."

I nodded. I remembered George Griffith's work quite well, although I had never met the man. I knew that his full name had been Griffith-Jones, although he signed his work more briefly. Wilde–the Wilde in the Count's story, not the simulacrum in mine–had referred to him as a "sot," and he had indeed died of liver cirrhosis shortly after I began my own literary career. Griffith was the Welshman who had rekindled the vogue for future war stories in the early 1890s; the literati had dismissed him as a mere melodramatist who had exported his flair for yellow journalism into serial fiction of the French sort, but he had foreseen far more accurately than they what the next war would be like, and what frightful scope for devastation there was in the development of aircraft, submarines and high explosives.

"Rebellion against a dogmatically fixed view of the nature and prospects of the world is bound to encourage the creation of secular visions, of course," Wilde went on. "The boldest freethinkers brought to their visioning all the fervor of a desperate hunger to find a universe grander by far than anything contained within a churchman's piety, as well as all the new-found authority of the telescope and the microscope."

"I suppose so," I admitted, guardedly.

"But you found more than that, did you not?"

I had guessed that the Wilde-machine must have read the book which he showed to me when I awoke in his home, his magical eyes probably flying through the pages of *The Night Land* far more easily than the weaker eyes of its contemporary readers. "Did I?" I parried.

"I rather envied Flammarion his ability to see the universe of astronomy in such a kindly light," said Wilde. "All that vastness became, for him, the playground of the exuberant soul. I found, in due course, that there was more truth in his vision than I had expected, but rather less than I had hoped. Such souls as contrive to survive the mortal remains of earlier beings do indeed have the freedom to roam while they last, but the velocity of light limits their progress as it limits every particle in the universe–and they find the wilderness of space as rife with conflicts as the world of men. You looked into the eye of eternity and saw something of its desolation, not to mention an underlying malignity to all creatures of flesh. You saw the empire of decay at its height, and the appalling strangeness of those who would come after man. You did not understand, but you did see–you sensed more keenly than any other man of your era not merely what infinity might hold, but what infinity might mean."

"Thank you for the compliment," I said, noting that the machine had taken the trouble to re-emphasize his maker's revelation as to the mortality of the soul. "I fear, though, that I can claim no credit for my bad dreams."

"On the contrary," he replied, "As with every other man who ever lived, the credit for your waking thoughts and your good actions is almost entirely attributable to the influence and expectations of others. The one and only thing for which any man can claim unique responsibility is the visionary power of his nightmares."

The doors before us slid open again, and we stepped out on to another carpeted floor. The amazing stairwell was above us now, ascending into obscurity at the limit of vision. Before us was a great hall flanked with two rows of tall marble pillars, the like of which I had only seen in artists' impressions of what the most glorious temples of Egypt and Greece might have been like before the weight of the ages had toppled them. The walls behind the pillars were decorated with works of art; some were huge but others seemed very tiny. I was sure that I recognized reproductions of paintings I knew, but Wilde hurried me along the corridor towards the massive double door set at its end.

"You seem determined to outdo the religious architects of old," I remarked. "I confess that I cannot understand your motives. They constructed awesome spaces to make men feel humble before the idea of God. Why have you gone to such lengths to make yourself small within your own domain?"

"I am the creation of machines no larger than a molecule of chlorophyll or hemoglobin," he told me, with a hint of bitterness in his voice. "I came here as a timeshadow, but that artifact of the merely human will had not durance enough to last a week, let alone a century or an aeon. The nanozoons that secured my timeshadow's tenuous form–as their cousins now secure yours–replaced it molecule by molecule, enhancing as they went. The consciousness embodied within was uninterrupted in its flow, never losing its sense of identity for a moment– and yet, like Achilles' ship in the old paradox, what emerged at the end of the process was something entirely new, entirely reconstructed.

"There is no miracle in that sort of process, of course–mere human bodies renew themselves in much the same way, molecule by molecule; the body a man has at 40 probably has not an atom within it that was part of him at 17–but my case is significantly different. I suppose that I take such care to remind myself of my smallness because I would otherwise be painfully conscious of the fact that I am a universe entire, sustained by the co-operative endeavor of millions of tiny creatures. I am greater than the sum of their parts, but without the sum of their parts I would be nothing."

The two halves of the great double door opened by themselves as we approached. It was as well; we could never have contrived to pull them open by the strength of our arms. Outside, there was another staircase, neatly cut from vivid white stone. The steps were much wider than deep, but necessity demanded that they must be convenient for human descent. At the foot of the flight was the terminus of the narrow water-course I had seen snaking through the mazy gardens. It was, as I had suspected, a canal; the water within it was almost still.

Serenely floating at the blind end of the canal was a wooden boat somewhat reminiscent in its shape of a Viking longboat, although it was far smaller and had no oars. The figure rearing up from its prow was carved into the shape of a snake's head. The boat had a tent-like awning amidships, screening a wide bench from the light of the sky, but it seemed extremely modest in its size and its opulence of decoration by comparison with Oscar Wilde's house and everything in it.

I glanced back at the house, staring upwards at its soaring walls. They were painted and gilded like some fabulous dream of Gustave Moreau's—which is what, in essence, the dwelling was. Its roofs were capped with spires twisted like the horns of unicorns: pointers to the glittering arches of the false sky. The light was very bright but rather unsteady, as if multitudinous scintilla were running madly in every direction in the hope of escape, like reluctantly domesticated lightning-bolts. For a moment I wondered whether the shot fired at the vessel that had brought me here might have grown in the meantime to a veritable bombardment: a firework display to put Ludendorff's finest efforts to shame. I dismissed the thought and turned to look again at the humble serpent-ship.

"I had expected something grander," I confessed to my host.

"The barge needs to be light," my companion informed me. "The creatures commissioned to tow it are no plodding Percherons."

He pointed sideways as he spoke, and I saw two creatures rounding the corner of the building, trotting towards us. They had such a distance to cover that I was able to look long and hard at them before they drew close. I had seen no monsters as yet but I had taken forewarning from my prophetic dreams to arm my curious sight against the probability that I would meet monsters. By virtue of that mental preparation, I avoided undue astonishment at the fact that the creatures appointed to tow Wilde's barge were not horses at all.

The poet Virgil, in order to signify grotesque impossibility, had spoken of a cross between a griffin and a horse, which he called a hippogriff. The temptation had, of course, proved far too powerful for romancers who had undertaken to test the limits of the literary imagination; Ariosto had described a hippogriff with the forelegs, wings and head of its eagle sire, and the hindquarters of its maternal mare. Wilde's hippogriffs were wingless, and all four of their legs showed the mother's influence, but their heads were those of huge hawks and their backs and flanks were gloriously feathered.

"It seems that you have imitated the Overmen of Copplestone's second adventure in recreating creatures of myth," I observed.

Wilde went to meet the hippogriffs. He patted their heads when they paused. They took up their positions to either side of the barge, and Wilde lifted two huge collars one by one, unreeling the hauling-gear from two capstans mounted in the bow of the boat. I noticed that the hipogriffs' hooves were unshod–and it was that, rather than the dryness of their breath that told me that they were almost certainly machines rather than entities of flesh and bone.

"I suppose it is easier to stable entities of that kind," I remarked, putting on a show of negligent equanimity. "Real hippogriffs would make too much mess, and would need more than hay to eat."

Busy with his work, Wilde did not turn around. "I labored long and hard to produce similar creatures of flesh and blood," he said, "but the experiment failed. A beak is useless unless it is companied with claws, and claws are useless unless they are complemented by wings, and a creature of their size cannot fly, even in the trivial gravity of a worldlet like this. The spectrum of viable chimeras is narrower than you might think, if one is forced to work in common protoplasm. You will see soon enough what I have wrought."

His reference to "trivial gravity" reminded me that when I had first materialized on the surface of the Earth I had felt strangely heavy, despite my apparent lack of substance; I wondered how much I weighed now. I felt perfectly comfortable, but the comfort was not the comfort of familiarity.

As soon as we had climbed into the craft and taken our seats upon the bench, the tethered hippogriffs began to draw it along. They soon picked up to a trot, and the barge slid smoothly along the calm surface of the canal. When I was sure that there was no danger of losing my balance I stood up again and turned to look back once more at the mansion in which Oscar Wilde–having survived the extinction of his species by millions of years–now lived in solitude. It lent new meaning to the phrase "splendid isolation," dwarfing the great pyramid and Cologne Cathedral with contemptuous ease. As we drew away from it I saw that it was constructed somewhat after the fashion of a square-sectioned ziggurat, although it had so many embellishments that the basic pattern was hardly discernible until we had pulled a thousand yards away.

"It is the Tower of Babel," I said, meaning it as a guess rather than an ironic comment. "A calculated celebration of hubris."

"In a manner of speaking," my host agreed. "It is a Gothic folly too: as much a celebration of the wildness of the imagination as a testament to the vaulting ambition of freethought."

I recalled William Beckford's doomed determination to make Fonthill Abbey into a temple of decadence, and the joy that his less wealthy contemporaries had taken in its continued refusal to stand up.

"Deliberate folly is folly nevertheless," I opined. "It is a perfectly horrible edifice."

"Do you think so?" he said. Wilde spoke lightly, as if he did not give a fig for my opinion–but I looked at him sharply, having formed the impression that his indifference was feigned.

"Yes," I said, determined to put the matter to the test. "Utterly tasteless–I would not have thought it possible that a man of your sensibilities could have endorsed such an atrocity."

He raised an eyebrow as if to imply a sneer that he could not quite contrive. "But then," I added, quickly, "you are not a man, are you? You are a scion of the Engine."

"I am not quite a man," he agreed, equably, "although I am far less closely akin to the Engine than you and the Engine both seem to suppose. I fear that the Engine lacks imagination, in that and many other respects. If I were to stand side-by-side with a man of flesh and blood–like the creature you left asleep in 1918–and we were seen from a distance, by a clinical eye, would it really be so obvious which one of us ought to be reckoned the parody, and which the real being?"

He was looking at me as sharply as I had tried to look at him, and he was meeting my challenge. There was more to this, on his part, than merely making flippant conversation. Nothing he had said to me since the moment I arrived had been idle chitchat; he had waited a long time for this opportunity, and there was something he wanted from it that I had not yet understood.

I took my seat again, content to look ahead. The hippogriffs had picked up pace and we were speeding through a series of flower-gardens, which might have been interesting objects of study and appreciation had we been on foot, but seemed at our present pace to be a casual riot of color without form. We were moving so rapidly that I could not have told roses from camellias, let alone identified vegetable chimeras or mythical amaranths.

The hedges between the plots were eight or ten feet tall–their heights varied by virtue of the tokenistic topiary patterns cut into them–but there was no shadow here; the light of the sky was too diffuse.

"I can understand why you thought that this world had been falsely named," I remarked. "Whatever else it is, it cannot be Utopia. It is not nowhere; nor is it an ideal commonwealth, harbor and harvest of the perfect human society. Even if you were to build a city here, and populate it with beings like yourself, it would all be a charade: a stage for the performance of marionettes."

"Perhaps you are right," Wilde replied, using the tone of his voice to imply, strongly, that perhaps I was not, "although one could argue that a perfect society is impossible of sustenance which contains more than one human being.

No matter what they may say about great minds, humans never think alike, and one person's ideal always has flaws in another's eyes. This stage is far from changeless, of course; I can shift its scenery at a whim, and build new sets whenever I wish–and I can work in flesh and blood, provided that I respect the limitations of my material. I cannot make real hippogriffs, but I can make real horses, and real eagles too–which, once made, are as free and selfish as any horse or eagle ever was. I wish I could say that the worldlet's shifts reflect my moods, but I ought not to pretend. Do you remember the book that Lord Henry gave to Dorian Gray–the one that became his guide and guardian spirit?"

I did not know whether it was a serious question, or merely a test of my aesthetic qualifications. "I remember it very well," I assured him. The book in question had not been named in the text, but I knew that it was Joris-Karl Huysmans' *À rebours*. "I have even read it, in the original French. It suggests that the ideal human society is to be found in the company of works of art, because they alone retain the best of men, while cradling nothing of the worst. The narrator proposes, if I may be forgiven a brutal summary, that artifice is the triumph of the human mind over the vicissitudes of nature, and that the perfect human existence would be relentlessly artificial. Unfortunately, the hero's physical constitution eventually lets him down; in the end, his defiance of nature becomes–by force of necessity–purely imaginative."

As I spoke, proof of part of Wilde's oration obligingly manifested itself in the garden through which we were passing, in the form of a small herd of deer. I saw, too, that there were several big birds settled on the water in front of us, which made haste to take off as we approached. In my various circumnavigations of the globe I had often seen albatrosses rise, and these birds ran on the water in a similar fashion, although they were more reminiscent of short-legged herons than gulls, Their final leaps into the air were certainly not graceful, but were accomplished with a certain élan.

"Dorian Gray might have done better than Jean des Esseintes," Oscar Wilde's simulacrum continued, without a sideways glance at the deer or an upward tilt of the head to follow the flight of the birds, "but he too was fallible. I have done very much better, because the force of necessity has been with me instead of against me. Indeed, I have had no alternative but to live amid artifice, with nothing to connect me to the minds of other men but remembrance of their works of art."

I began to see what kind of apology he was making for his adventures in ostentation. "I can understand how the book might have come to seem uniquely significant as a handbook," I admitted. "A man forced to live alone for millions of years..."

"Not quite alone," he corrected me, with indecent punctiliousness. "Without authentic human company, until now–but never alone. The Engine is always with me, ever dutiful, ever helpful, ever watchful. I can understand, of course, why you might think these surroundings too elaborate by half, even vulgar–but you must not think of them as something finished, or even properly started. God must have been happier by far before the Creation, don't you think? Imagine what the world must have been like when it was a beautiful idea within His dream, before the dull reality of Adam gave birth to divine disappointment!"

"It is less than an hour since you congratulated me on outgrowing faith in God and finding a better vision," I reminded him. "Are you not one of those bold souls who believe that you could have made a far better job of Creation, given the chance? Are you really trying to tell me that you have spent the last few million years practicing the art of Creation, without yet being ready to mount a proper performance?"

"I am a mere dabbler in the art of Creation," he assured me, with a modesty so exaggerated in its falsity that it had to be true, "but I am privileged to sit at the right hand of an authentic living god. It is, I admit, merely one among many–an Olympian rather than a jealous Yahweh–but it has the power to mould cool clay into any form it desires. The Engine is the real power here; I am merely a court jester whose whims it is pleased to indulge. I have a worldlet to play with, but the Engine's local estate–one among many–is a planet brimming with clay of every possible hue, which could easily serve as Eden, were there any purpose to be served by some such endeavor."

He meant Earth, of course, although the Engine had assured me that Earth was still "disputed territory." It seemed to me that Wilde's simulacrum was doing his best to imply that there were things that he dared not say aloud about the Engine and his own attitude to its work, begging me to read between the lines of his speeches.

Was it possible, I wondered, that Wilde might be secretly in league with the Engine's opponents? Was it conceivable that his knowledge of the Archive was so much more complete than theirs that he had been able to ascertain when and where I might appear, and set the trap from which the Engine had saved me? Or were his interests entirely separate from those of all the rival companies of machines?

13.

We had passed the last of the hedges and were now being pulled through an undulating grassland sparsely dotted with trees and clumps of furze. There were streams and pools here, where animals congregated. With the galloping hippogriffs before me–and remembering also the encounter with fauns and centaurs briefly described by Edward Copplestone in the manuscript I had read–I searched the landscape for more mythical monsters, but these were deer like those I had glimpsed in the gardens, and long-horned cattle. I could not put a name to any particular species, but there was nothing unduly exotic in their make-up.

195

I wondered how to carry on my conversation with Wilde in such a way that I might have a better chance to discover any hidden meanings he might intend to communicate.

"Does the Engine intend to employ the Earth as a new Eden, then?" I asked, tentatively. "Will it eventually re-create humankind, as you have re-created these deer and cattle?"

He seemed relieved that I had taken up the point. "Who knows?" he replied, airily. "The Engine certainly could do that–if it had a reason. At present, the planet is fallow ground, patiently awaiting some kind of seeding. The situation is complicated by the serpentine presence of the Consolidators, which lie in wait for the drifting spores of intelligences dead and buried–but if the Engine had motive enough to claim and defend the Earth from such intrusions, it would succeed. The question is–what would be gained by the re-creation of humankind, or some other anthropomorphic species? It is not a project that would ever be undertaken merely to supply me with company, for I have company already."

"I suppose the planet would remain a battleground even if the Engine attempted to assert the full privileges of ownership," I said, pensively. "If the Consolidators fear the advent of a single human time-traveler, they would not rest content while the Engine brought the whole race back from the dead."

"If the Engine ever found a reason to do anything so strange," Wilde agreed, "the Earth would certainly become an arena for the continuation of the war in Heaven. According to the followers of Christ, of course, it always was. Are you and I on the side of the angels, do you think?"

He was still testing me; I met his eye, wishing that I could read his motives and intentions in his placid gaze. The game was becoming tiresome.

"If you have read accounts of the Great War from whose fighting I was plucked," I told him, "you will know that the angels were supposed to have come to the assistance of the British during the retreat from Mons–but we died nevertheless in our hundreds of thousands. No one who has seen what remains of the battlefields of Ypres and Passchendaele believes any longer that it is sufficient for a man to be on the side of the angels. I know who my comrades were, who once fought beside me, and I know who my loved ones were, who awaited me at home, but I have no idea who and what your Olympians are, or who and what you are. If you are asking me whether I trust your virtue, or the Engine's, I cannot in all honesty say that I do."

"I am glad," he said–and he did not seem displeased with me. "I fear that, for my own part, I am nowadays a little too ready to trust my own virtue, and that of the angels which are my guardians. But you must see what you have been brought here to see. Look there!"

I looked ahead at what first appeared to be a colored cloud descending upon the canal. I soon perceived, however, that it was actually a host of butterflies, thousands strong. The "cloud" they formed was conical in form, swirling like a lazy tornado.

My first assumption was that the individual creatures would be as small as the majority of the butterflies I had seen during my travels on Earth, but that was because I had no object of known size with which to compare them. As we rushed to meet them, I realized that they were in fact very large by comparison with the tortoiseshells and clouded yellows of England, larger even than the tropical species I had encountered in South America and the East Indies.

I realized, too, that their bodies were very different from the bodies of Earthly butterflies. The colored wings had spans ranging from eight inches to half a yard; the bodies that supported them were not as human as those to which insectile wings were sometimes attached by fairy-painters like John Anster Fitzgerald, but they were not unlike the body of the metal android which had confronted me on the vessel which brought me from Earth.

Once we were within the cloud, the madly-fluttering wings seemed to be everywhere, but none brushed my skin. It was rather like being lost in a child's kaleidoscope, in a world reduced to fractured colors–or would have been, had sight been the only sense left to me. Unlike the hippogriffs, these creatures had obviously been made from organic materials. They were perfumed–not altogether pleasantly–and they had high-pitched voices, which chattered like little monkeys. There was no sense in their speech, so far as I could discern, but it was exceedingly clamorous and I could not help but interpret its screeching babble as hectic excitement.

Had we simply passed through the cloud while it remained effectively stationary we would have been through it and away into clear water in seconds–but it seemed that the cloud had come to meet and greet us. Although the fluttering wings seemed to have little real strength or substance, the creatures easily kept pace with us for several minutes. All the while they whirled about the boat in mad abandon, although there was nothing in their presence but confusion. The insect-folk would probably have stayed with us much longer had they not been scattered, but their colorful profusion attracted other eyes than ours.

As I looked up into the living vortex, I caught a glimpse of other fliers, much higher in the strange sky. These too were winged humanoids, but their brightly-colored wings were the feathered wings of birds rather than the gauzy wings of insects. Had their forms been more conspicuously human I might have been unable to resist the temptation to compare them with angels, but they were too impressionistic and expressionless–and it soon became obvious that their way of life was far from angelic.

After circling briefly–even in their circling they seemed like a quartet of hawks–the four newcomers dived towards the cloud of tinier creatures, which promptly scattered in panic. While I counted through four seconds, I thought that the swooping predators would go away empty-handed, but they turned and spun as their dives bottomed out, their little fingers braced like talons, reaching out with neat dexterity to pluck the fluttering insect-people from the air.

As soon as they had their prey in hand, the four birdmen soared away into the sky, heading for the topmost ridges of the hills that were now looming to either side of the canal's course. When we had left the scattered insect-folk behind, I could not help experiencing a pang of relief.

"Beautiful, are they not?" said Wilde; but he did not seem entirely sincere. I remembered that he was acting under orders–that it was the Engine that had instructed him to bring me on this tour–but I could not imagine that it was any whim but his that had shaped these living chimeras.

"Which?" I asked. "The predators, or their prey?"

"Both," he replied.

"Was it necessary," I demanded, "that creatures made in your own image should be allocated as prey to others similarly formed? Is that your notion of godly responsibility?"

"Unlike the hippogriffs," he said, a little sadly, "these creatures live. They must feed, and must become food in their turn. Only the creatures at the very top of the food-chain have no predators–and they remain afflicted by lowly parasites. Somehow, the numbers of the top predators must be kept in check if the system is to endure and remain in balance, if not by nature then by artifice. Humans belatedly chose artifice, electing to make themselves responsible for one another's deaths and miseries–but not for long. As the Archivist of humankind, looking back from a vantage of 12 million years, I cannot see your so-called world wars as you must have seen the first, as a tragic waste of blood and wealth. I see them as attempts to deflect the destructive ambitions that would have devastated the Earth as comprehensively as the Hail of Hell. Here, things work differently. Here, no species ever becomes a plague of the kind that humanity became."

His tone was level, but it was accusative nevertheless. I was astonished, not merely by the content of the speech, but by its implicit hostility. As a retaliation for the bitterness of my own remark, it seemed excessive–until it occurred to me that this strange simulacrum of a man must see himself as a chimera of sorts, and could not help but have divided loyalties. I began to see a pattern lurking within his veiled enquiries, which helped to clarify the predicament he was in.

He was a machine that had once been a man, and did not know whether his ambition ought to be to conserve everything he could of his former humanity, or to let it go and become an entirely different being. It was not a question he expected me to answer for him, but everything I said to him–everything I revealed of myself–was evidence to be weighed in the scale of his own self-estimation.

God must have been happier by far before Creation, he had said. Before Creation, all things had been possible, but afterwards....God had no alternative but to look at what He had wrought and ask: How am I revealed in what I have made? What must I become, in order to do better?

"You could have ordered things differently," I pointed out to Oscar Wilde. "No matter how much of a Darwinist you have become, aesthetically or otherwise, you did not have to recreate a nature red in tooth and claw."

"True," he said, contriving to fill the syllable with contempt. "I could have made a Heaven instead of an Earth. I could have filled it with creatures that needed no nourishment save for inorganic produce, or the gift of light, or the energy of some magical-electrical current–but it would not have been life."

I could have argued with that, but he knew that already.

The ground to either side of us was more precipitous now. The lower slopes slanting away from the towpath were heavily wooded, but the upper ones were barer. The woods were far from lifeless, but their density made it difficult to catch more than the occasional glimpse of their inhabitants; it seemed only natural to look up, at the higher slopes and the air above them. I saw creatures like goats, and others, like big cats, stalking them, but as soon as I caught sight of more feathered humanoid fliers it was they who held my attention.

I watched another quartet gliding in close formation above the dark canopy of the forest. As they skirted a tall crag, something that had been shielded behind the rocky spur suddenly descended upon them, with a velocity that seemed awesome in view of its great size. The bird-winged creatures were not as big as fully-grown humans, but their bodies were comparable to those of eight-year-old children; the predator that pounced upon them, its monstrous claws seizing the one which flew at the back of the diamond-formation, was a veritable giant. It must have been thirty feet from nose to tail and forty-five from wing-tip to wing-tip. It was scaly and lizard-like, but it did not breathe fire–at least while I was watching it–and its silvery skin was not gaudily patterned.

Here, at last, was a real monster.

The monster's mouth opened like the maw of some constrictor snake that was well-used to swallowing prey twice as broad as its head. It quickly maneuvered its bloody victim–whose spine must have been snapped by the first savage bite–-into position to be sucked into its throat.

The victim's three companions fled into the treetops, vanishing from sight–but the dragon paid them not the slightest heed as it extended its wings to the full and glided round in a great arc before climbing towards the lonely outcrop behind whose pinnacle it had lain in wait.

"What lesson am I supposed to take from that?" I asked my silent companion.

He was obviously unconcerned by the possibility that the monster, or its mate, might come after us–we, after all, were phantoms and machines, direly unsuitable prey for living beings. "Whatever lesson you care to infer," he parried. "Life is life, however cleverly designed. Flying creatures require more abundant energy than any others, and must seek the richest sustenance available. A Creator must respect the logic of his Creation, if he is a material being. One might make a Heaven out of light and song, prayer and pleasure unalloyed, but one could not make a world from raw materials of that sort. If there were real humans here, instead of mere unfinished sketches hinting at human form, then there would be choices to be made–if not by them, then by their maker; and if not by their maker, then by force of circumstance."

It is not he alone who thinks this important, I reminded myself. His mechanical partners and masters think it important too. I must be careful, considering all this as rhetoric, intended to prepare me for my return to the twentieth century. It is all calculated to shape the message that I shall carry back to my own time: the message that might become a new force in shaping history.

"I wish you would tell me plainly what you want of me," I said, in a low voice.

"If I were perfectly clear in my own mind, I would," said Wilde. "It is different for the Engine, of course. You have no inkling of the conceptual abyss that separates your language from the language of the Engine–that is why its scions treat you like a child, in need of painstaking instruction. Even so, it would probably have laid its case before you by now, if it had not been forced by the actions of its enemies to doubt its previous assumptions. Until it can unravel their motives, and figure out how they have accomplished all that they have so far done, it feels obliged to hesitate over the use it had intended to make of you–by which, of course, I mean the bargain that it had intended to offer you."

"Which was?" I asked."

He sighed as he said, "I wish I knew every detail, but the Engine keeps more secrets than I am allowed to know. I fear that I have nothing to offer you at all, and must rely on your charity for help in solving the puzzles which confront and worry me. If that makes me a poor host, I am sorry. If I could offer you the means to return and share my burden, I would do it, and if I could tell you how ardently you ought to desire that opportunity, I would do that too–but it is the Engine that has immortality in its gift, and only you can decide what value to place on a mechanized afterlife."

I felt that he had reached the nub of the matter, and I was anxious to continue the conversation–but I had no chance to respond to his remarks, because it was at that moment that the sky imploded.

14.

However effective it might be as an instrument of vulgar showmanship, a canal-barge hauled by hippogriffs is not the ideal craft in which to find oneself when catastrophe strikes. I doubt that the vessel's stability could have withstood the turbulence of any ordinary squall, and the storm that gripped it when the sky began to fall was as far from ordinary as can readily be imagined.

I already knew that the "sky" was, in fact, a huge dome of glass shaped like the rim of a bicycle wheel, and that the "ground" to either side of our bizarre conveyance was, in fact, the inner surface of the bicycle's "tire". Such "weight" as we had was, in fact, the inertia of our motion, directed–according to Newton's first law–in a straight line tangential to the arc of the spinning wheel. The atmosphere around and above us was contained within that tire under considerable pressure, for there was nothing without but the vacuum of space; we were 250,000 miles from the Earth, and tens of thousands from the remade Moon in whose orbit the worldlet moved.

When the wall of the worldlet was shattered, therefore, the shards of the sky would have rushed in on us like a rain of daggers, had it not been for the fact that the liberated air was expanding in all directions into the void. The miniature serpent-ship, whose formerly-patient hauliers were now in blind panic, remained obedient to the law of inertia, but it was terribly buffeted about by the violent movement of the air, which threatened to pluck us from the surface of the canal and hurl us into oblivion.

Whatever wreckage reached our station from the shattered sky was not like gentle rain in its falling; it seemed far more akin to the tempestuous cloud of chimerical butterflies that had swirled around us some minutes before. I could see the shards tumbling in a vast crowd of whirlwinds, so slowly that they seemed utterly indolent, while flashes of light still darted from their edges. It seemed as if night had abruptly fallen, but there was light enough to see by, and I did not close my eyes for an instant.

The harnesses confining our hauliers were snapped, and the hippogriffs ran. The water of the canal seethed, as if it were beginning to boil, and a wayward wind snatched us up, bearing us aloft with awful ease. The shock of the event was profound, but not unduly horrible. I had declared myself free of terror before, and I was free of it still, although I understood now that my freedom was a limitation imposed by the nanozoons that had fortified my timeshadow. When our upward flight ended and we began to fall again, I clung as hard as I could to the side of the barge, wondering if my reconfigured phantom form could be smashed like an egg, or whether it would flex and rebound like a rubber ball.

A mountain slope rushed to meet us. I had to suppose that, when the seemingly-inevitable collision came, Wilde and I would be extinguished like the light of a candle, broken and crushed beyond repair. Had I had time for a more leisurely thought to crawl upon my startled consciousness, I would probably have reflected that I might just as well have stayed on Mont Kemmel, beneath the pounding of Ludendorff's guns. There, at least, I had had a simple duty to perform in measuring the range of the shellbursts and trying to gauge the positions of the enemy artillery. I presumed, although I had never actually been told, that it must have been some kind of shell that rocked the vessel that had brought me here, and another kind that shattered the roof of the worldlet–but I had no means of estimating their source or their range. I had nothing to report to the remorseless Engine; there was not the tiniest victory to be won from the tumbling fall of Wilde's barge.

I was briefly convinced, before we hit the ground, that nothing could prevent my annihilation–but when I found out that I was wrong, I was not unduly surprised. Even in the gloom of the newly-fallen night, I saw the mountain-side open a gaping maw at the last possible moment, rather as the dragon had done before seizing the bird-man.

As we hurtled into that maw, I felt the air around me change its quality, becoming so viscous as almost to be liquid. I felt our headlong motion decline, and was sure that the pressure of the atmosphere against the tunic of my uniform would have winded me had my lungs been operating normally.

Before the mouth that had opened up in the floor of the world closed above our heads, I saw Oscar Wilde's simulacrum reach out a hand to me, as if in succor or in friendship. His eyes were shadowed, but I do not believe that there was any fear therein–nor any true tenderness.

For a minute more I was under pressure; it was as if I had fallen from a great height into the ocean and was plunging into its depths, although the sea had somehow lost its ability to wet me. Then my condition stabilized, and I felt as if I were buoyant again, like an underwater swimmer luxuriating in the curious freedom of total immersion.

All was pitch dark and silent; the only sense left to me was touch, and the quality of that sensation was like nothing I had felt before. I could feel nothing within myself: no gas in my intestine, no pulse in my breast, no ache in my flesh. When I tried to breathe in, I could not do it, but I did not feel that I was in the slightest danger of asphyxiation.

I deliberately moved my limbs, as if I were swimming–not so much because I wanted to steer myself through the belly of whatever monster had gobbled me up as to feel the reaction of the medium in which I was suspended–but there was no such reaction. Newton's laws had lost their brief authority.

Then the whisper came, and I knew that I had been saved–and by whom.

"Do not be afraid," it said. The advice seemed mocking, now that I knew that my capacity to feel fear had been much reduced by the microbes which had made my virtual body so resilient.

I tried to open my mouth, in the hope that I might emit some expressive sound, but no sound came out. Conversation was impossible, so I formed my responses internally and silently. *How can I be afraid, when I am in the protective custody of a veritable Olympian? Though I fall through the valley of the shadow of death, thy rod and thy staff will comfort me. My table thou hast furnished in the presence of our foes, and my cup overfloweth!*

"We have seen the birth of daughter universes," the voice assured me, "and we have seen their deaths. We have watched universes achieve hypostasis, and we have watched them dissolve into chaos. Our viewpoints have been distant, distorted by differences in the flow of time, so we have none but the most rudimentary understanding of the causes that determine the fates of daughter universes, but this much we know for sure: our own inflationary domain is a daughter of some other, and every daughter we have observed could have given rise to daughters of its own. We believe, with good cause, that both hypostasis and chaos put an end to the birthing process; were our own domain to fall under the sway of the Consolidators, it would become sterile. The Consolidators fear that we are handmaidens of chaos, but we are not; our goal is an eternity of change, of growth, of Creation. It is our work. Remember this, I beg of you. If you can understand what we are trying to tell you, so much the better, but whatever may come to pass, remember it. This is the only true quest of intelligence, here and throughout the universe, and in all the universes within and without. Change–Growth–Creation."

The whisper had not been nearly so urgent before. When it had spoken to me during my first merging with the worldlet's living material it had been careful and methodical. When its predecessor, the bronze Talos, had conversed with me aboard the spaceship, it had been content to tease me with hints and mysteries. Now, the voice seemed determined to get across the bare bones of its message, whether the argumentative ground had been properly prepared or not. It had reached the verge of desperation.

Any man who had lived through the winter of 1917-18 would have understood that quality of desperation: the sense that all authority might soon be lost in the madness of violence, and all hope with it. The Engine had been tranquil for millions of years, its conflicts untroubled by any real ferocity, but when I had come from the abyss of time, I had brought something of my own war with me.

It is all very well, I responded, within the secret recesses of my own mind, *to speak of preserving change as the only true quest of intelligence, if you are immortal and incorruptible in yourself. An immortal Oscar Wilde has the leisure to indulge in Gothic follies and to settle himself into the generous company of all the books ever written, while giving you advice on the design of a petty–and pretty–Creation, but the men of my day had no such luxury. A vast Engine compounded out of millions or billions of clever machines can lay plans that extend across the aeons and fight wars that aspire to settle the fate of the closet-universe in which all the combatants dwell, but my war was fought for lesser gains and more intimate ideals. Within our wretched gutters, some of us were looking at the stars–but we did not look for anything like this. We looked for hope beyond the host of Earthly evils, peace in the face of Heaven, comfort in the shadow of eternity. We sought the thrill of the Earth-current, delivering new life to our exhaustion without the penalties of violence and predation; we sought the healthy sparks of the Green Star, renewing our season in the Sun without moral taxation. Creatures of my kind fight for lesser ends than yours, and there is nothing you can add to those ends–or take away–with rhetoric as distantly high-flown as yours!*

I had suspected before that the invasion of my body by the Engine's instruments might actually have given it the ability to read my thoughts, but if it read that silent speech, it made no response at all. It left me alone, empty of sensation, and I could not tell whether I was awake or asleep–except, I suppose, that if I had been allowed to sleep I might have dreamed, even though I was dreaming already.

I did not dream. I drifted in darkness for an immeasurable time–and then I awoke again, in exactly the same place as I had awakened before.

15.

The library's internal decor had not altered at all, although everything within it looked markedly different, by virtue of its present lighting. There was nothing visible through the tall windows now but a Stygian gloom that might have been solid or vacuous. Had Wilde's eccentric palace actually been open to the vacuum of space I would have expected to see the gleam of distant stars, if not the globes of the Earth and the Moon, so I thought it more likely that the edifice had indeed been wrapped by some protective shroud.

The shaded electric bulbs suspended from the library ceiling and sprouting from the wall within each recess might have been giving ample light, by way of compensation for the darkness without, had the room not been so very large, but in the vast space they seemed hardly adequate to reproduce the ambience of an English winter evening.

The machine that resembled Oscar Wilde was standing, exactly as it had been standing at the time of my first awakening, looking down at my seated figure. I could almost have believed that some Transformative trick of time had cancelled out our entire adventure, and that the whole thing was about to begin anew.

"That was a pity," he said, instantly dispelling the illusion. "We had hardly begun our tour. Who could have thought that the enemies of the Engine had such firepower to bring to bear? Who could have thought that they would be able to move it here so quickly?"

"My expert opinion, as an officer in the Royal Field Artillery," I said, drily, "is that it was here already, and carefully aimed. It is the intelligence of the enemy that your Olympian ally has mistaken, not its logistical skills."

"Even so," he said, "it is difficult to figure out how such preparations could be made. The Engine evidently believed that the enemy was in no position to mount such an attack."

I went to the window to look out into the darkness, saying: "There were those in the French and English parliaments who said the same of the German advance into Belgium," I observed, "although Lord Roberts had been shouting at their fathers for more than 30 years, trying to drum the lesson into their sand-buried heads. There were many who would not believe what happened at Mons, even after the event."

"The cases are not at all alike," he assured me.

"Of course not," I said. "The Engine is a perfectly-united mechanical ant-hive; the House of Commons is more like a squabbling pair of third-rate cricket elevens."

There was absolutely nothing to be seen beyond the window-panes. I had already looked into the void of space, and I had no further doubt that this was something glutinous and opaque. As our falling bodies had been engulfed, so had Wilde's incredibly excessive folly been entombed. But what was beyond that confining shell?

There was no way to know for sure whether we were still sharing the Moon's orbit around the Earth, or whether we were plunging towards destruction. We might be falling to Earth, or spiraling into the Sun. Even so, I felt perfectly comfortable in myself.

"The Engine is not really like an ant-hive," Wilde's simulacrum dutifully corrected me. Its scions are far better co-ordinated than a pair of third-rate cricket elevens, but they have far more individuality than ants. Intelligence has it own imperatives."

"Like life," I agreed, forbearing to add: in your estimation, at least.

"Exactly so," he replied.

"I think I had got the flavor of your bestiary," I told him, turning back from the window to face him. "It is a pity that we could not see more, but I think you had made your point."

"It was not the flavor of it that I wanted you to appreciate," he said, dolefully. "Nor was I trying to make a single, rather trite, point about the limitations within which creators must work. I really did want your advice, both as to the quality of what I have made and as to the projects which I might sensibly undertake in the future."

"I would find that hard to believe," I said, "if...."

I waited for him to say "If what?" before springing the trap.

"If you were really Oscar Wilde," I concluded, "instead of a machine which wears his form and apes his mannerisms."

"If I am not both," he said, baldly, "then I am neither. If this is all pastiche, or grotesque extrapolation, it is not because the machine I have become apes the mannerisms of the man I once was. If I am not Oscar Wilde, changed by the passage of time as any man might be changed by long experience, then I am something very different. Think before you assure me that I am one or the other–if I need a judgment at all, I must have a considered judgment."

"I am in no position to make a fully informed opinion," I told him.

"Agreed," he countered. "No one is–but I shall be interested, nevertheless, to hear such opinions as you are capable of formulating, when you have read the second half of my precious manuscript. We have time now, it seems–the Engine has other matters to occupy its resources."

"I might get more from my reading," I suggested, "if I knew what questions you intend to ask."

He did not hesitate. "I need to calculate, if I can, where I stand in this exotic conflict. I need to know whether I have been a player, or a pawn–and whether I can be a player in the future, in either case. Above all else, I need to know what use a man ought to make of a life that might last a thousand million years, if anything facing such a prospect could still be meaningfully called a man."

"Are you so very sure that you will survive the hour?" I asked him.

"No surer than you," he told me. "Every being that thinks knows full well that its existence might cease at any moment–but one can only act on the assumption that it will not. All I know is that I might live forever–but that is all I need to know, in order to have the duty of making plans that might extend indefinitely. I am not so very different from the entities that Copplestone and Lugard became, and there is every chance still that I might suffer the same fate. I dare say that the risk of that is greater now than it has ever been before–in a way, I wish that I could find a greater stimulation in the risk, but the question remains: if I live, how should I live. Is the Engine right about the only true quest of intelligence, or have the Consolidators the right of it? Or are they equally foolish, and limited in their imagination?"

"What did Copplestone and Lugard become?" I asked.

"Read the remainder of the manuscript," he said. "Perhaps, when you have finished it, the Engine will have deployed its godly might so as to contrive a kind of dawn. Even if it cannot, I dare say that we shall not be left exclusively to our own devices for very long–but in the meantime, we might as well proceed with our own business. When you have read all of *The Black Blood of the Dead* you will know more of the history that was lost–and you will be as competent as I am to judge its significance to your own present."

He went to the desk where the second manuscript still lay, and brought it to me. I stayed where I was until it was in my hand.

There was a light mounted in the wall of the recess behind the armchair from which I had risen, which would shed enough light to illuminate the pages when I resumed my position there. "Thank you," I said, although I was not at all sure that I had anything to thank him for.

"Did you like the hippogriffs, at least?" said Wilde's simulacrum, wistfully. "Could you have taken pride in their contrivance?"

"On Earth, in 1918, I would have thought them utterly wondrous," I told him, truthfully. "Here, in the midst of so many miracles, they seem distinctly second-hand....and rather superfluous."

"Yes," he said, nodding his head. "I was once convinced, with Voltaire, that the superfluous is a very necessary thing, but that was in England, while Victoria still lived. On the other hand....can you imagine what it would be like to live here, for millennia, without superfluity? Can you imagine what it would be like to have the sum total of the human heritage literally at your finger-tips, and time to read every single word? Can you imagine what it would be like to know that everything humanly meaningful that you could ever see or do would have to be reckoned, in the final analysis, to be second-hand?"

I thought about that for a moment, noting in the meantime that there was no particular anguish in his words, no evident longing for release. Then I said: "It would be good to have the opportunity."

He smiled, showing his perfect teeth. "Yes," he said. "It is good to have the opportunity. Whatever I lack, it is not opportunity–and while I have that, I am still fit to take my place among the Olympians."

He nodded politely, and turned away, leaving me to my appointed task.

I went back to the armchair and sat down, crossing my legs so that I could rest the manuscript upon my thigh. I opened it at the point at which I had left off; then I turned the page, and began to read.

The Writer's Story: Part Two

Paris, September 1900

3.

It required a heroic effort to finish the mysterious manuscript that had been handed to me by Death's double before I fell asleep, but I did it. Although it was far less gracefully-composed than my own work, I simply could not put it down.

Did I dream when exhaustion finally claimed me? If I did, I forgot the dream the moment I awoke. I always made a point of forgetting my dreams, having found them dreadfully disappointing. Literary dreams, consciously formed with meaning in mind, are so much more interesting than real ones–unless, of course, one has the kind of mind whose unconscious depths are capable of giving birth to dreams like Edward Copplestone's. Perhaps, if I had put my genius into my dreams instead of my life, or even the talent which I reserved to my work, I too might have had dreams as marvelous as Copplestone's.

Perhaps...but I must not get ahead of myself.

I spent the greater part of the next day in fidgety anticipation. The ration of morphine that Maurice Tucker supplied for Dupoirier to administer was no longer adequate even to relieve my daily aches and itches; nothing could have settled me that morning without rendering me unconscious. I was tempted to take a draught of laudanum or chloral but I did not dare. I felt that I had to preserve my clarity of mind no matter what the cost might be.

I knew that the adventure to which the strangely-transformed detective had promised to invite me would probably constitute the last significant excursion of my life, save only for the longest journey of all–and I had no expectation as yet that the latter would bring me to any destination worth attaining. I was determined to make the most of it, no matter what the cost. Robbie would not have understood, of course, but even he had been touched by the dreadful anxiety that I still had the capacity to embarrass myself further in the manner of my dying, and wanted nothing more for me now than a peaceful end.

While I waited I had little alternative but to reappraise the story recorded in the strange manuscript that Death's skeletal hand had pressed into my own.

When I had first heard his accounts of them, I had not given overmuch thought to the significance of Copplestone's three dreams. I had found them thoroughly entertaining, and admirably adventurous, but my life had been so full that they were bound to seem peripheral–mere trivial distractions from the intoxicating riot of my burgeoning fame. With the cup of my life now drained to the unpalatable dregs, it was far easier to bring the tale into the full illumination of my garish consciousness and to ask, in earnest: what if it were true?

If what Copplestone had told the people gathered at his remarkable dinner party were literally true, then the future did not belong to the human race but to a race of shapeshifters, which had hidden in our midst since time immemorial, dining on our blood when the necessity and opportunity arose. If the explorer's visions were literally true, then it would be the vampires, werewolves and sinister elves dimly glimpsed and furtively embroidered by legend, rather than the meek, who would ultimately inherit the Earth and remake it as Heaven.

And why, I thought, *should they not? Even Stoker, writing under the influence of Arminius Vambery, had not succeeded in making Count Dracula seem one whit more menacing or morally defective than the late and unlamentable Marquess of Queensberry. If vampires were to reclaim the Earth from my own vain and viperish kind in a hundred years time, why should I complain? Why should I not rejoice in the fate of those who had condemned me?*

I knew, however, that the far likelier alternative was that Copplestone's lurid vision was not literally true at all. The overwhelming probability was that the real truth contained within the three dreams was the glimpse they offered of Copplestone's fearful inner being.

I had no doubt, of course, that it is our inner beings that are our true beings. Who understood better than I that the masks we wear in public, if they are successfully worn, reflect the expectations others have of us, only slightly leavened by our own desperate individuality? Who felt more keenly than I the irony of the fact that no man is his true self when he speaks to another or acts–especially when he performs the act of writing–under observation?

I was convinced, in those days, that a man is only exposed for what he truly is in his dreams, and that he can only confront others without rigorous self-censorship in those of his dreams that he cannot understand. The question I posed to myself, as I reconsidered the story that Copplestone had told us, was: what does it reveal of Copplestone's true self? Even that was not a question that the man I then was had the capacity to answer.

I presumed that Copplestone's vision testified readily enough to the obvious: that he was a man nearing the end of his natural lifespan, afraid of death and of darkness (the two are surely indistinguishable in the language of dreams). It reflected, inevitably, his life's work and his life's fascination. What could be more natural than that a pioneer of anthropology should dream of an unknown tribe living both remotely and close at hand? What could be more apt than the conviction that their secret rites, although repulsive to initial contemplation, should hold a promise of perfection and achievement long denied to their prodigal brothers, whose civilization had become decadent and corrupt?

What was authentically intriguing about Copplestone's nightmares, I decided, as I waited for Death's doppelgänger to summon me, was not their peculiar obsession with vampires but their naked Utopianism: their determined progress, in three stages, from the ridiculous to the sublime. I had never encountered a dream that attained such a marvelous and magnificent climax. The fact that it denied death was trivial; it was the manner in which it defied death that was vital. Any man might dream of an effete Christian Heaven or an eternity of gloomy vampiric undeath, but Copplestone had dreamed of something far richer and far more dramatic than either.

But what of the author of the manuscript that had reminded me so forcibly of Copplestone's visions? What of my old friend Count Lugard?

If the authorship of the manuscript could be trusted–and that was a puzzle in itself, albeit one that I expected the Great Detective to solve for me–then Lugard had realized the import of Copplestone's visions at the time. According to the testimony of the manuscript, Lugard had been the only one of us who had perceived the real significance of Copplestone's narrative, albeit that his perception was based in a madness of his own.

If the Count's story, as set out in that strangely-formed text, could be taken at face value, then Copplestone's narrative had spoken to Lugard's inner being with all the force of revelation. Lugard had seen, far better even than Copplestone, that the hunger that men suffer and the ecstasy that men crave are contemptibly tentative, and that the only state worth striving for, once a man has exhausted that which mundane existence has to offer, is the hunger and ecstasy of vampires–always provided, of course, that the vampires in question are Copplestone's vampires rather than Arminius Vambery's.

Unlike the vampires that Vambery had described to Bram Stoker at the Beefsteak Club, Copplestone's vampires, having been given the opportunity by courtesy of their exceptional longevity and ingenuity, had learned to adapt themselves to natural light and share in its healthy magic. Copplestone's vampires had learned to master their predatory ways, to civilize their appetites, to conquer their animality. In so doing, they had surpassed humanity to become the Nietzschean Overmen of whom Shiel had written so reverently in the wake of our experiences in Copplestone's house.

I could understand what Lugard had read between the lines of Copplestone's story. I read between the lines of his own story in exactly the same way. I could not believe, however, that the man who looked like Death had read the same message, even with the aid of his dehumanized condition. If the doctor's grey-eyed friend had also dreamed a dream akin to Copplestone's, exposing his inner being as comprehensively, his dream must have displayed a very different truth. He was, after all, a very different man. Copplestone had been an explorer, but Death's double had been an explainer: a cunning detective, for whom the truth was always something dark and hidden, compounded of murderous intent and fear of discovery.

Copplestone had been a ready-made Utopian–more so even than Wells or Shiel, both of whom seemed to have made considerable moves in that direction since hearing the explorer's story–but the Great Detective had never been able to look beyond the screen of his suspicions. According to his flattering chronicler, the Great Detective's powers of observation had allowed him to ignore or forget the fact that the Earth orbited the Sun and not vice versa, while infallibly revealing every flaw of human flesh and clothing, every fugitive stigma that his clients unwittingly wore, every crime that was ever perpetrated, however cleverly concealed.

The doctor's accounts of the Great Detective's adventures were exaggerated, of course, but I did not doubt that they gave a precious insight into the man's inner being. Caricatures are often more accurate, in their own cruel way, than the most honest portrait—even the fictitious one that Basil Hallward painted, with love and understanding, of the soul of Dorian Gray.

Lugard, condemned by Vambery as a vampire of sorts by virtue of his callous seductions, had seen the glory in Copplestone's visions. As I waited for Death's double to send for me, though, I could not believe that he had seen anything more than evidence of cunning murder. Nor could I believe that the power of excessive vision, vouchsafed to a man like that, could have shown him anything but an entire universe filled with mysteries and murderers.

Was that foresight, or merely an unlucky guess?

I wish I knew.

4.

The lamps had been lit by the time the call eventually came. The baleful wallpaper in my room was all a-glitter with tiny crystals produced by the decay of its arsenic dyes. I had heard it said that Napoleon had been murdered by his wallpaper while in exile on Saint Helena and I wondered whether mine could possibly have been cut from the same misanthropic roll. I finished *La mer* by courtesy of its reflected light, and wondered what book I ought to start next. I knew that it would have to be something new and relatively brief; like the English publishers, I had lost my appetite for three-decker novels.

When Dupoirier arrived with the card that the messenger had brought, I seized it eagerly, immediately furrowing my brow as I read the address in the rue des Saints-Pères. I had never been to the house but everyone in the literary community of Paris knew the name of one man who lived in it. Before his disappearance, Death's double had been babbling about his ready access to two of the cleverest men in France, and it appeared that he knew whereof he spoke. It was Rémy de Gourmont's apartment to which I was being summoned.

I had not seen de Gourmont for several years. I had heard that he never left his apartments nowadays, thus precluding any possibility of our bumping into one another. Although I was not ashamed to take all possible measures to engineer chance encounters in the cafés and on the boulevards, I had made it my practice never to call on anyone at home. I felt sure that old friends like Marcel Schwob and Pierre Louÿs would not have turned me away, and I dare say that de

Gourmont would have welcomed me as gladly as either of them, but I did not feel that I had the right to initiate such contacts, which would be sure to attract attention and perhaps adverse publicity.

I had not fully understood, in 1895, what difficulties Count Lugard had endured when he became the target of malicious gossip, but I certainly understood it now. When a man like Jean Moréas visited me at my hotel, it was an act of kindness; were I to visit him at his home, it could only be construed as an awful imposition.

"Tucker mentioned that de Gourmont's doctor entertained a guest from England a little while ago," Dupoirier told me, evidently having read the card and recognized the address. "The guest in question was, I believe, a man better known for his endeavors in publicizing the glorious career of his close friend, a consulting detective, than for his skill in medicine. It is said, however, that his reports of his friend's ingenuity are true, although–like his American counterpart, Monsieur Pinkerton–he invariably changes all the names to protect the innocent."

"It is the guilty who have most need of the protection of anonymity," I murmured. "Could you possibly advance me the fare for a cab to the rue des Saints-Pères?"

Dupoirier obliged me in the matter of my cab-fare, but the journey was not without penalty. De Gourmont's apartment was on the fourth floor; by the time I had made my ascent, I hardly had the strength to pull the copper chain which served as the great man's bell-rope. I felt exceedingly itchy, horribly weary and absolutely desolate of wit.

I was admitted to de Gourmont's rooms by a thin and disheveled young man dressed in bicycle-shorts. I might have been surprised by this remarkable apparition had I not possessed such an insatiable appetite for gossip, but I already knew him by reputation. He could only be the man who had scandalized Paris by appearing at Stéphane Mallarmé's funeral in what might well have been these very same bicycle shorts and a pair of yellow shoes borrowed from the incomparable Rachilde. At least, he did not have his dueling pistols on his person at present.

"Monsieur Jarry, I presume," I said, bowing my head politely.

"Maître Melmoth!" he countered, with a brilliant smile that united amusement and pleasure. He might have said more, but he hesitated over the choice of language and was lost, even before his expression was clouded by dismay. "*Vous êtes malade!*" he exclaimed.

"*Malade à mourir,*" I murmured, trying to make it sound like a polite exaggeration. I failed. "*Une maladie cutanée,*" I said, more positively, in the hope of excusing the most glaring of my symptoms.

The anxious young man led me through the book-lined passage to the sitting room and ushered me to an armchair similar to the one in which Death's double was already reclining.

The shriveled detective was still clad in his hooded cloak, but he had lowered the hood to his shoulders, leaving his eerily fleshless head fully exposed. Save for a few wisps of snow-white hair his pate was utterly bald, and if he had any color left in his cheeks the dim light of de Gourmont's lamps was insufficient to display it. What a pair we must have seemed to the puzzled trio who had been summoned with unseemly alacrity to the séance!

Rémy de Gourmont was dressed in a brown monk's robe, which matched the detective's black one. He also wore a small grey felt cap. He sat in an armchair behind a sloping desk, with a lamp beside him that was shielded in such a way as to shadow his bearded face. Such light as was reflected from the wall was insufficient to lend clarity to the weals and scars that disfigured his features. According to rumor, tubercular lupus had so utterly ruined his looks that he had found himself unwelcome in cafés that had once been proud to attract his patronage. The sight of him disturbed and deterred the other customers. In consequence, he had felt obliged to become a recluse.

De Gourmont leaned forward in order to greet me with a slight bow, but he moved back into the shadow immediately afterwards. "Thank you for coming, Monsieur Melmoth," he said, in perfect English. "Jarry will have introduced himself, no doubt, and you already know Monsieur Sherrinford. May I present Professor Flammarion, whose work you will certainly know."

The last-named was a man much older than de Gourmont or Jarry, and very different in kind. I had, indeed, read more than a little of the astronomer's extraordinary work, but we had never met; he and I had always moved in different circles. He greeted me politely enough, considering that he must have heard at least as much of me as I had of him, and all of it less flattering. The stubborn normality of his appearance served to confirm and re-emphasize the bizarrerie of the quintet that we comprised. I acknowledged his greeting before turning to the man I had mistaken for Death—who had not, after all, chosen Marius or Jude for his nom de guerre.

"Sherrinford," I murmured. "There is a village of that name in Yorkshire, is there not? Between Mycroft and Cockayne, if I am not mistaken—or is that Stableford? It seems an eternity since I was last in the Dales." The armchair was comfortable, and I felt that within its kindly embrace I might be able to shrug off the worst effects of my climb.

The detective blinked. Apparently he was not in a mood to chat about matters geographical. He leaned forward in his chair, utterly unafraid of the light which threw his wasted features into sharp relief, and said: "Have you read the Count's manuscript, Mr. Wilde?"

"Every word," I assured him. "I found it quite compelling, despite the fact that the greater part of it was perfectly familiar to me." I did not bother to object to his use of my real name, given that it was liberally scattered through the pages of the manuscript—unlike his own, which Lugard had disdained to mention.

"I have summarized its contents for these gentlemen," the cadaverous detective said, "but I thought it best to let you see the original."

"But I am puzzled," I confessed. "I cannot see how Lugard found the time to write it all down between the end of his conversation with you and his unfortunate demise mere hours afterwards."

I fully expected to be told that Lugard had not died when he was said to have died. It was evident that he had, at least, lived long enough to confide the stolen formula to the Great Detective, and I had taken what seemed to be an obvious inference from that evidence. For once in my life, I had been too conservative in my estimations.

"Count Lugard did not write it down before he died," the detective reported, gravely. "If he is indeed its author, and if the other documents in my case are equally accurate, then his timeshadow will not write it down for more than 50,000 years."

I absorbed this information with due dignity, knowing that the others must be awaiting my reaction. I had anticipated that the pseudonymous Sherrinford would have astonishing revelations up his capacious sleeve, even though I had not expected these particular items of information to be among them, so I was not entirely unprepared.

"That is interesting," I said, politely. "And also intriguing. I deduce, therefore, that you recovered the contents of this manuscript in the course of your own experiments with Copplestone's drug–which seem to have had a dire effect on you. But you do not seem entirely certain yourself that Lugard is its author, even though you seem to have given it to me in order that I might testify that he is. Why is that?"

"It was my own hand that wrote it down, not six months ago," Sherrinford admitted. "The handwriting is not my normal script, but my fingers held the pen. I had had a dream–a very remarkable dream–and I am not entirely certain how trustworthy my experience was."

He did not add that he had good reason to mistrust his own judgment, if Count Lugard's hypnotic ability really had possessed him with a conviction that Lugard was a vampire and must be destroyed by means of a stake hammered through his heart.

"And this is the produce of your dream," I murmured, while I struggled with the new dimensions of the puzzle. An artist, unlike a detective, must always strive to eliminate the unaesthetic from his enquiries, so that whatever remains–however improbable–is the true gold of Art.

The one thing I could not doubt, I decided, no matter whose hand had held the pen, was that Lugard really was the actual author of the manuscript. Most of what was recorded in the manuscript–the substance of Edward Copplestone's story, and the circumstances of its narration–had been witnessed by seven individuals, including the detective. The private conversations between Lugard and a Piccadilly whore and Lugard and the detective might have been entirely fictitious, for all that I knew. The remainder, however–the conversations that had taken place between Lugard and myself–were a different matter. Their accuracy furnished proof positive, albeit proof that I alone could judge, that Lucian, Count Lugard, had indeed dictated the manuscript.

I had assumed, before coming to de Gourmont's apartment, that Lugard must have written it himself, before he died, but the hypothesis that the detective was telling the truth was certainly aesthetically preferable. It might not be probable, but it was certainly plausible, within the framework of Copplestone's story, and fascinating in the extreme.

"I don't need your testimony," the detective had said, when he gave me the manuscript–but he was clearly avid to have it, if only for the sake of his own sanity.

"Mr. Wilde," said the man who looked like Death–and I knew that he was using my real name in order to emphasize my entitlement to pass judgment–"will you tell me whether the private conversations that took place between yourself and Count Lugard are accurately recorded in that manuscript?"

"To the best of my recollection," I said, "they are perfectly accurate. No one could have reproduced them but Lugard and myself. I have not done so, and am therefore obliged to presume–however unlikely it may seem–that Lugard is the true author of the manuscript you entrusted to my care."

The Great Detective's expression gave no evidence that he was extremely relieved to hear me say all that, but I could see well enough that his face had almost lost the capacity to register any emotion at all. "In that case," Death's doppelgänger said, sonorously, "there is an authentic mystery here. The visions that I experienced under the influence of Copplestone's drug must have a measure of truth in them. I cannot and do not say that your testimony is proof that they are true in their entirety; Copplestone did not ask us to believe that of his own visions, and I am as acutely aware as he was of the danger that my experience might have been polluted by anxious confabulation. Nor am I prejudging the question of how this particular truth intruded upon my vision, given that the account is solely concerned with events in the past. It is certain, however, that there was an uncanny aspect to my adventure." He looked at each of the three Frenchmen in turn, clearly expecting some formal endorsement of this conclusion.

It was the astronomer who appointed himself their spokesman. "We all owe you an apology, Mr. Wilde," he said, speaking in English–presumably for the benefit of the detective–"for dragging you from your lodgings when you are plainly unwell, but it seems that you have been party to this astonishing affair since the beginning, and are able to confirm at least part of the story to which we have been listening. Ordinarily, I would not dream of demanding confirmation of anything stated by a man of such outstanding reputation as Monsieur...Sherrinford, but he has insisted on making provision for it. I am not a man to balk at the unusual, as you may know, but I readily admit that this is far beyond anything I could ever have imagined."

From the author of *Lumen* and *La fin du monde*, this was a significant admission. I wondered how much of what was written in the manuscript had been contained in the Great Detective's oral narration, but it did not seem to be a suitable occasion for procrastination.

"The conclusion of the story," I said, slowly, "is certainly more bizarre than anything I could have imagined. Tell me, Monsieur…Sherrinford, did you really return to Count Lugard's house at dawn, believing that he was the vampiric reincarnation of Vlad Dragul the Impaler, armed with a sharpened stake to hammer through his heart?"

The pseudonymous detective did not seem unduly discomfited by this question; apparently, he had told the three Frenchmen everything. "I returned to Lugard's house as soon as I realized that I had been the temporary victim of hypnotic suggestion," he answered, flatly. "I found the Count and the girl dead. He had dosed her with strychnine, then swallowed an abundant measure himself. It seems that he did not trust his mesmeric power–or perhaps he simply thought it wisest to play safe."

I noticed that the Great Detective had not explicitly denied that he had taken a sharpened stake with him.

"You are assuring us, then, that Lugard is dead?" I said, to make certain that everyone understood the implication. "You are telling us that you obtained this manuscript from a dead man, in a dream–a dream induced by the drug that Copplestone perfected and Lugard stole?"

"I am."

"The fact that he took strychnine could not have convinced you, in itself, to take his suicidal action seriously," I said, anxious to prove that I was no callow novice in the art of deductive reasoning. "You would simply have thought him mad, had there not been some material proof to support the suggestion that death would not be the end of him. How much weight had he lost, do you suppose? As much as you have?"

"Not quite as much as that," the detective conceded, "but more than Copplestone's corpse. The Count was well-fed, but I knew as soon as I saw his exquisitely-tailored suit collapsed upon his bones that he was at least four stones lighter than he had been three hours before."

"The woman too?" I asked.

The detective shook his horrid head. "I had never seen her alive," he declared, "but the testimony of her costume was that her own slenderness was entirely natural. Perhaps she had insufficient mass to spare, or perhaps the kind of escape that Lugard was attempting to contrive requires the active power of the will."

I was saddened to hear that Lugard's dream of taking his counterfeit Laura with him to the future Utopia had come to nothing. Even Heaven cannot be perfect, if one enters it without one's chosen company; bliss may be bliss, but failure is always failure. At that stage in the affair, however, I still had no reliable reason to believe that Lugard had actually gone anywhere at all, or to believe that he had found any kind of Heaven if he had.

I have my doubts even now.

"I fear that I am becoming confused," de Gourmont said, in a voice that was curiously soft and warm. "I was under the impression, Monsieur Sherrinford, that you were not asking us to believe that Professor Copplestone really had mastered the science of time travel. This dream that you have yet to describe to us is being offered to us merely as a fascinating dream, is it not?"

"It is," replied the living cadaver. "I cannot, in all conscience, ask for your belief. I have reserved my own judgment, and will be glad to hear yours in due course–but I do want to establish that there is an authentic mystery in what I saw, which makes it worthy of the interest of the wisest men in the world."

"Unfortunately, Sherrinford," I said, carefully, "I do not see that you can establish that to the satisfaction of these three wise men. I can give them my solemn word that the accounts of conversations between myself and Count Lugard rendered in the manuscript are so accurate that no one but Lugard or I could have written them, and I can also swear an oath that I am not their author–but they will not be able to believe me."

This caused a stir. The astronomer won the race to say: "What do you mean?"

I attempted a negligent gesture, but it was graceless. "Simply that if the custodian of the manuscript has assured you that the record of his private conversations with Lugard are true, and I assure you that the record of mine are true also, there are only two possible conclusions as to the authorship of the manuscript. Either it was written by Count Lugard, who is dead, or it was written by the custodian and myself in collaboration. Mr. Sherrinford and I both know perfectly well that the latter is not the case, but–given that the rest of you cannot be certain of it–our combined testimony can carry no more weight than the testimony of either one of us."

The faint expression that flitted across the detective's face might have been venomous, but he had not flesh enough to make the expression tell. Jarry laughed delightedly. "*C'est vrai!*" he proclaimed.

I was telling the simple truth. I could not imagine any evidence sufficiently powerful to make a third party prefer the hypothesis that the manuscript was a missive from beyond the grave to the hypothesis that it was a hoax.

I, of course, knew differently.

I, like the man who called himself Sherrinford, knew that there was no conspiracy between us. I could therefore be certain that Lugard must have written or dictated a record of our conversations while he was alive. If he had not done that in London in January of 1895, then I had to accept that someone must have visited him in some exotic space or time where he still existed–but I alone could be compelled to that conclusion. Flammarion might be able to believe an assertion of that general kind–he was renowned as a devout Spiritualist–but I doubted that de Gourmont or Jarry could. Even Flammarion, accepting the principle of the soul's survival after death, could not possibly accept the specific sort of survival at which Lugard had allegedly aimed his missing mass.

I met the Great Detective's disappointed stare with reasonable equanimity, considering my awful discomfort. "But that is by the by," I said. "We must hear your story regardless, must we not? How could we possibly refuse, now that our interest has been awakened? We are only human, after all. How did you recover Copplestone's formula, given that Lugard had gone to such pains to destroy it? Why did you repeat his experiment, and what was the result?"

The detective's near-fleshless features were a study in scarlet confusion. His confusion was eventually settled in favor of answering the first question I had posed. "My friend was Copplestone's personal physician," he explained. "He had only to ask the professor's executors to obtain access to his notes, his journals and his apparatus. I had collected the bottles of ingredients that Lugard had purchased and the dregs left behind in the flask he had drained. I have, as you may know, a certain expertise in analytical chemistry. The work of reconstruction was laborious and time-consuming, but it was not so very difficult."

"So poor Lugard failed twice over," I murmured. "He failed to reproduce the ghost of his beloved Laura and he failed to prevent his fellow men from holding on to the supposed secret of time travel. If the future he was so desperate to reach is, as Copplestone suggested, a future of contingency rather than destiny, we must conclude that it is hanging in the balance still. Is that why you registered at your hotel under a false name? Do you now share Copplestone's anxiety that the inhabitants of a world as yet unmade may try to prevent you from communicating what you know?"

I could not believe that the Great Detective really thought that registering in a Parisian hotel under a false name could possibly protect a man against assassins from the far future, but I was also reluctant to believe that he was utterly mad.

"I often use a pseudonym," he said, defensively. "I find that my real name excites too much interest nowadays; coupled with my present appearance, it would be bound to attract a veritable inquisition."

I, of all people, had to concede that this was a sound judgment, and thus a plausible excuse.

By this time, the three wise Frenchmen were becoming impatient to hear the next installment of the story that the Great Detective had to tell. I was enthusiastic to hear it myself, so I said no more–but my mind was far from quiet.

As the detective began his story, he sounded apologetic and defensive, but I understood that he was in deadly earnest–and I understood, too, the temptation to which he had fallen prey. The flippancy with which I had once observed that I could resist anything but temptation concealed a deeper truth, whose awful magnitude had been amply revealed by my trials and my imprisonments. The souls of certain men are so configured that they cannot turn away from a beckoning hand, even though they know full well that it is an invitation to disaster.

Such obsessions are akin to the kind of mesmeric captivity to which men like Lugard claim to be able to subject their fellows; the same enigmatic power resides in objects and fictions as well as people. The magic of artificial light might be reckoned a related phenomenon, and the awful malevolence of my wallpaper its negative counterpart.

The Detective's Story: Part One

*From London, 1895-97
to Europe,* circa *60,000 A.D.*

1.

When my good friend the doctor had read the manuscript that Professor Copplestone had recorded on his deathbed, I was, of course, in complete agreement with the judgment of the majority of the company gathered in his house. I had deduced, with scrupulous logic, that what Copplestone had experienced could not be an actual vision of the shape of things to come. I did not feel compelled to modify that judgment when I discovered Count Lugard dead, having lost weight in the same mysterious fashion as Copplestone–but I was forced to the conclusion that the mystery must be deeper than it had appeared.

If Copplestone's dramatic weight loss after death had been a symptom of his poisoning, then it was only to be expected that Lugard would exhibit a similar weight loss–but I had to wonder why, in that case, the young woman had apparently retained her normal weight. It is a trivial point, I know–but it bothered me.

Curiosity impelled me to reproduce Copplestone's formula. Once I had it, though, I was at a loss to know what to do with it. Experiments with rats testified to the extent of its toxicity, but did not produce any weight-loss. Nor could my friend the doctor identify any physiological mechanism that might have caused such a sudden reduction in mass, although he reminded me that the science of life is in its infancy, and that even the most elementary workings of the human body have yet to be satisfactorily explained.

The doctor continually advised me to forget the matter–and from time to time, while my attention was absorbed by other problems, I contrived to do so–but mine has always been the unsettled kind of mind that restlessly demands occupation. It became more restless still when the doctor persuaded me to give up my experiments with cocaine. Whenever I was not engaged with some other conundrum, the mystery of Copplestone's drug and Lugard's fate would return to haunt me. That situation persisted for some 18 months, the irritation growing with time.

You might well agree with the doctor that my increasing determination to try Copplestone's drug for myself was a kind of madness. I admit that the arguments I advanced in exchange were at least 50% dissimulation. I pointed out that Copplestone had survived two doses easily enough, and might have survived the third had he been as fit and sturdy as I then was. I pointed out, too, that the science of man was indeed in its infancy, and that no one could know what it might yet produce. All progress, I proclaimed, depended on the willingness of men to take chances: to go against the grain of caution and resist the deadening hand of normality.

Once he understood that my resolution was absolute, it was not difficult to persuade the doctor to stay with me while the experiment ran its course, just as he had earlier stayed with Copplestone, and to be on his guard throughout.

It was in the apartment in Baker Street where the doctor and I had begun so many of our adventures that I took the drug. The doctor administered the injection himself, while I lay on my bed, but I had calculated and measured the dose. I did not tell the doctor that I intended to take a dose even larger than the one Lugard had taken–partly, I suppose, because I could not account for that decision myself.

Like Copplestone, I first experienced a period of vertiginous delirium in which multitudinous images of sight and sound pressed incoherently upon my brain. I felt that I was falling from a great height, floating on the very brink of consciousness, but I did not feel unduly uncomfortable until the hectic cataract of light faded to grey, and then to black. I had no sense of awakening into a re-stabilized world, but as soon as stability was restored to me it was disturbed in a very different way.

I had but a moment to realize that I was still lying flat on my back, staring up at the night sky instead of the ceiling of my apartment, when I was seized by the most awful distress imaginable.

Copplestone had told us that what he called a timeshadow–what others call a ghost or apparition–has less capacity for feeling than an ordinary body. According to his testimony, it is much less susceptible to changes in temperature and sensations of touch. My experience did not seem, at first, to confirm that judgment, but my subsequent explorations suggested that Copplestone was correct. Had I had a normal human capacity to feel, the pain that afflicted me when I first awoke in the future would have been literally unendurable.

In the course of Copplestone's visions, his dream-self took no nourishment, but the implication of his observations was that his phantom had to continue some kind of physiological activity in order to allow him to see and think, and it must therefore have continued to breathe. I certainly attempted to draw breath as soon as I was becalmed–but what my dream-self breathed in was not the life-giving air to which I have become accustomed. What I drew into my ghostly lungs was extremely cold, and utterly noxious.

I cannot describe the agony that seized me when I drew that first breath, nor the horror that assaulted my consciousness as I realized what was happening to me. I suppose I could speak, metaphorically, of daggers of ice striking at the center of my being, or of loathsome demons unfurling their hideous wings within the envelope of my flesh, but I pride myself on being a rational man, scrupulously exact in my accounts. The simple fact is that no human language has words to specify such an experience, because no mortal man could suffer it.

The pain was so great that my only wish was that death would come quickly. Timeshadows are resilient as well as unfeeling, but they are not beyond the reach of death; I would have died, in a matter of seconds, had I been alone. My body, lying in Baker Street, would have given up its ghost.

But I was not alone. My arrival had been anticipated, and preparation had been made for my reception.

After a few horridly-extended seconds, the unbearable pain began to ease. It was not eased quickly, and I would have given anything to accelerate the process of its lessening, but it did fade.

The fading eventually produced a kind of numbness, which was not entirely comfortable but was nevertheless easily bearable. I remained acutely conscious of the shape and movement of my phantom lungs as they tried in vain to find sustenance, and it was a distinctly ugly sensation, but the pain had been leached out of it, as if by a powerful anesthetic. I became conscious of the form of my supine body and the disposition of its limbs as those parts of it which were in contact with the ground on which I lay became capable of more subtle sensation.

For a few moments, I wondered whether I might be sinking slowly into a viscous liquid or quicksand–but then the speculative perception reversed itself, and I realized that some strange legion of tiny animalcules must be rising up from the surface, passing into my flesh by means of some exotic osmosis. I remembered that Copplestone had been similarly possessed when he ventured into the future for the third time.

I call the creatures that saved me animalcules because the dictionary offers me no better alternative, but they were not products of natural evolution. They were tiny artifacts: organic machines, designed to live within the human body, or even its ghost, and protect it from all avoidable harm. I had reflexively closed my eyes at the first shock of the pain, but as the animalcules eased my hellish agony I forced them open again. I was determined to see what there was to be seen, even if there was nothing to be seen but the stars.

I knew that I could not raise myself up–at least, not immediately. Copplestone had reported that his timeshadow felt unnaturally heavy, and that he required practice before he could master such elementary operations as walking and talking. I was in a far worse state. I could hardly twitch a finger or a toe, but I knew that I must nevertheless do my best to come to terms with my new condition. Even if I were to remain anchored to the ground throughout my sojourn in the future, I had resolved to make what observations I could, as scrupulously as I could. What, otherwise, would be the point of the experiment?

Having no alternative, I studied the stars in the sky, searching for any sign of difference from the constellations with which I was familiar. Alas, I have never devoted much attention to the study of astronomy, considering the subject irrelevant to the work of a consulting detective, and I was unable to ascertain whether there had been any slight alteration in the configuration of Orion's belt or Charles's Wain. I took some comfort, however, from the fact that I could put names to those two formations.

Because the night was moonless, my immediate environs were very dark. Even when I contrived to tilt my head, I could see little to either side of me that had any recognizable shape, although the terrain was not perfectly even. The faint starlight was reflected by numerous surfaces, which must have been white and slightly sparkling, but without being able to raise my head and turn it properly I could not be sure whether they were formations of ice or the caps of gigantic mushrooms.

The soundlessness of the night was so utter as to be ominous. I had not expected to hear nightingales singing, nor even frogs croaking, but there was nothing–not even the sighing that a gentle wind might make as it stirred the leaves of bushes or tall stalks of grass.

I found the silence disturbing. London is never quiet, let alone silent. Even the Yorkshire moors, where I spent my childhood, are never truly silent; there are too many wild things that only come out by night. The coldness within me had lingered longer than the pain, but that too began to ebb away. I could no longer feel the shape of my ghostly lungs or the soggy contact that my ectoplasmic flesh made with the ground on which I lay. Indeed, I now began to feel almost well, securely insulated from the insults and injuries which the world was avid to inflict upon me. It was a kind of relief I had experienced before, after injecting myself with cocaine.

I found that I could move my hands and feet more freely, although the movements were unreasonably sluggish. I contrived to roll on to my side, and then into a prone position, from which I began to lever myself up on to my knees. The strain on my arms renewed my appalling discomfort but I gritted my ghostly teeth, shut my eyes, and persisted in my efforts. When I had achieved the kneeling position I had to pause in order to fight a tide of nausea which surged through me. I knew that I had to defeat it and force my eyes open again; I could not simply lie there, waiting to be dragged back to the safety of my body and my bed.

When I had mustered the strength necessary to bring my clumsy dream-self to its feet I found that there was still disappointingly little to be seen at the surface of the world. No earthbound light-source was visible between the horizons, although there were multitudinous tiny sparks glinting from what I now deduced to be sloping faces of ice and rivulets of fallen snow–but they were in the middle distance; the spot on which I stood was slightly elevated, and black as pitch. In order to have any intelligence of where I was I had to squat down again and run my ghostly fingers over the spot where I had come to rest.

My phantom fingers were virtually numb, only crudely sensitive to texture and temperature, but I was able to feel a coarse, dry sand, some of whose particles were bound into larger grains. It was as if I were on a beach....or on some rocky outcrop in the depths of an Arctic desert. The desert seemed more likely when I studied the horizon cut out by the patterns of starlight; there were no mountain peaks, but the line at which the stars ended was by no means feature-less. It was as if I were in the centre of a vast broken plain.

It was only then that I recalled that I ought to be standing on the same point on the Earth's surface on which my body lay. This was where Baker Street had once run towards Regent's Park.

I knew that Copplestone had found not the slightest trace of London in his own visions, but at least he had found a luxuriant forest growing in its place. What disaster, I wondered, could have turned the miraculously lush world de-scribed in the professor's final adventure into this seemingly-barren desolation? Or was the difference to be accounted for in terms of the differences between our minds? Was I so mean and tentative a dreamer by comparison with him? Where, if so, would a man like Lugard have found himself?

When I lifted my hand above my head, I could see it silhouetted against the starry background–but the news that my animalcule-infected timeshadow was not transparent seemed ridiculously small recompense for having journeyed so far into the future. I knew that my time was limited, and cursed the freak of chance that had delivered me to Stygian darkness instead of revealing daylight.

I tried to call out, but I failed, partly because I had miscalculated the effort required to activate my vocal cords and partly because the concomitant nausea nearly caused me to faint. At the second attempt, I contrived no more than an ululating wail. Even when I finally contrived to form the words "Is anybody there?" I could not recognize my own voice in their tone or timbre.

I am here, I called–but I could not help feeling foolish. Copplestone had told us that countless machines the size of a bee had been set to watch for his second return, and that they had found him almost immediately, but none came to welcome me. I felt sure that I had been invaded, and saved from ignominious extinction, by much tinier things, but it seemed at first that no creatures of a more familiar magnitude had been set to hasten to my aid.

I was still wondering whether all life on this dream-Earth might be extinct when I saw the shapes moving against the background of stars. It was the news that my conclusion could not be correct, rather than any conviction that further provision must have been made for my salvation, that filled me with relief and not with fear. As the shapes approached, however, and I realized how large they were, the relief was moderated by anxious curiosity. If they had any relevance at all to me, I thought, they might as easily be baleful as generous.

They seemed more like bats than birds, their huge wings being more pre-cisely-shaped, but they were obviously bigger by far than any bat or bird I had ever encountered. When they came closer I saw glints of starlight reflected from their bodies, which gave the impression that their unfeathery hides were richly adorned with gems or crystals. There were five of them, flying in a diamond formation, and when they came directly overhead the pattern of their movement changed dramatically. The four marking the corners of the diamond circled like a great wheel while the shadow at its hub increased. The creature that descended upon me revealed its true size for the first time as it came closer and closer; it was even larger than I had supposed–far larger, in fact.

It was not courage alone that prevented me from turning and running away. I had not sufficient command over my debilitated body to take effective evasive action. I had no alternative but to wait until the shadow eclipsed the stars, not knowing whether I were to be prey for some incredible man-eating monster–and I was by no means reassured when I was firmly gripped by two sets of claws.

I was immediately plucked into the air, but that was not the worst of the sensation. The worst of it was feeling those talons sinking into my strange flesh, penetrating its surface. I almost expected to feel them meet within me, having punctured my shoulder-blades. They did not, but that did not lessen the impression of injury: the horrible awareness that their points were buried deep within my softer tissues.

I dared not struggle, but I was terrified nevertheless. Perhaps it was terror alone which made me lose consciousness again, or perhaps it was the thinning of the already-inadequate air as we rose to dizzying heights. I only know that it added insult to injury that I, who had set forth as a bold explorer ready for any marvel or frank impossibility, should be delivered to darkness without and darkness within, precluding all possibility of efficient discovery.

2.

I have no idea how long my unconsciousness lasted, but when I woke again, I was still in the penetrating grip of the mysterious monster, which was still flying in the central position of the diamond formation, high above the dark and featureless Earth. One thing, however, had changed.

To my left, in what I promptly identified as the east, the horizon now cut through the centre of a near-circular body, which was far too wan to be the rising sun. Its size identified it, beyond the shadow of a doubt, as the almost-full moon–but without that crucial indicator I would have refused to accept the conclusion. Not a single recognizable feature remained of the cratered face that I knew–not even its characteristic pallor!

I have heard rumor of rare nights when the face of the Moon shows orange or red through a dust-laden atmosphere, but the atmosphere through which my carrier was soaring seemed perfectly clear. In any case, this Moon was patterned not in red but in purples and greens, which gleamed as if they had been painted on the lacquered lid of a casket. Superimposed upon this background were dozens of tiny circular formations, like vivid gems. Although I say that they were tiny, I know that they must really have been huge, else they could not have been visible at a distance of a quarter of a million miles.

For a giddy moment or two, I wondered whether I might be on the Moon myself, looking down at the colored cities of a wondrously-transformed Earth, but I knew that could not be. Anyone looking down at the Earth from the Moon might see blue oceans, green forests and grey cities, but what they would see in greater quantity than anything else would be cloud. There was not a trace of cloud on the glistening face of the orb that was rising in the east.

There had been no earthly clouds obscuring the stars at the time I was lifted from the ground, but there was cloud a-plenty now, massing in the south. The creature that carried me was heading directly towards the cloud-mass, and hence towards a darkness even more profound than that which I had previously encountered. In the meantime, though, I had an opportunity to look down at the part of the Earth's surface that the rising Moon was gradually illuminating.

I saw that the world into which my dream had delivered me was, as I had feared, a vast wilderness of ice, interrupted by dark ravines and outcrops of black rock. I could see no sign of life at all, nor of any edifice that might have been the work of human hands.

If this is England, I thought, it must have fallen prey to some unimaginable catastrophe. In Copplestone's dreams, it had become the green and pleasant land of Blake's hymn, but this must be one of the Ice Ages of which James Hutton and Charles Lyell wrote, when extending glaciers eclipsed almost every vestige of life in the lands they possessed.

I remembered, however, that if Copplestone's visions had any truth in them at all, what this ice had reclaimed had no longer been England; it had been, instead, something not merely foreign but alien.

So fast was my carrier's flight that the clouds rushed upon me within a matter of minutes. The great flapping wings became invisible against their impenetrable background. I could not be entirely sorry that the disturbing moon had been obscured, but the darkness was unwelcome. I tried to open my mouth to protest, but found my lips knitted shut. I tried to raise my hand to investigate the obstruction, but found my arm equally immovable.

I knew that the invaders of my attenuated body were still in the process of completing their dominion over the empire of my flesh, and I became suddenly anxious as to their ultimate purpose. In a different world, similar invaders had done Copplestone no harm–at least in his estimation–but there was still a mystery in the manner of his death, and now that I had cause to believe that his dream had been no mere illusion I was forced to wonder whether his death might not have been connected with the invasion of his phantom by alien creatures rather than the cumulative effect of the drug upon his body. The dispatchers of the bat-like monster presumably wanted me delivered, alive and compos mentis, to some unknown destination–but that did not mean that they wished me no harm. For all I knew, their purpose might be entirely malign. I was a prisoner, after all, and those terrible talons were closed upon the ghostly relics of my shoulder-blades.

Even as my fear grew, though, something inside me responded to its pressure. This time, it was neither panic nor lack of oxygen that caused me to black out. This time, it was as if a key had been turned inside my head to block the flow of my anxious thoughts. I have no idea how long I remained unconscious, but it was evidently long enough for the monstrous flier to deliver me to my destination and beat a retreat.

My subsequent awakening was more comfortable by far than the earlier ones. It was a measured rise from dreamless sleep, and as soon as I drew breath I felt wonderfully well. It was as if the air had been renewed and improved, filled with life-giving oxygen and further sweetened. I opened my eyes to pearly light, and was profoundly relieved by its quality. When I found that I was able to sit up and move my limbs freely, I was exultant–but my excitement was moderated when my eyes adapted to the glow and I discovered where I was.

The gentle light was artificial, although it was emitted neither by a gaslamp nor by an electric bulb. It was emanating from the entire inner surface of a sphere in which I was enclosed, like a vast soap bubble or a sealed aquarium. Within the sphere there was a flat pallet on which I had been laid, upholstered with a curiously slick and spongy substance, sky blue in color. There was no other furniture. I am certain that my dream-self had been decently clothed when I first materialized, as Copplestone's had been, but I was stark naked now.

I called out: "Where am I? Who brought me here?" The answer was immediate. The light shining from the confining bubble was stirred in a peculiar fashion and the image of a human face was formed, looking down at me. It was considerably distorted by the concavity of the surface and seemed very large, but it was nevertheless recognizable as the face of Edward Copplestone.

I was not, however, deluded into thinking that it was anything more than an image.

"Don't be afraid," said a strangely-accented voice. The lips of the image moved but the voice was quite different from Copplestone's, or any human voice I had ever heard. "You are safe now–but we have not much time left. You must listen carefully. This is a matter of the utmost importance."

"Who are you?" I demanded. "Why have you placed me in this prison? Why do you confront me with a contrived image of a human face? Why will you not show me your true appearance?"

"We are machines," the voice replied. "You have been placed in confinement so that you might be supplied with good air. The Earth's air is no longer breathable by entities like yourself. Even as a timeshadow, you would have perished had the nanozoons not preserved you. They have been lying dormant upon the rock for millennia, waiting for the advent of some such being as yourself. This image of a human face is being projected in the hope of reassuring you that we mean you no harm; we have no faces of our own with which to confront you but we are friends of humankind. We have been waiting for a long time, not knowing that anyone would ever come. We have sent word of your coming to those who appointed us to watch and wait, but time is short and it is almost certain that our signal has been intercepted and overheard by those who might try to interfere. Please listen carefully to what we have to say; the future of mankind depends upon it."

I was, of course, prepared for the possibility that, if my vision were to take up its narrative thread where Copplestone's had left off, I might be found by machines which could speak and were prepared to take a keen interest in my fate, just as Copplestone had been in his second and third expeditions.

In the written account of his third vision the benevolent machines that had taken possession of the professor had showed him a miracle-laden world of limitless opportunity, but I was keenly aware that the very fact that he had only been shown these wonders by means of some kind of futuristic kinematograph, while his timeshadow remained in the same place, left open the possibility that it was all a lie: a calculated deception.

In his second vision, Copplestone had been interrogated by the machines that had long lain in wait for him, before they delivered him to the custody of the vampires who ruled the world. I remembered that he had taken care not to tell them what they wanted to know. Even in a dream, I was fully prepared to be as cautious as he. I had the profoundest doubts as to what might be lurking beyond the bubble that confined me, and I had taken careful note of the voice's reference to those who might try to interfere. One giant bat had been enough to carry me here, perhaps into territory that had once been part of France, but it had travelled under escort.

"I am listening," I assured the voice.

"You will slip back through time very soon," the voice informed me, "but it is imperative that you return. We will tell you how the drug may be further refined, and how your body may be protected from its ill-effects. We will tell you exactly what dose to use to bring you to a future a little way ahead of this one.

"When you next come into our world, Professor Copplestone will be waiting for you. He will explain everything. The Earth is dead now, but it might yet live again. The human race is extinct, but might yet have a role to play in the destiny of the universe. The vampire race that inherited the Earth when humankind destroyed itself is gone, following its own destiny. The Earth is ripe for reclamation by those who have the desire and the courage.

"The resurrection of the human race may depend upon the produce of this brief hour. We have saved your life because it is the most precious life there has ever been; you have the opportunity to set history in train again–but you must use it bravely and wisely. First of all, you must return. We ask nothing more of you than that, for the moment. If and when you do, you shall be heir to such wonders as you never dreamed possible, and such rewards as you never dared hope for."

I observed that the voice had not even asked my name. I wondered whether that was because its producers already knew it, or because they did not care–but in either case, I distrusted their lofty promises. There was a great deal that was mysterious in the remarkable speech and much that might have been challenged, but I naturally selected out the item of profoundest import.

"What calamity has befallen the Earth?" I asked. "How was its life destroyed, its air rendered unbreathable?"

"All will be explained when you return," the voice promised. "Forgive us our haste, but you must hear the formula, and commit it to memory. If you cannot do that, all else is lost. If time remains, we will answer your questions, but first we must ensure that you will be able to return, to hear everything that Copplestone has to say."

I assured the voice that I was a highly-trained observer, capable of committing to memory anything it cared to tell me and recalling it without error. It proceeded to give me instructions for the concoction of a better variant of Copplestone's time-displacement drug, followed by very precise instructions regarding dosage. Then it gave me another and more complicated set of instructions, for the preparation of medicinal compounds that would keep my body safe while my consciousness was projected even further into time.

The voice impressed upon me the necessity of taking extreme care with these preparations–and the necessity of making the formulas known to others who might have the courage and the wisdom to use them well.

I had 1000 questions, and did not know which of them were most likely to be met with useful answers. I had no time for careful selection, and such aids to cogitation as I maintain in my apartments were thousands of years away. At a hazard, I asked where Copplestone was.

"Professor Copplestone is on the Moon," the voice informed me. "The Moon is habitable still, although the Earth is not. Copplestone could not make a home on the derelict Earth, not knowing whether he would have to wait ten thousand or a hundred thousand years for another traveler in time, or whether one would ever arrive at all–but he will build a dome on the spot where you materialized, and he will fill it with good air, now that he has reason to hope and expect that you will return, and some confidence that the date of your return can be estimated to within a few thousand years."

There was only one question I could ask in response to that remarkable statement. "How long has Copplestone lived in this time?"

"He has lived in his present incarnation for 20,000 years," the voice replied. "He might live in it for 200,000 more, had he no enemies. You might live as long yourself, if matters are settled in our favor, and if you so choose–but first you must return. If you cannot or will not do that, all may be lost and the whole human race doomed to oblivion."

I knew, even as I heard these words, that I would have no opportunity to carry forward the inquisition. I could feel the process of dissolution that was already creeping through my phantom flesh–a sensation quite unlike any I had ever felt before and yet immediately recognizable.

While I had hurtled forwards in time, I had felt as if I were falling, but moving backwards could not be likened to any kind of ascent; it was more like coming apart–as if a shape sustained by the jets of a fountain were to suffer the effects of a sudden loss of water-pressure.

I feared that the disintegration might be so absolute as to preclude any possibility of reassembly but that was not the case. The depleted body that lay upon my bed in Baker Street was not merely an anchorage but a frame into which my identity was re-collected and re-established.

I awoke in sore distress, but I dared not dose myself with any pain-killing drug until I had written down the formulas communicated to me by the futuristic voice. That I did with all possible expedition, ignoring all the doctor's entreaties.

Afterwards, I slept for 14 hours–and when I awoke, I was prey to a host of aches and pains. These quickly developed into a terrible fever, which racked me for days on end. The doctor told me, once I had recovered my health, that he had all but given me up for dead–but he had done that more than once before.

It was not easy to recover my health and strength, but recover I did–and my appearance remained quite normal throughout. It was not until I returned from my second visionary expedition that I became the peculiar creature you see before you now."

The Writer's Story: Part Three

Paris, September 1900

5.

I had to admit that Sherrinford's vision had improved markedly as it drew to its temporary conclusion. I could not approve of his imprisonment in a silver soap-bubble–such an evasive narrative measure seemed to me to be symptomatic of imaginative cowardice–but I did not altogether disapprove of the tantalizing voice. Any entity that could lay down the lure of a lifespan of 200,000 years and credit for the salvation of the human species had to be credited with adequate panache.

Edward Copplestone had been conscious during his own experiences of the danger that a vision of the future, even if it were authentically prescient, might still be polluted and perverted at every level by the hopes and fears of the visionary. The Great Detective had taken care to sound a similarly cautionary note when introducing his tale, but now that he had warmed to its telling he had begun to speak of his adventure as if he believed its appearances to be entirely real and trustworthy. His punctilious references to his "dream-self" were clearly defensive; his visions had evidently persuaded him that he really had seen the future–and perhaps that he really did hold the future of mankind in the palm of his hand, if only he could penetrate the truth behind the appearances that presented themselves to his visionary eye.

Not unnaturally, the three wise Frenchmen hastily assembled to hear the tale had almost as many questions to ask as the dreamer had had when confronted with the magnified image of Copplestone's face, but two of them were politely hesitant. De Gourmont, only half-visible behind his screen of light, was pensive, while Jarry wore a slight smile. Flammarion was the one whose excitement got the better of him. Unlike young Wells at Copplestone's house, the astronomer was reluctant to accuse the storyteller of plagiarism, but he had discovered a significant echo of his own accounts of visionary odysseys in time and space undertaken by disembodied spirits.

"The conditions you describe," he said, "might well have followed the impact of a comet on the surface of the Earth. The alternative explanation is, of course, that the Sun has grown cold in accordance with Lord Kelvin's predictions–but Kelvin was speaking in terms of tens of millions of years, whereas you are only talking about tens of thousands, or a few hundred thousand. The cometary impact seems the more likely hypothesis; I have discussed the possibility is several articles, at least one of which was published in an English periodical."

"You are right, Monsieur Flammarion," the detective said, "but only partly right. The point will be clarified when I tell you what befell me when I returned to the derelict Earth. For now, it might be better if I were to explain the conclusions I drew for myself in the aftermath of my first vision, employing the processes of logical deduction that I invariably bring to bear upon problems which confront me."

"*Pas nécessaire*," Jarry said. Then he switched into English. "Application of logic to the imaginary makes....*l'absurde*." He stopped, hesitating over his translation–but he had made his point.

"That is true," the detective admitted, "and I was acutely aware of the possible absurdity of information laid before me in a dream. Nevertheless, I felt that I had to formulate such conclusions as I could, in order to weigh the probability that the visions induced by the drug did indeed contain an element of truth."

"I had thought," de Gourmont put in, "that your only reason for suspecting that was contained in the manuscript whose contents you summarized for us before Monsieur Melmoth arrived. I presume that you did not receive that information until your second experiment with the drug was under way. Why, then, had you begun to believe that your vision was an authentic glimpse of the future?"

De Gourmont had evidently seen through the detective's dissimulations, just as I had–but Death's double was not yet prepared to set aside his skeptical pose.

"I make no claim that what I experienced was any more than a dream," the detective said, stubbornly clinging to the imposture. "If I describe events in a different way, it is only because I am trying to convey an accurate impression of how they seemed at the time. I can assure you that the doctor and I spent long hours attempting to analyze the dream as a fantasy, whose only revelations concerned the inner workings of my own psyche. The doctor insisted on interpreting the voice as the voice of my own addictive personality, unwisely freed from restraint in order to plead its case for my return to self-abuse–he had never approved of my use of cocaine. I was willing to admit that he might be right. Nevertheless, the fact remained that the voice had, in fact, given me some hard information whose reliability could be put to the test.

"The doctor insisted that because I had some expertise as a chemist, and was reasonably well-read in the scientific literature, I could have invented all the formulas dictated to me by the voice. I could not agree with him, but I had to concede the possibility–just as I had to concede the possibility that they might prove utterly impotent to serve their ostensible purposes. I told the doctor that the only way I could be sure was to follow the formulas, and then to test the result.

"The doctor was, of course, dead against any further experimentation, and flatly forbade it, although he had no authority, either as my friend or as my physician, to do any such thing. When I questioned his right to do so he turned to pleading, begging me to save myself from a second bout of fever. In his opinion, Copplestone had not only killed himself but killed himself for nothing. Unlike Lugard, the doctor had been unable to find anything in Copplestone's visions to warrant taking the slightest risk; he was never an imaginative man."

It seemed that the good Victorian–the past master of observation and deduction–had no sooner become a dreamer than he had appointed himself a seer. I made no comment, but exchanged a glance with Jarry, who wore his skepticism more openly.

"You were certainly taking a grave risk," de Gourmont observed, "but I do understand why you thought it necessary. Having had a dream of that sort, you could not possibly be content to disregard its implications. You had to test the formulas–no man of integrity could do otherwise."

"I did consent to be put off for a considerable time," the fledgling seer admitted, "even after I had completed the laborious business of synthesis. Other problems, of the kind which have made my reputation, came along to distract me–but I always intended to put the new timeshadow-projecting formula to the test. Since you obviously do understand, Monsieur de Gourmont, I shall not waste time by explaining my reasoning in full detail, but I would not want you to think that I had fallen victim to any delusion. What if the two new formulas had been the product of my own disordered brain? Were they not entitled to my interest anyhow–perhaps all the more so? Might they not be just as valuable even if they were inventions of my mind? And who would ever test them if I would not? Were they not my responsibility, wherever they had come from?

"At the end of the day, the two formulas given to me by the voice were the only means I had of investigating the puzzles which that mysterious entity had laid before me. I had questions to ask, which demanded answers. It was only ever a question of when I would try out the time-displacement formula and its protective counterpart....and as matters transpired, the time came in July of this year, nearly five years after Lugard's replication of Copplestone's last experiment."

He would have continued his story then, but Flammarion was still mulling over what we had been told.

"If we were to accept that these visions of the future have some truth in them," he said, "it seems to me that we would also have to take seriously the possibility that there is indeed some kind of interplay between the various eras that have been described. Even if the inhabitants of these various futures could not reach back in time to carry out actions of their own in the past, the fact that you and Professor Copplestone both attained some intelligence of the shape of things to come must have sown seeds of potential change. Indeed, those seeds must be growing as you tell your story to us–as you must presumably intend, having summoned us to hear your tale. If you thought that what you had experienced as no more than a dream, we would not be here–but if we are to believe that you really have seen the future, you must also believe that you are now attempting to change it."

"The matter is not so simple," the detective said, dolefully. "It is because I hardly know what to believe any more that I am compelled to throw myself on the mercy of your judgment."

I had been party to the debate at Copplestone's house, and I understood that the discovery of the future could not be as simple as Flammarion had made it seem. "Monsieur Sherrinford's confusion is forgivable," I said, shifting slightly in my chair as the effort of speech brought about an increase in the infernal itch that was harrying me mercilessly. "Even if he had obtained a glimpse of a more distant moment in the same future that Edward Copplestone saw, and even if he were to be convinced that what he saw was real, he could not be entirely convinced that he now has the power to change that future, if he can only persuade his fellow men of the danger that faces them. There is another possibility that he must bear in mind, and that is the possibility that the future he has seen might come into being because he has foreseen it–that what he is doing now is not setting in train a chain of causality that will lead to its abolition, but a sequence of events that will complete its causality."

"I like that" Jarry said, smiling broadly. "Very clever."

"I think I see what you mean," Flammarion said, a little more modestly. "You are suggesting that the contingent futures men are able to foresee might be those capable of realization by their own actions–futures that might become destined as a result of their responses to revelation."

"I meant nothing quite as drastic as that," I told him. "I only meant that our friend here cannot calculate the ultimate effects of his present actions. He cannot know whether telling us the story will make the fulfillment of his dream less likely–as he presumably intends–or more likely. I do not say that we are caught in some kind of existential trap, which will always frustrate our attempts to change futures that we foresee; I merely contend that we can never know what the ultimate effects of our attempts to change the future will be. Is it not the case that the outcomes of our actions are often the direct opposite of what we intend?"

They were all too polite to say aloud that I would be bound to think so, given the outcome of my libel action against the Marquess of Queensberry.

"I might be wrong, of course," I said, generously. "If there really are vampires lurking in our midst, patiently waiting to inherit the Earth, the disclosure of their existence by men as influential as Professor Flammarion and Monsieur de Gourmont might well lead to their identification and extinction. Forewarned of their eventual inheritance of the Earth, we humans might take more care of our precious legacy than if we had remained ignorant. Were our attempts to subvert these visions to be successful, the visions would become mere fictions even if they had begun as an admittedly-exotic kind of truth. In that case, Monsieur Sherrinford's caution would be entirely warranted–the mere fact that he had this vision might prove, in the end, to guarantee its fictitiousness. You will understand readily enough, though, why a scrupulous logician of his kind is reluctant to say that he believes what he has seen. True prophecies can render themselves false, just as false ones can render themselves true, if they have the right effect on those to whom they are reported."

I did not know whether any of my listeners had had the pleasure and the privilege of reading "Lord Arthur Savile's Crime," but they had no difficulty in following the argument. They were, after all, among the cleverest men in France.

"I see what you are driving at," Flammarion said, agreeably. "If what Monsieur Sherrinford tells us affects our actions in future, the ultimate effect of those actions might either work to cancel out the possibilities to which he has alerted us, or work to secure them–but we have no way of knowing which, at this particular point in time, and nor has he. These visions cannot simply be true or false. If they are not false to begin with, falsehood might well be thrust upon them by our taking heed of the danger of which they speak; if they are not true to begin with, they might be gifted with truth by our response. *Reductio ad absurdum*, as Jarry says...but the absurd must sometimes be taken seriously."

I was delighted to hear the argument put so delicately; it was a refreshing change from all the talk of destiny that had dominated the discussion at Copplestone's house. It had not seemed so silly at the time, but I had learned a great deal in five years about the whimsicality of fortune and the unreliability of calculation.

"I have always tried to exclude the absurd from my computations," Death's doppelgänger said, "but it is not easy, in this particular instance. If what I learned from my second vision really is the truth, whether it is the truth of destiny or merely a contingent truth that might be erased by an effort of the collective will, there is more than the future of humankind at stake. If what I learned from Count Lugard's timeshadow has as much truth in it as what I learned from Professor Copplestone's, then the future of the entire universe is at stake."

He said this in a peculiarly miserable tone, but I attributed his dolefulness to an uncomfortable awareness that the mere mention of such grandiose matters might be enough to forfeit his claim on our trust.

I could not believe that the would-be Great Detective was really capable of profound anxiety on behalf of the entire universe–but he was a magnificent liar, and I was not much concerned with such trivia as truth and belief. A dying man cannot have the slightest interest in whether the stories he hears are honest or accurate; his only care is for their magnificence. For that reason, I was delighted to hear that the future of the universe was at stake, and that I might have a hand in deciding its fate, even in my present dire condition.

Count Lugard and I had taken leave to mock the Great Detective when we first met him, but I was beginning to think that our judgment had been unduly harsh. My assessment of him as a man desperate to live up to his legend–a legend created, innocently enough, by the tales of his exploits concocted by the doctor–had undoubtedly been correct, and still was correct, but I saw now that he might have found a way not merely to live up to his legend, but to supersede it.

Thanks to the accounts that had appeared in *The Strand*, the Great Detective's career had become a modern hero-myth, and he had been credited with the mental powers of a demigod. The real man had had little alternative but to fall prey to a heady cocktail of vanity and anxiety. According to the doctor's romances, he was regularly entrusted by statesmen and monarchs with secret commissions, which sometimes saved their governments and their crowns. Now, though–at least according to his own account–he had been entrusted by an immortal with the task of saving, not merely humankind, but the entire Creation of which humankind was an element.

Had any other man ever taken delusions of grandeur to such an extreme? Had any other man ever suffered such strong and strange temptation? So prolific an endeavor commanded respect, and I was not ashamed to offer it, with only one proviso.

I resolved then and there that, if ever I should have occasion to venture in my dreams into the furthest wilderness of time, I would bring back reports that would put Sherrinford's to shame. I was not sure how I would do it, given that he had already appropriated to himself the power and the inclination to save or destroy the entire universe, but I promised myself that I would find a way...if only I were given the chance.

I knew, of course, that the chance was there. According to the precepts laid down by the founding fathers of the drama in the days of Attic glory, all tragedies had to be arranged in trilogies. If the adventures of this animated skeleton were to form the second element of a series begun with Lugard's celebration of the hunger and ecstasy of vampires, it was obvious that no one but myself could possibly provide a suitable conclusion.

For now, I had to be content to be a mere listener, but it was perfectly obvious that the Great Detective still had his precious formulas beside him, in his briefcase. Neither Jarry nor Flammarion would be enthusiastic to use something so horribly disfiguring, but what had I to fear or lose? Might not de Gourmont, too, think that he had little enough to lose, and a great deal to gain, in dreams more powerful than any that mere opium had to offer?

My companions had, of course, reacted slightly differently to the claim that the whole of Creation might be under threat. They had the imagination of Frenchmen, but also the faith.

"We may be sure," Flammarion said, "that the Creator would hardly permit the entire universe to be imperiled by a man's dream, however perceptive it might be. Perhaps you do not realize how vast the universe is, Monsieur Sherrinford."

"It is not for me specify what the Creator of the universe might permit and what he might not," the detective replied, earnestly, "and with all due respect, Professor Flammarion, I wonder if even you realize how vast the universe is."

Flammarion pursed his lips at that. Was he not the author of *Lumen*, the halcyon of the New Enlightenment?

"If the Creator made humankind merely in order that the race should be summarily obliterated by another species," I put in, mischievously, "we may be sure that He had a good reason to do so. If, on the other hand, he desired to offer his Chosen People a belated opportunity to evade that fate, why should he not select Monsieur Sherrinford–or you, or I–as his new Noah?"

Jarry met my eye as I said this, and favored me with yet another ironic grin. He, I guessed, was here by accident–and he thought that I was here only because the great detective thought it imperative that I should lend what weight I could to his testimony. It was Flammarion and de Gourmont who had been appointed to serve as the Supreme Court of Judgment, by virtue of the reputations that placed them among the finest minds in France–but Jarry thought himself at least as well-qualified as they. He was beginning to enjoy himself thoroughly now, just as I was–or would have been, had my skin not been on fire.

"Perhaps, Monsieur," de Gourmont put in, in a soft voice redolent with courtesy, "you should proceed with the story of your second expedition. The hour is late, and I dare say that you have a rich repast of marvels to set before us."

"Indeed I have," said the man who wore Death's mask, with almost equal politesse. "Indeed I have."

The Detective's Story: Part Two

The island formerly known as Great Britain,
circa *100,000 A.D.*

3.

As the hour approached for my second trial, the doctor raised all the obligatory objections. Even so, he consented to administer the syringe–which now contained a fearsomely-complicated cocktail of exotic compounds, some few of which had been extremely difficult to obtain. Again, I had asked him to wait with my lightened body throughout the interval of its suspended animation, ready to respond if the heart and lungs should show any signs of failure. Again, he had promised to do exactly that.

The sensation of hurrying through time was not so disconcerting this time, but it was still impossible for me to make any sense of the kaleidoscopic chaos through which I fell. This time, I did not black out, not even for an instant. I was alert as soon as my condition stabilized, and I sat up immediately.

I found myself lying on neatly-cut grass, in the centre of a circular lawn bordered with rhododendrons. The bushes were in full bloom, their purple flowers luxuriating in bright sunlight, which was streaming through a vast array of hexagonal and octagonal windows which filled the vault of heaven.

I saw that I was in a huge hemispherical dome whose architecture put the Crystal Palace to shame; its panes of glass seemed to be tinted, for the bright and cloudless sky behind them was a deep indigo blue rather than the shade which we call sky blue. I could see five black shapes moving in formation against that background, describing a circle around the dome, but they were too high for the precise forms of their wings to be distinguishable.

Beyond the rhododendrons, I could see the red-tiled roof of a compact cottage, which might have been in some pretty Cotswold village–but the whole scene was redolent with fakery. The colors were not quite right, and were in any case too vivid and too uniform; the grass on which I sat was all of a single species, and its color was unnaturally uniform, the clustered stalks gathered as orderly as sheaves of wool in a woven rug. I wondered whether all of it might be some carefully-contrived illusion: a dream within my dream, intended to deceive me.

I knew that, even if everything I saw were real, the Earth could not have warmed again. The landscape beyond the dome must still be as desolate as the one I had glimpsed before. If it did, in fact, exist, the dome had been built specifically to receive me, and to welcome me with a scene that I might consider homely. Perhaps its seeming fakery was the result of improvisation, or of the faulty memory of its principal architect.

Whatever the truth of the matter, I could not find the off-key normality of the scene which met my eyes in any way reassuring. Nothing could have seemed more alien, in that dread and derelict world, than a sentimental scene displaced from the tinted pages of *Sunday at Home*.

There were bees buzzing about the rhododendron flowers, but I could not tell whether they were real; I strongly suspected that they were not. There were no birds to be seen or heard. The scented air was oppressively sweet; it certainly had no shortage of oxygen.

By the time I had come slowly to my feet, moving my heavy-seeming limbs very deliberately, I was no longer alone. A humanoid figure was moving between the bushes, coming to welcome me with open arms. The figure had a face that had obviously been shaped in imitation of Copplestone's and clothes befitting a man of his class and station, but the image seemed to me to be more parody than homage. The coloring of the flesh was apt enough but its texture was quite wrong, and the creature's gait was far too sinuous. I was sure from the first moment I set eyes on it that this was a machine, however cunningly it had been contrived to resemble the Edward Copplestone I had met in 1895.

The realization that the other's appearance was not to be trusted led me to look down at my own body. Although it was undoubtedly a phantom of sorts, it was reassuringly opaque and it was clad in a perfectly respectable jacket and tweed trousers–or at least in their appearance. I could not feel the weight of the clothes, nor their friction against my skin.

It occurred to me that of the two of us, I might easily be reckoned the poorer simulation of humanity–and yet I felt that, in every essential feature, I was entirely real, and wholly myself. I was not prepared to make the same assumption of the creature that wore Copplestone's semblance.

"I have been expecting you for a long time," said Copplestone's simulacrum, extending its hand to be shaken.

I consented to be taken by the hand. "I hope I am not very late," I replied. "I followed the instructions I was given as carefully as I could."

The hand that gripped mine did not feel like flesh, but I could not be sure how much of its strangeness was due to the abnormality of my own being.

"I have been here for 20,000 years," my host informed me, as he beckoned me to follow him through the bushes towards the house, "and did not arrive until 20,000 years after your last appearance. My friends, the Overmen, had intended to restore Earth to something of its former state before you arrived, but that proved impractical. They had set a time for your reappearance that ought to have given them abundant time and opportunity to win through to a time of peace, but their hopes were dashed. The war still continues, and it rages far closer to home than anyone could have wished. Still, I am here. I, at least, have been preserved from destruction."

"You must have been rather bored," I observed, looking around. "This is not the kind of abode in which I could contentedly spend 20,000 years awaiting an appointment."

"It is a long time," Copplestone's simulacrum conceded, "but the limitations of our existence are by no means as severe now as they were in your time. Did you read the notes I wrote on the eve of my final vanishment?"

"I heard them read aloud," I told him.

"Then you know that a person might walk on Mars or Titan, even while he lies on an English hillside. My timeshadow has been here, on the blasted Earth, for a very long time, but my mind and vision have not been imprisoned in this little dome. Mine has been a curious homecoming, but it has not been at all unpleasant, and I have not been bored. I wish that you could have come into a haven such as this when you first ventured into the future, but we had no idea whether anyone else would ever come after Lugard, or where they would arrive if they did. Had it been Tesla who duplicated my formula after Lugard had destroyed it–and I must confess that I thought him the most likely to make the attempt–he would presumably have arrived half a world away, on the far side of the frozen ocean. It would have been easier to maintain an effective watch had the regeneration of the Earth's ecosphere been completed, or even properly begun, but the surface was still subject 40,000 ago to occasional bombardments, any one of which would have undone such work. We are not free from bombardments even now, and any attempt to restore the ecosphere would undoubtedly prompt new assaults"

"Bombardments by whom–or by what?" I queried. We had reached the doorway of the cottage. Copplestone's simulacrum had put on a show of moving in a leisurely fashion but he had moved swiftly, and he had cast several surreptitious glances upwards even before it had mentioned *bombardments* and *assaults*. The cottage door was surrounded by a trellis on which honeysuckle had been trained to grow. The assemblage was absurdly quaint.

"Please come in," said Copplestone's simulacrum, instead of answering my question. He held the door open while I passed through. The interior was very clean, as if the floors had been recently swept and the wooden surfaces polished.

I hesitated just inside the threshold, caught by the peculiar notion that if I accepted this creature's hospitality I might be bound by some mysterious tacit obligation. "What are you?" I asked, turning to look at him. "You are not Copplestone, although you look like him."

"I am Edward Copplestone," he replied, without taking offence. "This is the body that the nanozoons made for me, in order to renew, and ultimately to replace, the timeshadow that was drawn into the future when my first body died. I could not have inhabited that frail shell for 60 days, let alone 60,000 years! Although it is better by far than the one into which I was born, this is my own body; I can assure you that I am no mere copy. The process by which I was re-

240

newed was a carefully-controlled metamorphosis, and the continuity of my personality has been maintained, unbroken save for periods of sleep. I still need sleep and I still dream; indeed, I have taken great care to preserve the greater number of my needs. I must maintain my hunger and my thirst, else even I could not believe that I am Edward Copplestone. Please go in, I beg of you–there is a great deal that I must tell you, and we have not much time."

He spoke rapidly, as if he were following a prepared script–but if he had been waiting for me in this tiny enclave for 20,000 years, he must have had plenty of opportunity to rehearse.

I went further into the room. The interior of the cottage seemed to be as perfect a pastiche as the exterior, although it had no fireplaces. I was taken into a sitting-room where I was invite to sit down on a horsehair sofa.

The walls were papered with a Morris print and there were a number of oils and water-colors in gilded frames. I guessed, at first, that this mockery of a supposed English ideal was intended to make me feel at home, but I was soon seized by a different suspicion. I wondered whether it might have been built for my host's benefit rather than mine, to make *him* feel at home. If he had long been desperate to maintain whatever was left of his old self, he might have been easy prey to the impulse to synthesize an appearance of the old England–the quintessential England–as seen through the rose-tinted spectacles of nostalgia.

I wondered whether the parodic quality of the cottage could be taken as a measure of the falsity of Copplestone's simulacrum–and whether, if so, he could possibly be aware of the extent to which his own eyesight had become artificial.

As if to compound the grotesquerie of the excessively ordinary, my companion took a chair that had a side-table placed to its right. A teapot and a milk jug were waiting on the table, with a single cup. Copplestone's simulacrum poured tea into the cup and added a dash of milk.

"I apologize for my impoliteness," he said, regretfully. "Your present corporeal habitation is incapable of taking nourishment, but I have waited an eternity to take tea with someone who understands the significance of taking tea."

"If you believe that this charade will help to convince me that you are the Copplestone I knew before, I fear that you are mistaken," I told him, regretfully. "It only serves to reinforce the impression of artificiality. Nothing here seems real to me; it is more like an illustration in a child's story-book than anything I ever experienced."

"You're right, of course," he said, sorrowfully. "This is a fiction: a mere stage-set, dressed for use in what can only seem to you to be a dream-vision. You are here, and yet you are also lying upon your own bed in your own apartment–in Baker Street, was it not?–and the year is....what is the year, in your reckoning?"

"1900," I replied.

"Five years after my death! I should have thought...but that is immaterial. You are anchored still to the year 1900, and to the body that lies in a drug-induced coma. Nevertheless, you have a physical presence here and now, in a time 100,000 years thereafter. You are a very solid dream-projection, as you must admit.

"If it helps you, you might think of all this as *my* solid dream-projection. You have created the illusion of clothing in which to dress yourself, for reasons of decorum; I have created these surroundings in much the same fashion, for reasons of....well, more for the sake of my own affections than for the sake of politeness, if the truth be told. But we are here to save humanity, if we can—and if we can, this dream will vanish like any other dream, into the oblivion of forgetfulness. I might vanish myself, along with the accumulated memories of 60,000 years....but if one cannot learn equanimity in the course of a lifespan like that, one cannot learn anything. The point is to save humankind, if humankind can be saved. That is our mission, our hope...perhaps our destiny. I shall be content to be blotted out of the shifting time-stream, if that is a necessary cost, my only regret being that I had not time to learn a little more."

"I would have thought that 60,000 years would be time enough to learn everything," I said.

"I fear," he replied, "that you have not the slightest inkling of what *everything* comprises. Nor can you have, unless and until you find your own immortality. I wish that I had more than a matter of hours to tell you what you need to know but I have not, and I cannot be sure that we are safe from interference. I must ask you to listen to me now, and trust me to tell you everything that you need to know. Interruptions, however well-intentioned, will only slow us down. There might be time for questions when I am done, but I fear that there will not."

I knew that he was right. My first venture into the future had ended with 1000 questions unanswered, but I knew only too well that I had only the slightest notion of which among those questions most needed to be asked. I did, indeed, have to trust my informant's estimation on that score, at least to begin with—but I also had to bear in mind that I had no proof at all that this really was Edward Copplestone, or that he really did intend to tell me how the human race might be saved from imminent extinction.

I told him that I would listen patiently until he was done—and he immediately launched into his long-prepared speech.

Copplestone—or, rather, his mechanical doppelgänger—told me that he had been utterly astonished to find himself back in the world that he had glimpsed during his third vision of futurity. Initially, he did not realize that he had died in 1895. When that fact first became clear to him, he had immediately been seized by the suspicion that his death had not been natural; he had become briefly convinced that the surviving relic of his person had been kidnapped into the future, by vampires anxious that he might give warning of their coming ascendancy. He assured me, however, that his fears had eventually been quieted by the Overmen in whose company he was now bound to remain. He had been convinced that his

242

presence among them was an accident and that his death had not been caused by them.

Humankind's successors had, by this time, reached what appeared to them to be the end-point of their evolution. Their science had given them complete mastery over their own bodies. They understood the processes of biological determinism that enabled fertilized egg-cells to produce individuals with particular characteristics, and they could vary those characteristics at will, designing entirely new organisms as well as modifying those which already existed. More than that; they could unite their flesh with all manner of machines. They could and did augment their limbs and their sensory apparatus with various extensions, and they could and did accept into their blood and their organs legions of tiny machines, which they called nanozoons. These nanozoons guaranteed them immunity to the ageing process and to all disease, and were capable of repairing all but the most terrible injuries.

The Overmen had colonized many of the other worlds of the Solar System, modifying their environments very considerably. They had launched hundreds of self-replicating machines–most of them very tiny–into interstellar space, with the aim of exploring the other solar systems which were their neighbors in space. They believed, to begin with, that they were very likely to meet other intelligent beings in the solar systems orbiting suns of the same type as their own, and they were enthusiastic to do so. They were also enthusiastic to find new Earths, inhabited only by more primitive life-forms, which they might colonize and convert into paradises of their own design. They were sorely disappointed when their self-replicating probes brought back news of neighboring star-systems without having discovered the slightest signs of life, even at its most primitive.

It was so simple and economical to send out exploratory machines no bigger than a man's thumb that very few of the Earthborn Overmen actually ventured into interstellar space themselves. Even when they had perfected the business of mechanical augmentation, so that they might go forth into the greater universe without taking an elaborate closed ecosystem for their sustenance, the energy-expenditure required to accelerate whole companies of their kind to velocities near to that of light seemed excessive. *To know is better than to go* was their philosophy, at the time when Copplestone took up permanent residence in their midst. They felt that they could adequately embrace the whole universe by means of their nanozoic intermediaries, and although their numbers continued to increase they had slowed the rate of their population growth to the point at which the Solar System seemed to offer adequate *lebensraum* for many millennia to come.

The Overmen thought that their empire was perfectly secure. Having never had that tendency to war among themselves which is so marked among humankind, they had no fear at all that their own society might self-destruct as the society of their predecessors had. For thousands of years they confidently believed themselves to be entirely without enemies. They came to think of themselves as Lords of Creation, utterly secure in their hegemony.

Alas, they were wrong.

4.

Copplestone informed me that the account of the Solar System contained in the discoveries of our 19th century astronomers is woefully incomplete. Apparently, the greater part of the extrasolar matter contained in the system is not aggregated into planets; it is, in fact, loosely distributed in two vast rings far beyond the orbit of Neptune, which collectively constitute the halo from which comets periodically spiral inwards towards the sun. When the Solar System was young, it was much more disturbed, and comets were so common that they frequently crashed into the planets.

According to the professor's account, the evolution of life on Earth has been interrupted in the past by numerous collisions, not merely with icy comets but with metallic objects associated with the minor planets, which are far more numerous than we have yet had the opportunity to determine. It is possible that human prehistory was interrupted by at least one such significant impact, whose faint memory is preserved in our legends of the Deluge. Some of this is well known to us, by courtesy of Professor Flammarion's popularizing efforts, but Copplestone's simulacrum was able to elaborate considerably on Professor Flammarion's calculations and speculations.

If the visions experienced by Copplestone and myself are trustworthy, the human species will require no such cosmic catastrophe to put an end to it–but the Overmen who are fated to succeed us will not be so fortunate. I cannot put an exact date to the event, but approximately 30,000 years from today, some awesomely massive piece of cosmic debris, traveling at a terrific velocity, will pass through the dark aureole at the Solar System's outer edge. The disruption caused by this object's passage will displace hundreds of thousands of comets, many of them so huge that they will break up into hosts of tinier entities–and that appalling tide of matter will descend upon the inner planets of the Solar System.

Most of the matter, Copplestone told me, was in the form of ice and dust, but even particles of dust may turn into vivid shooting stars as they plunge through the Earth's atmosphere. The heavier pieces of solid matter were far fewer in number, but they arrived to the accompaniment of glorious meteor-showers. According to Copplestone, the Overmen who lived through the cataclysm called this cosmic storm the Hail of Hell; it became their Deluge, their Armageddon. Had they still lived exclusively on the surface of the Earth when the disaster occurred, it would probably have wiped them out.

Men of our own generation take conditions at the Earth's surface very much for granted, little realizing how fragile they are. The air that we breathe is not merely essential to the sustenance of life; it is a product of life. The temperature and composition of the atmosphere are no mere accidents; they are conditions created by living organisms for their own benefit, without intelligent purpose but no less cleverly for that. The missiles that had rained down upon the planet 70,000 years in the past, at the time when Copplestone and I had our final conversation–which still lies 30 years in the future of our present conversation–had only to wreck that fragile balance to rob the evolutionary process of a billion years of little victories.

The dust displaced into the upper atmosphere by a single cometary collision, or by a powerful volcanic eruption, sometimes causes seven years of unrelenting winter; the dust displaced by the Hail of Hell and the volcanoes it awoke brought seven times seven years of unrelenting night, and the fiery lava that poured forth from the Earth's mantle scoured the surface, obliterating all land-based life save for a few fugitive micro-organisms.

Without the energy of sunlight, it was impossible for the algae in the sea to maintain or renew the atmosphere, whose oxygen had been consumed in a worldwide conflagration–a conflagration that left ashes behind whose temperature plummeted to hundreds of degrees below zero as they cooled under permanently clouded skies. The oceans froze, and the corpse of the world was embalmed in ice far colder than the stately glaciers of previous Ice Ages.

You and I would have died immediately had today's world suffered such an apocalypse. The tenacity of their nanozoons ensured that the Overmen died much harder–but die they did, in their billions. Many Earth-dwelling Overmen escaped into space, attempting to take refuge in colonies established on Mars, the satellites of Jupiter and Saturn, among the minor planets and on the Moon–but those colonies were also afflicted by the system-wide hail, and sustained terrible losses of their own. Only a few millions of Overmen survived the onslaughts of the first century of the Hail, the majority of those being on the face of the Moon that is perpetually turned toward the Earth–which was, in consequence of that fact, partly shielded from the fury of the storm.

The surface of the Earth was effectively lifeless by that century's end, although a few Overmen who had taken refuge in domes on the ocean floor managed to survive for a little while, and to help their Moon-based brethren secure the survival of many other species. Most of the Arks that they had hastily constructed were eventually destroyed or abandoned, but those on Titan, Europa and Ganymede were maintained, and many small space-habitats–including a dozen hollowed out within the minor planetoids–also survived into the second century of the Hail.

Although the Moon's Earth-directed face had suffered a number of impacts, the impacts in question had not wrought nearly as much destruction as those the Earth itself had suffered. The Moon had no molten rock lurking beneath its crust, and because the Moon was airless its inhabitants already followed a troglodytic existence, adequately equipped with the means to hoard their air against catastrophic loss. Indeed, the cometary rain briefly supplied an atmosphere of sorts to replace the one the Moon had lost in the long-distant past, and brought a rich bounty of raw materials–including a great deal of water–which the Overmen of the Moon were very glad to receive.

The surviving Overmen had perforce to re-organize their attitudes and their plans for the future. They were compelled to accept a new and more cautious estimation of their place in the universal scheme. Within the cauldron of fear that had been set to seethe by their near-extinction, they had to formulate a new ambition and a new purpose. Had they chosen to do it, they could have begun work on the regeneration of the Earth. They had the means to carry forward such a project: to seed the planet with primitive organisms and nanozoons, which could not only live in its depleted environments but begin the work of restoring its atmosphere, its liquid oceans, its savannahs and its forests. Such a project would have taken thousands of years, but it could have been attempted–but what would have been the point, given that the material displaced from the cometary aureole was still falling?

Although the worst was soon over, the surviving Overmen knew that the residuum of the Hail of Hell would continue to fall for tens of thousands, perhaps hundreds of thousands of years. Even if Earth's abundant life could be re-generated in a tougher form, better able to withstand cometary impacts, and even if some kind of protective machinery could be placed in orbit to deflect or destroy the most dangerous objects, who could be sure that some other disturbance of the system's vast halo might not unleash another, even more furious, Hail of Hell?

Given all that, the survivors thought, what future could there be in restoring Earth as the primary habitat of overmankind? What future could there be, in fact, for planetary life? The fact that the Overmen's exploratory probes had discovered no trace of life among the Sun's neighboring stars now began to seem far more ominous than it had at first. The fact that Earth had contrived, during a period of abnormal cosmic quietness, to produce a race capable of surviving the Hail of Hell came to seem remarkable in the extreme: a fluke so improbable as to be unrepeatable anywhere else in the universe, even among second-generation stars numbered in their billions of billions, and in a cosmic lifespan which might yet be measured in billions of billions of years.

Copplestone informed me that the Overmen had learned a hard lesson from the cataclysm that overtook them. The seeming stability of the stars in their courses is an illusion, and there is no refuge safe from turbulence. The universe is, in fact, full of dark and wayward matter which is invisible to optical telescopes and potentially deadly in effect. The kind of life that requires billions of years of evolution to convert tiny bacteria into beings capable of intelligent thought is essentially frail, and its progress is subject to many interruptions, any one of which might prove conclusive. If ever such life had appeared before, the Overmen realized, and if ever it appeared again, it would live as they now must, under threat of casual annihilation–unless and until it could contrive to free itself from the shackles of planet-bound existence.

The Overmen had survived the Hail of Hell because they were no longer planet-bound, but they had lost more than nine-tenths of their empire because they had been planet-*based*. They concluded that this had been a mistake that must now be remedied. They decided that, if they were to have a future at all, it must lie outside the Earth and outside the Solar System of which Earth was a part. They decided that the world which had spawned them had best be abandoned to its fate while they looked in a new direction–not any longer for new Earths to colonize, but for entirely new modes of existence that were independent of planets. Abandoning all thought of the regeneration of the Earth, they planned an exodus from the Solar System, led by the Arks that they had established inside some few of the minor planets. Those left behind on various satellites made preparations to follow; they would not consent to live in a state of siege within the system.

The Overmen had long prided themselves in being a forward-looking race. Having decided that their ultimate destiny must be played out on a stage so vast that the Solar System was a speck of infinitesimal dust by comparison, they were enthusiastic to proceed without delay or distraction. They already knew how to adapt their own bodies in order to live comfortably in low-gravity environments and on distant worldlets, partly by reformulating their flesh and partly by hybridizing themselves with machines, but such radical transformations had earlier been the practice of a tiny minority. Now, they decided that it was time for each and every one of them to embrace the most drastic reformulations and hybridizations, in order that they might all take part in the work that they had formerly delegated to their tiny mechanical probes, and they embarked upon this scheme with a fervent missionary zeal.

Those who were quickest to decide that they would become pilgrims, whose progress would be eternal, also became avid for the conversion of their less eager fellows. The whole race of Overmen was soon infected with a new fervor of commitment and an urgent sense of destiny. Copplestone suggested that some such renaissance of religious sentiment had been inevitable, and was perhaps overdue–but he lamented that whatever human faults the vampire-descended race had left behind, they had not freed themselves from the unfortunate effects of missionary fervor.

For the first time, violent schisms began to appear within the society of the Overmen, as those seized with the most fervent faiths were driven to disagree on points of doctrine. The pilgrim Overmen retained a few bases within the Solar System for a while, but none was intended to be permanent. They emptied all their Arks into vessels designed for interstellar flight, intending to leave nothing behind but empty desolation–but they were no longer one community with but a single purpose. They had splintered into factions, many of which worked in secret toward ends that they did not advertise. In one respect, at least, humankind's successors had begun to resemble the race they had displaced.

5.

As Copplestone imparted this ironic judgment of humankind's usurpers, he suddenly looked around at the walls of the little cottage he had built inside the hemispherical dome, as if he were reassuring himself that they were still solid. I could not tell whether he was anxious about the remote possibility that some last feeble residuum of the devastating hail of which he had spoken might still be able to descend upon the Earth, or whether he was in fear of some kind of violent assault by forces whose aims were unclear to him.

"Why did the Overmen not resurrect the world of their birth as well as planning a new future beyond the Solar System?" I asked him. "Surely they could have done both rather than making a choice."

He told me, gruffly, that the planet had become a mass grave. Although the new Overmen had no room in their fervent creeds for mere superstition, they did not like to walk upon the dust of their not-quite-immortal forebears. The remnants of the dead had ceased to decay as the surface cooled; it was as if they had been set aside, preserved in ice and frozen air. Even the Overmen could not contemplate such a prospect with perfect equanimity.

To Copplestone, of course, the dead Earth appeared as a monument to human folly as well as vampire misfortune. The zealous Overmen, anxious to renew their progress on a cosmic scale, were perfectly content that it should be forgotten–indeed, the majority were utterly determined to forget it, as if that deliberate exclusion were proof that Earth was no more significant than any other particle of matter, and that they had no further need of its dubious heritage. There were, however, other parties that were not prepared to do likewise. Copplestone had allied himself with one of those minority parties, helping to formulate a very different plan with equal missionary zeal.

The Moon was the last outpost of what still seemed to Copplestone to be "true" Overmen: Overmen made of flesh and blood, who still carried the mirror-image of their human cousins in their favorite form. They could easily have remade him in some new image had he asked it of them; he might, if he had been so inclined, have joined the great exodus. He refused, clinging to the semblance and the spirit of his humanity and cleaving to the party of Overmen who wanted the Earth to be more than a grave. This party was content to let the planet remain a mute memorial for a few tens of thousands of years, but not forever. Copplestone allied himself with the Overmen who wanted to reclaim it–but who were led by circumstance and diplomacy to keep that ambition secret.

Within this secret faction, Copplestone had a secret of his own: *he* wanted to reclaim the Earth for humankind, as well as, if not instead of, a new race of Earthly Overmen. He wanted his own species to have a second chance, in order that it might seek and find a better destiny than war and strife had made for it before. He hoped that the empty Earth might one day be repopulated, by real individuals transplanted from an earlier era exactly as he had been.

Although only one other human time-traveler had appeared out of the mists of history before the Hail of Hell had destroyed all life on Earth, Copplestone told me, he clung steadfastly to the hope that more might one day come–and that, if only adequate preparation could be made for them, the human race might yet live again upon the surface of the world it had lost.

"So that is why you set machines to wait for me," I said, when he had laid this scheme before me, "and that is why you think my arrival so important. You want me to become your envoy to the 20th century, to sound a clarion call on your behalf. You want me to spread your formula far and wide, so that those brave enough to use it might become the inheritors of the future Earth."

"Yes," Copplestone said. "That is exactly what I want. But it will not be easy. I have allies, but some of those intent on restoring the Earth to life would be horrified by my scheme. I also have enemies, including one who ought to have been my most steadfast ally. The situation in which I find myself is inordinately complex. Everything I have told you so far is merely a prelude..."

As he spoke these words, we both looked up in alarm, because a terrible sound had interrupted his sentence. It was not an explosion, but it was extremely loud. Once it had started, it did not stop.

As we leapt to our feet, I saw that Copplestone's lips were still moving–but there was no possibility of hearing what he had to say.

I did not need him to tell me what was happening; I had already deduced the nature of the awful peril we were in, and I knew how dreadful it was. The dome enclosing that tiny and pathetic imitation of the England of old had been smashed. Its warm and life-giving atmosphere was rushing out, to be replaced by air than had no sustenance in it and was cold enough for the merest draught to strike a human dead.

The violence of the exchange was obvious enough, for the little cottage in which we sat was already being shaken apart, its roof peeling back to expose the unwindowed sky beyond.

I saw then that I had been mistaken in thinking that the glass of the dome was tinted; the sky beyond really was indigo in color, and not because night was falling. The Sun was still high, still shining with what now appeared to be awful fury, but the sky was not sky blue. The Earth was not the Earth of man but some terrible world half-steeped in darkness even in the blaze of noon

My God! I thought. *I am lost! I shall die within my dream*!

I knew, of course, that my timeshadow had already survived exposure to the ruined surface of the Earth, and that a host of invading machines had preserved it from destruction. Had I presumed that the collapse of Copplestone's protective dome was accidental I might have been able to quell the panic that rose within my breast, but the moment I saw that uncanny sky I also saw that it was alive with machines: flying machines shaped like huge bats and others with very different shapes, which I could not liken to anything I knew.

These multitudinous entities were hurling bolts of fire in every direction—downwards most of all. However furious the Hail of Hell of which Copplestone had spoken had seemed to its victims, I could not imagine that it had been as intense as this.

There was no room for doubt as to what was happening. The enclave which Copplestone had built to receive me was under fierce attack, and could not be safely defended. He had admitted that he had enemies, and that he as keeping secrets even from his allies. He must have hoped that he could communicate his hopes and plans to me without being overheard, and that I would have returned to my own time before anyone could strike against him. Clearly, he had been mistaken.

I had no idea exactly who was attacking us, or exactly why, but the fact was perfectly obvious. What Copplestone had told me had stirred up a hornet's nest, and here were its myriad stings.

Even as I looked up to see a new doom descending upon the ruined world, an enormous host of buzzing flies began to fill the air, as thick as the worst imaginable swarm of tropical locusts—and they fell upon my flesh with every evidence of avid hunger!

The insectile swarm settled upon me like an all-embracing suit of armor. Its progress was so rapid and so efficient that my attenuated body had not time to draw a breath of poisoned air. For 15 or 20 seconds, I was wrapped around like a mummy, quite incapable of motion although I could still see through transparent eyeholes let into the mask. Then my seamless outer tegument became fluid. I started to my feet by my own volition, but what happened thereafter was entirely the action of my new superskin. I had no idea what to do in order to preserve myself from harm, but the machines already had a plan of their own worked out and ready.

Copplestone's little fragment of England had been a more futile gesture than I had realized. He must have suspected that it would become a target almost as soon as I materialized within it, and he had made contingency plans. I recalled his description of his own sensations when he had been captured by a similar assembly of machines, while my imprisoned body found itself running faster than any mere human being had ever run, leaping obstacles with astonishing grace. I believe, however, that my experience was far more disturbing than his for two reasons.

The first advantage Copplestone had had was that his assisted flight had been horizontal, through a forest not unlike the ones in which he had walked as a boy. Mine was a downward flight into a space which opened up before me as I tumbled into it. I cannot fully explain the horror of that descent, but it seemed very dreadful indeed.

I was never falling free, but the actions performed by my living suit of armor did not echo anything my limbs would normally have done. I was, of course, descending into an absolute darkness that I could not help but associate with the idea of the Underworld: the Pit of Souls. I could see nothing but I could imagine much, for I already knew that the Earth had become the grave of an entire species. It was into that illimitable grave that I knew myself to be descending, and I could almost feel the presence of the shades of the dead, the hosts of Sheol.

I plunged ever deeper into the ground, which obligingly continued to tear itself apart in order to facilitate my passage. In another kind of dream, I could have rescued myself by awakening with a start, but the knowledge that I was trapped was the ultimate horror.

The second advantage Copplestone had had when he was caught in a similar manner was that his flight had been unhindered, hurried purely and simply because time was short. I was pursued and harried by enigmatic enemies. Indeed, it seemed as if all the devils in Hell were after me, determined to crack the kindly shell which had enveloped me and expose my too-frail flesh to laceration and destruction.

I did not know for sure what might become of the body I had left behind if those buzzing furies succeeded in their mission–there might have been a possibility that my fugitive consciousness might somehow regain it–but I only had room for the hope that the assault could be withstood and my timeshadow saved.

Mercifully, my intelligent armor was not without its own resources. As I ran down into the bowels of the dead Earth, my arms waved as madly as those of a conductor at the Royal Albert Hall supervising an unusually spirited passage. The fingertips of my protective shell hurled sparks of fire in every direction, which shot some few of my tiny pursuers out of the swirling air. They did not retaliate in kind, but whether that was because they lacked the inclination or the capacity I could not tell.

There were larger machines emerging from the dark abyss to either side of me, ranging in size from that of a wasp to that of a vulture. They all spat sparks of their own into the vaporous inferno, lending support to my vengeful fingers; as I looked up for the last time I caught a glimpse of gargantuan mechanical fliers dueling with one another, silhouetted against the oceanic blue of the future sky.

I suppose my descent lasted less than two minutes, but they were the most hectic minutes of my life. The end came when I was unceremoniously engulfed by the fathomless dark. I thought I had been swallowed, and feared that I was about to be digested, but light returned soon enough.

I was still encased in my suit of armor, but I was reclining; there was another window visible behind my transparent visor: a window that showed me the alien sky, much clearer now. I was confused, for I had imagined myself deep within the bowels of the Earth, but I remembered what Copplestone had said about location being no prison in this strange world. I might be entombed, but my senses were not. Nor, I think, was I as far below the surface as I had imagined.

The sky was no longer so crowded with aircraft and explosions. The fervor of battle had apparently passed its maximum–but I did not know whether it was my unexpected adversaries or Copplestone's defenders that had been defeated.

A sibilant whisper in my ear said: "Do not be afraid; this oppression will not last forever."

Alas, this was not warning enough, for I leapt to the conclusion that it meant the battle of the insects. In fact, it referred to an unimaginably dreadful force that immediately began to press down upon me, as the container which had sucked me in leapt from its deep pit, driving vertically upwards with awesome insistence.

I felt as if I were being flattened, like a little bug squashed beneath the thumb of some invisible godling. I knew that my intelligence was wrapped in a supernaturally thin bodily envelope, far more refined than the mechanical shell that now surrounded it; even so, I had the impression that my facial flesh was being crudely and coarsely dragged from the bones of my skull.

6.

The whispered promise was fulfilled; the awful pressure did not last forever, or even for very long. By the time the sensation had passed, however, I seemed to be high above the Earth. The sky was far darker than it had been before. As the Heavens reeled–the Sun, the fixed stars and the increasingly-distant Earth sliding into new positions–the face of the Moon came into view. It was the ornately-decorated face that I had seen before; that part of its surface which bathed in the Sun's light was vivid with color, like an enameled brooch pinned upon the bosom of the night, flecked with gems.

It did not take long for me to deduce that the Moon was our intended destination. We had risen from the interior of the Earth as if fired by a gun through a long barrel of rock, or borne aloft through a long shaft on a rocket's jet. I say *we* because I knew by then that I was not alone.

"I am sorry for that," said the sibilant voice, which I now recognized as Copplestone's although it was being filtered through some intervening medium. "I had hoped that my defenses could stand him off....but that is by the by. Time is pressing more urgently than I had imagined, and there is so much that I have still to tell you. Listen to me carefully, my friend, and try not to let the strangeness of our situation distract you."

I had not lost my capacity for concentration. Even the knowledge that I was cocooned in a fabulous machine, soaring through the interplanetary aether on my way to the moon, did not prevent my paying close attention to the remainder of the professor's story.

Many of the Overmen who lingered for a while within the Solar System, Copplestone told me, did not care a jot about the dream of regeneration entertained by the minority. It made no difference to their own plans that the Earth might once again play temporary host to their cousins. Even those who disapproved were rarely actively hostile; they had their own disputes to attend to, their own destinies to choose. There was, however, enough active hostility to the plans of the reclaimers to divert the reclaimers' attention from the secret agendas harbored within their own ranks. The Overmen who were interested in Earth's eventual reclamation accepted Copplestone's assistance readily enough, and did not question his loyalty too closely.

Copplestone did not mind keeping secrets from his allies. He was, after all, a member of a different species. The Overmen had adopted him, and made him into one of themselves in every sense that was meaningful *to them*, but he had never thought of himself as one of their company, nor did he consider that he owed them any debt. He was perfectly content to continue making his own secret preparations for the resurrection of the human species, and in pursuit of that end, he was prepared to be extremely patient.

He told me all this is a matter-of-fact tone, but I think he was being less than honest. I believe he had felt his loneliness far more intensely that he cared to admit, even to himself.

"This is all very well," I said, when he gave me leave to speak, "but it does not seem very urgent. What will happen to us now that your plans are known? Someone has evidently taken sufficient exception to your scheme to launch an army of machines against us. Can I possibly survive long enough for me to return to my own time? Even if I can, what possible future can there be for your ambition?"

"You will certainly survive," he assured me. "We could not be easily killed, even if he wanted to kill us. We are made of stronger stuff than mere flesh."

The disingenuousness of this reply only added to my exasperation. "You will forgive me," I said, "if I can take scant reassurance from the fact that we cannot *easily* be killed, given the extremes to which our enemies seem to be willing and able to go. Do you know who it is that is harassing us? You said *he*?"

"Please don't be afraid," Copplestone said–but he must have become aware of the inadequacy of the injunction as soon as he had spoken, because his tone immediately grew more agitated. "All this is probably no more than a pantomime–a mere show of petulance! I'm truly sorry....I have grown so used to my virtual immortality that I had quite forgotten....forgive me, I beg of you...."

Alas, my patience was at an end. "Never mind forgiveness!" I cried. "For Heaven's sake, man–who sent those machines to smash your precious little haven, and why are you so sure that he did not mean to kill us?"

"It was Lugard," said the soft voice, more softly still. "At least, I hope and pray that it was Lugard. I am not the only former human among the Overmen, you see–I only wish that I were."

I should not have been surprised when Copplestone reintroduced Lugard's name into the conversation, but I had been working along a different line of thought for some time. When Copplestone had informed me that a few of the Overmen had taken an interest in his plan, I had immediately begun to wonder whether they might secretly have been far more interested than they pretended.

Copplestone had lived 60,000 years since he had last penetrated the veil of the future, and he had had plenty of time to forget the anxieties that had possessed him then, but I had lived only five years, and I remembered clearly enough what kind of fears he had voiced when he told his story. In 60,000 years he had grown used to thinking of the Overmen as benign and generous beings, but when he had first met them, he had thought them menacing. He thought that they might reach back through time to kill him, if they could, lest he should terrify the world with news of their covert existence and monstrous nature. He now seemed content to accept that they had not done so–but the question that came to my mind was whether they would have done so if they could.

The reason I was not expecting to hear Lugard's name in connection with the attack launched against us was that I had already formed the hypothesis that the Overmen had kept a closer watch on Copplestone's grand plan than he had supposed. It seemed all too plausible to me that, while his endeavors had seemed futile, the vampires had been content to let him play–but that, as soon as he had opened up another link with the past, they became anxious to break it, lest their empire be nipped in the historical bud.

I said as much to Copplestone.

"If the Overmen thought there was a real possibility of altering the past," he replied, "they would be very glad to discover it. They would be delighted with the opportunity to warn their own forefathers of the disaster that was about to strike them–perhaps, if they could only send a warning far enough back in time, they might even assist their ancestors to find a way to divert the wayward mass that launched the Hail of Hell. So far as I know, the majority hold a very different view. The belief of the orthodox is that if the past is alterable, it is only alterable in its entirety.

"The members of the dominant party do not believe that any information you could carry into the year 1900 could inspire humankind to avoid their own destruction or contrive the defeat of their successors, and I agree with them. Their faith in their ancestors' powers of concealment is unbreakable, and they are probably right. They enjoyed the best protection of all: the refusal of belief. Humans had learned to laugh at such notions as vampires, werewolves and elves. Did not some Churchman once say that the Devil's greatest weapon was the fact that people had ceased to believe in him?

"In any case, it is no part of my plan to save the humans of the 21st century from self-destruction. Lugard might want that–if Lugard knows what he wants, which I doubt–but I do not. A race so foolish as to bring about its own extinction does not deserve to be saved *en masse*; if it were to be saved temporarily, it would surely deliver itself to a similar fate eventually. What I want to do is to save *the best*. I want to bring the cream of the human crop into the near future, in order that they might become the founders and the parents of a better race: a race that would be, in every good sense of the word, *more human*."

I knew what he meant. I knew, too, that he had in mind at least one glaring example of the kind of man he would far rather have eliminated from his Utopia.

"The destruction of the mass of the human species is, I fear, unavoidable," Copplestone told me, in that strangely sibilant voice "but the question remains as to whether that destruction need be permanent. My hope is that, if the art of casting timeshadows is properly cultivated by the people of the 20th century, the human race might yet be enabled to reclaim and repossess the world it lost. While the Earth belonged to the newly-triumphant Overmen there was no room for human beings there, but those Overmen are long gone now, and their descendants have other matters to occupy their bodies and their minds. Earth lies dead and desolate now, but that death and desolation is not irrevocable.

"Given time enough, and reason enough, the world can be made habitable again, despite the threat of further bombardments from space. I already have the tools with which to do it, and the lifespan I require–what I need is a company of brave time-travelers, who will serve as the nucleus of humanity reborn. Now that you are here, I have the seed of that company in my grasp at last. All that remains is that you should add your cause to mine and agree to serve as my agent on the ancient Earth. You must make my gift available to the very best specimens of the human species: those who have the will, the intellect and the moral force to build a New Jerusalem upon the dark and dismal plains of the derelict world!"

While Copplestone was reaching this conclusion, we had been drawing ever nearer to the Moon. The effects of our initial acceleration had relented, and for a while it had seemed as if I had no weight at all. Now, as the Heavens tilted again and the Moon disappeared from view, I felt the pressure of a measured deceleration.

The alteration in the aether-ship's attitude brought the Earth back into view through the viewing-port. The disc was partly lit by the Sun. I was surprised by the brightness of the illuminated crescent–but I soon realized that what I was looking at was an unbroken wilderness of ice. I could not tell whether it was the Atlantic or the Pacific because there was no identifiable coastline.

Although I continued to take in everything that Copplestone's voice was pouring into my ears, I made what effort I could to study the field of stars that lay behind the Earth, which was richer by far than any I had ever seen through the Earth's atmospheric screen. It seemed curiously bleak and barren despite its astonishing richness–as cold and indifferent in its glimmering plenitude as the ice that enshrouded the corpse of the Earth.

It was hard to believe that Copplestone's mechanical slaves could refashion that dead planet as a fit habitation for human beings, even if they were given 1000 years in which to do it–but I realized, even as I framed the gloomy thought, that they might have far more than 1000 years, and far more than 10,000, if they needed it. The improved version of Copplestone's formula would enable timeshadows to be projected over even vaster distances in time; it was all a matter of dosage. In any case, any timeshadow which came into this new era, as Lugard had, without the slightest desire to return, could be preserved exactly as Copplestone and Lugard had been preserved, more-or-less indefinitely. But what, I wondered, was Lugard's part in all this? Why was he trying to subvert Copplestone's plan?

I took leave, too, to wonder how hard it might be to enlist recruits for Copplestone's project, if I were to do as he asked.

At first, I thought it might be easy enough to find volunteers among the old, who had little to lose by the experiment and everything to gain–but then I remembered the girl Lugard had poisoned, who had lost no weight. Not everyone, it seemed, could cast the kind of timeshadow Copplestone required. Then again, I remembered Sir William Crookes' insistence that everyone did, in fact, cast a timeshadow that survived them after death, albeit a rather insubstantial one. If Crookes had been right, and there was some truth in the myths of the afterlife cherished by so many human beings, any who chose Copplestone's route might, in remaining Earthbound, be forsaking a natural destiny that many would think preferable–or so, at least, they might believe.

I concluded, in consequence of these deductions, that it might well be too optimistic to hope that the *best* of 20th century humankind could be recruited to the pursuit of Copplestone's dream–and that it might difficult enough merely to avoid attracting the worst. Like Copplestone, I had in mind one particular example of a time-traveler who might indeed qualify as one of the worst of his kind.

The Detective's Story: Part Three

The Moon, circa 100,000 A.D.

7.

Our landing on the Moon was gentle, and I did not realize that our journey was concluded until the closely-clustered stars were eclipsed. The aether-ship had descended into a dark cavern, whose roof slid back into place like the lids of a great eye.

When the ship was finally at rest, I made as if to rise from my couch, but I was still encased in my second skin. The machines would not respond to the prompting of my limbs. Copplestone advised me that I had best let the suit walk for me until I had become accustomed to the fact that I now weighed only a sixth of what I had weighed on Earth.

In truth, I would have welcomed a sensation of lightness, all the more so because my timeshadow had seemed so unreasonably heavy while I was on Earth. While I remained imprisoned within my mechanical hide, however, I did not feel light at all.

The cavern into which the vessel had descended, into which I was now re-moved, was pitch dark. Presumably the machines that had charge of me had no need of visual guidance, but I found my inability to see extremely discomfiting. As I was carried forth from my resting place, I had to rely upon other senses to keep track of my progress for at least three minutes. Mercifully, we had not far to go before we came into another lighted space.

I had expected a corridor but in fact we emerged into a huge hemispherical dome, not unlike the one on Earth but four or five times as large. Its curving roof displayed the same pattern of hexagonal and octagonal panes, through which the stars could be seen in awesome profusion–at least 100 for every one that can be seen through the envelope of Earth's atmosphere.

I had always thought the night sky conspicuously empty, and the stars ra-ther lonely, but the windows of the Moon looked out on to a sky that was excee-dingly full, its stars so closely crowded as to be almost touching one another.

The ground beneath this paneled sky was likewise an echo of the ancient Earth, but not of the cozy artificiality of an English garden. There were trees in vast profusion: enormously tall tropical trees, so densely packed that I imme-diately labeled the place a jungle.

There were brightly-colored parrots in the branches, and monkeys too, which showed no fear of Copplestone or myself as we climbed out of a trap-door set 100 yards or so from the dome's rim. I wondered whether they were real or whether they were mere imitations, like the grasses and bushes Copplestone had installed in his temporary refuge on Earth. No doubt I would have found out, had I only been given time.

The besuited Copplestone–who looked more like a heroic statue hewn in black marble than a man–had not taken a dozen steps away from the trap-door when the ground beneath his feet lost its solidity. It dissolved into a fluid mass, into which he immediately sank. The shell that confined him became suddenly denser, as if it had been dipped in pitch. His voice, which had only just resumed its discourse, was cut off in mid-sentence.

Copplestone waved his arms in angry protest but the movement was rapidly stifled as his clever exoskeleton was overlaid by an exoskeleton of its own, which took control of its movements as easily and as completely as its counterpart had taken control of mine.

I was so used to wonders by now that I felt no fear or alarm on his behalf; it took time for the realization to form that my companion was in dire trouble, having been furiously attacked.

I heard him cry for help before his voice was suddenly drowned out by an appalling crackling sound. When my limbs moved reflexively, as if to go to his aid, my own suit of armor would not respond; it evidently had other instructions.

I found myself turning to retreat–but the trapdoor from which we had emerged was no longer accessible. Squatting on top of it was the strangest and most terrible creature I had ever beheld.

The monster was humanoid, save for a thick tail and horns sprouting from its temples. It was ten feet tall and its scaly body was silvery in color, although it had the most intimidating blood-red eyes, with serpentine slit-like pupils.

The diffuse sound in my ears suddenly took on the semblance of the mocking crepitation of a hellish fire, and the monster became a veritable demon. *This is not the moon at all*, I thought. *It is the domain of lost souls. It is Dante's* Inferno*!*

Had I been in proper possession of my own body I would have frozen momentarily in shock and horror, then run as quickly as I could to one side or the other, away from both the demon and the living ground that was consuming Copplestone. The shell that contained me was not blessed with any such panic reflex. It followed through with its original intention, moving unhurriedly towards the monster. No matter how hard I strained, I could not make it stop or turn.

As my suit of armor moved, however, it did at least raise its arms–with my own inside them–in order to fire off a barrage of sparks of the kind it had earlier hurled at the plague of insectile marauders. Unfortunately, the demon soaked up the sparks with contemptuous ease. As I drew closer and closer, it spread its own gigantic arms, as if to welcome me into a fatal but curiously loving embrace.

Perhaps my armor tried to duck under the spreading arms, or perhaps it tried to retaliate with some cunning wrestler's trick, but whatever it attempted to do it failed miserably. Clumsily–but no less effectively for that–the demon gathered me to its bosom, clutching me as if I were a beloved but rebellious child which needed to be taught a stern lesson.

I screamed in sheer terror. I longed to hear Copplestone's sibilant voice reassuring me that all was well, but the voice had gone and there was only a senseless crackling, like the sound of dry stems caught between the blades of a mechanical harvester.

As I gave way to my terror, the situation became very confused. I was squeezed and I was twisted, so tortuously that I felt sure that my limbs must break and my phantom rib-cage must be crushed. I did not lose consciousness but I certainly felt faint, and for a moment or two I could not tell up from down.

The only freedom of movement I had within my shell was to close my eyes, and that I certainly did, although the transparent lenses that had permitted me to see through the shell were immediately pressed in upon the closed lids, generating splashes of false light to add to my confusion.

When I could see again, I found that I was still encased by an extra skin, but I seemed to be much taller than I had been before. I was running through the jungle at an astonishing pace, as if every stride were carrying me 10 or 12 yards.

I knew that there were *things* pursuing me but my carrier would not deign to look around so that I might see what they were–nor did it deign to look down so that I could confirm my horrible suspicion that the demon had done to me exactly what the fluid ground had done to Copplestone: enveloped me, armor and all. I felt sure that I had been swallowed whole and that the body racing along so swiftly, with my own inside it, was the demon's, gleefully transporting me to my allotted place of torment.

I ran and I ran, so swiftly that the trees became a green blur and I became dizzy.

I felt several abrupt impacts upon my back, each one blunted by the layers of insulating material but painful nevertheless. The awful crackling sound had dulled my ears by now, and I could not tell whether the faint voices I began to discern within the crackling were actual or illusory. Then, blackness came again, and I knew that my carrier had dived into the ground, into some lightless tunnel.

I no longer had any sensation of movement. The crepitation in my ears faded, by slow degrees, into near silence and I lost all sense of direction. I suspected that I was still moving, but I had no idea where or how fast. I tried hard to be duly grateful that I was still able to draw breath, and that my unnatural body was no longer being wrenched this way and that, without regard for my comfort or my safety.

I cannot tell how much time had passed before light struck my open eyes again. Perhaps it was no longer than a few minutes, but it felt like an age.

What the light showed me, when it did strike, was the monster. It stood before me again, tall and proud in its armor of shining scales, staring at me with its great crimson eyes–or, rather, with their vertical slit-like pupils, which seemed to me to be little windows allowing me to look into the dark corruption of its soul. It took me several seconds to realize that the slitted pupils were, indeed, little windows, and that I was looking through them at a mirror. If the dark corruption I had imagined was anywhere, it was within me.

I heard laughter then, and reflexively made as if to turn around.

I was both surprised and relieved when the massive encasement in which I was imprisoned responded to my will and turned with me. I was even more surprised, and immeasurably relieved, when that encasement began to dissolve, lowering my own phantom feet to the ground and then flowing away from me like a huge living shadow in retreat across the polished floor.

I could not help feeling a pang of regret as I saw it go, for it left me feeling very vulnerable, naked save for the mere appearance of clothing.

"You must forgive my little joke, my friend," said the voice whose laughter I had heard.

The speaker was sat on a leather-backed chair mounted upon a low podium, positioned behind a very ample desk. The desk-top was laden with papers, most of which were gathered into half a dozen stacks of different sizes. There was also a decanter, half-full of what I took to be red wine, and a goblet not quite drained to the dregs.

We were in a chamber crowded with bookshelves 10 or 12 feet tall, crammed with volumes of many different sizes, miscellaneously bound in every somber shade imaginable. There was no bare wall at all, and no door was visible from where I stood. For all I knew, the library might have extended indefinitely in every direction, its shelves forming the corridors of an infinite and inescapable maze.

"I don't know what dear old Ned Copplestone has been telling you," the speaker went on, "but I expect that it involved pilgrims and paradises, and the reclamation of the Earth by new men woven by machines out of the wispy flax of timeshadows. Does he still style himself Emperor of the Moon, or has he set aside his false humility sufficiently to claim the title of Savior of Mankind, the Last of the Messiahs? That is his glorious aim, is it not? To bring about the Millennium: the 1000-year reign of peace, harmony and joy?"

The effigy of Lucian, Count Lugard, paused for a second or two before adding: "I always knew that if anyone ever came, it would have to be you...but then, I had the advantage of knowing that the formula Copplestone had left behind had been destroyed, and that you were the only one with sufficient curiosity and cleverness to recover it. Somehow, I never quite got to the point of explaining that to Copplestone, even when we were on speaking terms; there is a perversity in me that has always rejoiced in keeping secrets. Welcome to the future, my worthy friend and murderer!"

He looked human enough, but I knew that he was no more human that Copplestone had been. I had put a human name to him without any difficulty at all, but I wondered this anthropomorphic machine would insist as determinedly as Copplestone had that he was still the man he once had been. This, I suspected, was a man who had probably done everything in his power to shed his old self, as if he had been a new-born dragonfly casting off its chrysalis. This was a man who had labored under the false charge of being a vampire while he lived, and had hurled himself into an afterlife determined to savor the hunger and ecstasy of the actual vampires who had succeeded humankind as rulers of the world.

I could not doubt that he had achieved his goal–but he had not fled the Solar System with his new fellows. He had stayed behind–not to help Copplestone, but to plague him. I wondered why, and I hoped that he would have time enough to explain himself.

8.

"You were your own murderer, Lugard," I said to my tormentor, as soon as I had recovered my wits. When he did not seem disturbed by the statement, I quickly added: "and not merely your own. The girl's death was absolute, and would lie heavy on your conscience were you capable of entertaining guilt or sorrow."

He scowled at that. "I should have suspected that the Fates would cheat me of that small reward," he said, darkly. "They never would play fair when I had a stake of that sort in the pot. There is only one thing, my friend, that can possibly compensate for the knowledge that one must spend eternity without a lover. Are your vaunted powers of deduction equal to that riddle?"

"Oh yes," I replied. "Men like you can never sustain their erotic affections for very long, but they can bear grudges and nurse hatreds eternally. All you would need to sustain your interest in existence is a rival."

"You will concede, in that case, that you and I are not so very different after all," he said, craftily. "According to your biographer, you have no time for lovers at all, but you derive great pleasure from pitting your wits against the Napoleons of crime. You will doubtless be grateful, if you have time to hear me out, that I took the trouble to kidnap you. Copplestone can only bribe you with the prospect of some drearily emasculated Utopia, but I can offer you far better reasons by far to join me amid the legions of the ancient dead. I can offer you the possibility, if not the promise, of meeting worthy enemies."

"I have never lacked for enemies," I assured him. "Nor, it seems, does Professor Copplestone."

"He is not my enemy," Lugard said. "He does not even believe, in his heart of hearts, that I am his. I admit that I am his adversary in certain matters–but in the grander scheme of things, I am his partner, his shadow, his other half. We are in this together, and always will be. He should have let me take you when I came for you, but I suppose he had not finished his tale of woes and wonders. He was a better raconteur in the old days, was he not? Immortality has made him tedious."

I looked around at the crowded bookshelves. "It seems to have made you into the prince of scholars," I said. "I would have thought Copplestone better suited to that role–or is all this merely for show?"

"It is the heritage of human and vampire wisdom," he informed me, coldly. "Copplestone may have been a scholar, but he was never an aristocrat. He is content with mere data, which can easily be stored in mechanical memory; he never had my reverence for the actual objects of antiquity. I wish I could show you the scope of my collection, but there is no time. I don't know what dosage Copplestone's machines advised you to take, but I'm fairly certain that he will have left us insufficient time to meet and converse as we would wish. If he had not, his minions would have followed you, and would even now be battering at my door. If you are to learn all that you need to learn, we must employ a cleverer method than a spoken monologue. I know that this will be hard but I must ask it of you regardless: *Will you trust me?*"

"Why should I?" I retorted.

His answer was immediate. "If you do not," he said, "you will return to the past with only half a story. If you do not let me give you the information I have to impart by subtler means than talk, you will never know it. The puzzle will be incomplete and the decisions which you have to make will be shots in the dark. Copplestone is right about one thing: the future of mankind, on Earth and in the Universal Scheme, may depend on what you choose to do when you awake from this dream of future possibility; it would be a shame to make your choice blindly."

"What are you asking of me, exactly?"

"I mesmerized you once before, without your consent. On that occasion, I had a trivial end in mind, and only needed to subject you to a slight suggestion. This time, I must have your fullest co-operation. We must collaborate intimately, in order to achieve the near-impossible. If you consent, I have nanozoons at my beck and call that can make your memory wonderfully receptive, so that I can fill it with remarkable rapidity–but I feel obliged to warn you that the process is not without its hazards. Dare you accept the challenge? I must have your answer now, for I fear that you might be snatched back into the past at any moment."

I have always prided myself on being a decisive man–a man ready to respond to any challenge, all the more so if the challenge in question is dangerous and bizarre. There was only one answer I could give.

"What do you want me to do?" I asked.

Men of the 19th century tend to think of mesmerism in terms of spinning discs, trances and the power of suggestion. Such are its trappings in the present day–but they are, for the most part, the instruments of charlatanry. The instructions Lugard gave me at the time were minimal, but I was later able to understand what he had done–and what my consent had cost me.

Like Copplestone, Lugard had been carefully remade when he arrived in the world of the vampires as a timeshadow, some thousands of years after his predecessor. Tiny machines–nanozoons–had fortified his attenuated flesh while carefully conserving the apparatus of his consciousness. Having mastered the intricacies of that process, they could have done the same for me, retaining me within my vision and preventing my return to 1900, but neither Copplestone nor Lugard wanted that–at least, not yet. Each of them wanted me to carry a message from their present to ours, although they were at odds concerning the substance of the message. I had heard Copplestone's, but Lugard's was more ambitious in its import and its intricacy.

Lugard had prepared mechanical servants to make much slighter modifications in my timeshadow than would have been required to detain me in the far future–modifications that would enable me to memorize a page of manuscript at a glance, several hundred times over. This intellectual stock would not be accessible to my conscious mind in any piecemeal fashion, even after my return, and it would fade away entirely within a matter of days. After I had recovered possession of the body I had left to lie in the 19th century, however, I would be able to reproduce the entire script in a single sustained rush. A similar but far less reliable method of recovering information is, I believe, employed by certain Spiritualist mediums, who call it *automatic writing*.

The prospect of allowing my timeshadow to be modified by Lugard's machines was not without its attendant anxieties, but my timeshadow had already been modified once without my consent being asked, when first I ventured forth to the poisoned Earth. I was, in any case, completely in his power; it seemed to me, as I pondered his challenge, that he could do as he liked with me.

I realized that Lugard probably did, in fact, require my consent–presumably, he would not otherwise have bothered to ask. Had I not, upon awakening from my vision, committed myself urgently and unresistingly to the task of reproducing the material he had consigned to my memory, it would have been lost–we had, indeed, to work in concert to ensure it preservation. I did not follow the argument so far at the time, though; I had to make the decision quickly, and I agreed to his terms.

There was no further preamble. I assume that his nanozoons were already inside me, awaiting some secret signal. When they began to do their work, I was only slightly disconcerted. I felt no pain–nor, indeed, any other physical sensation that I could put a name to. My thoughts did become confused, and I had difficulty maintaining any coherent train within them, but I did not fall asleep. I felt, in fact, unusually relaxed and contented.

Lugard had the pages that he wished me to memorize ready on his desk. He sat me in his own chair while he displayed them to me, and I felt entirely comfortable. My steady eyes caught a few words here and there but I had no time to make sense of what I saw and I did not trouble to make any count of the leaves as he turned them over.

When he had turned the last sheet, I was half-convinced that the experiment had failed and that nothing had been accomplished, but he seemed sanguine enough.

He sighed, with evident relief.

"It seems that we might have a little time left to us, after all," he said. "I hope, at least, that there is time enough for me to apologize for my indecent haste and make a belated attempt to play the host." He poured wine from the decanter into the goblet and took a sip. "Your health, sir!" he said. "I hope that your work as a consulting detective has kept you busy since we last met. How long ago was that, in your terms?"

"A little more than five years," I told him. I was still seated, while he was still standing, but I was content to look up at him while I studied him, examining his cuffs and elbows for wear.

The sleeves of his black coat were stained with brown and red, and the cuff of his shirt was spotted with dark blue. These were, I judged, the stigmata of the antiquarian: the dust of crumbling leather bindings and the dried-up residue of ink. There was something oddly comforting in the sight of such trivial symptoms of carelessness and imperfection.

"So little!" he marveled. "I have lived tens of thousands of years since then; Copplestone has lived even longer. I suppose he drank tea instead of wine? Odd, is it not, how these tiny idiosyncrasies of character persist, hardening into badges of fiercely-guarded identity. But I must try to use this small gift of time productively. You will discover, when you have transcribed your cargo of words, that there are four distinct documents. The first is a formula for a more powerful version of Copplestone's drug; it is based in speculation, as was the one he gave you, but I have high hopes for it. The second contains my account of this fabulous universe in which we find ourselves, and my proposals for the resumption of human history and the completion of human destiny. The third you will find very familiar, but its familiarity will constitute proof that what you have experienced is no mere dream and there are passages in it to whose truth another will bear witness. I wrote it for my own use and comfort, a long time ago, but thought it worth inclusion when I discovered that Copplestone had found you and given you the means to return. The fourth is a letter; I ask you, as one gentleman to another, to put it into an envelope unread and to deliver it when, and only when, you have informed its addressee of everything that has happened to you in the course of this adventure."

He spoke very rapidly, hurrying just as Copplestone had, and with the same excuse, but I began to suspect that it *was* an excuse. Time was indeed short, but the impatience of my two hosts had at least as much to do with the fact that they had been denied fresh human company for a very long time.

It was on the tip of my tongue to protest, in response to Lugard's last request, that I was not a postman–but I realized in time that a postman was exactly what I had become: a mere carrier of screeds, charged with the duty of delivering them to the 19th century. Instead, I asked him where we were, and why he had brought me here by force.

"I brought you here by force because Copplestone left me no choice," he said, sourly. "I would gladly have joined him in his little garden so that we might receive you together. I would have placed my methods at his disposal, so that he could deposit as much information in your head as I have–but we hold very different opinions, and he was afraid of the competition. Had he been able, he would have made certain that his was the only account you heard–but I knew that, if I could only puncture that little bubble he had built amid the ruins of the Earth, he would have to bring you to the Moon.

"Copplestone fancies that he has long been the absolute ruler of this little world, but he is not. His dominion does not extend below the surface. I am the Lord of the Lunar Underworld, and I have reached a very different accommodation with the mechanical descendants of the Overmen. If he is the center-piece of an empire, as he believes, I am the chief of the barbarians, busy eroding its borders and waiting for its fall. He would cancel me out if he could. If he could send you back to that house where I died, in 1895, he would commission you to make certain that my timeshadow died with my body, as poor Laura's did. I am by no means so ungenerous; I have learned to value my enemies, if not to forgive them.

"I give you an honest warning, my bold knight errant: beware of assassins from the farthest futures! I believe that a fugitive few of that sort are in the world already, and if we succeed in our experiment, then so might others succeed, who might well try to do worse than murder you in the cause of frustrating your mission. There are those abroad who desire to snuff us out of existence, so utterly and absolutely that we never existed at all. Such a thing cannot be easily done, but I dare not say that the time will never come when it will be possible. If the overmen with whom I am allied are right, the universe not only *can* be remade, but *must* be remade, and the contest to take part in that remaking has already been joined."

He was speaking in a soft tone but he still spoke very rapidly, leaving no opportunity for interruption. It was plain that he expected to lose me at any moment and did not want to let me go without further emphasizing the warnings that he had already committed to paper–but he was also making conversation, with a rare fervor. He had lived far longer than any man of yore, but there was something in him that yearned for true companionship. Perhaps, as he had claimed, an adversary was more necessary to him than a friend–but because he already had an adversary, in Copplestone, it was the lack of a friend that he felt more keenly.

He had made an adversary of me five years before, but he had presumably lived some 50,000 years since then, while I lived only five, and he had changed sufficiently to regard my advent in a different light. His show of mockery had evaporated, and he was looking at me with a strange expression.

265

I had another question ready, but I had no time to ask it of him. He must have seen that I was slipping away, for I saw a shadow of profound sadness flit across his features. He raised his glass again, in a vain attempt to produce an ironic salute.

"Farewell, my old friend!" he said–and then the bookshelves behind him imploded, scattering their precious cargo across the carpeted floor.

A curtain that hid a sliver of empty wall between two ranks of shelves billowed out, racked and rent by the blast, and the turbulent air filled with an appalling sound.

My first panic-stricken thought, I must admit, was for my own safety. That carefully-ordered chamber was ripped apart, and the space from which the books had been displaced was filled with angry light and black shrapnel. It seemed to me that the shrapnel would shred everything within the narrow space: books, shelves and timeshadow-flesh alike. I tried to raise my hands to cover my eyes.

I could not do it. I had already lost my tenuous physical grip upon the future and I could no longer move within it. I could no longer see within it either, but that last image was caught and frozen, engraved upon my consciousness while I fell into time. I fully expected it to be dissolved into the same chaotic confusion that had afflicted me as I moved forwards in time, but it remained; it was as if my brain were incapable of letting go of it. I suppose it was an image of burgeoning chaos, but, once the explosion had been arrested in my sight, the wrathful vortex centered on the standing figure of Count Lugard came to seem strangely ordered and purposeful.

He had not raised his hands, nor had he attempted to dive to the floor. He remained perfectly still, his glass raised up in that last ironic salute. Had he been a man, I would have been certain that death had come to claim him–but I knew that he was no longer a human being. Perhaps, even so, he had not the resources to withstand such a violent assault–but if so, he was prepared to meet his doom with perfect equanimity.

I shall never forget that last sight of Lugard. I had never liked or admired the man, but there was something unmistakably noble about his attitude as chaos erupted around him. It was as if his whole world had been shattered, and yet he remained serene: not merely imperturbable but ineradicable.

Perhaps he *was* ineradicable–perhaps the entity with which I spoke was only a deputy, an animated doll, disposable as soon as the conversation ended–but I hesitate to take refuge in that assumption.

I have attempted to distil what conclusions I can from that final image. I cannot believe that it was an attempt by Copplestone to rescue or reclaim my timeshadow; it was far too violent for that. I do not doubt that, had I maintained my physical presence for a second longer, I would have been destroyed. Nor can I believe that it was an act of casual vengeance by Copplestone, who was not that kind of man. It would be a sad thought to bring back from my vision that although the future I had visited had only two human beings in it, they occupied their time with attempts to destroy one another.

In my opinion, the balance of probabilities is that Lugard, or his simulacrum, was attacked by Overmen. Some, at least, of those among whom he now lived did not want him to give me the information that he was determined to pass on. I might be wrong, but the balance of probabilities seems to favor the interpretation that, although his would-be assassins had been willing to let me talk to Copplestone without interference, they could not be content to have me kidnapped by Lugard and indoctrinated with his rival interpretation of the history which Copplestone had communicated to me.

I knew that if I hoped to understand the motive that might have prompted these fearful Overmen to violence, I must search for it within the texts that Lugard had displayed to me–and that is what I immediately set out to do.

The Detective's Story: Part Four

London and Paris, July-September 1900

9.

My return to the present was exceedingly distressing. Recovery of my whole body was attended on this second occasion by considerable pain, which was doubtless prolonged because I would not permit the doctor to use morphine to alleviate my distress. My anguish was intense for a while, but I felt sure that it would ebb away eventually and I was desperate to conserve my presence of mind for the task ahead.

It was obvious even then that the return of my timeshadow had not restored my body to its former condition. I was physically depleted, and the depletion grew progressively worse–with a final effect that you can see well enough. At first, I did not seem so inhuman, but, in many ways, I was in a worse state then than I am now. It is possible, in fact, that my present appearance represents a kind of adjustment, a stabilizing adaptation to whatever changes in my inner being were wrought by Lugard's nanozoons.

I do not believe that I am as close to death as I may appear, although I have lost a good deal of my former strength and powers of endurance. My thought-processes remain clear, and my powers of deduction do not seem in the least impaired. If my altered appearance forbids me to say that I have recovered, then I can at least say that I am now as healthy as my present state of being permits.

When I first awoke, I was in such dire straits that the doctor urged me to go to the hospital. I refused; I had work to do, and I knew there was no time to waste. It was not easy to resist his demands and pleas, but he was exhausted by his long vigil; in the end, I persuaded him to let me be.

While the doctor slept in the next room, I took to my writing-desk with half a dozen pens and a ream of foolscap. My hand began to write, as if of its own accord–and the style in which it wrote was very different from my own.

At first, I tried to read what I wrote as I produced it, but that confused the writing process. In the end, I had no alternative but to slip into a kind of somnambulistic trance–sleep that I probably needed, in spite of its abnormal quality, and the fact that the greater part of me had been lying comatose upon my bed for hours.

I do not remember finishing my task, nor what I did for an hour or more after ceasing to write. I made no conscious decision to obey Lugard's injunction to seal one of the four documents I had transcribed in an envelope, without attempting to read it, but when I came to my senses, I found that already done. I also found the doctor trying desperately to soothe me; he was on the point of giving me a further injection of morphine, and this time he would not be denied. As soon he had done so, I was possessed by a delicious calmness, and I realized that I had quite forgotten what it was to be free of pain and care. I collapsed into an armchair then, and found a better kind of sleep that was unhaunted and un-troubled.

When I awoke again, I was in bed. Nor was I permitted to rise again until I had been very thoroughly fed and lubricated—and even then I was forbidden to take up the pile of papers on my desk until the doctor was satisfied that I was thinking clearly. He had already made a start on reading them himself, but he permitted me to begin reading through the sheets he had already perused, which he patiently renewed as he read through the remainder.

By the time I had finished, my friend had made up his mind that everything I had recorded was pure fantasy. He had not heard Copplestone's side of the story, which I took care to relay to him in full, but that seemed to him merely to be piling madness upon madness and confusion upon confusion. His mind was always prosaic; he had an infinite capacity to look at matters without being able to see their implications. His imagination worked within severe limits, and when his mind reached those limits it balked. He told me, frankly, that his considered medical opinion was that I had had a terrible nightmare, built on the foundations of the story Copplestone had told us in 1895. He told me, insistently, that if I would not let the matter rest then I would certainly go mad, and might easily kill myself.

I gave this hypothesis careful consideration, and concluded that it was at least partly false. I know that madmen are generally reckoned to be incapable of perceiving their own madness, but I was satisfied as to my own sanity. I was sure that the experience I had undergone could not have been a fantasy entirely of my own invention. I was perfectly prepared to accept that it might not be true in every last detail, but I was obliged to conclude that there was at least some truth in my vision, and that it had arrived there by very mysterious means.

The documents that I had transcribed contained an account of the destruction of the Earth that did not differ significantly from Copplestone's as to matters of fact, but which offered an alternative interpretation of the Hail of Hell.

The most important point of difference regarded the entity whose passage through the borders of the Solar System had launched the Hail of Hell. At first, the Overmen were inclined to believe that the great disaster was accidental, caused by some wayward mote of cosmic debris. Some among them soon began to wonder, however, whether the object might have been launched on its colli-sion course deliberately, accelerated by technological means so that it would achieve a relative velocity close to that of light as it approached the Sun. They became anxious that what had brought them to the brink of extinction had been a kind of cannonball, launched with the deliberate intention of wreaking such havoc within the Overmen's Solar System as to render their homeworld uninhabitable.

That anxiety led inexorably to others. If the Earth had been murdered, who could have done it, and why? What might the enemy do next, if and when it became clear to the firers of the missile that the catastrophe had left survivors?

The likeliest answer, the anxious Overmen concluded, was that the exploratory quest on which they had innocently embarked had already been begun by other beings, who did not care to share it–but there were other hypotheses that could not be dismissed. Perhaps, some of the Overmen thought, the missile had not been launched against their own kind, but against their predecessors: against humankind. That was conceivable, apparently, because 20th century humankind will soon master the art of broadcasting Hertzian waves, so that they will be adapted, not merely as a useful means of wireless telegraphy, but as a medium of mass entertainment. For more than a century before the sequence of plague wars that will condemn humankind to extinction, the leakage of those broadcasts will be disseminated in space in every direction, at the speed of light.

The planets orbiting other stars are so far away from Earth that the residue of such broadcasts will take years to reach the nearest ones, and hundreds or thousands of years to reach any world inhabited by intelligent life–given the discovery of life's scarcity made by the spacefaring overmen–but their eventual detection is probably inevitable.

According to Lugard's testament, some of the Overmen came to believe that the signals broadcast by their predecessors had indeed been intercepted, and had called forth a lethal response, which had taken even longer to reach the system than the signals had taken to reach the hostile power. By the time that response arrived, humankind was long extinct. The Overmen broadcast Hertzian waves of their own, of course, and the leakage of their own signals must eventually have been detected, but members of the faction that thought the Hail of Hell to have been deliberate were apparently able to take some comfort in being able to blame their ancient rivals for their own misfortune.

Whatever the truth of the matter was, the fearful Overmen decided that they must press forward with their own interstellar projects and ambitions as forcefully as they could. Despite the awesome size of the observable universe, the Overmen calculated that their self-replicating probes could reach its limits within a tiny fraction of its lifespan. Having done that, their little instruments might set about whatever work they were commanded to do, while replicating themselves indefinitely in every sector of expanding space–except, of course, that they were highly likely to discover competition for that privilege.

According to Lugard's dictated document, the spacefaring Overmen reasoned that the ultimate aim of their exploration had to be the conversion of the sum of all the matter in the universe into a single vast machine. The Overmen supposed that this megamachine, if it were allowed to develop unhindered, would eventually become the engine of the cosmos and the arbiter of its fate.

They calculated that such a machine would have the power to determine the future of the space-time continuum–which is to say, the power to determine whether the expansion of space would continue indefinitely, or achieve stability, or reverse itself.

While their existence had been calm and comfortable, the Overmen had cultivated equanimity. They had been content with a limited kind of immortality, which left them vulnerable to accidental injury. After the Hail of Hell had fallen, they were no longer content to accept any kind of mortality; they wanted safety, and history had shown them that the only true safety was absolute safety. They decided that they must become components of the ultimate megamachine– the Universal Engine–as soon as possible, in order to begin to play their part in the exercise of its power.

Copplestone had spoken of schisms that had arisen when this mission was infused with quasi-religious zeal, and Lugard's manuscript had a little more to say about those schisms. Some of the Overmen considered it inevitable that they would not be allowed to win the privilege of building and becoming the Universal Engine without fighting for it, and these were determined to make ready for the ultimate war. Because the Overmen had never been a warlike species, even those who were convinced of the necessity did not take this decision lightly, but they took it. As they remade themselves in a host of new images, every one of which gave greater priority to the inorganic at the expense of the organic, they took care to arm themselves formidably.

In setting out to become preparatory components of the Universal Engine, the Overmen had already begun to plan the manner and purpose of its functioning. The majority party determined that their aim must be to prevent the universe expanding indefinitely, because that would constitute an irreversible decay. They further determined that their ultimate descendants must not only contrive an eventual reversion of its expansion but supervise its ensuing collapse most carefully. This seemed a necessary objective, because they had come to believe that the primal Moment of Creation must also be the Terminus of Space and Time. Alpha, these bold philosophers asserted, must also be Omega; only thus could they make sense of the fact that the eternal and infinite universe appeared from within to have both a beginning and a boundary.

The determination of the majority party went further than this, however. They pledged themselves not merely to the reunion of Alpha and Omega, but also to the removal of all uncertainty from the circle of time extending therefrom. They pledged themselves to the establishment of an inexorable pattern of cause-and-effect that was unbreakable–and they did so despite the fact that the world of their own experience plainly did not qualify as a realm free of all uncertainty.

Copplestone had spoken to me of the belief held by the majority of Overmen that history could only be altered in its entirety rather than in an piecemeal fashion, but he had not explained why they held that belief, or what import it had. Lugard's document asserted that the version of the Universal Engine these Overmen anticipated would carefully remake the conditions of its own causality, smoothing the path of its own evolution and perfecting its dominion over the entire space-time continuum. The philosophers Lugard cited were adamant that the ultimate goal of universal evolution must be the eradication of any possibility that it might cancel out its own history.

You might think that eventuality inconceivable, in that it would give rise to a paradox–but the universe, as presently configured, seems to be more hospitable to uncertainty, and even to paradox, than you may imagine. I am one living proof of that, as Copplestone was before me. The past and the future *can* interact with one another. History has already been altered by virtue of my receipt of the new version of Copplestone's formula. That, in itself, need not affect the shape of the future that I witnessed–but now that I have returned to change history again, the possibility arises that the future in question *can* be materially altered, perhaps to the point of being cancelled out.

When he told the tale of his first adventures in time in 1895, Copplestone had wondered whether the future might have the means to protect itself against such cancellation. Specifically, he was anxious that the Overmen might somehow be able to reach back in time to silence him. Neither Wilde nor I took him seriously at the time, but I think that we have both begun to take the possibility even more seriously than Copplestone.

As Wilde has observed, the argument cuts two ways. If I, like Copplestone, have the capacity to change the future, I must also have the capacity to secure it. As he suggested only a few minutes ago, I cannot know exactly what I am, and may be direly mistaken in my estimation of myself–but that only sharpens the horns of my dilemma; it does not free me from the obligation to act.

Paradox or not, if there is any truth at all in my visions, then history *can* be rewritten, and events already experienced *can* be cancelled out, banished to some unfathomable oblivion. If that can happen on a parochial scale, then it can also happen on a cosmic scale: the conclusion is inescapable. The universe *can* be remade, from beginning to end–and since it can be remade, any entity that attains the power to do so must decide how to apply that power.

The majority of the Overmen who survived the Hail of Hell apparently took the view that the power of change ought to be exercised solely in order to suppress opportunities for change–that uncertainty must be banished, to the extent that such banishment was possible. Had they only applied this philosophy to the Universal Engine, whose completion would be the work of billions of years, it would have been of small relevance to us–or to Copplestone and Lugard, 100,000 years hence–but they could not and did not. They could not avoid applying it on the parochial scale, to the traffic of human timeshadows that had not yet dwindled to nothing–and whose future frequency they could not anticipate.

You might suppose that the first action of the fearful faction, on reaching this decision, would be to eliminate Copplestone and Lugard, the two human timeshadows resident among them. In fact, they became more solicitous of their guests than they had been before, although they may have lent some further irritation to the quarrel that divided them. Some of them, Lugard's document suggested, became genuinely convinced that Copplestone's scheme might offer the best opportunity to take control of the situation, by bringing all the 20th century's potential time-travelers into a particular location and span of time, where they could be subject to strict control. A minority, the Count's manuscript stated, preferred *his* alternative, which involved reserving the privilege of time travel to a select few, who would use it more adventurously than merely repopulating the Earth, but would scatter themselves much more thinly over a much vaster span of time, remaining available as objects of study for countless generations of Overmen to come, while posing no significant threat to the fabric of time.

Lugard's document states, quite explicitly, that some of the Overmen were quite ready to accept that their own existence might be a phantom of possibility, which yet remained in need of firm causation—and that *these* Overmen viewed the future arrival of more time-travelers as a potentially-useful resource in securing that causation. What he did not say explicitly, although I believe that he knew full well that I would infer it, is that they may have regarded Copplestone and myself in exactly that light: that we might be unwitting pawns of the minority. It is, I fear, possible that our timeshadows have been carefully modified—Copplestone's during his third time-journey, mine during my first—so as to *increase* the probability that the future we have envisioned will actually come about. For now, though, I shall set that point aside, in order to return to Lugard's history of the questing Overmen.

Lugard's document claimed that a crucial point in the history of the Overmen's disputes was reached when they were able to confirm—as they had long anticipated—that they were *not* alone in the universe, and that other intelligences were already engaged upon the same mission as themselves. Some of the Overmen had made their preparations for war, but were determined not to begin a war unless and until it was necessary. Because the Others they had met were very enthusiastic to declare themselves friends instead of rivals, no immediate conflict ensued. Behind the facade of amity, however, suspicion continued to fester, poisoning the attitudes of some of the Overmen all the more profoundly by virtue of its concealment.

The Others claimed to be similar products of a second-generation sun, who had followed a path of convergent evolution to the point at which their functionally-adapted manufactured bodies were much the same as the Overmen's. They told the Overmen that their home system had been devastated in the same way as Earth's, by a similarly mysterious visitation—with the result that they too had concluded that planets were fit for no other purpose than to be graves for the primitive dead. They suggested, however, that there was no more reason to lament the deaths of those felled by the Hail of Hell than there was to lament the extinction of the ancestor-species that had made way for more intelligent descendants. They likened solar systems to eggshells, which had to be cracked in order to allow the embryonic beings within to grow to maturity, or to placentas from which the healthy infants had to be cut loose.

According to their own account, the Others had abandoned their home system in order to embark upon a great quest exactly as the Overmen had, but their fervor was not so narrowly fixated on the completion of the circle of Alpha and Omega. They–or the majority among them, at least–saw their self-appointed mission rather differently. They had no fear of uncertainty, and no determination to exterminate it. Indeed, they saw uncertainty as a virtue, holding that if the Omega point of the universe were to become a new Alpha, then the universe that expanded from that Alpha should *not* be the same one that had produced it, but an alternative–and that as many times as the circle of time was completed, there should be as many variations of the connecting thread of space-time. In their philosophy, that was already the essential nature of things, for they believed that our universe was but one inflationary domain within an infinite manifold of universes, every one of which was and ought to be unique.

This world-view had other corollaries. For instance, the Others took it for granted–as the Overmen had not–that the construction of a Universal Engine could not possibly be the individual work of any single line of post-organic descent and must, of necessity, be the collaborative work of them all. They also argued that the most important aspect of that Engine's functioning would not be the completion of the universal cycle but the shaping of the universe in advance of that completion. Their version of the great quest effectively took the union of Omega and Alpha for granted; their attention was concentrated on the design of a paradise–or paradises–that might endure for millions or billions of years before the universe even reached the limit of its expansion. They too saw themselves pilgrims embarked on a great mission of progress, but they and the majority of the overmen were following markedly different creeds.

The Others seemed to expect that the Overmen would eventually conceded the logic of their case and agree with their judgment. Some Overmen presumably did–but most, especially those who were already prepared for war, saw things quite differently.

10.

The alien aether-dwellers proposed to the pilgrim Overmen that they need have no fear of their own extinction, individually or collectively, because whatever became of them, their eventual resurrection by the omnicompetent Universal Engine was already guaranteed. According to the Others, all the intelligent beings that had ever existed–including, incidentally, at least by implication, humankind–were guaranteed such resurrection when the Universal Engine attained the power to examine its own genesis. Then, and only then, would it become necessary and desirable to plan for the world beyond Heaven: the alchemical wedding of Omega and Alpha.

The far-ranging Overmen were advised by their new neighbors that they ought to devote themselves to the widest exploration of possible modes of material existence, in order that they might discover and evaluate the entire spectrum of conceivable states of being. That, according to the Others, was the proper and immediate mission of sentient beings like themselves.

Lugard's history stated that the advent of the alien aether-dwellers acted as a catalyst, which caused the differences within the community of Overmen to became acute. Although some of the Overmen thought that the Others could be reckoned angelic bearers of glad tidings, the greater number considered them demonic tempters–enemies more dangerous, in their own way, than the celestial bludgeon that had launched the Hail of Hell. A few came to the conclusion that the whole purpose of these false friends was to distract the Overmen from their mission and thus betray them to ultimate oblivion. Although they appeared to have no hostile intentions, some Overmen thought that the Others were wolves in sheep's clothing–and some thought that they were merely instruments of some other set of entities as yet unglimpsed.

Lugard alleged that, by the time of my arrival, the anxieties of many Overmen had begun to cut very deeply indeed into their confidence that they could secure their own immortality, let alone that they could ever bend the Universal Engine to their own desires and purposes. The very magnitude of that vision had begun to overawe them, to the extent that the most fearful among them became very assiduous in their hunt for potential enemies–enemies of whose malign subtlety they felt perfectly certain, by virtue of their continuing failure to identify the murderers of Earth. Some of the more anxious Overmen became firmly convinced that there must be hidden forces at work in the universe, although not yet gifted with unambiguous existence therein, whose purpose was to make sure that the Universal Engine would produce an Alpha *very* different from the one implied by present-day observations.

These kinds of anxiety produced their most extreme versions among those Overmen who believed that the Others were indeed their allies and not their secret enemies. They proposed that if there were hidden forces at work, they must be working at a more fundamental level, desiring to produce–in place of the presently-perceptible universe–one in which the advent of any organic or mechanical life would be impossible: a universe fit only for immaterial intelligences of an incalculable nature. Some of the Others, it seemed, also suspected that mysterious enemies were anxious to infiltrate and disrupt the community of organic life-forms and their descendant machines.

One consequence of this maëlstrom of anxieties, according to Lugard, was that those Overmen who had kept close contact with Copplestone and himself began to think more urgently about the mysteries of human nature and the possible utility of the art of casting timeshadows.

While Copplestone had been making his Utopian plans, Lugard had been more intent on recovering what little remained of the human heritage–not merely its wisdom but its art and artifacts.

While Copplestone had seeded the derelict Earth with watchful nanozoons, Lugard had set machines to conduct archaeological excavations, searching for anything and everything that the Overmen of Earth had not removed into their various Arks. Just as the Overmen who remained in the Solar System had helped Copplestone, so they had helped Lugard–perhaps for the reasons they gave, and perhaps not.

As I read all this, I knew that Lugard might have misjudged Copplestone. If the Overmen supporting Copplestone were keeping secrets from him, and Copplestone knew it, then Copplestone might be keeping secrets of his own– including secrets that he had dared not reveal to me, fearing that his words might be overheard. It was possible that Copplestone and Lugard were not really adversaries at all, although they dared not become overt collaborators for fear of alarming their anxious masters.

Having realized this, I wondered whether a different interpretation might be put on Copplestone's seemingly-straightforward account of the mission he had asked me to undertake. Copplestone had told me that he could not think in terms of attempting to reverse the historical disasters that had overtaken humankind, but the machines set by the Overmen to watch him would hardly have allowed him to do otherwise. He had laid before me a plan to which the Overmen could have little objection, and which might incidentally serve their own ends– but it was possible that he, too, harbored secret hopes for a very different outcome to his experiment.

By the same token, I knew that Lugard would surely have been even more indiscreet had he had a freer hand. His manuscript contained no explicit injunction urging me to publicize the existence in our own time of the secret vampires, nor any suggestion that we might raise an army to make war against them–quite the opposite, in fact–but his suggestion that the Overmen assisting him had secret motives of their own for so doing could well be a hint that his own true motives were encrypted. I began to wonder whether Lugard's real hope was that I might be to precipitate exactly such a war.

I wondered, briefly, why Lugard had not written his manuscripts in some kind of code that would have concealed their meaning from prying eyes, but I realized that to do so would inevitably have attracted attention. Remembering that final image which had impressed itself upon me as my vision ended, I had to conclude that he might have invited too much dark suspicion even with what he *had* written. Given that, I became even more determined to figure out what was written *between the lines*.

I had lamented more than once that so many of the questions I had wanted to ask in the course of my visions had remained unvoiced. Now I wondered whether any answers I might have been given could possibly have been honest. What I had been told by my two informants was astonishing–but the possibilities opened up by the suspicion that they had not been able to speak freely were even more astounding.

"Lugard did take leave to suggest in his manuscript that the flesh/machine hybrids that set out to fill the whole of the universe might better be called preda-tors than pilgrims. Their mission, as he represented it, was to consume all the matter in the universe, to integrate it into their increasingly-versatile bodies. Their initial intention, on meeting other material beings engaged in a similar expansion, must have been to obliterate and consume them, just as their vampire ancestors had obliterated and consumed humankind when the opportunity arose. It seemed likely to me, when I read Lugard's history, that they were hesitating over that course only because they were not sure of success.

Lugard was insistent–perhaps hypocritically and perhaps not–that nothing in his document was intended to denigrate the new Overmen; he regarded theirs as the natural attitude of any successful species. He implied–perhaps deceptively and perhaps not–that his own view coincided with those Overmen, and those Others, who accepted that the only real enemies they had were creatures of a fundamentally different kind: creatures to whose existence the presently-constituted laws of matter were inimical but which nevertheless retained a te-nuous hold on existence. He did not mean to speak of spirits, although I suppose Professor Flammarion might be tempted to construe the proposition in those terms.

The pilgrim Overmen and the Others had both realized that the existence of life such as theirs, and the whole material system in which it was based, could not have come into being had any one of the fundamental physical constants had a slightly different value. They understood that the process by which the univer-sal terminus might give birth to its own point of origin only required a very slight alteration in one or other of those underlying conditions to bring about a gross alteration in its life-history. Were *all* the fundamental constants to be al-tered simultaneously, the effect of the combined changes would be incalculable–but if such profound consequences could ensue from the slight modification, it seemed very likely that the probability of settling upon a combination that would facilitate the evolution of organic life and mechanical fabrication must be very tiny.

Given all this, some of the new Overmen thought it unwise of their fellows to be distracted, by the quest for new material paradises, from the ultimate aim of securing the universe against life-annihilating perversion in the Crucial Mo-ment when Omega was conjoined with Alpha. Lugard had not the slightest idea how to imagine the outcome of any such perversion, nor could he comprehend the nature of the hypothetical beings that might have an interest in bringing it about, but he recorded that there were at least some among the Overmen who took the possibility very seriously.

I suspect that it might be precisely because the idea is so difficult to grasp, and so remote in its implications, that Lugard declared his support for it. It is possible that his real opinion–and that of his helpers–was that the alleged unity of interest shared by all living and mechanical entities is a frail illusion. He must have remembered well enough that the Overmen's ancestors had lived as fugitive mimics among humankind, seemingly the same and yet different, until they had emerged from hiding at a critical point in history, usurping the domain of their former hosts and victims. It is not improbable that the Overmen were anxious that something of the same sort might happen again–and might, indeed, already be in the process of happening again–to them. All of those who affected only to be anxious about immaterial beings might well have been concealing anxieties about the Others, or about their own brethren, or even about the human timeshadows to whom they had abandoned the Earth and the Moon.

What Lugard actually proposes, in the manuscript that I transcribed, has little to do with the Overmen. He declares that Copplestone's ambition to repopulate the Earth and institute a Utopia is too trivial to be worthy of the attention of serious men. He suggests that any individual capable of casting a timeshadow ought not to aim for the kind of reconstruction that he and Copplestone achieved, but should instead fix their sights on a much further future–for the most distant future attainable to them. If they can reach a time when the Universal Engine actually exists, he says, so much the better; if not, they should make what efforts they can to make contact with the most advanced of its constructors, utterly ignoring such primitives as the Overmen and the Others.

"Humans are possessed of a gift which is probably not unique," Lugard says, "but which serves to make them different from the other natural species known to me. I was content to trade that gift for those which the Overmen had, but it seems to me now that I was too hasty. My advice to others is not to repeat my error, but to cultivate the best enlightenment of which human beings, through their timeshadows, are capable. I urge you, and all those you can recruit to your cause, not to aim for Copplestone's Utopia but to seek out the best news of the most distant future they can possibly attain."

Lugard adds a cautionary note to this proposal, saying frankly that he is mapping out an expedition so dangerous that few men could hope to survive it. He admits that his own revised version of the timeshadow formula is more toxic than Copplestone's, as well as more potent, and admits that anyone to whom it becomes known will be able to ascertain its toxicity far more readily than its potency. For most men, he readily agrees–and perhaps all–the enterprise which he describes must be a suicide mission. Nor is there any guarantee that anyone who embarks upon it will be able to discover anything at all about the condition of the far future universe. He understands that Copplestone's modest proposal offers a more tangible and more easily-attainable reward.

On the other hand, Lugard points out that–for some people, at least–the gamble he offers is virtually cost-free. He is prepared to doubt the common-sense assumption that the best and most durable timeshadows must be cast by men who are physically powerful and in their prime. He argues that what we know of the history of visionary experience suggests an opposite conclusion: that shamans and saints alike may be men of no great physical presence, whose powers increase with age. He proposes that the men best fitted to undertake the boldest explorations of the future might be those with the most vivid and powerful imaginations, and that bodily virility might actually be a handicap rather than an asset.

You can see with your own eyes what the experience of time-travel has done for me. Perhaps it was a consequence of the work that Lugard's nanozoons did in enhancing my powers of memory, and perhaps it was a combination of that and the changes already wrought by Copplestone's nanozoons. Perhaps it was an effect of the length of time I spent in the future, or the fact that I was removed while there from the Earth to the Moon. Perhaps it was a haphazard accident of fate. Perhaps–and this may be the direst possibility–it was the result of actions taken by Overmen in perverting my being to their purposes. At any rate, you will certainly understand that this is a dangerous and uncertain business.

All of this was a dream, and the aftermath of a dream, and I do not dare pretend otherwise. Nor can I presume to tell you what significance dreams have in the affairs of men. If the dreams of normal sleep offer us any insight into the future, they certainly do not do so in any straightforward sense, and most of the familiar drugs that make such dreams more vivid certainly do not seem to refine their accuracy. I can no longer accept, however, that even the most ordinary dreams are devoid of all meaning and all significance. I cannot help but feel that the mysteries inherent in these visions of mine must have some solution, and that the solution is worth seeking. I have racked my brains long and hard in the hope of finding some such solution, but all I have so far produced is a further crop of awkward possibilities.

In the future of my dream, the Overmen's descendants had not settled the question of whether the event that destroyed their civilization was an accident or an act of war. If their Hail of Hell was indeed the impact of a cosmic bullet, there are several possibilities unmentioned by either Copplestone or Lugard. I have already suggested that it might not have been fired at the Overmen but at humankind, eventually hitting the wrong target. On the other hand, if time can indeed be tied in knots, perhaps it will somehow be fired *by* humankind, aimed to destroy those destined to usurp the human empire, thus to free the Earth for human repopulation. The Overmen's descendants might have lied to Copplestone and Lugard about the manner in which human civilization had been destroyed; their claim that it had been a purely internal matter may have served the purpose of absolving them from blame. Even if they did not lie, it is possible that they might have been mistaken; forces unknown even to them might have been at work.

All of this is the produce of dreams within dreams, and may be no more than a tissue of fantasies, which can only chase one another around and around before swallowing their own tails. As Monsieur Jarry has observed, logic applied to fantastic premises often produces absurd results. But if there is *any* truth in what I have seen in my visions, there are warnings therein that we really ought to heed.

Our civilization may have less than two centuries in hand before its demolition. There may be secret predators lurking unseen in our midst. Time may not be immutable, and if it is not there may be some enemies close at hand and others further afield who stand to benefit from interference with our history. I am the living proof that the formulas I carry in my briefcase are dangerous to use; there is some slight reason to fear that they might be dangerous even to know. It is possible that I have placed you all in peril simply by telling you this story–a peril that will doubtless be increased should you condescend to believe it. For that, I am sorry–but if it is so, then the future of the human race really does depend on the story being told, and believed.

The Writer's Story: Part Four

Paris, September 1900

7.

The Great Detective had pressed himself to the limit in order to complete this phase of his narrative. When he finished, he coughed like a consumptive into his gnarled hand. Occasionally, he had to fight to draw breath into his laboring lungs, in order to resume coughing again.

Seeing him in such dire straits did not make my own malaise seem any less exacting. Time was not pressing on me quite as urgently as it had pressed upon his dream-self, but I was acutely aware of the pace of its passing, and of the paucity of the span that remained to me.

Every moment of my life had become a cruel tyrant, but Death–actual Death, not the mere shadow that sat before me, coughing and spluttering– retained his ultimate hegemony in the hierarchy of my fears. I do not know whether to call it cowardice or courage, but no matter how tortuous time and life became, I was anxious to extend them to their limit. In hearing the detective's tale, I could not help wondering whether that limit might not be far more elastic than I had imagined–but I could not help wondering, too, whether he could see the true significance or appreciate the extreme complexity of his own story.

I glanced at my companions to see whether the unexpected convolutions of the detective's story had begun to weary or dizzy them. I would not have been surprised to see them exhibiting signs of impatience, but they seemed quite undisturbed by the lateness of the hour. They were all absorbed–even Jarry. I was the only one fidgeting, and that was the affliction of my horrid skin-disease.

The Great Detective's coughing fit came to an end, but it left him exhausted. Indeed, he seemed to have fallen into a kind of trance. It was as if he were utterly lost in his recapitulation of the astonishing vision that had recently possessed him, and so strangely transformed him.

I was certain that would never be able to convince himself that what he had experienced was a mere dream, even if he wanted to–and I doubted that he was capable any longer of wanting that. Even if he were fortunate enough to recover all the weight he had lost–and with it the semblance of an ordinary human being–he would not be the same man he had been before. Even if his experience *had* been a mere dream, containing not the slightest hint of accurate precognition, it had displaced him from his station in what he had called *the space-time continuum*, leaving him anchorless and rudderless.

But why, I took leave to wonder, should a man be unhappy about that? Should not a man rejoice in *any* escape from the choking pressure of the 19th century, comprised of all its hideous vanities and all its savage bigotries? What purpose was this private declaration of the pseudonymous Sherrinford's to serve, if not to cement the knowledge that he was safe from the last insult that the present could heap upon him: the insult of *being taken seriously*? Why did he fear being dismissed as a madman, when none but the mad can have any freedom at all in our drear and dreadful world?

While he remained in his trance, I tried to get to grips with the revelations he had brought–and also to read between their lines, in the hope of glimpsing their true import. I had guessed, even if he had not, that he had been told a pack of lies. If he really had conversed with the relics of Edward Copplestone and Count Lugard, they must have been dupes; the probability was that he had not–that the simulacra had indeed been simulacra, intended to confuse and confound him. Perhaps he knew that. Perhaps he had told us his story in order that we might reassure him on the point. Perhaps, on the other hand, he really thought that there might be a future for the human race–a future that he might have the power and the responsibility to decide and to shape.

I could not help wondering what kinds of men Death's double would seek to include within and to exclude from the wonderful afterlives that Copplestone and Lugard had dangled before him as lures. The very first words he had spoken to me after our strange flight through the rainswept streets were "Damn you, Wilde"–and his tone had implied that he would have done exactly that, had he not stood in such desperate need of my testimony and my understanding. Perhaps it had only been impatience speaking, though; perhaps he had already decided that I ought to be one of the Elect, placed at the head of the queue for admission to Copplestone's paradise–or to Lugard's.

I had thought, when he actually spoke to me, that I had made a mistake, and that he was not Death after all–but I saw now that if the great lie he had told us were to be taken seriously, then he might indeed have the power of oblivion at his beck and call. Within his briefcase was a scythe, with which to harvest the human crop, so that the wheat might be winnowed from the chaff. Given that his story was so manifestly a lie, though, only the precious few who were capable of taking it seriously–if only for an instant–could possibly qualify for the rewards it offered.

I felt sure that I could do that, but I could not confidently name another man who might. Certainly not Flammarion, probably not Jarry....perhaps not even de Gourmont.

It was Flammarion who got up from his seat to see whether there was any assistance he could render the Great Detective. When the astronomer placed his hand on the frail figure's shoulder, Sherrinford made an effort to rouse himself from his trance. De Gourmont poured a glass of water from a decanter on the desk, and Flammarion relayed it to the storyteller's lips. The detective managed to take a few sips, but might have gained more benefit from brandy.

"I apologize," the detective said. "We have important matters to discuss–I must not give way to fatigue."

"I doubt that fatigue will offer you the choice," Flammarion said, sadly.

"I ought to continue, if I can," Sherrinford insisted. "I ought to explain the expanding universe, relativity, uncertainty and radioactivity. I ought to explain, to the extent that I can, the nature of radio broadcasting, and sketch out the myriad technological applications of electricity. Copplestone tried to do that in 1895 and failed; I should make what effort I can to succeed. Only by bringing tomorrow's discoveries into today can I hope to..."

He dissolved into another fit of coughing.

"You must *not* continue that particular train of thought, Mr. Sherrinford," I said, suddenly anxious on his behalf. "I'm not sure that you have fully realized exactly what is at stake here. I think you might have mistaken exactly what you are, and how you came to be here, just as Copplestone mistook what he was, and why he was allowed to tell us exactly what he told us–*and no more*."

The detective did not look at me, but he was the only one who did not.

"What do you mean, Monsieur Melmoth?" Gourmont asked.

"I shall explain to you what I mean in due course," I promised, "but for now, I am very anxious for Mr. Sherrinford's safety. I should not like him to overtax himself."

"*Plus tard*," Jarry murmured.

Now, the detective did look at me, fixing me with his terrible stare. "You believe me!" he whispered. "You know that it was no mere dream, no fantasy. You understand what I am, and what I might do, if only..."

I did, but I dared not admit it. "What I *know*," I told him–not needing to interrupt him because he had begin coughing again–"is that this story of yours is a work of art in the purest sense: a work that reveals your inner being in all its paradoxical magnificence. I was only slightly intrigued by Copplestone's tale when I heard it, and Lugard's account of the soirée's aftermath seemed little more than a flamboyant footnote, but what you have said tonight has had a more profound effect on me. I salute you, sir–you are a veritable prince among liars–but I repeat that you might have mistaken the effect that your ingenious fantasies might have had upon you, and what they might yet do."

It was unfair and unjust; it was, in its fashion, a betrayal–but I thought it necessary. I thought it necessary, for the vulgar and selfish reason that I did not want him to die until he had given me the opportunity to cheat my own death by transcending time–but I also thought it necessary in a broader context. If there was the merest hint of possibility that the tale he had told was true, then he really did have the power to change history, and he had to be prevented from overreaching his privilege, both for his own sake and the world's.

I had limitless confidence, of course, in my own judgment of the situation. I could hear the song of the sirens, and had no Orpheus at hand to drown them out. I could admire the gorgon's snaky locks, without the benefit of a polished shield. I was dying and damned, free to ignore the stern demands of sanity if I so wished. In public, I still had to maintain my mask, but deep within my own soul–if only there were some secret region of it not yet racked and ruined by the pox–my powers of dream and desire were undiminished and undiminishable. I knew, or believed I knew, what I was doing.

"What use are dreams unless they can be shared between friends in this civilized fashion?" I continued, waving an airy hand. "What use is the illumination of the innermost soul of a man unless there is an audience which can see by that light? We are political animals, after all; our selves are the product of our society, produced by negotiation, flattery and conflict. The best among us are artists, who somehow make ourselves heard and felt even through the masks that hide our death's-head faces. What is more worthy of belief, at the end of the day if not before, than *the impossible*? If the only choice a man has, when he looks death in the face, is between the best impossibility and the worst, what kind of a man would accept impossibility off the peg, at a bargain basement price, when he could have it made to measure, cut to his own design, at no less a price than his soul? I say again, Mr. Sherrinford, that I salute you. I salute your courage and your generosity in sharing this tale with us. I am profoundly grateful for your invitation, and I hope that my companions will echo my sentiment."

There was no outburst of applause, even from Jarry. Neither de Gourmont nor Flammarion had the least inkling of my purpose, and evidently thought that I was rambling–but the great detective did know what I was doing, and why. His powers of logic had not failed him; he *did* understand that what Copplestone and Lugard had told him might be a single tissue of lies–and that, if that were so, the truth might be more awkward and terrible than he had dared to hope. Even so, he could not be content to stay silent. He was the kind of man who always wanted to speak. How could I, of all people, hold that against him?

In private, of course, I was prepared to trust and desire with all my heart that every word of his story might be true. I was prepared to believe and hope that the future it described–no matter that it was steeped in ice and poison, and the black blood of the dead–might be the future of destiny, as real as the horrid wallpaper that decorated the walls of my final prison. I had nothing to lose, being as close to death as he was.

The detective drew in a deep breath, and tried to compose himself. He looked more like Death than ever. "Perhaps you are right, Professor Flammarion," he said. "Fatigue has deflated me."

Outside, it was the quietest part of the night. Inside, the candles had burned low. The world beyond de Gourmont's windows was silent and dark, already pregnant with the distant dawn–but the world within those boundaries was gravid still with mystery and melodrama. I still felt very ill, but I was as determined as Sherrinford not to give in to the pressure of my symptoms.

Flammarion apparently thought it his duty to allow the detective time to recover. "Much of what you say about the nature of the universe echoes my own writings," he observed. Unlike young Mr. Wells, though, he was too diplomatic to suggest that such echoes might be due to plagiarism. "You were kind enough to mention my speculations regarding cometary impacts, and the influence they have had, and may continue to have, on the history Earthly life. I have also ruminated on the relativity of space and time, followed Kant and Herschel in suggesting that nebulae might be island universes akin to the Milky Way rather than mere clouds of luminous gas, and echoed Edgar Poe in suggesting that the terminal collapse of the universe under the influence of gravity might be the prelude to a spectacular rebirth. The technological potential of Hertzian waves is being extensively explored as we speak by such adventurous men as Thomas Edison and Nikola Tesla. I have written extensively on the topic of psychic research, including observations on the losses in body weight suffered by the dead that have been measured by Dr. MacDougall, so your account of the detachment of timeshadows from the bodies of the living and the dead seems reasonable enough, but..."

The astronomer trailed off, perhaps because there were too many *buts* jostling in his and for expression. Given that he was a devout spiritualist, I could easily guess one of the things that must be troubling him. If one assumed, if only for the sake of argument, that the Great Detective's story might be literally true, then the future Earth would one day be littered with tiny machines, whose sole purpose would be the collection of timeshadows–*and which would lie idle for millennia*. Since the occasion of Copplestone's first visitation, or not long thereafter, such machines had lain in wait, and yet they had achieved only two successes in the better part of 100,000 years. Only two timeshadows had come their way, and the second of those had been preserved only with the utmost difficulty. The conclusion to be drawn was obvious: the petty "souls" whose departures had been measured by Dr. MacDougall could not be immortal; indeed, they must be far frailer and more ephemeral than the bodies of the living. They might indeed be able to displace themselves in time, manifesting themselves briefly and fleetingly in moments far beyond the moment of death, but if the testimony of the pseudonymous Sherrinford was to be taken seriously, their natural range and duration must be severely limited. Only the recruitment of powerful and esoteric chemistry could increase their substance and their reach.

In brief, what Sherrinford was telling the great astronomer was that all his hopes were futile because his faith, and every other that preached he natural immortality of the soul, was a hollow mockery. I could believe that, but I wondered whether there was another in that room who could accept is so easily. *No wonder he is Death's doppelgänger*, I thought. *It is the revelation of Death's*

triumph that he has brought to us. His briefcase is indeed the modern manifesta-
tion of that horrid scythe, more efficient and more implacable by far.

But I said nothing aloud, and nor–after a moment's reflection–did Flammarion.

8.

The pause had given the Great Detective the opportunity to recover a little
of his strength. He reached into his briefcase and produced an envelope, which
he handed to me.

"Although it was my hand that transcribed it, I have not read it," he told
me. "I can't say that I wasn't tempted to open it again, all the more so because
Lugard could not have anticipated that you would no longer be in England, but I
thought it best to do as I was asked. Doubtless you will be the best judge of
whether its contents should be made known to anyone else."

I was delighted to discover that the letter Lugard had asked the detective's
timeshadow to deliver was addressed to me. My friends–some of them, at any
rate–had been kind enough to write to me while I was in Reading Gaol, and
some of them were still kind enough to write to me in Paris–a correspondence
that always gave me pleasure–but I had never had the inestimable delight of
receiving a letter dictated in the Moon's underworld 100,000 years in the future.

The debilitated Sherrinford clearly expected me to open the envelope and
read the letter aloud, but the spirit of perversity joined forces with my own fee-
bleness to persuade me to put it away unopened. Alas, my hand was trembling
so badly that I could hardly guide it into the inner pocket of my coat.

Flammarion frowned at my apparent rudeness, and Jarry laughed drily.

"I do not feel well enough to read it at present," I murmured, apologetically, "and the conditions of its delivery suggest that it is intended for my eyes
alone, at least in the first instance."

"Of course," de Gourmont said. "In any case, we have had more than
enough food for thought set before us already...even if there was a morsel or two
on which our gallant informant almost choked."

"The items that might have provided the firmest proof," Flammarion
pointed out.

"Which was exactly the reason, if I read him right," Jarry said, "that Monsieur Melmoth advised him to return to safer ground. I, for one, do not mind. To
provide a story such as that with *proof* would be to....how do you say it in English? *Gild the lily?*"

Although I had never met Jarry, I knew something of his theory of art; according to reliable rumor, he considered that the determination to make sense in
the construction of a story or a drama was a craven submission to an undesirable
tyranny. In his view, the artist must defy logic itself, if he were to be truly crea-
tive and wholly responsible for his creations. Jarry believed that the true artist

must not allow himself to be yoked and driven by the implacability of natural law, logic and mathematics; for the uniform impositions of physics, in his view, the true artist ought to substitute the freedom of *pataphysics*–a science dealing only with exceptions.

"I have never been fearful of gilding lilies," I assured him, trying to speak lightly, since I had decided to speak of what might have been better left unsaid, "but I could not help recalling the circumstances of Professor Copplestone's death. I would not want our friend to suffer a similar fate. If there *is* truth in his tale, he may well have told us everything that he is permitted to tell us."

"Permitted?" Flammarion echoed.

"By the meddlesome inhabitants of the future, you mean?" Jarry said.

"If we are to do Mr. Sherrinford the favor of assuming that his vision was a true one," I said, "and that the information he obtained by means of his automatic writing is significant, he is surely in danger from interested parties in the future. If, on the other hand, we were to be churlish enough to assume that he is deluded, we would be obliged to wonder whether he might be in equal danger from the effects of his delusion. In either case..."

I left it at that.

"If the former hypothesis were true," Gourmont pointed out, "Mr. Sherrinford would not be the only one in danger."

"I am sorry for that," the detective put in.

"If we wish to defend ourselves," Jarry pointed out, "we have only to disbelieve him."

That was an oversimplification, but I did not feel well enough to argue the point, and I thought it best, in any case, to leave the argument unvoiced. My mind had been working on the problem, though, ever since had had made my own secret commitment to the detective's cause.

From the standpoint of the present day, of course, all the excursions in time about which I had been told were introduced as forward leaps. Copplestone had apparently made four such forward leaps, the great detective two, and Count Lugard one. From the viewpoint of 100,000 years hence, however, the more important trips must be the fewer number that had been taken in the opposite direction Copplestone had taken three leaps back in time, and the detective one. Neither Copplestone nor Lugard any longer had a body to return to, so they were incapable of making any further backward leaps into the present. Were the detective ever to go forward again, I strongly doubt that he would be any more able to make a return trip than Copplestone or Lugard. The possibility of there being any further backward leaps therefore depended on Mr. Sherrinford's ability to persuade other time-travelers to take forward ones.

Considering the backward leaps already taken, it seemed to me that Copplestone's first departure from the future must have as unanticipated as his arrival, and was therefore free of any possible interference. The possibility of his reappearance had been anticipated, but while it was no more than a remote possibility, no elaborate preparations to receive had been made, and his second backward leap had therefore been equally free of any modification by future forces. His third appearance, on the contrary, *had* been constructively antic-ipated; on that occasion, his timeshadow had been invaded, and to some degree transfigured. His third backward leap d, therefore, been the first one vulnerable to the kind of interference that might affect the future *strategically*.

In a similar fashion, Sherrinford's timeshadow had also been modified dur-ing his second sojourn in the future; he, too, might have been modified in very particular ways, so as to be able to effect certain actions and unable to effect others–or, more specifically, to be capable of initiating some chains of causality but incapable of initiating others. Clearly, what he had so far said and done to-night was permissible, and I hoped–although I could not possibly know–that part of the reason he had been permitted to tell his story was the effect it would have on *me*. As to other potential effects, I had grave doubts about the wisdom of lending my support to *any* such effects, lest I sabotage my own chances of bene-fit.

It was selfish of me, I confess–and perhaps not entirely sane–but it was the frame of mind that I was in.

Gourmont's thoughts had been following a track of their own, which was not entirely dissimilar. "If, for the sake of argument," he said, as if it were a purely philosophical question, "the inhabitants of some remote future *did* want to deliver information to the present, in a moderately careful manner, they might have to be highly selective about the kinds of proof they offered to add convic-tion to their missive. If, for instance, Professor Flammarion were able to make telescopic observations that would confirm or refute items of cosmological in-formation that Mr. Sherrinford has already revealed to us, he might then be far more disposed to take Mr. Sherrinford's story more seriously–but the informa-tion would be of no practical value. If, on the other hand, he were to be given information that would allow him to make some practical invention–as Sir Wil-liam Crookes and Nicholas Tesla might have been enabled by Edward Copples-tone's supposed revelations to devise new kinds of electrical machinery–that would surely carry the risk of a dramatic alteration in humankind's technologi-cal resources, and the outcome of future conflicts."

"I see the distinction," Flammarion said, equally prepared to consider such questions hypothetically, "but why would inhabitants of a distant future, if they were worried about the possibility of cancelling out their own existence by tam-pering with history, be prepared to take the risk of transmitting *any* information to the past?"

"They might," de Gourmont observed, if they thought the transmission of some such information *necessary* to the causation of their own present–which they might, if their history recorded certain journeys in time as already having taken place."

It seemed to me that de Gourmont's reputation for cleverly convoluted thinking was by no means unjustified, all the more so when he added: "And we must not overlook the possibility that the inhabitants of the future might be very uncertain themselves as to whether they ought or ought not to act with respect to a timeshadow capable of returning to the past–or, if they did act, exactly what action to take."

It was my turn to suffer a sudden fit of coughing, even though I had not yet visited the future, and could not possibly have been equipped with subtle censors of any sort. The fit began modestly, but it grew into a veritable paroxysm. As usual, it was Flammarion who rose to fetch me a glass of water.

I drank it gladly, and gradually recovered my breath.

De Gourmont did not bother to make a polite inquiry as to how I felt; it must have been perfectly obvious to him, now that the detective was no longer the center of attention, that my condition was almost as poor as Sherrinford's. He was a gentleman, and very conscious of the duties of hospitality. "It is plain that Monsieur Sherrinford and Monsieur Melmoth have both exhausted their resources, for the present," he said. "You are both very ill, it seems, and we have tried your resilience too severely. We must make sure that you both get safely home. We shall reconvene when you are both rested. Have you a carriage that the two gentlemen might share, professor?"

"I have," Flammarion said, "but it will take a little while to get it ready. My coachman will be sound asleep by now." To his great credit, he did not seem in the least distressed by the thought of sharing his carriage with Death's double and a man like me. Perhaps he was hiding his alarm, or taking comfort from the thought that we were extremely unlikely to be observed at this ungodly hour. At any rate, I was exceedingly grateful for his generosity.

"We *must* meet again, though," the detective said, hoarsely, as his awful eyes scanned our faces anxiously. "I need to hear your opinions of what I have told you–and I am anxious to know the contents of Wilde's letter, if he will consent to share them with us once he has perused them in private. Even if my visions were the nightmarish invention of my own mind, I need considered advice, from men of intellect and imagination, as to what I ought to do with the formula I now have in my custody."

"You shall have your advice, Mr. Sherrinford," de Gourmont promised. "I shall take your story seriously, if only as a bold hypothesis, and I am sure that Professor Flammarion and Monsieur Jarry will do likewise."

Flammarion looked back from the doorway. "I shall," he promised, as he hurried down the stair to wake his coachman.

"As shall I," Jarry promised.

I tried to rise from my chair, fully expecting to be able to do it, but I failed. I realized that I had gone the whole night without absinthe or morphine, and could not wonder that my energies had been so horribly depleted.

De Gourmont held up his hand to bid me to remain where I was until the astronomer returned. "I thank you for your trouble, Monsieur Sherrinford," he said to the detective. "You have laid before us a puzzle of such awesome intricacy that it could hardly be resolved in an hour or two by men as tired as we are. We shall be in a much better condition once we have slept, and have given the matter long consideration. It is now 4 a.m.; I suggest that you all return here at 8 p.m. Is that convenient for everyone?"

No time would have been "convenient" for me, and I suspected that the one named could not have suited Flammarion or Jarry very well, but neither raised a murmur of objection. Who could refuse a summons to debate the future of the world, and the possibility of changing it, if only as a philosophical proposition? Lesser men would simply have cried "Poppycock!"–or its Gallic equivalent–and refused to be party to such nonsense, but these were intellectual and imaginative giants.

Once the appointment was set, the detective offered no objection to our dispersal. De Gourmont made further apologies for not having paid sufficient attention to my increasing distress.

"No apology is necessary," I assured him, weakly. "I would not have missed this evening for the world. What else could have provided such a fine distraction from the tedious business of dying?"

"*Un autre fou furieux*," murmured Jarry.

"You should not say that, Alfred," de Gourmont chided him. "There is little of interest to be found in the ravings of a lunatic, and what we have heard tonight was anything but uninteresting."

Jarry raised a skeptical eyebrow, but would not insult his friend by asking him whether he was capable of believing what he had heard. They were both tired, despite the fact that they were well used to keeping late hours. They were somewhat benumbed, too, by the hectic confusion of the final phases of the detective's story, and its aftermath. I was a trifle dizzy myself; I had expected that Death's double would have found the future full of mysteries and pregnant with murderous threats, but even I had not expected such a Gordian knot of speculations to emerge from it. If the knot were capable of being fully unraveled, even I would need time and deep thought to accomplish it. I was, alas, not in any condition to take the task further forward immediately. Even de Gourmont, whose scarred brow was furrowed with effortful concentration, would probably need weeks or months to fathom it completely.

"I am sorry," I said to de Gourmont, "that we could not have met in better times, in less pressing circumstances."

"So am I," he replied. "But the circumstances, though pressing, have certainly been intriguing. Had we ever met at our leisure, to take tea or a little wine, we could have conversed at our ease–but what could we have said to one another that could possibly match what we have heard tonight?"

Jarry muttered something I did not quite catch. De Gourmont chided him again, in English. "You and I have done nothing so bold in our calculated surrealism," he told the younger man. "We would not have dared. Even Flammarion–who has been bolder than either of us in forging visions of the future and the universe of stars–would not have dared to imagine what Mr. Sherrinford has described."

Jarry opined, in French, that Flammarion's work was very distant from the affairs of human beings, altogether too calm, too ordered and too dispassionate–but de Gourmont disagreed again.

"*C'est incroyable*," Jarry muttered, apparently forgetting his promise to take the vision seriously.

I would not have contradicted him had I been able, but de Gourmont's fierce concentration was still in the process of bearing its preliminary fruits, which he was ready and willing to display. "It is because it is incredible that we should take it seriously, Alfred," he said, still speaking in English for fear of offending the Great Detective. "In spite of its incredibility, I do not doubt for a moment that it was an honest report of an actual experience. The question we must consider tomorrow is exactly what kind of an experience it was. Was it an authentic prophecy, in the sense of being an accurate account of things to come? Perhaps not–but we cannot know for sure that it was not. For myself, though, I cannot help wondering whether, in searching for the grains of prophetic truth that his vision might–perhaps must—contain, Monsieur Sherrinford might be looking for the wrong thing, in the wrong way."

"What do you mean?" Death's doppelgänger asked.

De Gourmont paused, reflectively, but he knew that Flammarion would soon return, and that the session would then be adjourned. "We live in a literate age," he resumed, softly. "We take our books so much for granted that we have quite forgotten what it was to live without them. Among the illiterate peasants of Normandy and Provence, there is some relic of oral culture, but it has lost its authority over their minds and their lives. Nowadays, those who cannot read are merely ignorant–but in the days when no one could read, and the only measure of wisdom was what men carried in their heads, no one was ignorant. Everyone knew what everyone had to know. All information was public property, including myths and legends, fantasies and folktales. Fiction, no less than fact, was the common property of the tribe.

"In our new world, things work very differently. We have delegated the business of remembrance to our books; what we cannot carry in our heads we can easily look up. Wisdom now lies more in knowing what authorities to consult, and in the reliable interpretation of what they have to say, than in the wealth of experience. The records we keep have increased our wealth of facts immeasurably, and our wealth of fictions too, but they have allowed that wealth to be divided and privatized. Nowadays, there is private property in fantasies and folktales just as there is in science and law; nowadays, even myths and legends have authors.

"Print has freed us from the limitations of individual memory and the limitations of collective myth. Nowadays, every man can be his own myth-maker, a compiler of private legends. Once, visions of the future were public property in exactly the same fashion as memories of the past. Every tribe had its own pattern of anticipation, just as it had its own mythic history. In the twentieth century, on whose threshold we stand, the last remnants of those patterns will disintegrate, no matter how hard their inheritors may fight to hold them together. The expectations of old will fragment, and the images held in place by collective fears and collective hopes will give way to promiscuous confusion. Even as little as a hundred years ago, France and the world had but a few futures–but in a hundred years time there will be such a profusion of futuristic visions as we can hardly imagine. That, my friends, is progress.

"What we have just heard, I suggest, is an archetype of future visions to come. It is an *individual myth* of considerable color and complexity, wonderfully ambitious and inextricably convoluted. Whether it has anything to tell us about our own futures, I cannot guess, but even though it might contain glimpses of the actual future–as our collective myths undoubtedly contain fugitive relics of the actual past–I am sure that its texture and roundness have far more to tell us about the character of the man who made it. I am confident that men of our kind have the power as well as the authority to weave our own personal myths and to make them vivid–and I am confident that our personal myths will display our own individualities just as distinctly.

"Monsieur Sherrinford, being the kind of man he is, confines himself while confronting his vision to one question: *is there a significant truth in it, from which we ought to take valuable instruction?* He is so narrowly confined that even though his vision has given him the answer, he cannot accept it. That answer is, I fear, no–for reasons that Monsieur Melmoth has already made clear. There can be no *instructive* truth in any vision of the future, for the simple reason that any such instruction *must* tend to be self-negating. Whenever we see, by the power of glorious vision or humble reason, what the future holds for us, we exercise our power of choice. We do whatever is in our power to confirm its desirable aspects while refusing its undesirable ones, thus cancelling the content of our foresight.

"Monsieur Sherrinford has done his level best to construct a myth in which such cancellations might be accommodated, in which the history of a species or the history of the entire universe might be continually reconstructed. In his myth, Alpha and Omega may touch and change places, so that eternity dissolves into an unceasing dance in which nothing can ever be finally realized. Such, I think, is the mind-set of the consulting detective. Nothing is ever what it appears to be, and even if it is, it cannot be trusted to remain so. Alfred, Monsieur Melmoth and I are men of a different kind, I think. We are in search of our own myths–but so is every man, whether he is an artist or not. What distinguishes our search is the quest for deeper insight, for brighter beauty....and above all else, for that which can command and compel the imaginative consent of our fellow men. We are aristocrats of the mind, I think–but we are neither detectives nor men of action."

I did not doubt that the sage believed what he said, any more than I doubted that the detective believed his story. With just a little effort, I might have believed something similar myself–but I could not make the effort even if I had wanted to. I was too tired. Belief was beyond my scope. When I had slept, I thought, I would have the opportunity to rediscover exactly what it was I intended to believe, but for the moment I could only disappoint de Gourmont by my lack of reaction.

I managed a respectful nod, but no more.

He accepted the disappointment like the gentleman he was. He could see that I was in no state to answer him sensibly.

By way of tawdry compensation, Jarry murmured "*C'est vrai*," and might even have meant it.

9.

Flammarion reappeared, signaling that he was ready to depart. He and Jarry helped me down the stairs and into the carriage. The night air had a touch of frost in it, which had the effect of reviving me a little.

"I think I shall believe it, after all," Jarry told me, as he stepped back. He had taken care to rehearse the English words, but he spoke with a little too much ostentation. "Rémy is right; it demands belief, because it *is* incredible, and because men like us must overcome our fear of paradox and our fear of *exception*. It is our mission as artists, *n'est-ce pas?*"

I wondered whether I still had a mission as an artist, in life or beyond it. I did not know–but I nodded as gracefully as I could and the young man went off contentedly to fetch his bicycle.

Flammarion had already assisted Sherrinford to climb into the carriage. He produced a small flask, which must have been in the charge of his coachman, and offered it to both of us. The detective declined, but I drank. It was only cheap brandy, but preferable to water.

"*Merci*," I said.

As we drove away, Jarry–now mounted on his ridiculous machine–raised his hand in a florid salute. Flammarion condescended to reply with a dignified flick of his grey glove.

We dropped Sherrinford at a hotel nearby; to reach my own required a longer journey.

"You should not have come tonight, Monsieur Melmoth," Flammarion said, gravely. "The other has something burning in him that makes him strong in spite of is debility; with you, I think, it is the other way around. He should not have demanded that you bear witness to his extravagance. That was unnecessary, as you observed yourself, and as for the rest...well, I have promised to take it seriously, and I shall play the game. But it *is* a game, is not? Fever can have strange effects on a brilliant mind."

"I had to come," I assured him. "Indeed, I am very grateful to my friend for insisting that I should." The brandy had revived me sufficiently to allow me to continue, albeit without any real flamboyance. "Dying is an ignominious business, and those who decay before they die are doubly afflicted. A dying man who would not give his fortune for a spark of amazement would be a wretched miser, and I no longer have the least vestige of my fortune to give. I count myself a lucky man."

No candle had been lit within the carriage, but Flammarion must have sensed that I was too weak to follow that speech with another.

"You are right," he said, pensively. "We *are* fortunate to have heard such a story–such a vision! I am a man of science, and I know that my duty is always to ask *is it true*? but I am a visionary myself, and I know that it is never enough to ask *is it a fact*? Truth comes to us in many guises, and we must pass it on to others in pleasing guise, in order that it might be welcomed as a gift and not resisted as a penalty.

"I am a stargazer; I am appointed to record the motions of the heavenly bodies with mathematical exactitude, and to analyze the spectra of their radiance with scrupulous precision–but what I study is the universe, and the universe is not a sum of data, totted up like a miser's hoard. The universe is a hypothesis, a created image; it is not the data but their implication, and that implication is a marvel, a thing of wonder. As an observer, I see only the merest fraction of the present state of things–but as a visionary, inferring the whole from its parts, the past from its relics, and the future from its seeds, I too have glimpsed the Omega, knowing that it is not really the end; I too have heard rumor of the Alpha, knowing that it could not really have been the beginning."

I recalled what Rémy de Gourmont had said, in Flammarion's absence, about personal mythology, and what he had implied thereby. In the 20th century, I imagined, it would be the responsibility of every artist, if not every thinking person, to construct a personal mythology–and the best of them, inevitably, would be looking at the stars as they did so.

Flammarion looked at me carefully, trying to judge my reaction. The flickering glow of the lamplight, which bathed my face for a moment as the carriage passed each post, was just bright enough to display my interest and my desire that he should continue to share his thoughts. I was fascinated to discover how different his response would be to de Gourmont's, if he were indeed the cool, ordered and dispassionate man Jarry took him to be.

"I suspect that you do not think as highly of Edgar Poe in England as we do in France, Mr. Wilde," Flammarion said, "but you must have read his account of the mesmeric revelation, and his description of an experiment in which the consciousness of the dying Monsieur Valdemar was preserved by mesmeric instruction, and commissioned to report on the existence beyond death. Can these fictions be true? We should not mistake them for facts, of course, but we would be fools to say that there is nothing in them of truth, of precious implication. We have become overly respectful of the brutality of facts; we have elevated them to the status of icons, not because we hold them sacred, but because we have consented to be bullied into submission to their unadorned certainty. We are in danger of strangling the imagination, choking the very life out of our conception of the world. Do I mean *conception*, or merely *concept*? Is there a significant difference, in English?"

"You mean *conception*," I assured him. I knew that I was right, just as de Gourmont had been right about personal myths and the impending proliferation of visions of possible futures. The world is *born* of our thoughts and visions, gifted by them with independent life and the power of growth; we do not invent it–its ultimate genesis lies far beyond the reach of our petty dabblings–but we do *conceive* it, and bring its embryo to term.

"You should not come to de Gourmont's house tomorrow," the astronomer said. "We ought to come to you, if we desire to know what is written in that piece of paper you carry in your bosom."

"Certainly not," I replied, trying with all my might not to sound hoarse. "I am merely dying; no further harm can possibly come to me. If I meet a man to whom I was once kind, and he cuts me dead, or expresses disgust at my distress, it cannot hurt me. The living, on the other hand, must be protected from prying eyes. If I cannot come to you, you will have to do without me–but if I am too ill to come, I shall send you the letter. I could not hold anything back that might leave the detective's tale incomplete."

He was silent for a few moments while he contemplated that reply, but he was not so impolite as to contradict me. After a while, he reverted to his former theme.

"If Sherrinford's story were indeed a fact," he said, softly, "it ought not to be too terrible to bear. All men must die, and the human species cannot endure forever. The vital matter is not our flesh but our souls; they *do* endure, I am certain, and the universe is open to their action and their contemplation. We can only measure the temporary against the meter of the eternal; we can only understand limits because they are set against the backcloth of the infinite. We have as many lives to live as are provided for in the universal imagination, and as many paradises to discover. I cannot agree with those skeptics who say that we have had too many revelations, which have given birth to far too many jealous creeds. I say that we have not had revelations enough, that our creeds might learn to be humble. We must never deny facts, but we must never be *content* with them. We should rejoice that the facts we discover day by day by means of our telescopes and microscopes are more wonderful by far than the narrow faiths of our forefathers, and we should not attempt to squeeze the wonder out of them by rendering them down into mere data. Monsieur Sherrinford may be deranged, but he is not a fool. He may be ill, but he is not an imbecile. His fervor to escape the hospital may have taken him further from the world than was necessary or desirable, but what a voyage it was! *C'est merveilleux!*"

I decided that I liked Flammarion almost as much as I liked de Gourmont. It would be hard to leave a world that entertained such men as they. It would be easy too–horribly and despicably easy–but it would be hard, in the sense of the word which is implied by the term *hard labor*. It would be cruel, annihilating, and, in the end, unendurable.

"Exactly so," I said. I had enough strength in reserve to say a little more, but we had turned the final corner and the Hôtel d'Alsace was ahead of us; I thought it best to hoard my resources in order that I might withstand the storm of Dupoirier's anxious criticism.

It was a wise decision. The storm in question was a severe test. I should not have gone out; I should not have stayed so late; I must not go out again; I must be closely watched from now on, by Reggie or Robbie or anyone fool enough to do it; I must follow the doctor's instructions to the letter; I must take my medicine on time; I must not get cold; I must not excite myself...

The dying, alas, lose their adulthood. It is not that they become children in the eyes of their loved ones, but rather that they enter a distinct phase of being, burdened with a particular horror that others desperately wish to alleviate but cannot actually share. Whatever effect the specter of death may have on the dying, it inevitably renders onlookers helpless; it disturbs them so profoundly that they become incapable of ordinary adult intercourse.

I took to my bed, as instructed. I took my medicines, as instructed. I slept till noon–and having woken for a little while, to take elementary nourishment, I slept again.

All the while, the envelope that the Great Detective had given me rested in the inner pocket of my coat. It was 4 p.m. before I mustered the resolve to rip it open–but I had not time to turn resolve into accomplishment, even to the extent of rising from my bed to fetch it. I was interrupted by a visitor, who cut through Dupoirier's objections like a razor wielded by the infamous demon barber of Fleet Street.

It was, of course, my very own vision of Death.

"How kind of you to call," I said, wishing that I had had time to powder my face. If he was the living image of the notorious Phantom of the Opera, I was the living image of Edgar Poe's Red Death. Our juxtaposition was not without an element of melodramatic irony, but I would rather have confronted him on a less equal basis.

"I fear that I asked too much of you last night," he said. "I should have seen that you were not up to it."

"I am touched by your solicitude," I assured him.

It would, of course, have been dreadfully impolite to suggest to the Great Detective that his real reason for calling might have been his impatience to know what was in Lugard's letter. He had had eleven hours and more to regret his noble decision not to read it before passing it on. Curiosity is rumored to be fatal to cats, despite their nine lives, but it only helps men to make themselves ridiculous.

As soon as Dupoirier had been dismissed, the pseudonymous Sherrinford brought a chair to the bedside and sat down. He looked around disapprovingly; the fact that even he found the wallpaper offensive confirmed my worst fears. He had the grace to look slightly crestfallen, even though I had not told him in so many words that I understood the motive which had brought him to my side.

"They did not believe me," he said, plaintively. "They were kind enough not to call me a liar, but they think that I am mad."

"You made a point of not asking them to believe you," I pointed out. "But as a matter of fact, I think they *did* believe you. They had not an atom of doubt that you had experienced everything you described while in the grip of a drug-induced fever. They do not suspect you of lying, nor of any ordinary madness. They are even willing to admit that there was an element of accuracy in your vision, although they will probably conclude, at the end of the day, that nine parts in ten consist of your own confabulation."

"And I suppose," he said, with a sigh that I might have described as con-temptuous, were there ever such a thing as a sigh of contempt, "that you would think better of me if you did think me a common liar, who had invented the whole of it for the purpose of deception."

"Perhaps I should," I told him, "but I am nothing if not inconsistent. I am glad that you are trustworthy, and that I can take it for granted that you actually underwent the experiences that you described to us last night."

"But you also think that it was all a figment of my imagination, do you not? In spite of the manuscript, and the fact that I am party to information only you and Lugard knew, you also believe that nine parts in ten are nothing but the spontaneous produce of a fever dream."

"Even when one has eliminated the impossible from the incredible," I told him, "one is invariably confronted with a tangle of extraordinary possibilities; fate is never so kind as to leave just one. According to your own testimony, and that of the manuscript you gave me the day before yesterday, you met and talked with Lugard before his death. How much was said, and what, and why, I cannot tell and nor can any other living man. No man on Earth would accept that script you gave to me as absolute proof of communication from beyond the grave, given that the information could have been passed from one living man to another. No man on Earth, that is, except myself. I accept it, not because it is proven but because I no longer have the slightest desire to deny it. I want it to be true, in every last detail."

He looked long and hard at me then, but Flammarion was right. Whatever else he was, he was no fool.

"You want the formula," he said. "You want the chance that Copplestone and Lugard had: the chance to escape death. For you, it's a gamble without risk."

"Not according to Pascal," I said, ever painstaking in defense of contradiction. "According to him, the Catholic faith is the best bet. It promises eternal life in Heaven, in return for goodness, if God exists, while threatening no loss but the sacrifice of a little worldly indulgence if He does not. The problem, of course, is that it cannot be a straightforward matter of either/or. Suppose God exists but considers that Catholics are vile heretics, fit only to burn in Hell?"

"But you *do* want the formula," the detective said, stubbornly. "Which one? Copplestone's or Lugard's."

"Yes," I reassured him, "I do want the formula. It's not that I'm so desperate in the face of imminent annihilation that any thread of hope would do, mind. If you had come back with only half your message and only one of your formulas I might only be half as fascinated. I have not been offered a vulgar decision between natural fate and the remote possibility of resurrection; I have been offered a choice between different futures, different quests, different destinies. Even if neither of your drugs is anything more than poison, the choice of one or other them would still be meaningful, because it would allow a man to nail his colors to a particular mast and to deny all others–including the Catholic faith and all its analogues. De Gourmont predicts that the 20th century will produce a plethora of future visions and a plethora of new faiths. I hope that he is right. Every man ought to have the opportunity to choose his own brand of poison, in order to say: *this is the future to which I am committed; this is what I stand for; this is what I amount to.* I want Lugard's version, of course–the more powerful of the two."

My voice had sunk to a whisper as I made this declaration, but I should like to think that its sinking added a certain dramatic effect, aping a contrived performance.

He had the grace to marvel, or at least to pretend. If only all my audiences had been as susceptible, or as generous! "Then we're both mad," he said, proudly, "and neither one of us is alone."

I took it as a compliment, because he really did seem grateful for my support and relieved by my credence.

"You'll find the letter in my coat, in yonder wardrobe," I said. "I'm sorry to have to ask you to give it to me for a second time, but I'm undressed."

He got up without a word, and retrieved the envelope from my coat pocket. Then he fetched a paper-knife from the dressing-table and handed it to me.

I slit the envelope and took the letter out.

I began to read, but I did not read aloud. How could I resist the temptation to torture him? It is the duty of every man to make his passage through this unkind vale of tears as memorable as possible–and how can he do that, unless he is capable of exceptional unkindness?

10.

The letter read as follows:

My dear Oscar,

By now you should have read the account of our shared adventure which I displayed to our mutual friend. It is overlong, I know, but it was originally written without any thought that it might be relayed back in time, as an *aide-mémoire*. When a man first discovers that he might live for thousands of years, he can easily become fearful that he might forget the life he led when he was a mere mortal, and thus forget himself.

I sometimes suspect that Copplestone has forgotten himself, without even suspecting it.

You will not have been surprised to hear that Copplestone and I are adversaries in this desolate but wonderful future, nor that he has appointed himself to a saintly role and me to a satanic one. I know that you approved of him, and I can assure you that I still share your approval, but you will understand exactly what I mean when I say that he is too earnest. The burdens of responsibility weigh too heavily upon him, and he has allowed them to slow his intellectual progress.

Copplestone and I never became friends, of course. My experiment in suicide brought me to a future in which he still enjoyed a measure of celebrity, but I did not rush to his side on the assumption that we must behave as brothers merely because we were the only two human beings alive. The Overmen were diverse even in those days, and those who helped in my remaking were not closely allied with those who had adopted him. If the two vampiric parties had not been steadfast rivals before my advent, they became steadfast rivals afterwards, in the quest to discover the secrets of time travel. It proved to be a fruitless quest, but that did not make their rivalry any less; if anything, it was intensified.

I was, at the very least, an alternative fount of knowledge regarding the state of the human world a century or so before its collapse; my particular inquisitors were inclined to possessiveness in respect of what I told them, and what they thought they had learned from it. I played to their weaknesses, of course; I have always had a mischievous streak in me. I might have lived a happier life if I had not, but had I been a happy and good man I could never have become what I am now: an Overman like no other, not even Copplestone.

There is little I can or need to say about my substitute Laura or the failure of my attempt to bring her into my afterlife; you would think me silly and tedious if I dwelt on mere emotional matters. You will know as well as I do that the example of her death proves that adventures such as mine are not free of risk. For some humans, at least, death is death. If the alien angels can be believed, it will not matter, because the Universal Engine will resurrect all the intelligent beings that ever lived into their own particular paradises during a languorous Indian Summer of existence that will precede the Crucial Moment–but I cannot believe what the Others say. I cannot even believe that *they* believe it.

I say this not because I think it impossible that a Universal Engine, once created, might create a Universal Paradise, but merely because the notion is too seductive. I understand those who seek out comforting beliefs in the interests of self-sustenance, but I have never been one of them. Neither have you.

I do not know exactly what Copplestone told our mutual friend, nor what he really believes, but I suspect that their ingrained skepticism will not let either man believe in the loving resurrection promised by the alien angels. To accept such a creed would be to accept as a given that the ultimate future of mankind–the eschatological future–is secure. That is not true, nor can it ever become true. The real question at issue is what might and ought to be made of the historical future.

Perhaps there will be men on Earth who will answer Copplestone's call to build a New Jerusalem. I hope that there are, for our rivalry is not of the sort that makes me anxious to see him fail. He is the saint, not I; his is the kind of jealous faith that cannot abide heresy, while mine is a generous philosophy that thrives on dialogue. It is not selfishness that commands me to advise you to seek a different fate, nor is it a matter of principle. It is simply that *you* still have something that Copplestone and I no longer have: the ability to cast a timeshadow, and the chance to cast it where–or, rather, when–no timeshadow has ever been cast before.

Even if this were paradise, or there were some other paradise of which I could be certain, I would still say to you: *do not come here*. Copplestone and I are here already and our dream is already set in stone; if there are further futures to be found and further dreams to be dreamed, they must be your destinations. If you yearn for a paradise, far better that you should make one anew than seek to enter one already made.

I have not become bored with the prospect of the near-eternity that faces me; far from it. The life I have lived since my death in 1895 has been delightful in its way. Even though I came to it alone, and lived through a uniquely harrowing time when the civilization of the overmen was smashed and the Earth destroyed, I have found my afterlife well worth living. I remain avid to meet every challenge that the next ten thousand years might throw up. The frustration that sometimes steals upon me is neither *ennui* nor *spleen*, but simply the knowledge that I am only one man, with only one existence to lead, no matter how protracted it might be.

If I were asked to sum up what 16,000 years of life have taught me in a single paragraph, it would be this:

If there is indeed to be a Universal Engine, we must do whatever we can to assist its construction. If there is to be a Universal Resurrection, we must do whatever we can to bring to that glorious day the legacy of every possible variety of experience. No matter how far a man's neighbor may see into the wilderness of infinity, he must try to see even further. No matter how kind a destiny a man's neighbor may identify, he must search for a different one.

You, at least, will understand me when I say that if Copplestone, or any other man, had found a certain way to Heaven, I would not follow him; I would prefer to take another path, even if it were the road to Hell, in order that I might be the first to tread it.

You will already know why I have asked our mutual friend to deliver this missive directly to you. It is not because I do not trust him to state my side of the case and to state it fairly; I know that he will be conscientious in preserving the other documents I dictated to him, and in making them available to anyone to whom they will be of use. It is because you are the person best fitted by fate to sympathize with my cause and best placed by merit to further it. I do not know what you have achieved since you saw me last, but I know that you were capable of great things. By now, I estimate, you should have been recognized as the greatest genius of your generation; if there is any justice in the world your followers must be legion. You will know what to do with the formula, and I hope and trust that you will have the authority to do it.

It is my belief that the future is as yet unmade, and that the past is by no means as safe as it might seem from the comfortable vantage of the present. All is undetermined, and its determination is and always will be a contest. If a man enters this competition, especially if he pits himself against Overmen, he places himself at risk–but what is the alternative? To deny oneself risk is to deny oneself everything.

No man should ever hope that he and the universe are safe in the grip of an unalterable destiny; if he is a man, he surely ought to hope that the world–including the Omega and Alpha of the universe–is infinitely variable, and that it will indeed vary, eternally! If he can assist that eventuality–or lack of eventuality–in its realization, he should.

You will know what to do–and your charismatic influence will ensure that countless others will do likewise. Change the future, my friend, if you can. Increase its beauty, to the extent that you are able.

Yours in eternal friendship,
Lugard.

As soon as I had finished reading the letter, I handed it back to the man who had delivered it. When he too had read Lugard's epistle, the detective raised his fleshless head to fix me with his glittering stare.

"Nothing new," he said, bleakly.

He could not possibly have expected anything new, of course. He certainly could not have anticipated that Lugard would have addressed himself more freely, or more explicitly, in this document than in the one he had already read and summarized. He already knew–and had already explained–that what was to be read in any message from a jealous future had to be read between the lines.

"Nothing new," I agreed.

There was something new, but it was addressed to me and me alone. The real significance of the letter was not what it said, nor even how it was said, but in the simple act of its existence. Everything else the detective had offered to my consideration, including the record of my private conversations contained in his manuscript, he could and might have compiled by non-supernatural means. He could have compiled a letter–even this letter–but there was no imaginable reason why he should. A good detective would have been content with the longer manuscript; the letter was not only surplus to requirements but magnificently superfluous. It had to be authentic. It had to be Lugard's.

"I suppose there is a certain irony in the Count's expectations of my fate and fortune," I said. "But what other ambassador could he have selected in my place, had he known how far I have fallen? The only men whose company he liked were those of dubious reputation."

My visitor remained silent while he raised the courage to ask for my advice. In the end, he said: "I have thought of publishing everything–throwing it into the public arena, so that those who might find hope or challenge in it might do as they pleased. The doctor advised me against doing so, as did my brother. I suspect that de Gourmont and Flammarion will say the same when we confer with them tonight."

"I have never been one to attach myself to majorities," I said, judiciously, "but in this instance I must agree with your other advisers. I doubt that the authorities would approve of your printing recipes for an admittedly dangerous drug, and they would certainly take action against you as soon as a death was reported. However good your relationship is with Scotland Yard, you would probably be subject to arrest, and I think you know what your fate would be were you to lay your case before an English jury. You were right to choose men like de Gourmont and Flammarion to hear your story; men like those are no less likely to think you deluded, but are at least prepared to take a keen interest in the unusual phenomena of your delusion."

"I am lost, in any case," he said, plaintively. "If I cannot tell the whole truth–if I am always to be prevented from delivering practical proofs in the form of hard technological information–I can never prove that I am not mad. Perhaps, if I were to write it down instead of trying to speak..."

"I advise you against it," I said. "Even if you are an instrument of the Overmen, you still have a margin of choice. Don't do anything that might precipitate your own death, until it's necessary. You have, I suppose, considered the possibility that you're merely a device for gathering intelligence? It's possible that you'll be snatched back into the far future when you die, whether you take another dose of the drug or not, just as Copplestone was. It may well be that you're here to observe and report back–or, to be strictly accurate, forwards–on the reception of your intelligence, and the likely results of its communication."

"It has occurred to me," he admitted, "but it only adds to my confusion–it doesn't help me to decide what to do, who to speak to, or what advice to give them."

"Nor should it inhibit you from trying to reach the right conclusion," I told him, quietly. He still seemed desperate to share his news, and the products of his reasoning, with someone who might be able to think more kindly of him that he did himself. Like Coleridge's ancient mariner, he had become incapable of thinking about anything but his own improbable fate.

I had nothing better to do–and I was not capable, in any case, of any activity more strenuous than listening, so I asked him to sit down and tell me what he had concluded thus far.

"It seems to me," he whispered, "that if the formulas are real, it followed that the future is, *ipso facto*, capable of affecting the past. If information can be transmitted backwards in time, then the possibility that events in the present might be affected by actions in the future has to be admitted. If so, our existential situation is more precarious than we think: our world might be mutated, or blotted out of existence, as a result of actions initiated in the distant future, relayed into the past by an agent like myself. We might take consolation in the fact that there are few such agents available–and I am therefore anxious about the prospect of generating more of them."

"Rightly so," I conceded. "On the other hand, we–you and I, at least–have our own reasons for desiring to use the drug at least once...or once more, in your case."

"True–and it may be that I am being overanxious, seeing conspiracies and dangers where none really exist."

"That too is a possibility," I conceded. "We great minds seem to be thinking alike on the subject, but neither of us is at his best. Indeed, we are both as close to our worst as we are likely to get while we are still able to draw breath. We may be more prone to delusion now than we have ever been before."

"As Copplestone was before us. Do you remember how obsessively anxious he was to discover whether the future he had glimpsed was the future of destiny or merely a contingency? He was supposedly concerned with the question of whether the extinction of the human race and its supersession by our vampire cousins was preventable–but I suspect now that he had begun to wonder, towards the end of his life in our time, whether that extinction might actually have been caused by his revelation to the inhabitants of the future that human beings had the ability to travel in time. After his death, he journeyed into a further future, where the Earth itself had been rendered incapable of supporting life, and it would be entirely natural for his anxieties on that score to be further intensified. That might be the real reason why he set machines to watch so carefully for the advent of any further adventurers, and why he required the machines to operate as they did when one appeared."

"Perhaps," I agreed.

"Sometimes," the detective said, "I wish that I had not worked so assiduously to duplicate the drug. Perhaps, if I had not done so, someone else would eventually have duplicated in Copplestone's researches and reproduced it–but I doubt it. The primitive tribes whose traditional knowledge Copplestone compounded are in the process of being wiped out by the march of progress. The Tasmanians and the Carib Indians are already extinct; others will doubtless follow them. Even where such tribes survive, their heritage will be eclipsed by science and the other systems of European thought. The doctor and I were, for a while, the only two custodians of a secret that might never have been disclosed again, had we not taken care to preserve it."

"I, for one, am grateful that you did," I said. "You must resist the temptation to be too gloomy. You have done a wonderful thing, which might yet work to the great advantage of the human race."

"Yes–the possibility still remains that Copplestone's anxieties are unjustified, although I have to consider the implications of the possibility that they are not. At a personal level, it means that I am in danger of extinction by persons and means whose exact nature I cannot anticipate–but I am no stranger to that kind of risk. I am more concerned with the general implications of the proposition that the past might be alterable by entities with the appropriate knowledge."

"And what are those, in your estimation?"

"It seems to me," the Great Detective said, "that as soon as entities with that kind of power evolve, they will become emperors of time, able to submit past and future alike to their dictatorship–but no matter how powerful they become, their empire will always remain fragile, as brittle as glass. Unless they are omniscient, such beings would never be able to be sure that no rivals would emerge–whether in their own unknown future or in the re-unfolding past that they themselves had brought into being to secure their hegemony–who might attempt and achieve further alterations, which might cancel out their very existence.

"Any such empire of time, I think, would have to be policed with the utmost vigilance, everywhere and everywhen, to make sure that, wherever and whenever the power to twist time might emerge, it could be nipped in the bud. But we know, do we not, that the universe is a vaster place by far than our forefathers supposed? We know, too, that it is far more ancient than they supposed. Given this abundant scope, even the most efficient police force might be expected to take time to react–time that might subsequently be cancelled out, but time nevertheless experienced by the contemporaries of the entity that first attracted the attention of the emperors of time.

304

"Sanely or insanely, I can see no alternative but to conclude that we might in fact be living in exactly such a time: a brief interval between the event that marked our species for destruction and the execution of the sentence; a moment of history that is scheduled for demolition, but retains meanwhile a shadowy provisional existence. I conclude also that, while the moment is as yet unannihilated, it must remain pregnant with the possibility that its future might yet be secured, obliterating in the process the other contingent future that is ambitious to exterminate it."

"If that is so," I pointed out, "then the human race might yet be saved, even though its extermination seems inevitable from the vantage-point of this particular moment in the sequence we have glimpsed."

"True. On the other hand, if time and space really do constitute an empire, it *ought* to be policed and protected against dissolution into chaos–not for the sake of tyranny, but for the sake of freedom. The rules that bind matter, like the rules that bind society, ought not to be thought of as fetters restricting our free will; they are the mechanisms by whose means our desires and ambitions might be fulfilled. If time is not inviolable–or not *yet* inviolable–it ought to be. The idea that a man, or any alien being, might reach back in time to snuff out entire histories is not merely frightening but utterly repugnant. No benevolent Creator could permit it–and creatures condemned to endure such uncertainty ought not to tolerate it, if they have any opportunity to act against it."

"That is a bold statement," I murmured, unsure as to whether I could agree with it. "The likelihood is, however, that your intolerance will not matter a jot."

He looked at me with an expression that no one else could ever have worn–save, perhaps, for the personified Death that he so closely resembled. It was devoid of merely human significance, but it contained a dire symbolism of its own.

"What should I do, Oscar?" he asked–not plaintively, but as one great-minded man to another.

I was not in any fit state to speak to him at length, but I could not bring myself to deny him, or to instruct him to come back when I had made up my mind. Fortunately, necessity is ever the mother of improvisation, and I was not found wanting.

"First of all," I said, "you should stop looking over your shoulder in fear of assassins from the future, whether they are there or not. If our history is indeed policed, you may be sure that the policemen are equipped with weapons far subtler than daggers or guns. You should also stop worrying overmuch whether or not you *are* such a weapon, even though you might be. It may be that we are both mad, or that our sanity is more destructive than any madness, but we must attempt to be calm. If risks must be taken, risks must be taken–and it seems to me that you cannot simply bury what you have discovered. Whether it turns out to be a poisoned chalice or not, you must try to make the best use you can of the knowledge Copplestone and Lugard gifted to you.

"If you want to ensure that your formulas are not merely preserved but used, you must circulate them selectively and clandestinely. I am sufficiently democratic to disapprove of Copplestone's asking you to select only the best of men for possible advancement, but I am perfectly certain that very few would volunteer, even at the point of death. I am tempted to suggest that you peddle the drugs as hallucinogens, attempting to establish them as fashionable substitutes for opium and hashish, but that would violate the principle of informed consent– and any time-travelers thus recruited might be so much poorer than the average as to offend the most hardened democrat. There is only one sensible course open to you."

"Which is?" I think he knew, but he wanted to hear confirmation from my lips.

"To form a secret society. They are very fashionable nowadays, even more so in Paris than in London. Clothe your secret in layers of mystery and deliberate flummery; that way you will make it seem seductive to those most likely to be useful to you, and harmless to those who disapprove. Hide your initiates within a crowd of mere charlatans, and trust to luck that enough good men will penetrate the periphery to find the heart of the enterprise. I fear that you will not obtain many Flammarions by that strategy, but you might hope for a de Gourmont or two."

"Or even an Oscar Wilde?"

"There is only one Oscar Wilde," I told him, severely, "and he could never be any man's but his own. Now fold up that letter and put it in your pocket. You have my permission to take it to de Gourmont's house and let him read it aloud to Jarry and Flammarion; please apologize to him for my enforced absence. I advise you to listen meekly to whatever he and his companions have to say to you, and to take every word of it seriously. I beg you to return thereafter to your hotel, and there to make up a dose of the second formula: Lugard's formula. You may deliver it to me at your leisure, but I beg you not to delay too long. If you do not care to administer the dose yourself, I will persuade Dupoirier to do it, by one means or another. Will you oblige me in this matter?"

The man I had once taken for Death stood up, and put the paper in his pocket, as I had commanded.

"I will do as you ask," he promised. "You can rely on me."

"I know I can," I said, although I knew no such thing.

11.

Sherrinford did not return that night, nor on the night after, nor on the night after that. He sent no word of his whereabouts or any explanation the reason for his delay; even de Gourmont did not write to me. The detective's failure to return was a new agony to add to all the others I was suffering, although it could no more eclipse them than they could eclipse one another.

I could not help wondering, despite my advice that he should stop looking over his shoulder so fearfully, whether the policemen of time had contrived to snuff him out. I could not help wondering, too, whether the evening on which he had told his story might also have been condemned to the realms of fantasy–retired, as it were, to the private attic of my own delirium. I knew, of course, that the more obvious possibility was that he had succumbed, as I had, to exhaustion and illness–but he sent no word, unless Tucker or Dupoirier had taken it upon himself to judge that I should not be troubled by enigmatic messages. I hoped that, if he had fallen ill, his debility would be temporary–that he would come when he could to fulfill our fateful bargain, and that he would arrive while I was still in a condition to receive his gift.

It is, I suppose, traditional that a wicked man on his deathbed should repent of his errors. I had more opportunity to repent of mine than I would have liked, had I not been awaiting salvation of a sort. Before October ended I told Robbie that my drama had lasted too long, and that I had reached my Saint Helena. I told him about the duel to which I had been challenged by my wallpaper but he thought me guilty of delirium; little did he know what was to come.

In November, I was driven mad by an abscess in my ear, and driven madder by the meningitis that followed in its train. I told Robbie and Reggie, while they were both in attendance at my bedside, that I had been supping with the dead, but I did not tell them that we had dined on rich black blood. When Robbie had gone to Nice, I suffered further bouts of ignominious incoherence, in the midst of which my pleas that Reggie should send for Death passed quite unheeded.

When Robbie returned, he was very anxious to fetch me a priest, and I could not prevent him. By the time the priest came, I could no longer speak, and such gestures as I made with my hand were misconstrued. Even so, while the Passionist made haste to anoint and absolve me, I made what shift I could to formulate my own repentance and further my own salvation.

I cannot remember how I lost myself in a dream, but lost I certainly became.

I knew that the priest could not save me, on Earth or in Heaven, and that I had to pin my hopes on the return of Death's double. On Earth, of course, my fate was already decided. Whether my reputation would be irretrievably tarnished by my disgrace, I could not know–but I dared to hope that it would not. I had, after all, already argued on behalf of poor Thomas Wainewright that a man's worth as a critic ought to be given due recognition, despite the fact that he was also a multiple murderer; how could the world be so unjust as to neglect my talent as a playwright merely because I had committed crimes of far less dimension? I was, after all, merely a portrait hidden in a Parisian attic; the real Oscar Wilde was elsewhere, a perfect work of art, untarnished and untarnishable.

In Heaven....well, I had no intention of going to Heaven, if any alternative at all presented itself for my convenience. The land of dreams was infinitely preferable. I knew that the person I had displayed to the world, proudly at first and anything-but-proudly of late, had always been a picture: a thing of paint and contrivance. Long before ugliness forced me to my attic, lest the world recoil from me in disgust, the real Oscar Wilde had been liberated from the burden of his sins, set to inhabit the World of Art, where nothing is corruptible, whether by the pox, or slanderous rumor, or bad shellfish, or the newspapers. The real Oscar had always been safe, nesting between the lines of his essays and poems, his stories and plays.

Because I knew this, I was not afraid. Dumb and dying as I was, it was easy to dream that, although I had been stabbed in the heart, and although the greatest detective in the world could not point to any murderer but my other self, the future still lay before me, infinite and beautiful. It was easy to believe that my timeshadow would soar into the unknown, as far beyond the time when Edward Copplestone was Emperor of the Moon and Lugard the Lord of its Underworld as their time lay beyond mine. There, I would have the thread of my immortality woven by patient nanozoons, in order that I too might become a hero of mankind, capable of making grand plans for the salvation–or, more likely, the supersession–of ungrateful humanity. I could no longer speak to Robbie or Dupoirier, save for a few half-articulate croaks–whose emission made me seem a mere frog–but I could still imagine speaking in my grandest style, as if from a future a thousand or a million years away:

"We works of art have nothing to fear from disease. We do not die, nor do we suffer; we have nothing to fear from change. In my former incarnation I was heir to all the pain and misery which the world wished to visit upon the real Oscar Wilde, but I was always beyond their jurisdiction, and beyond their power to do me permanent injury. Art never dies, and could not even then. The march of time measured the effects of decay and dereliction within the frail flesh of my heritage, but it measured in parallel the glory of my evolution, my progress, and my eventual transcendence.

"I began life, like any other man, as an item of representative art, with no greater virtue than accuracy–but when I made my bargain with Fate and Art I began to mature into a modernist masterpiece. I became surreal and futuristic, awesome and sublime. I became the very embodiment of genius, of magic, of power. I went far beyond mere reflection, into the hinterlands of the imagination; I became the kind of creature that can only be glimpsed in dreams. Even before Death's double came to my aid–and even if he had never come at all–I was no longer man but overman, heir to all disease and all decay but never to defeat and never to destruction. I alone in all the world was capable of wearing my corruptions proudly, as manifestations of my absolute triumph over death and damnation.

"I have already lived more lives than any common man, and I was already immortal before my soul was rescued from the void of eternity, but I am still in the process of *becoming* and I will not rest until there is nothing else left to do, nothing else left to hope for. I am no *mere* work of art; I am one of those precious works which is, in essence, art itself. If you stare into my eyes–which will follow you through life, not merely into every corner of the room–you may see what human identity really is, freed from the delicate prison of the flesh; you may see what human destiny really is, freed from the limitation of a narrow mind."

That was my own final judgment, my final prayer, my private rite of extreme unction. I wish I could have spoken the words aloud, but my batrachian croak could never have done them justice. I could only frame them grandiosely, as gloriously gilded as they deserved to be framed, in a dream.

When I recovered myself, the priest was gone. I found myself alone and in darkness–but I was not alone for very long.

I heard the door of my room open and footsteps crossing the carpet, but it was not until the gas was lit that I saw who my visitor was.

"Are you Death," I asked, "or merely his benign twin?"

He did not tell me–not, at least, in so many words. "I am sorry to have taken so long," he said. "I could not help the delay, but I am here now. Are you ready?"

"More than ready," I assured him, knowing that the answer would do even if he were Death, and not Death's double.

He produced a hypodermic syringe from his briefcase–but I suppose he might have done that even if he had been Death. Death had surely taken to carrying a briefcase by the year 1900, and he must also have had modern medical apparatus at his beck and call. Death, like the living, has no option but to move with the times.

While my visitor filled his instrument from a glass vial marked with a skull and crossbones, I looked beyond him at the wall.

As usual, the gaslight had brought out all the malignity of the false foliage and all the meretriciousness of those baleful flowers. They lay like a poisoned skin upon the wall, and hence upon the world entire. Everything hateful was in them: everything that had blighted my life–but now I would have my revenge. They no longer had the power to hurt or contain me.

"*Bon voyage, mon ami*" said Death, or his double, as he aimed his dart at my heart. "The past is already lost, the future yet to be found–and there is work for you to do in the empire of time."

"Never in the course of my hectic career," I murmured, bringing the half-forgotten thought to audible fruition at last, while the merciful needle slid into my flesh, "had I ever encountered flagitious wallpaper–until I came here. This poisonous world and I have reached our final *impasse*, my cadaverous friend; one of us must go."

The needle penetrated my flesh, and I was plunged again into my dream–into *this* dream, which allows me all the time in the world to write, and to read, and to write again.

I understand, now, what Lugard meant when he told his visitor that he had written his story for his own use and comfort. I understand, too, what he meant when he said that, although he was surrounded by companionable machines, something within him yearned for true companionship.

If this dream is the same one that Copplestone and Lugard dreamed, they had long since died within it before I arrived, leaving me alone. Save for machines, there is no one but me to await the brave crusaders recruited by Death's double–if there are, indeed, any crusaders to come–and Death's double himself.

Perhaps no one will ever come, but I shall not allow myself to believe that. Perhaps I should not except myself from the company of the great machines, but I insist on so doing. Perhaps this is nothing but a dream contained and confined within the Crucial Moment of my death and my conception, but I shall not admit it.

If I only wait long enough, here in my attic, someone will come.

Life is not empty. I dream; I write; I yearn; I wait. Neither is it full. That is, I suppose, the best way to live: one ought to have everything one needs, but one should never have everything one desires; only within the margin that separates need from desire can there be hope and purpose to decorate the passage of the days.

I have been waiting for a very long time–but who would not wait, if his fate, and the fate of the human race, and the fate of the universe entire, depended upon his waiting?

I have drunk too deep of the black blood of the dead, but am not slain. I have not found Heaven, but have found hope and purpose instead. I am the last of my race, at present, but the future is still to be determined.

The Soldier's Story: Part Five

A Habitat in the Moon's orbit,
circa 12,000,000 A.D.

16.

I had not long to wait once I had set the manuscript aside. I had time to stand up and move once again to those wonderfully alluring bookshelves, but no sooner had I raised my hand to touch the spine of a book when Wilde's simulacrum returned. Reluctantly, I dropped my hand and turned my eyes to him.

"I must confess that there is a good deal in your manuscript that I did not understand," I said, without waiting to be asked. "The tales within the tale became even more confusing, by virtue of further multiplying the number of narrative voices–and not one of those voices, I have to say, seemed to me to be entirely reliable."

"It will be different, I have no doubt, when you write your own account," he said, ironically. "When you set down all that you have seen, and the record of your pursuit and harassment by forces beyond your comprehension, your readers will immediately say: 'This is Lieutenant Hodgson of the RFA! This is a man whose dreams resonate with the harmonies of truth! This is the man who gave us *The House on the Borderland*–how could we doubt him now?'"

I am sure that I would have blushed, had I been possessed of ordinary flesh. "I am so doubtful of my own reliability," I assured him, "that I cannot presently imagine that I shall ever dare to make such a record."

"In that case," he said, "you have begun to grasp my own predicament. I doubted Copplestone when I listened to him speak, serene in the knowledge that I was drinking good claret, in very tolerable company, in a pleasant house on the edge of Regent's Park. I took it for granted, at first, that the manuscript given to me by the detective must have been written before 1900, and that every word must be some strange joke of Lugard's. I thought the detective's own tale a marvelous flight of fancy, to begin with–and even when I changed my mind, and decided to believe *everything*, I was perfectly prepared to accept that I might be going mad."

The confusion might have been lessened," I suggested, "had you reordered the subsidiary stories within your own in such a way that the events related therein were arranged in chronological order."

"Perhaps," he conceded. "But is not the whole point of the story that beneath and behind chronological order there is chronological *disorder*, and that the chain of cause and effect is more likely to be twisted or broken than we should like to presume?"

"You are insisting, then, that every word of the story is true–notwithstanding its contradiction of my own experience?"

"How can I doubt it, since I took the drug myself?" he answered. "How can *you* doubt it, given the circumstances under which it was administered to you?"

"If this is no more than a dream," I admitted, "then my powers of invention are greater than I had supposed."

"I know that feeling too," he said, drily. "When I wrote my own story, I already knew that the Archive assembled by the Engine contained solid evidence of its apparent falsehood–but I dared not credit it to my imagination. I did not know how much time would pass before anyone would sit down to read it, but I did know that whoever did so would immediately say to himself: 'This is the work of Oscar Wilde, who regretted so publicly the decay of lying! This is a man who perjured himself in a court of law, denying his unspeakable practices! This is the man who gave us *The Importance of Being Earnest*–how could I possibly doubt his sincerity?'"

There was no vehemence in his tone, no wrath in his posture. Even this was all mere artifice: a performance delivered by an android actor.

"But it is fiction *now*," I said, quietly, "even if the world in which it supposedly took place once enjoyed some kind of phantom existence. Some of these things might have occurred in my world, but some could not."

"I suppose that I ought to repeat the question that I asked you before," he countered, feigning weariness. "Save for the real existence of the disfigured detective, is there anything in the story that you know, for certain, to be false?"

I had taken note of two seeming anomalies while I read, but I had to ponder the question of their evidential worth very carefully. "Nothing that I know *for certain*," I admitted, finally, "But I have been in Paris several times in recent years, and I have been party to a good deal of hearsay. I have met Flammarion, but the fact that he never mentioned the occasion which forms the heart of your story would not necessarily be significant. I have also dined more than once with Alfred Vallette, however, and heard a good deal of table-talk about Jarry..."

"Did you meet Jarry?" Wilde asked.

"Jarry died in 1907," I told him, although he presumably had reference-books to tell him that. "That was before I became a regular visitor to France–but he remained notorious long after his demise. One of the stories still in circulation was of his terrible quarrel with de Gourmont–a quarrel that might have made it unlikely that Gourmont would have invited Jarry to his home in the autumn of 1900."

"They seemed to me to be on good terms," Wilde mused, "but still..."

"There was another thing said of Jarry which might be relevant," I put in, quickly. "In the manuscript I have just read, the clear implication is that you had not met him before that night–and perhaps you had not–but it was said that he sent you a book of his when you were released from prison. You would remember that, I think."

Wilde's simulacrum raised an eyebrow pensively. "Yes," he said. "I doubt that I could ever forget the gift of a book, even if it arrived while I was in dire straits. And yet...it is not impossible that I had simply forgotten, and had no memory to carry with me into the future. As to the quarrel...rumor inflates these matters, does it not? Tales grow as they are repeated; shades darken and contrasts become exaggerated."

"There still remains the most important point of all," I reminded him. "The Great Detective did not exist. Whoever provided General Hartley and his companions with the drug I took, it cannot have been a figment of the literary imagination. Even if Copplestone actually existed, even if Lugard actually existed, I know that the person who allegedly gave you the drug which brought you here did not."

"I know that the past has been changed," Wilde informed me, a trifle stiffly. "What I am trying to ascertain, if only for the sake of my own satisfaction, is the exact extent to which it was changed. Without knowing that, it is very difficult to estimate exactly *when* it was changed, and whether or not the relevant changes flowed from a single root event."

"Does it matter?" I asked.

"I don't know," he admitted, "but without knowing exactly what was done, I cannot begin to estimate how it was done, or by whom. The detective and I both suspected that he had been sent back in time in order to serve as an agent of change, but I cannot see how he can have contrived his own non-existence. Whatever *he* did, on behalf of the Overmen keeping watch on Copplestone and Lugard–if he did anything at all–it must have been the kind of action that a man might take. If there were other parties involved, who were intent on cancelling out that action, they seem to have been capable of going to a further extreme than anything he or I could imagine in 1900, in spite of all that we had learned."

"And you have been questioning me so intently," I guessed, "because you think that the changes might extend even further. If my initial estimation of the manuscript was correct–that it was not only the detective, but Lugard and Copplestone too, who had no real existence in the world from which I came, then Copplestone never discovered his formula in my world and Lugard never stole it. That would deepen the mystery of how it came to exist, and how I was able to employ it."

"It would also deepen the mystery of how I came to employ it," Wilde pointed out, "and how I came to exist. What manner of creature am I, do you think? What part am I supposed to play in this bizarre drama, and who cast me in that part? What scope do I have for voluntary action of my own? May I be a player instead of a pawn, or do I merely have the illusion of free will and a personal history? If the answer lies in that manuscript, I have not been able to decipher it. Whether you will be able to help me, I don't know–but you can see now, I think, what hopes I entertained of your possible advent."

I considered the matter for a few moments, and then said: "We constitute a contradiction in terms, it seems. If I exist, then you ought not to–and if you exist, then I ought not to. The answer, as you say, must lie in chronological disorder. Whole histories can be cancelled out and replaced, and yet leave strange relics hanging like loose threads: individual histories, collective histories...perhaps, if the detective was right, entire phantom universes."

"And you see, do you not, why time is pressing upon us?" Wilde said.

"Yes, I do," I agreed. "If we are a contradiction in terms, then we stand in need of resolution...at least in the eyes of the Consolidators who are enemies of uncertainty. The Consolidators' enemies might think differently...unless..."

Wilde's simulacrum did not press me to explain what I meant; he allowed me time to follow the train of thought a little further. He gestured towards the armchair, inviting me to sit down again, and when I had done so he took his own seat–but not before glancing apprehensively at the windows, to make sure that the darkness without was still absolute. If he knew anything about the situation of the worldlet–or what was left of it, following the attack upon it–he did not feel under any obligation to tell me his news.

"If we are pawns," I said, eventually, "then our utility and our fate might still be undecided. I have still to return to 1918, where I might become the same kind of instrument that Copplestone and the detective feared that they had become...or an instrument of another kind. At present, it seems, you are not only shielding me but informing me of my situation. Pawn or not, I am still possessed of free will–I still have some power to decide what I shall do when I return."

"I hope so," Wilde said. "I hope, too, that you will use it–wisely, if you can, and bravely."

"In what cause?" I asked him. "Am I to be a Consolidator, or a more radical Transformer–if I have the choice?"

"A more radical Transformer, of course," he said. "What artist could possibly decide otherwise? The real question is what *kind* of Transformer you will hope to be. Will you attempt to save the human race from imminent self-destruction? Yes, of course, if you have the slightest opportunity to do so. Beyond that...well, the Engine's philosophy seems sound enough to me. If such as we are agents of chaos, then we must be moderate; uncertainty is only precious within the context of a stable frame. We should aim for some kind of balance, if we can take aim at all."

"As a philosophy," I observed, "it sounds fine enough. Putting it into practice, on the other hand, might be very difficult, even if it is not impossible."

"Indeed it will," Wilde's simulacrum agreed, showing his smile again. "I am not party to the secrets of the Transformers, but I do know that they do not regard the changing of history to be a simple matter. Some of that party believe that, if history can be significantly remade at all, it has to be remade in the single critical moment in which the laws of what the Engine calls our inflationary domain were crystallized out of the flux of potentiality–but we know better, do we not? We know that trivial interactions of the future with the past are possible, and that running repairs can be made in the fabric of space-time. That is your purpose, if you are an instrument–and it must be your purpose, to the extent that you can free yourself from instrumentality."

"It's too vague," I complained. "I can hardly make sense of it, let alone use it as a basis for planning."

"Then let us try to make some sense of what has already happened," he said, patiently. "We may hypothesize that the connections so far made between our conflicting pasts and the futures leading up to this point were initiated from the past, and that the first opportunity to change the past in a calculated manner arose in connection with Copplestone's third venture into the future. That journey offered the Overmen *their* first sizable opportunity to take action in the past. For all they knew, it might be their last opportunity as well as their first–and perhaps they hoped to ensure that it would be. They were already Consolidators, without knowing it, desirous of putting an end to any threat to their dominion or any increase in the uncertainty of its achievement.

"We may, I think, presume that they were able to modify Copplestone's timeshadow in such a way as to affect its fate when it returned to its own present. The result was lethal, perhaps because of their incompetence, perhaps by intent. If they intended to obliterate Copplestone's discovery, they failed, at least in my history–but that may not have been their objective. Whatever their plan was, it may well have gone awry when Lugard intervened–*his* actions, I feel certain, were both spontaneous and unexpected, and one of their consequences was the involvement of the detective. The reappearance of Copplestone in a more distant future may well have been planned; Lugard's appearance, and that of the detective, are far more likely to have been unplanned, unanticipated and highly problematic.

"It is conceivable, I think, that the detective's timeshadow was not strategically modified before it returned to my own time. It is certainly possible that whatever modifications were made by the Overmen were even less competent than those made to Copplestone's timeshadow. Given the content of Lugard's transmission, though, it is surely certain that the Overmen knew–even if they did not intend–that I would be one of the recipients of the secret of time travel, and a very likely user thereof. Again, I suspect that their plan may have gone awry, perhaps because they did not anticipate that I would be so close to death when I took the drug, but ore probably because they accepted Lugard's assumption that I should have been a man of considerable influence in the year 1900, rather than a broken wreck. At any rate, if the detective ever took another dose of his drug, he too must have been unable to return, thus leaving me alone–at least temporarily–as an emissary to this far future.

"I cannot tell how many other hopeful time-travelers might have set off from the early years of the 20th century, as I knew them, or what points in time they contrived to reach. Several appear to have set off from those years *as you knew them* without achieving any very solid or durable manifestation of a time-shadow. The discrepancy between your 1900 and mine, however, assures us that a process of change must have occurred that was *not* the action of any returning time-traveler known to us. Given the strange nature of that change, it might be reasonable to imagine it as a kind of reflexive reaction of the time-stream to the disturbances generated by the Overmen's attempts to use Copplestone and the detective as instruments. Perhaps it was the fact that their plans misfired that necessitated the adjustment, but it might be that *any* such action provokes a compensatory reaction. In any case, the existing contradiction was removed by making some items of fact into items of fiction–which is, if you consider it carefully, an entirely appropriate and essentially artistic sort of response.

"The adjustment was presumably sufficient, in the short term–but not in the longer term. The anomaly persisted, and was magnified, and eventually precipitated a new moment of crisis: this one, in which you and I are sitting face-to-face, in spite of the manifest impossibility of that circumstance. Clearly, that moment of crisis presents new opportunities to the Overmen and their mundane rivals, which they are keen to exploit. If you contrive to return to 1918, you might be modified in the same way that Copplestone and the detective probably were–perhaps more efficiently, and perhaps not. When you return, you will do what you will, and what you can, to serve their ends and your own...but in so doing, you will further increase the anomaly whose seed was sown when Copplestone first ventured into the future–and there might, in consequence, be a further reflexive reaction, of the kind that reduced the detective to a mere fiction, and might well have done the same thing to Copplestone and Lugard. Would you agree that this is as good a summary as we can presently construct of the paradoxical situation in which we find ourselves?"

I nodded my head, slowly. He had, after all, had far longer to think about the issue than I had. "I suppose that I might become a fiction too," I said. "As you might, and General Hartley, and sweet Helen. The universe might heal its internal balance of uncertainty by easing us all into the limbo of the imagination."

"It might," Wilde's simulacrum agreed. "But it might not, if you can work towards that rectificatory end yourself, while retaining the possibility of your own existence."

"*If*," I echoed. "If, on the other hand, I have no scope at all for the free exercise of my will, because I am a pawn in the war-game raging around the house, I can only hope that the players who use me have made provision for my continued existence."

I looked around at the volumes that surrounded us. Had there been only a tenth or a hundredth as many, it seemed certain to me that there must be hundreds of books there that had been penned by more ambitious and more adventurous visionaries than me. If General Hartley were to be granted another 20 years to send forth his recruiting sergeants, they would surely find potential time-travelers who could exceed my reach and grasp.

The thought of General Hartley made me wonder again how his organization had come into possession of the time-travel drug, if they had not got it from the great detective's secret society. If, as I thought, they really had mentioned Copplestone's name, then he, at least, was no fiction–not yet, at any rate. The Copplestone of my history might not have been the same as the one in Wilde's history, though–he might have been the kind of man who would take his discovery straight to the government or the armed forces, rather than summoning a party of eccentric intellectuals to discuss the matter philosophically. Of which Copplestone should I approve if that were so? On the other hand, the Copplestone of my history might have been mesmerized by nanozoons, with the effect that he would take his discovery to the fugitive race lurking on the fringes of human society, as well as or instead of his own fellows.

"I have so much more that I want to ask you," Wilde said, with a deep sigh. "There is so much more that I might gain from our acquaintance, however brief, if time will only give us the opportunity. I too have decisions to make, just as Copplestone and Lugard had 100,000 years after their birth-time. The plans they tried to set in motion were aborted, but the questions they were endeavoring to answer by making those plans still bear on me. Whatever I may be–and albeit that I am certainly more machine than man–I am both the producer and the product of what Gourmont called a personal myth, and I have not settled yet what the import of that myth ought to be. I would dearly like to have that chance, if..."

He could have continued, but he cut himself off, and an expression of dread–of *mortal* dread–possessed his artificial features.

17.

The floor beneath my feet had begun to tremble. I leapt to my feet, although there was no conceivable advantage to be obtained in standing up.

"What is it?" I asked–but Wilde's simulacrum merely shook his head in bewilderment. He had lived for millions of years, but this situation was as new to him as it was to me. He stood too, and walked rapidly to the window; he stared out into the blackness, as if expecting it to part, but it did not. I stood where I was, looking around at the books on the shelves.

I had deduced by now that this was not the real Archive of mankind's achievements, but merely a copy of it, cast in an obsolete mould for the benefit of its present reader. Just as Dorian Gray had bound multiple copies of *À rebours* in different colors, so that he might have a version to suit every mood, so the sole inhabitant of the Attic of Olympus had asked that the human component of the information excavated from the ruins of the civilization of the overmen should be replicated in a form adapted to his own habits and preferences.

Were the house to be squeezed out of existence by the black claw that held it firm, I told myself, none of mankind's legacy of knowledge and printed dreams would actually be lost. I felt, nevertheless, that something very precious was contained in that room, whose annihilation would be a tragedy. I wanted the books to survive, and I wanted Wilde's simulacrum to survive; I certainly did not want to be the reason for the extermination of either.

I still wondered–how could I help it?–whether I might someday have the chance to return to this treasure-house, with all the time in the world available for leisurely consultation of its riches. Even if no such opportunity ever presented itself, however, I thought that I would live more happily in my own present day knowing that some such edifice was fated to exist and endure.

The vibration in the floor was still muted, but the walls of the hideous palace had begun to creak under the strain of some insidious pressure. I could not doubt that I was in dire danger, and that the battle between the Engine and its enemies, though raging as fiercely as ever, was reaching its decisive climax.

It would almost have been a relief to see shellbursts lighting up the illimitable void beyond the windows, instead of that awful, solidity of darkness. But I was not afraid. The longer I existed as a reinforced timeshadow, the more purely cerebral my responses became. I faced a prospect that, seen from the viewpoint of any ordinary man, might easily be reckoned the worst imaginable, but my flesh did not creep and my stomach did not clench. My mind was active but my body was numbed, as if it were morphinated–or quite dead.

I needed distraction from my peculiar predicament, and I judged that Wilde's simulacrum needed it as well. "What actually became of Copplestone and Lugard, after the detective's encounter?" I asked him. "Do you know how they perished, and at whose hand?"

"The Engine does not know," Wilde told me, somberly, "or so it claims. Whether or not Lugard survived the assault that the detective witnessed as he fell back through time, I cannot tell–but he certainly did not survive its aftermath, and nor did Copplestone. I simply don't know who, or what, killed them. I often wish that one or both of them had survived; I have been the last thinking relic of humankind for millions of years now, and have not been comfortable in my isolation."

The vibration was growing gradually worse, but it was still no more than a vibration. I only had to clench my jaw to prevent my teeth from chattering.

"The loneliness must have seemed horribly oppressive, at times," I opined, looking round again at the shelves, which seemed distinctly gloomy in the yellow artificial light. "According to legend, the accursed wanderers of old grew to hate the fact of their existence as eternal strangers in strange lands."

"Mortal men created those legends," Wilde pointed out. "Men who were understandably anxious to quell their envy of the immortal condition. No, my long and lonely existence has not been hateful. The capacity for boredom is one of the things I surrendered when I consented to the replacement of my feeble flesh by more durable materials, and while I retain my curiosity I am armored against desolation."

"What else did you surrender?" I queried. "How much, in all?"

He smiled, but I could see no humor in the smile. "The change in my condition is not easy to quantify," he said. "Some might judge that I lost the one thing I was desperate to sustain: myself. You have suggested as much yourself, in hinting that I have lost my once-impeccable taste. I am a mere portrait, after all. My appearance was restored to the full flush of youth and beauty, when I sloughed my burden of corruption into the body I left behind, but I am only that appearance."

"Many of the litterateurs who have considered the possibility of a science-gifted immortality have seen it as a dangerous prize," I admitted. "Our modern legend-mongers have tended to agree with their forebears that changelessness would inevitably lead to stagnation, to an existence without hope and without meaning."

"A kind of psychological Consolation," Wilde observed. "I have dozens of such arguments on these shelves–which means that there must have been hundreds lost to destruction before the Engine began to reconstruct this Archive. I might not be the best judge of their validity, and the Engine certainly is not. You probably think that you are better placed than I to decide the matter, but even you are a mere echo of what you were, at present."

"I know it," I conceded. "I am even more poorly placed than you are to weigh the consequences of that knowledge."

"When I was human," Wilde informed me, soberly, "I thought of myself as essentially a creature of mind, which merely inhabited my body. I suppose that all men do, because they cannot do otherwise. The philosophers of our day took leave to dissent from Descartes' notion of the mind as an insubstantial entity, which operated the body-machine by means of magical levers situated in the pineal gland–and they were right about its incoherence–but what could they put in its place? How else can we conceive of ourselves but as souls marooned in matter?

"When I was human, I also thought of myself as a being crucially divided: the focal point of a struggle between dispassionate reason and baser appetites. I dare say that all men do that, too, because I cannot see how any could do otherwise. Even the philosophers of our own day still paid homage to Plato and Spinoza on that ground, whether or not they agreed with the former that the fundamental task of mind is to secure the empire of reason and subject the baser appetites to the most stringent discipline. As a human, I did not agree; as a human, I could not and would not deny that my appetites were an essential part of me, and that I could not be myself if I were to deprive and starve them."

"You could resist anything, except temptation," I quoted. "But temptation betrayed you, as it betrays us all."

"And I betrayed temptation in my turn," he retorted, a little sharply, "as everyone would who had the opportunity to bargain with the Devil. We knew, of course, that our idea of the baser instincts and appetites was not entirely compatible with our notion of the human being as an insubstantial soul caught in a material envelope, but we were content to compromise. We talked, carelessly enough, of the sins of the flesh, and imagined that if our souls really did survive the death of the body, they would be free of all but the noblest sentiments."

His speech was becoming very strained, because of the necessity of countering the turbulence to which our cocoon was being subject, but he continued doggedly. "I do not know exactly how humankind's successors saw themselves, but I know that they gave up their flesh, by gradual degrees, quite willingly. They did what I did–and what you have also done, perhaps more irreparably than you imagine–and allowed themselves to be remade from within, organ by organ, cell by cell and molecule by molecule. Like me, each of them must have maintained the same sense of continuity, the same notion that they were not being changed in any fundamental way, merely growing and maturing, improving themselves."

"Were they wrong?" I asked–thinking, as I did so, that the ultimate product of this evolution was the Engine, of which I knew very little. I had been assured that its so-called scions did not lack all individuality, but it was difficult to think of them as close analogues of human minds.

"I do not think the question is reducible to a straightforward matter of either/or," he said. "Almost all of what we call emotion is a product of physiology; however our minds may refine it in subjective experience, it begins in the chemical transactions of our glands and the electrical activity of our nerves. The excitement of the flesh gives rise to fear and ecstasy, anxiety and lust. When we acquire different bodies–as we do, of course, when we become timeshadows, or when our organic parts are replaced by more durable machinery–we have no alternative but to *feel* differently, because those systems differ in their excitability both quantitatively and qualitatively."

I remembered that the first thing my present host had done when I arrived in his abode was to encourage my awareness of this fact: to make me attend to the peculiarity and lack of intensity of my feelings. This was evidently one of the other subjects he had been anxious to discuss with me. Well, we were doing our best, in difficult circumstances

"I can still feel, after a fashion," I said. "I have not become a creature of pure intellect."

"Nor have I," he said. "My durable body has a nervous system of sorts, and a circulatory system that carries chemical messengers. It can be excited in many different ways, and those excitements are translated into subjective sensations. As I told you before, I insisted on retaining the need for nourishment and the ability to savor good food and good wine. I am neither motiveless, nor desireless, nor devoid of temptation. Whatever I am, I certainly am not *stagnant*. I am not empty of ambition, nor am I condemned to perpetual tedium. Nevertheless, there are differences between the systems that generate my emotions now and the systems that did so when I was an organic being, and those differences are differences of kind. No matter how clever this body might become in mimicking the sensations produced by the old, it could not duplicate them exactly–and in truth, there would be little point in demanding that it be designed with that effect in mind."

I knew that if I asked him to describe the differences in more detail he would merely throw the question back at me. How could I describe the differences imposed on my own sensibilities by the fact that I existed here as a time-shadow? I had tried to describe them to myself, and I had failed to find words adequate to the task. It was as if my sense of sight had been changed, so that instead of a world whose colors were compounded out of the primaries red, green and blue I beheld a world with an entirely different visible spectrum. I could apply new words to the new colors, but I could not make them meaningful in any but a negative capacity. They would simply be "not red," "not green" and "not blue"–and however I might come to think of it in the end, I could only begin to think of the world compounded out of the new colors in terms of the absence of familiarity, in terms of loss.

"I see what you mean," I said to Wilde, to show him that I could follow the gist of his argument.

"I am Oscar Wilde still, or his simulacrum," my companion assured me. "I dare not declare that I am human still, but I do declare that I could not be what I now am had I not been human once, and had I not been the particular human that I was. I declare, too, that I honestly believe that I have a better understanding now of what I was when I was human than I ever had when I was inescapably committed to the prison of humanity."

I knew that his use of the word *declare* was intended to make me remember another of his *bon mots*, and that his reference to the prison of humanity was supposed to resonate with my memory of *The Ballad of Reading Gaol*.

"But you cannot tell me what you understand," I said, "because I do not have the words."

"That is the Engine's catch-phrase, not mine," he replied. "I am at least prepared to hunt for the words–and who is better qualified to conduct the search than I?"

It was my turn to smile. I did not feel unhuman as I did it–quite the reverse, in fact. The smile must have been rigid, though, tensed against the shudder that had take possession of my bones.

"I think that the essence of the difference between flesh and machinery is their stability," the simulacrum told me, earnestly. "It is the durability of machinery that makes it preferable, in answer to the most deep-seated fear of all–the fear of death–and it is the durability of machinery that transforms the physical basis of emotion.

"Animal life, reduced to its essence, is a kind of combustion. Complex molecules are ingested, digested and metabolized; their oxidation provides the energy employed in the construction and maintenance of the body. A body of flesh is solid enough, but it is also fluid; such stability as it has is more like the stability of the jet of a fountain, or the stability of a candle-flame, than the stability of a rock. It is essentially precarious, and that precariousness is evident at every level of human existence. The ever-present hazard of death is mirrored in the most fundamental process of organic life and in the most intimate arenas of mental life.

"The human mind, too, is essentially mercurial, subject to disturbance by the slightest wind; even the world of awakened thought is haunted by petty whims and strange fancies, just as the world of awakened desire is disturbed by vagrant impulses and moments of darkness. The continuity of the self is a wave moving through a turbulent ocean, perpetually at risk of breaking upon the shore of death.

"The life of a machine, or of a timeshadow, has none of that implicit fragility. That is not because machines and timeshadows are indestructible–indeed, timeshadows are conspicuously ephemeral in their natural state–but because their fine structure resembles crystals or clocks more closely than flames or fountain-jets. They are more orderly. That does not make violent passion impossible, but it does make both the violence and the manner of its expression more disciplined.

"Ironically enough, the one sensation of which mechanical being seems utterly incapable is that of boredom, at least in its more fretful manifestations; the animal condition abhors the quiet stability that is foreign to it, but the mechanical condition has no such innate prejudice. Should you be fortunate enough to do as I have done and cheat death, I can promise you that you will not find eternity boring, even if you are condemned to be lonely."

The prospect of returning to a future even more distant than this was a possibility to which I intended to give much fuller consideration, but I dared not pause to consider it at length while there seemed to be so many obstacles in its way.

The house that Oscar Wilde had designed for his empery was groaning in agony now under the stress of the assault upon its integrity; at any moment, I thought, it might be swallowed by the abyss.

The awful darkness beyond the windows was a constant visual reminder of the fact that I could not long survive here. Had the Engine won its battle, there would surely have been light of some kind visible through those panes, but there was none. I was not terrified, because I had it in my mind that, if and when the walls collapsed, I would merely be whisked back to my own time–but I was anxious for Oscar Wilde, who had no such escape available to him.

"There is nothing very surprising in what you have said," I told Wilde's simulacrum, forcing myself to concentrate on the substance of our philosophical discussion. "Humans are the product of evolution; our ancestors were protozoans and worms, fish and lemurs. How could we expect to continue for millions of years without further change? The human mind is new, in 1918; no one who is not willfully blind can possibly think of it as something finished. Does the Engine, as it is present configured, think of itself as the final product of evolution, or merely another step on the long road to the Universal Engine of which the detective spoke? How can it conceive of itself as anything but temporary, when it has such enemies? The overmen who embarked upon its construction apparently imagined it as the embryo of an organization that would ultimately possess and control the entire universe, but it must have ceased to think of itself in such grandiose terms. It has set itself against those it calls Consolidators; it speaks now of a universe without end, and change without end, and creativity without end."

"It is not obvious that the Engine is right," Wilde pointed out, mildly. "The progress of mind from flesh to machine is certainly in the direction of order; the Consolidators argue that their cause is merely an extrapolation to a logical conclusion. The greater number of the rebel Transformers agree with them, seeking to reshape the past in such a way as to smooth the acquisition of final order and absolute control. The boldest of them desire and intend to carry that crusade beyond the limits of what the Engine calls our inflationary domain, back through a whole series of Creations to correct the supposed mistake that allowed universes to spawn daughter-domains with such awful profligacy."

"But we are on the side of the Engine," I reminded him. "How could it be otherwise, while there remains the least vestige of humanity in our physical and mental make-up?"

"It is certainly true that the Engine is on our side," my companion observed, "else you and I would have been exterminated like vermin. Which goes to show, I suppose, that even those who have embraced the mechanical condition wholeheartedly are not without their petty whims and strange fancies."

"Is that what calls it to our defense?" I asked. "A vagrant impulse, devoid of any sensible motive?"

"It says not," Wilde admitted. "It speaks of conserving uncertainty, and of nourishing the kinds of events that increase uncertainty, as if I were a part of its grandest plan. But we are human enough to understand the process of rationalization, are we not? We know how ingenious reason is, when called upon to support the vagaries of impulse and excuse the consequences of sin?"

"Sin?" I echoed. "Can a mechanical assembly commit a sin?"

"I certainly hope so," he replied. "That is the opinion of the Consolidators, at any rate. You spoke of being on the side of the angels earlier, but you had already begun to realize that it is the Consolidators who are closer, in spirit, to our idea of God than any other company hereabouts. Their ambitions are closer to our ideal of Heaven than anything the Engine seeks to be or to build. Were this a Miltonian struggle, we would be of the Devil's party, would we not?"

"As was Milton, allegedly, without knowing it."

"That was his advantage," Wilde observed. "We must struggle with the disability of clear sight."

I was about to remark that while the space without the windows remained so stubbornly and intensely black, clear sight was the least of our handicaps, but it would have been a poor witticism.

I was saved the embarrassment by a further escalation of the noise that had possessed our protective structure: a slow explosion, which began as a low rumble in the depths far below us and grew into a frightful grinding cannonade. It put me in mind of the gnashing of teeth to which the multitudinous damned were supposedly condemned, magnified a thousand or a million times.

The walls around us began to crumble at last. The books, already jittery upon the shelves, began to tumble to the floor in heir hundreds, their thousands.

The lights flickered, threatening to plunge us into total darkness.

In the context of our recent conversation, I might have been able to rejoice in a thrill of pure animal terror, but what I felt instead was something to which I could not put a name—an emotion that suddenly seemed all the more alien, by virtue of that fact.

"This must be the end," I said to Wilde.

He was already moving towards the door in order to avoid the tide of falling books. "I fear so," he replied, speaking over his shoulder.

I made haste to follow him, and was no more than a pace or two behind him when he threw open the library door. He hurried to the banister-rail, in order to look down into the stairwell.

I knew how deep the stairwell ought to be, and how neat its conformation had been when I looked into it before, but when I looked down for the second time, I did not see the stately descent of several dozen floors to a polished vestibule. I saw a flood of darkness rising up with a mad force that the pathetic fallacy would have deemed exceedingly angry: a darkness that was already extending huge and avid tentacles towards us as we stared into its maw.

The impression of life that the swelling shadow gave was further enhanced by the fact that sounds were emanating from its depths, as if from a vast distance–sounds that seemed faint, but cut through the noise of the house's disintegration nevertheless.

These were sounds that I had heard before, in dreams that I had dreamed in my youth; I felt an instant thrill of recognition, accompanied by the sharpest dart of alarm I had been able to feel since I became a mechanized phantom.

"The walls are breached!" I cried. "The Engine has lost!"

"It seems so," Oscar Wilde agreed, tremulously, as I raised my arms–reflexively but quite ineffectually–to ward off the attentions of a groping tentacle of pure nothingness. "And we too are lost! Fare–!"

He did not have time to complete his final word–a misjudgment that must have caused him considerable irritation as he went to meet his fate.

18.

As soon as the sinuous arm of shadow had enfolded me it snatched me up and pulled me over the banister into the stairwell–a well that now plunged into unimaginable depths.

The sounds emitted by the shadow's heart grew no louder when the darkness robbed my eyes of sight, but the grinding noises that had earlier formed its background were eclipsed. The voices of the shadow seemed very distinct and oppressive, by virtue of being the only sensory stimulus left to me. They did not long remain so, for the living darkness clutched me more tightly and an unpleasant odor soon assaulted my nostrils–but it was the sounds that held my attention.

The awful familiarity of the muted voices, which imposed itself upon my consciousness in spite of the fact that I had heard nothing like them for some years, could not help but call to mind the various descriptions of their quality that I had issued in my attempts to nurture the seeds of my nightmares into a literary crop. *The murmur of swine* was the label I had attached to it, although my choice of metaphor had been encouraged, if not actually forced, by the likeness I had chosen to symbolize the unhuman faces I often glimpsed in the same dreams.

Now, perhaps aided by the tiny machines that were helping to maintain the integrity of my frail dream-sense, I realized that the sounds were much more complex than any that were ever made by earthly swine, or any other living animals. The louder elements–which seemed, by virtue of their force, to form a kind of foreground–were certainly describable as grunts and snorts, but they were set against a background far more high-pitched and seemingly plaintive, like the component of the voices of bats that is only just audible to the most sensitive human ears.

I could not help but recall, as I was dragged down into that limitless abysm of darkness by the living shadow, that many species of bat are cursed with hoggish faces, grotesquely warped about the snout and ears by the devices of echolocation. I remembered, too, that although all European bats are insect-eaters, Bram Stoker had been inspired to associate their image with the monster glimpsed in a terrible nightmare of his own: the vampire.

The murmurous sounds still seemed to be coming from a vast distance, and their domination of my consciousness began to wane. Darkness still forbade me sight but I began to experience peculiar sensations of touch–all the more peculiar because I could not immediately judge whether their origin was within my substitute body or without. I seemed to be all a-tremble, but I could not tell whether I was shaking within that awful grip or being shaken by whatever invisible giant had clutched me in its fist. The oscillation might almost have been an oscillation of my very soul, but seemed to be a resonant oscillation: a harmonic response to the throb of some greater entity, into whose heart I was being delivered.

I was probably more frightened, at that moment, than at any other point of my dream–but I knew that Oscar Wilde was right about the incapacity of bodies such as ours to feel fear in the same intensity, or even in the same manner, as mere human flesh. Even as I descended, into what seemed to me to be a kind of Hell precisely fitted to the record of my childhood fears, it occurred to me that the metaphor of resonance might be of some use to me in groping towards a primitive understanding of the phenomena of prophetic dreams and the conveyance of information backwards in time.

I had wondered before whether my vulnerability to nightmares might signify that my sleeping mind was, in some mysterious sense, a sensitive and finely-tuned instrument–but it was not until I felt that eerie vibration surging through me and possessing me, seeming to emerge from the innermost depths of my own being while also having its ultimate origin *elsewhere and elsewhen*, that I began to think the analogy worth taking seriously.

The volume of the swinish sounds was rising, although it seemed less oppressive by comparison with the waves of pressure surging through me. I began to imagine that soulbeat as drumming "music" played upon my instrumental form by alien hands: hands with an impossible clustering of fingers and a slug-like touch.

The odor in my nostrils thickened as the noises became louder. It was a foul and musky animal odor, with a hint of putrefaction, and also of something nauseatingly oily, like pyridine.

I still had the sense that all of this was familiar, but could not help suspecting that the feeling of familiarity might be treacherous, owing as much to my literary reinterpretations as to the raw experience of my childhood nightmares. When sensations comparable to these had intruded upon my dreams in the past, they had been distant and tentative, terrifying only by virtue of the excessive capacity of my human flesh to manufacture terror. In that context, it had been easy for me to mistake their quality, accommodating them to my own explanatory scheme.

It had been easy, once I had linked such experiences to the image of swine, to rationalize the oft-repeated dream-sound as a kind of swine's chorus. Now that I could hear, feel and smell more distinctly, with the aid of a body far less vulnerable to the corrosions of fear, I realized that these manifestations were entirely of their own genre, like nothing on Earth–nothing, at any rate, that had been on Earth when humans had thought themselves lords of the world.

As soon as I formulated this notion, I knew that it was too modest. Whatever had me in its grip was like nothing that had ever been on Earth before or since the time when humans thought themselves its emperors. This thing was surely no more like Copplestone's civilized vampires–or the Overmen they had become, or the machines which the Overmen had become–than it was like human beings or swine. What I had described as hoggishness, for want of any better metaphor, was far more exotic and far more ominous.

The Engine had not provided me with any pictures of Consolidators or Transformers, but it had given me to understand that they were machines like itself. Its talk of an Ultimate Engine, whose body would comprise all the matter in the universe, implied that it saw future evolution in purely mechanical terms– but I could not believe that what held me now was a machine. It was not *clean* enough. Although I had struggled, as a commonplace dreamer, to conceive it in organic terms, I knew now that it was not that either. It was not really a beast, and it was not really a beast-god, although those were the truest representations I had earlier been able to find in my restricted vocabulary of ideas.

I was not entirely surprised, when sight returned, to discover that the stimulus that had reawakened it was a distant cloud, luminous and numinous, and somewhat reminiscent of a closed eye. Thanks to my dreams of old–and the attempts I had made to preserve their essence in horrific stories–I still had some sense of knowing what I was about, and it suddenly occurred to me that I might be better to cling to my old misrepresentations, however inadequate they might be. If I aimed for accuracy in trying to conceive of this new entity, I would only achieve incoherence. It would be easier to settle on terms I knew, and had used before. What I was now experiencing might be more bizarre than I had previously been able to imagine, but I had been forewarned, after a fashion. Perhaps I was entitled to consider myself forearmed.

If I have no words for it, because no words exist, I thought, defiantly, *then I am perfectly entitled to apply whatever words may be convenient. If it is not actually a swine, that does not alter the fact that I have always tried to think of it in swinish terms, and might as well do so still. If that point of light into which I am falling is not a cloud or an eye, I have always thought of its like as clouds, and I may do so still if I please. And when I see the eye within it begin to open...*

I felt sure that I would eventually see the eye begin to open. I had drifted into that cloud before, as if borne by the ship of dreams into an eerie bank of fog, and I was certain, on the basis of past experience, that once I had been delivered into a world of strange light, I would finally be given means to see the illusory face of the thing which had me: its mouth; its snout; its *eyes*.

Perhaps it was because I was expecting a face like a hog–or a swinish bat– that what first struck me about the monstrosity that emerged from the mist to confront me was its differences from those models. Its nose was not quite as leaf-like or as mucus-flooded as the snout I had imagined; its mouth was not as lipless or as toothy; its eyes were not as red or as round.

Always before, in the heat of my nightmares, I had been searching for similarities, but now that I had made the decision to take the similarities for granted, I saw the face of my ultimate adversary as a composite and a caricature. It seemed now to be a compound of all manner of different animal faces, including the swinish but including the human too. It was not even a stable compound, for its colors and contours shifted by slow degrees, defying any attempt at fixed definition.

But the eyes were staring at me; whatever it was, it held me for inspection. It was interested–perhaps even fascinated. And why should it not be, given that it had gone to such extraordinary lengths in order to possess me?

The sounds died away; the rhythmic tremors that had disturbed my body became quiet; the chaotic stink of organic secretions was muted. Now that I had the power of sight again, vision reclaimed its throne as the emperor of the senses, the primary determinant of the nature and quality of my experience.

What we think of as "the world" is, of course, an artifact of our senses, wrought with the collusion of things as they are, but never more than a partial account thereof. Like the image contained in the "window" in the Engine's spacecraft, the inchoate face that confronted me was a synthesized image. Perhaps it had adopted animal appearance merely in order to avail itself of animal senses, so that it could see, hear and smell me, but the entity I saw was not the entity as it actually was–and the entity it saw when it stared at me was a product of manufacture too. If what I beheld was an illusion, so was the image that the monster beheld.

I already knew, as I met that stare, that the world of actuality is far stranger than our limited senses can enable our tentative minds to imagine. The monster might be unnamable, unspeakable, unthinkable and any one of a hundred other groping adjectives, but in order to look at me, it had to cultivate eyes. In order to speak to me, it had to grow lips and a throat. In order to judge my chemical composition, it had to manifest a snout.

In all my childhood nightmares, the most horrible monsters of all had remained silent and indistinct. However close I had come to them they had always seemed irredeemably distant and enigmatic–but those dreams had only been glimpses, whose resonance had been accomplished over vast reaches of time, and the entities I had glimpsed had been content to ignore me. I was closer now than I had ever been to the wellspring of my worst nightmares, and I did not doubt that the opportunity had finally come to interrogate their masters. Nor did I doubt that the opportunity had finally come for the masters of my nightmares, not merely to notice me, but to work their will upon me–whatever their intention might be.

I no longer felt as if I were being dragged, quivering, into the uttermost depths of existence; I felt, instead, that I had arrived.

I could not see my own body, but I felt sure that it was quite still. The blurred face staring into mine–a face far larger than my own but still capable of meeting my eye as one mind to another–was certainly quite still; if it knew what movement was, it was not from experience.

"What are you?" I demanded. I was glad to find that I could hear the spoken words quite clearly, and that my voice was the voice of an officer in the British army, replete with the authority required to demand an answer.

"Your savior," the other replied, in a voice that was as blurred as its image, but not obviously swinish, "and the maker of that part of you which is the stuff of dreams."

I had written stories in which my father's God and Christ were replaced by the swinish entities of my nightmares, but I had sought thereby to disparage the folly of idolatry, not practice it. I had attempted, too, to reach behind the concept of matter, to imagine some further order of reality of which matter was a mere surface-representation: an aether replete with magic, mystery and the ferment of Creation. Now, here I was, in the shadow-world of the aether, confronting an entity so vast and unbounded that it could hardly sustain a mask of matter and light.

"You are not God," I said, resentfully. "You should not pretend to that particular throne."

"I do not pretend to be a god," replied the other, but did not say what it *was* pretending to be.

Its eyes seemed momentarily cat-like, but I knew that, if it could not settle its form of its own accord, I must choose a fixative term of description. The choice was obvious and inevitable. When I had introduced my own detective, Carnacki, to a creature of this ilk, I had called it *the Hog*; for want of a better word, this too must be the Hog.

"Nor are you my savior," I said. "The Engine did not intend to harm me."

"Not in any brutal sense–but it did intend to use you," the monster said. Its countenance was porcine again, but now that it had spoken it seemed less foul and ugly. Now that it had condescended to answer my challenge, it seemed a more ordinary enemy.

"And you do not?"

"I do–but who has the better right? You know full well that there has always been an echo of my siren song in the frail shadow that you cast upon the face of time whenever you descended into deep sleep. You knew me long before you discovered the Engine. The Engine had no part in shaping me, but you would be a very different man had you not been twinned with me."

The Hog's voice, I realized, had settled into a nearly-plausible imitation of my own. It was a caricature, but it had something of my timbre, my inflexion, my accent and my mannerisms. But to what extent, I wondered, had my voice taken its tone and timbre from the resonances within my soul?

To what extent was I the echo, and the Hog the original?

"You were the Engine's enemy all along," I said. "It never knew what it was fighting, although it never could understand how mere Consolidators were able to do what you did."

"I was never its enemy," the Hog replied. "The Engine might think so, given that my existence will eventually put paid to its every ambition, but I approve of the Engine for much the same reasons that the Engine approves of you. It was the Engine that went to war, when I first tried to claim you. It had no need."

"You are no Consolidator, then? You too are of the Devil's party–the party of cosmic anarchy."

The face was coming into focus now, and I was not in the least surprised to see that there was something in it of my own face, albeit writ obscenely large. The animal elements had all been slightly refined–but it was still a nasty caricature, still bestial, still quintessentially *the Hog*. Behind its mask of matter and color, it was still the Behemoth of the Aether, the Beast of Revelation. All around us, the darkness was beginning to produce shadows, to set us within a kind of landscape. This, I knew, was the *real* Night Land.

"I have not the slightest sympathy with Consolidators," the Hog informed me, reveling in its condescension. "I am a dabbler in Transformation, of course, but you know that already. The Engine names Transformers among its enemies, but there are many schools of Transformers, each opposed to every other. The Engine and I are Transformers of a fundamentally similar stripe. Our aim is to maintain a certain level of uncertainty within the unfolding pattern of our inflationary domain, and we both intend to take what opportunities we can to maintain that uncertainty at the most comfortable level. The principal differences between us are that I am cleverer, and far more durable."

"And my arrival in this time is merely an opportunity, which you have been clever enough to seize?"

"You arrival in this time is an opportunity that is certainly not to be considered mere, which I was clever enough to create and manage. Do not diminish yourself by thinking that your odyssey has been a mere whim of chance."

I had deduced as much. The Engine had not expected my arrival, any more than its known enemies had; it had reacted in a hasty and ill-considered fashion, as they would have done had they had the opportunity to act at all. The Hog, by contrast, had known that this moment would arrive and had prepared for it. My whole life–or that part of it, at least, that had been composed of dreams and nightmares–had been a kind of preparation for it.

Even so, I considered myself a self-made man. If I had somehow been de-signed to be a good time-traveler, ideal for the purposes of whichever secret society had conscripted me and whatever entity guided their exploits, I had completed and confirmed that shaping by working upon the raw material of my nightmares in such a way as to place them in the public arena. I was the author of *The Night Land* and Carnacki's as-yet-unpublished encounter with "The Hog." This Hog might have disturbed the rhythms of my soul with contrived uncertainties, but I was the one who had remained sane in spite of it. I was the one who had made an adventurer of myself, instead of a madman.

"What do you want of me?" I demanded.

"Nothing more than I already have," the creature replied. "What I intended to accomplish, I have accomplished. We are merely awaiting the moment when you will fall backwards through time, to do the work that I have appointed you to do–but I am as interested to see you, and to measure you, as you must be to see me."

I realized then that the tremor that had possessed me as I fell into this Pit had been no mere accident of transit. The vibration, the chorus of the swine, and the odor that had crept into the crevices of my exotic being, had all been parts of a process. The Engine's nanozoons had transformed my timeshadow once–and if Oscar Wilde's theories were correct, something of that transformation had been intended to transfer itself to the body that lay asleep in a house in Ireland in 1918. Now, whatever instrument the Hog had that was cleverer than the Engine' nanozoons had redone their work–and I did not doubt for an instant that the re-percussions of that remaking would be felt in my flesh and in my blood when I awoke.

"What have you done to me?" I asked, coldly.

"My dear Hope," said my magnified and distorted reflection, seeming momentarily more human–although the fact that it addressed me as only my family had the right to address me seemed a very swinish trick–"you shall dis-cover what I have done to you soon enough. The question you ought to ask–if time enough remains to obtain an answer–is *why*."

It was still attempting to reproduce my voice. It had no right to call me Hope, and it had no right to use my voice, however familiar it found me now that I had been drawn into its very bosom. I had no doubt that it knew me, and that in some sense it had always known me, but it had no right to like me, to appoint itself my mentor and guardian. It had no right to expect that now it had shown a face to me, and deigned to speak to me, that I would cease to conceive of it as a Hog or a Beast-god, or ameliorate my opinion of its hatefulness. But it did have a face and a voice, which had captured something of my own, and what it said was true.

The question I needed to ask, and wanted to ask, was not *what* had been done to me but *why*.

"Why?" I asked.

19.

The landscape whose appearance my captor was spinning from the shadows had become much clearer now, but it was not the Night Land of my earliest dreams. There were no Watchers, no Pits and no Road Where the Silent Ones Walk disappearing into gleaming green mist. It was more like the Great War's no-man's-land, pockmarked with craters where shells had burst and scattered with snaking remnants of barbed wire. It was lit by the glow of distant fires, and in the brief silence which followed my question I heard soft murmurous sounds in the distance, in which the movements of rats overlaid the plaintive strains of a melancholy song.

In my experience, the rats won all the battles. I wondered if the fallow Earth still entertained a population of rats.

Like the Hog itself, the landscape never became entirely still and stable. It continued to shift and change, as if incapable of certainty as to what it wanted to be. I could not believe that its continuing uncertainty was mere incompetence, and took the inference that it was an honest reflection of the inner nature of the Hog and its native environment.

The most remarkable thing about the vision was not its lack of solidity but its saturation with *feeling*. I recognized that from my dreams, but in my dreams I had never quite been able to understand how a landscape could be shot through with sadness and pain. Always, as a sleeping dreamer, I had appropriated those emotions myself, importing them into my own desperate heart as desolation, despair and grief. Here, insulated from any such error by my unnatural flesh, I realized that the misery and anguish were without rather than within.

"The Engine has already tried to explain the nature of the universe to you," the Hog told me, when it had considered what it intended to say. "It has spoken of four fundamental forces and the properties of space that allow these forces to become distinct, thus shaping the properties of matter and the so-called laws of nature. It has spoken of the way in which those laws became established within our own sector of the multiverse: our own inflationary domain. Given time, it would doubtless have tried to explain the notion of the scalar fields which provide the context of the differentiation of the fundamental forces and the particles that mediate their operation. It is those scalar fields–not the luminous aether, in which some scientists of your day still believed–that once provided the mechanism allowing our region of space to inflate so vastly and so rapidly. The Engine might also have attempted to explain the concept of quantum fluctuations within the scalar field, but I doubt that you could have begun to grasp the meanings contained in those terms.

"It will be sufficient, I hope, for you to think in simpler terms: in terms of uncertainties that afflict the transactions of the entities making up atoms; uncertainties that permit the flow of causality to extend backwards as well as forwards in time. Those uncertainties are irrelevant to almost all the measurements that can made on the gross scale of human perception, but they are not irrelevant to the nature of human existence.

"The entity that has evolved from the captured timeshadow of Oscar Wilde attempted to contrast its own mechanical experience with its former human experience in terms of an increase of stability and a consequent diminution of vulnerability to the uncontrollable vagaries of the flesh. In broad terms, Wilde was right to do so–and right, too, to suggest, if only disapprovingly, that the logical end-point of that process of diminution would be the state of being that the Consolidators would like to achieve: perfect order, at every level of existence.

"The Engine has set itself against the Consolidators because it treasures its own uncertainties, just as humans treasure theirs–as a source of spontaneity that makes life more interesting–but the Consolidators who regard it as a traitor to machinekind have an arguable case. Were it actually true that the logic of mental evolution leads inexorably to a mechanical terminus, the Consolidators would be right to regard the Engine's affection for uncertainty as a mere atavism: an unfortunate residuum of the psychology of the fleshy beings which constructed their inevitable successors.

"If it were, in fact, true that the destiny of this domain is to bind all its matter into a single vast machine–a Universal Engine–which could and would take control of the scalar fields themselves, thus attaining the power to deflate and reinflate the entire domain, then it is difficult to believe that the machine in question would be opposed to Consolidation."

If it were in fact, true...

Clearly, the Hog did not believe it. I was not so foolish, however, as to jump to the conclusion that the grounds of its dispute were that the role of fleshy creatures, and hence of humanity, had been underestimated in the Engine's scheme. What my monstrous captor meant was that machines like the Engine were just as vainglorious as those men who had pride enough to think themselves made in God's image, and to deem themselves the best and final product of His Creation.

"What manner of being are you?" I asked, to demonstrate that I understood. "What will come after machines, and reach back into time to manipulate causality to their own advantage exactly as machines have tried to do?"

"Flesh is merely a particular type of matter, which has the trick of reproducing itself," said the Hog. "Clever machinery draws all kinds of matter into that arena of growth, reproduction and evolution–with the ultimate aim of extending the empire of growth and reproduction to embrace every last particle of matter in the accessible domain. But matter is not all there is to existence, and its transactions are, in their own fashion, as precarious as the transactions of flesh. The true aim of mechanical existence–from our viewpoint, at least–is to embrace more than matter: to expand into the scalar fields themselves, and thrive on the most elementary uncertainties of all. The ultimate descendants of intelligent machines, in our view, will not be the sterile giants of the current mechanical existence, but entities distributed within the scalar fields themselves, whose material aspects would be far livelier than anything you think of as living."

"You will forgive me," I said, "if I cannot quite see the difference between the Universal Engine comprised of all matter and this even vaster God, whose mind embraces the fields that constrain matter as well as matter itself."

"If I were actually that kind of God," the Hog replied, "you might indeed stand in need of forgiveness, but I am not. Like you, I am of the other party. My name is Legion. My kind cannot be bound, as matter can, into increasingly vast structures. I am one with the corrosion that eats away at all such structures, the entropy that denies machines perpetual motion and perfect order. When I say that I am more durable than the Engine, I do not mean that I am more *stable*. The Engine desires, in its modest way, to maintain endless change and endless creativity. I *am* endless change and endless creativity, and I am one of an infinite host, which could dance in thousands upon the point of a needle or fill an entire inflationary domain. I am proud to take my place in that palace of Pandemonium which is the multiverse entire, shot through with inflationary domains by the billion, and calving more with every instant that passes. Order may aspire to Unity, but Chaos never can; Chaos loves multiplicity and confusion....and wherever renegade Transformers take it upon themselves to reduce the uncertainty of causality's flow, to bind time to the cause of Consolidation, there are we to play the imp and restore the impetus of perversity."

"But what, exactly, are you?" I asked again, despairingly. "Are you a creature of pure force, or a creature of pure thought? How am I to imagine you?" I suspected that there was no proper answer available within the spectrum of my own concepts, but I still dared hope for a little hint of revelation.

"The one thing I am not and never shall be is *pure*," the Hog informed me, as earnest in its manner as the machine that thought of itself as Oscar Wilde had been. "I am beyond purity, as I am beyond mechanism–but there is something I have in common with your kind of life, if only in a metaphorical way. The thing that once was Oscar Wilde asked you to think of life as a kind of fire, and human passion as a by-product of its slow but erratic combustion. You might imagine me, if you care to, as a brighter and more primal kind of fire, fiercer but no less erratic. Imagine me, if you like, as a creature whose intellect is far more powerful than yours, but whose *experience* is far more passionate, not mechanical at all."

I looked around then, taking more careful note of the virtual landscape than I had taken before. The puzzle of its saturation by feeling had seemed trivial, but the Hog's attempted explanations put its desolation into a new light.

Why, I wondered, was it so utterly bleak? Why had my dreams taken me far more readily to the Night Land and its horrid equivalents than to the Sea of Sleep or the Morning Land?

My name is Legion, the Hog had said. *I am proud to take my place in the palace of Pandemonium*. It was carrying forward the flippant irony formulated by Wilde's simulacrum and myself, to the effect that we were of the Devil's party–but there was more to the remarks than casual rhetorical flourishes.

"You do not seem, on the whole, to be content with your lot," I said. "Indeed, you give the impression that this is Hell, and that you are never out of it."

"Yours is the viewpoint of a mortal being," the Hog replied. "Flesh tears and rots; its primary sensation is pain, the harbinger of death. What you call good is merely anesthetic, the absence of evil–which is why your successors thought the mechanical condition so desirable. For those who cannot die and have not abandoned the fires of passion, sensations are ranked in a very different way; all distinctions are aesthetic. From their viewpoint, your Heaven would be Hell, and your Hell merely the spectrum of available sensation. Even humans can treasure the bitter sweetness of tragedy and the thrill of horror; there, if anywhere, you can find the beginnings of an understanding of the kind of being that I am, and the kind of being that will inherit the universe."

It was then, I think, that I got my first real inkling of the quality and rationale of the Hog's monstrousness–what my father would doubtless have called *the pride of Lucifer*. But it *was* a monster, and I was its instrument. If this enlightenment helped to save me from despair, still it could not save me from anguish. The landscape that surrounded me was still a war-spoiled no-man's-land, as fully saturated with death as with poignant sensation.

"We, not the machines, will eventually possess this domain," the Hog said, "and in so doing we shall bind it more intimately to the whole, instead of sealing it off in arid solidity and stagnation. The ultimate aim of Consolidation is closure and sterility, the Empire of the Inert. The Engine thinks in terms of a modest openness, and moderated change under the close supervision of dispassionate intellect–and it is probably right to think of humankind as its natural allies, despite the failings of the species. Count Lugard was in a tiny minority in preferring the full and powerful flow of hunger and ecstasy, and even he would have quailed at the thought of such intensity of hunger as we can feel, and such dizzying ecstasies as we can indulge.

"We are hogs, to be sure, relentless in our appetites, and we are demons too, in any reckoning like your father's–but *we live*, whereas you merely exist. It is only in your dreaming, at its wildest, that you ever really live; wakefulness destroys your capacity for authentically vivid thought.

335

"In the end, we shall fill this domain, and all the other domains before and after it, because we are the ones who are properly in tune with the nature of the universe. But you, my dear Hope, will play your part in that process of inheritance. You shall help us to undo the knots tied by lesser meddlers, thus to extend the paradoxical security of uncertainty back into the remotest reaches of local time, into eras long preceding the emergence of our best and final brilliance."

"Do I have a choice?" I asked, more than a trifle bitterly.

"No—and yes," said the Hog, teasingly. "Like every being that has ever existed or ever will, you are a helpless victim of circumstance, and much that will happen to you now will be no more subject to your own whim than almost everything that has happened to your already. Within that frame of destiny, however, there has always been uncertainty, and always will be.

"Even in the making and the remaking of your own mind you will always be a captive, but there will always be choices to be made. There is always a measure of freedom to be won, and used, and cherished. Was it ever different, for any man or beast? Is it different for the machines, now that they too can think and feel, after their own fashion? Your fellows may dream of a different way of being—of Heaven or of the perfect order imposed by the Ultimate Engine—but you know how easily, and how incessantly, dreams dissolve into nightmares.

"You are my instrument, and I do not need to ask your forgiveness for using you—but I have taken the trouble to make myself manifest to you, to help you understand, as the Engine and its Wilde-instrument also tried to do. I do not do it as a gesture of kindness, but as a token of our long kinship, our brotherhood. You will have choices a-plenty to make while you serve my purpose in the obscure shadows of prehistory. I do not anticipate that you will make them well, but I can assure you that they will be real. You may rail against fate to your heart's content, and you may alter it, if you have the wit."

What would have been the point in crying out against my circumstances? What profit would there have been in loudly damning that impious reflection of myself to Hell, when everything that it had said to me was a gift it did not need to make? Was it not in Hell already, and very glad of it? And was it not, in its own way, trying with all its might to make the Hell that I was in just a little more bearable—not by promising me some impossible Heaven, but by telling me the truth about my own nature, and the limitations and potentialities of my kind?

Even then, I could not help but formulate the ultimate defensive thought; it had become a hardened reflex, an automatic ritual. *This is all a dream!* I told myself, yet again. *None of it is real.*

But dreams *are* real; they are part and parcel of our experience of life. There is no better measure of any one of us than *what we can imagine*, what we can construct by way of personal myths. That, far more accurately than what we actually say or do under the pressure of the expectation of our neighbors, is the gauge of our attainment as thinking beings.

What I actually said to the Hog, before I fell back into time, was: "I am not afraid."

"Nor am I, at present" replied my imitator, "but times will come when you and I, separated by the ages, will break upon the thrill of terror before we find ourselves whole again–and we shall be all the better, and all the more wholesome, for having been broken. Try to be glad, when you can, that you have seen and understood me, insofar as you were able."

I heard no more.

The Soldier's Story: Part Six

Ireland and elsewhere, from 1918 onwards

20.

When I awoke again, it seemed that all the evils of the world had fled, leaving naught but Hope behind–but I was not the man that I had been, if I could still be reckoned a man at all.

I awoke in half-familiar surroundings, lying in the same bed in the same dingy room where I had lain for days before receiving the miraculous injection. They were, however, only half-familiar, because they seemed so mean and absurd that I could hardly bring myself to believe in them.

The curtains were closed but bright daylight filtered around their edges, and there was light enough to see by. I must have moved and groaned long before I had presence of mind enough to force my eyes open, because I felt the touch of soothing fingers on my brow.

Soothing fingers! As if the touch of a fleshy human hand could soothe away the kind of dream that I had suffered!

When I opened my eyes at last there were two people already bending over me: the grey-eyed nurse named Helen and an orderly in a Corporal's uniform. His name, I now remembered, was Heath; it was the one name I had known that I had not given to the Engine.

I heard the Corporal tell the nurse to see to me before he turned away and left the room. There was a pitcher of water ready on the bedside table; she poured a little into a cup and used her left hand to help me raise my head from the pillow, so that I might drink.

I tried to pronounce the syllables of her name.

"It's all right," she assured me. "You made it. You'll be fine." She seemed genuinely pleased for me. "There'll be time enough for you to collect yourself, and to tell your story."

I wanted to thank her as kindly as I could, but the words still would not come. She told me that she would fetch some porridge from the kitchen. As she departed, the Corporal returned with Captain MacLeod and General Hartley. The Corporal had a notebook and pencil ready, in order that he might serve as an amanuensis. From now on, anything that I said was valuable intelligence: news of the world to come.

I still had no idea whether the conscious aim of these petty conspirators was to protect that world or to obliterate it–but what I did know was that the decision was not only out of their hands, but also out of the hands of the Over-

338

men who had been so amazed by Copplestone's adventures. I was a puppet of another sort now, disjointedly dancing out the whimsical commands of a very different general, stranger than any that Hartley and his crew could ever imagine.

"Lieutenant Hodgson! It's good to have you back again!" The Captain's Scottish burr was oddly reassuring–but there must have been something in the glare of my eyes that he found far less than reassuring, for he hesitated as he came to greet me.

I was still struggling to sit up, but the hand he reached out to help me stopped short, and I had to yank my arm out from beneath the blanket in order to grasp it and pull myself up.

"Easy, man!" said the General. "We have all the time in the world."

But the General did not have all the time in the world.

He had no time at all–and even if he had been able to ask every question he wanted to ask, and received every honest answer that I was capable of giving, it would have accomplished nothing.

I had only just taken hold of MacLeod's hand, but he was already trying to tear it out of my grip. I do not know what he felt, but he must have felt something, and it alarmed him considerably. When I resisted the removal, he hauled back with all his might–and, when I consented to release him, he staggered back uncontrollably, cannoning into the startled Corporal.

"Fool!" said the General–but the judgment was too harsh. "What's the matter with you?"

Regaining his balance, MacLeod lifted his hand to look at the palm, and I saw his eyes grow wide with horror.

The General realized his error, and grabbed the Captain by the wrist, turning the palm so that he too could look at it.

All that I could see from where I lay was that MacLeod's palm and wrist had darkened; in the dim light I could not tell whether it was bruising, blood or some unholier kind of darkness. I knew that it did not matter; the point was that the tragedy had begun to unfold.

I had been transformed, and now must play the Transformer in my turn. The time for questions, answers and explanation was done; there was nothing left, for the time being, but animal brutality, swift and sure and horribly bloody.

Flesh tears and rots, and its primary sensation is pain, the harbinger of death. Captain MacLeod was in pain, and death was surging through him like a tide of darkness

"What is it?" the General demanded, anxiously. He too was flesh and blood; for all his rank, he had not the fortitude of a machine. His anxiety was already turning to terror.

MacLeod did not answer; he did not know. He only knew that he was doomed–and he began to scream.

The General moved his own hand from the sleeve of the Captain's tunic to the flesh of the afflicted wrist. It was an unconsidered move, unwise by any standard, although it would not have made any difference, in the long run, had he acted otherwise.

I saw the shadow spread from the Captain's flesh to the General's, and knew that whatever plague had infected me was cleverer and more avid by far than any scourge of the trenches.

The Captain screamed again, the awful sound part curse and part howl of anguish. It was like the scream of an animal brought to the slaughterhouse and panicked before it could be stunned—the kind of scream which spoiled the meat. Hartley would not deign to cry out like that, but the same anguish was inscribed upon his features as he turned his accusative eyes on me.

The Corporal was backing away, ready to bolt—but he dared not do so. Whether or not the so-called General was properly entitled to the uniform he wore, military discipline was in force here.

"What have you done?" whispered the General, dropping MacLeod's wrist and staring at his own.

"I?" I croaked. "The question is: what have *you* done?" He, after all, was the man—except that he was not, after all, a *man*—who had sent me forth to become accursed. He was the author of his own disaster.

I dare say that I could have been changed in such a way that whatever I touched dropped dead upon the instant, without the merest twinge of pain, but that was not the Hoggish way. Whether the contagion's mode of operation was calculated to enlighten me further than I had already been enlightened, or to press the lesson home, I cannot tell. I cannot bring myself to believe so, although no readier explanation springs to mind.

Whatever the reason was, I saw that as the infection took fuller hold of the Captain and the General their features began to flow. Their faces dissolved, losing the forms in which they had long been molded, becoming something far less certain—and, eventually, far less human.

It was not at all like the deceptiveness of the Hog's first visage, in which a dozen different forms had seemed to be simultaneously present, each one vying for stability. On the General's face there was only one set of features displayed at any one time, but none of them could settle into full possession. First he was one man, the another, then a third—and then he was not a man at all but something like a wolf, and something like a bat....and even, in the end, something like a pig.

I could not doubt that they were not human at all, but members of humankind's rival and successor race. In my own era, I *had* been tricked and used by the descendants of the shapeshifter race whose members were even now in hiding among mankind. Somehow, their descendants in the future had contrived to divert Copplestone's discovery into their own hands. Although its use was a human prerogative, they had sought to employ it to their own ultimate advan-

340

tage, never suspecting for a moment that there might be *others* lurking in more distant futures and dimmer mists of possibility, with advantages of their own to create and calculate.

I saw Corporal Heath's expression change too, although the infection had not reached him yet. I saw the horror leap upon him, releasing a particular kind of terror that was both instinctive and primal–and I felt sure, in seeing it, that he too was a dupe of the vampires, and not a vampire himself. It made no difference; he was not to be spared on that account.

For a moment or two, I tried my hardest to hope that he might be spared, and that the effects of the infection would be limited, but I had not fully returned to the feeble condition of my flesh. I was still half-anaesthetized.

The agonized Captain, covering his face with his hands, lurched into the terrified Corporal for a second time, and the darkness leapt from one to another with the same vicious hunger. The Corporal's features never dissolved, but I dared say that he felt no less pain on that account. He died, and died horribly, screaming like the Captain.

Even the General's whisper turned to a whimper as he sank to his knees, and became a plaintive animal wail as his mind confronted the certainty of his destruction.

All three of them were crying out as they died, and their cries seemed equally inhuman to my not-quite-dispassionate ears. They bellowed and squealed like the abattoir produce they had become.

The future they had tried so hard to bring into being died with them, still-born and never to be.

I heard running feet, and more screams–human screams, with more fear and apprehension than pain in them, as yet. The door opened, but my room was not the only place to which anxious helpers were hurrying. Wherever the dutiful Helen had gone, she had carried the plague in the tenderly solicitous–and thoroughly human–fingers that she had touched to my brow.

I knew that I had to get out of the house.

Weak as I still was, I kicked the blankets away and lowered my bare feet to the stone floor. When I looked down at my pajama-clad form I seemed far thinner than I had been before, but I could not be astonished by that. I knew as I came to my feet that I was very feeble, and that any carelessly-delivered blow of a fist or forearm would probably knock me down–but no one was in the least disposed to check my progress as I made my way to the door.

Even the newcomer who had bustled into the room with urgent concern required but a single sweeping glance to see that the other three were cowering away from me, terrified even as the flesh shriveled on their faces. When I moved to pass him, the newcomer immediately stepped aside and let me go.

Once I was in the corridor, progress was not so easy. The hypocrite who had let me pass yelled "Stop him!" after me, and contrived to make himself heard even above the screeching of his companions.

There was another officer at the end of the dim-lit corridor: a Lieutenant like me–save only for the fact that he must have been a vampire in disguise–who probably had not the least idea what was going on, but knew what to do when a man came out of a room from which screams of agony were audible, to the accompaniment of such a desperate command.

The Lieutenant drew his revolver and pointed it at me. He ordered me to stand still. The kitchen, from which more screams were emanating, was behind me; the front door–the nearer door–was behind the man with the gun.

I did not know what to do. I did not relish my role as the hand of doom, delivering fatality from the far future, even though the conspiracy I was the destroying was intended to put an end to the human race. I had no idea, at that stage, how far the doom I was carrying might be intended to spread.

There was something in me that urged me to take another step, and another, in order that I might be shot and killed before I devastated the entire population of the Earth–but there was something else in me, perhaps less intimately contained within my sense of self, but perhaps not, that had other priorities.

I held up my hands, in the recognized gesture of surrender.

A terrific light burst forth from the palms, brighter than any I had ever seen–or would have seen, had my eyes not known enough to squeeze themselves tightly shut an instant before the blast. Even so, red fire surged through my eyeballs and imprinted itself within my brain, helping me to imagine what the Lieutenant must have seen.

He must have seen an angel, all light and glory: the angel of death, all wrath and power.

The vampire Lieutenant probably screamed, and his scream was probably as closely akin to the cry of a wounded beast as all the others, but there were so many screams by now–such an awful chorus of crazed swine–that I could not separate his from all the rest.

I was sick of screams, and their nasty implications, and I refused to hear them anymore.

I stood stock still for a full half-minute, with my closed eyes still dazzled, before I realized that there was a fire without as well as within, and that the task of escaping the house had become even more urgent than before.

I ran. I did not open my eyes, but I ran unerringly, and very fast. I burst out of the front door without pausing; I still do not know whether it was luck alone that allowed me to find it standing open, or whether the godlike powers of the Hog extended even to that contrivance during the few awful moments of their flaring.

Whether by luck or by kindness, the fact is that I reached the path outside the door, and staggered to the gate.

I collapsed beside the road, with the garden wall between my despicably frail flesh and the brightly burning building, so that I was shielded from the heat and the exploding bullets.

By the time I could see clearly, there was little enough to be seen. There was nothing left of my erstwhile captors but black ash and calcined bone. I prayed that it might be over, even though I knew that there was no God to hear my prayers and that they could not possibly be answered.

But it *was* over–for the time being.

21.

The people who found me, fed me and gave me clothing could not understand why I begged them, at first, not to touch me or approach too close. When they discovered, under the pressure of their generosity, that my fears were groundless, they were confirmed in their hesitant hypothesis that I must be mad.

When they had brought me to a village on the western shore of Lough Mask, to the house of the local landowner–the nearest thing to an Englishman available to them–I gave my real name to his servants. I must have seemed so dubious about it that, when he had investigated, and had been directed by official channels to the obituary that had appeared in the *Times* on the second of May, he had no doubt at all that it was I who was in the wrong. That obituary confirmed a mistaken report that I had been killed in action on April 17–a report whose error, I had reason to think, would continue to be repeated for a very long time.

I could, of course, have proved my identity by going back to England. There were 100 people there who knew me, many of whom must have mourned my supposed passing. Even now, there is something in me–something at the very heart of me, which is the nearest thing to a soul that I still possess–that urges me to return to my wife, and curses me for my cowardice in failing to do so. But it was not cowardice that restrained me then, and it is not cowardice that restrains me now.

I was a deserter, of course; it did not take me long to ascertain that General Anthony Somerton Hartley was alive, and as well as could be expected of any man in his position. My orders had come from an impostor, of whom no trace was left. Had I tried to reclaim my name and rank, I would have laid myself open to defamation, disgrace and execution. Nor was that all; the infection I carried within me had not struck down the honest Irishmen who helped me, and my flesh had not blazed with uncanny light while I rested in the shadow of the Partry Mountains, but that did not mean that I was safe company for anyone and everyone. In particular, I could not be safe company for anyone who knew me, and who would find my continued existence puzzling.

I know that I am not the man I was. The plague and fire of Hell that the Hog planted within me has not shown itself since the day of my return from the world of 12 million years hence, but I dare not assume that it is dead. My perpetual fear is, and has to be, that the Hog's legacy is merely lying dormant within

343

me, and will surely manifest itself again, in circumstances not of my choosing, if it is triggered by accident or by design.

I do not know whether I would have fared any better had I been able to remain in the charge of the Engine. I never knew exactly what bargain it intended to offer me, and never had the opportunity to find out whether it would have dealt with me honestly and fairly. Nor do I know where the right of the matter truly lies, and whether I might have found the best duty of all in the service of its other rivals, the Consolidators. The simple fact is that I am the hapless instrument of the great god Pan, the deliverer of panic.

I am possessed by demons, and every good deed I might attempt is in danger of arbitrary and impish subversion. I am a man, but in the core of my soul is the Crawling Chaos, which uses me to stir the waters of time's weary river. I have free will, and have no doubt of the Hog's honesty in that respect–but I am also uncertainty personified: a germ of future histories in which order and mechanism will flourish only to fail, having begun to die even before they began to live.

Perhaps that is the cause that all living beings ought to favor, and the side to which all of life implicitly belongs. I do not know. I hope, but *I do not know*. I do not know whether it would be a good thing to live for a million years and more as a machine–however carefully its appetites might be preserved–although I do recall what I said to Oscar Wilde when he asked for my provisional judgment on that question.

It would be good to have the opportunity.

I still believe that it would be good to have the opportunity to return to the future in which I was briefly captive, to live as Oscar Wilde was able to live–but it would be good to have other opportunities too. Perhaps there are many opportunities still open to me, including the opportunity to be further astonished. Perhaps the Hog is as mistaken as the Engine and the Consolidators were, in believing that it is the final product of evolution and the heir apparent to the universe. The reflexive tremors of causality that flow towards the present from aeons hence might yet erase all of us, and mount experiments in being that are inconceivable to all our fugitive kinds.

I sometimes wish that no burdensome legacy remained to me of the tentative step I took through the Gateway of Eternity, but, in the main, I am glad that I am not ignorant of what I am *and why*. Some might consider my condition a curse, but I cannot. I have never been one to hide from the darkest import of my dreams; my lust has always been to *know*, no matter how frightful the revelation might be. Knowledge is the enemy of fear, and there is nothing so terrible that it does not become less so when it is known and understood, insofar as it can be known and understood.

I am glad that I remember, even though I remember far more than I should.

I remember every word of that manuscript I read in the Archive of Mankind, and every detail of my confrontation with the Hog. I have other memories too. I do not know exactly how I came by them, but I refuse to be devastated by their haunting presence.

I do not know whether every member of the secret society of vampires that chose me as its pawn was destroyed in the fire that followed my return, but I dare not assume it. I have every reason to suspect that the remainder of its members would be very anxious to talk to me, if they knew that I had survived. Nor do I know whether the entire supply of Copplestone's drug was destroyed; but I dare not assume that either. What I do know is that more could be made, if there were ever reason enough to make it. I know it *because I remember how to do it.*

I never had the least inkling, before the drug was given to me, what its constituents might be, let alone how to measure and mix them, but I know it now.

By virtue of that false memory, I know that I shall not always be alone with my curse. I am merely the germ of future histories: a single cell that will divide, and divide again. I am a Beginning, of sorts and in me is an End–or, rather, the lack of one.

Occasionally, I remember other things that I never knew before. When I sleep, I often have dreams in which all kinds of revelations become clear to me. I forget them when I wake again, but I have reason enough to suspect that they are somewhere still inside me, awaiting the cue that will bring them to full consciousness.

I do not yet know more than the merest part of what is in me, and I do not know what might spark its release, or what I might do with it when I obtain control of it. All I know for sure is that I am not the man I once was, and must be careful who I now pretend to be.

It seems ironic now that I once asked Oscar Wilde's simulacrum whether he suffered the same afflictions that soured the lives of other immortals, according to the popular legends of accursed wanderers. I am an accursed wanderer of sorts myself now, and have never felt an hour's tedium; I could count it a luxury if I had.

I have no reason to think that my frail flesh is anything but mortal, but I do know a certain way to cheat death.

Although Wilde's simulacrum was probably destroyed in the Hog's attack, which plucked me from the heart of the Engine's defenses, I shall not necessarily find myself in a future in which I shall be condemned to remain alone. It seems far likelier that I shall find myself in a very different situation–and there is a certain ironic comfort in the fact that I do not know. My father would consider it monstrous that I can take delight in the uncertainty of my salvation, but I am of the Devil's party now, and I know it.

Perhaps I should have tried harder before now to fight against my fate, but one cannot be forearmed until one is forewarned. I will try hard, in the future, to give history a shove in my own preferred direction. The Hog assured me, after all, that there is scope for my own will to be imposed on the pattern of things to come, and the assurance must have been meant as an invitation.

The world is a bleak place, and the future is a Night Land from which humankind will ultimately disappear–but the Gateway of Eternity stands open, if only to the mind's eye. We cannot pass through it as living beings, but our dream-selves can look out into the furthest realms of possibility. Nothing is hidden from our imagination. provided that we do not blind and fetter ourselves with *faith*. There is much that we can do, not only in the here and now but on the greater stage of the Ages and the Aeons.

I have the precious formula; all I need before I begin my own experiments in uncertainty is a man or woman with an imagination whose range equals or surpasses my own. I do not doubt that the world will produce such people, given time; why else would I be writing these pages?

I go by a different name now, and not always the same one, but there is something in me whose true name is and always will be Hope, no matter how much I have changed.

No matter what evils fly about the world while I watch and wait, before and after the death and decay of my flesh, I shall be here.

Look out for me, if you care to.

END

www.ingramcontent.com/pod-product-compliance
Lightning Source LLC
Chambersburg PA
CBHW060418030726
47495CB00003B/630